"She is certain[ly]
one of romance's mo[st]
L[...]

ADELE
ASHWORTH

USA Today bestselling author of *Duke of Sin*

Duke of

Scandal

ENJOY A
PASSIONATE INTERLUDE
WITH ANOTHER SINFULLY
DESIRABLE HERO FROM
USA TODAY BESTSELLING AUTHOR

ADELE ASHWORTH

"A thrilling discovery."
New York Times bestselling author Lisa Kleypas

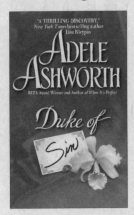

Also:
WHEN IT'S PERFECT
SOMEONE IRRESISTIBLE

EAN

A lady's heart is a tempting plaything for the **DUKE OF SCANDAL**

He stands apart from other men—a dark, tall, breathtaking figure of seductive masculinity. With a smile, he can topple the defenses of even the most proper maiden. And with a single whisper, she will be his.

A wife in name only, Lady Olivia Shea has returned to London in a rage, determined to confront her new husband, who vanished months ago with her inheritance on their wedding night. Yet this hauntingly familiar man who stands before her—this face and form she adores—is *not* her deceiving Edmund but the blackguard's twin brother, Samson Carlisle, Duke of Durham. Samson knows of his sibling's penchant for perfidy and he graciously offers to help the exquisite Olivia locate the missing rogue and recover her stolen fortune.

But Olivia fears that accompanying this mysterious, dangerous, eminently desirable man would be courting the most devastating sort of scandal—especially since it is now *Samson's* arms she aches to feel surrounding her, and his kiss she longs to taste...

Avon Romantic Treasures by
Adele Ashworth

Duke of Scandal
Duke of Sin
When It's Perfect
Someone Irresistible

If You've Enjoyed This Book,
Be Sure to Read These Other
AVON ROMANTIC TREASURES

ADELE ASHWORTH

Duke of Scandal

An Avon Romantic Treasure

AVON BOOKS
An Imprint of HarperCollinsPublishers

This is a work of fiction. Names, characters, places, and incidents are products of the author's imagination or are used fictitiously and are not to be construed as real. Any resemblance to actual events, locales, organizations, or persons, living or dead, is entirely coincidental.

AVON BOOKS
An Imprint of HarperCollins*Publishers*
10 East 53rd Street
New York, New York 10022-5299

Copyright © 2006 by Adele Budnick
ISBN-13: 978-0-06-052841-6
ISBN-10: 0-06-052841-9
www.avonromance.com

First Avon Books paperback printing: May 2006

Avon Trademark Reg. U.S. Pat. Off. and in Other Countries, Marca Registrada, Hecho en U.S.A.
HarperCollins® is a registered trademark of HarperCollins Publishers Inc.

Printed in the U.S.A.

10 9 8 7 6 5 4 3 2 1

For Mom,
who understands my passion for perfume
and all things scented

Prologue

Paris, France
January 1860

The Lady Olivia Shea, now married for slightly more than twelve hours to Lord Edmund Carlisle, stood at one of the tall, teal-draped windows inside their elegant room at the Hotel de Crillon on the Place de la Concorde, watching the sun peek above the horizon as it slowly began to brighten the winter ice that bathed the Jardin des Tuileries to the east.

She remained motionless, each slow breath from her lips fogging the pane in a small, predictable circle of moisture, her body cold from standing barefoot on the wooden floor, her mind numbed to all but the feelings of hopeless abandonment and building rage.

Only last evening she and her new husband had

arrived at the hotel for the beginning of their honey-moon retreat, the start of their new life together, or so she had thought. Blissfully happy, Olivia had dutifully changed into her bedding attire to await the consummation of their love and commitment, when Edmund had curiously remembered one final business errand to attend to before they left for Grasse on a month-long excursion—he needed additional funds for their trip. In the few hours that followed, while she waited for him to return, her earlier excitement and the natural trepidation felt by all virgins on their wedding night had come and gone. In its place she'd first experienced annoyance at his neglect, then panic, and lastly desperation when she started to evaluate all that had happened between them during the last three months—their chance meeting as two English aristocrats with so much in common while living among the very different French; their whirlwind romance where he acted the perfect, charming gentleman; his calculated courtship and desire for a quick wedding. Alas, sometime before the break of dawn the accepted the horrible, shattering conclusion that their entire relationship had been a sham and her new husband had taken her for a fool.

Why, Edmund? Why me? What did I do?

Olivia had yet to cry. Doing so seemed pointless, although she knew that soon she wouldn't be able to hold back her anguish and tears would spill like a never-ending fountain that originated from the depths of her heart.

Edmund had left her not at the altar, but waiting for him in their marriage bed. With a smile and a lie, he had tucked her in between expensive, scented sheets, kissed her sweetly, and departed with no apparent concern or remorse. Such a despicable act, in her mind, proved to be the greatest deceit. After the trust and affection she'd shown him, his final farewell was the ultimate humiliation. She suspected now that all his clever scheming and manipulation to get married quickly was to gain access to her accounts as her husband, made so much more sense to her through a dark night entertained only by her thoughts and the coming light of a cold and frosty morning.

Now, as the rising sun awakened the city that stretched out before her in colorless, charcoal gray structures and an ever decreasing flicker of torchlight, a plan began to take form in her mind. It was certainly true that she had much to blame in herself, that she had allowed her inheritance to be easily seized, but she wasn't as gullible as Edmund had clearly believed. She had resources, determination, skills he didn't know she possessed. Most of all, though, she had a keen wit and the will to use it.

Then and there, still dressed in her gorgeous hand-stitched bridal nightgown of imported white silk and Indian lace, Olivia made her most important vow of the many she'd proclaimed before God that week.

She would find him. Yes, she decided, fisting her hands tightly at her sides. She would find him, get her fortune returned to her somehow, and have their mockery of a marriage annulled. Then she would ruin him.

It might take some time, but she would find him.

I'm coming for you, Edmund, and you will pay.

Chapter 1

London, England
Late March 1860

It had been four long months since he'd been with a woman; probably a year since he'd touched a woman whose name he remembered. Tonight, though, he intended to seek out companionship regardless of the circumstance. He needed a toss between the sheets as he hadn't needed one in ages. Unfortunately, the circumstance to overcome was his very small selection of gently bred ladies flirting with discretion, snickering with intimidation, and prancing before him in a rainbow of richly colored gowns as they celebrated his distant cousin Beatrice's coming out. A typical party he felt obligated to attend, one of the Season's first, and not a great feminine offering for his trouble, to be sure.

The utter absence of female attention in his life of late was indeed a pathetic record, especially for him— Samson Carlisle, the most distinguished, roguish, scandalous fourth Duke of Durham. Or so he'd been told. What would his fellow noble rakes think if they knew of his recent lack of preoccupation with the gentle sex? He had his infamous reputation to uphold. Of course, nobody really knew him as they thought they did. Not even his closest friends. Yet he needed it to be that way.

Standing against a tall marble pillar of swirling bronze and gold, on the opposite side of the room of the elegant grand staircase, Sam steadily sipped a rather sour whiskey as he eyed the debacle on the dance floor before him. From his vantage point he could see most of the ballroom while still remaining relatively unobtrusive. He hated parties. He despised anything that drew attention to him, really, and nearly always being the highest ranking individual at any social function, not to mention one of the wealthiest, he tended to be the one person toward whom most people chose to gravitate. Sometimes it was obvious, sometimes not. Gentlemen wanted to discuss business propositions, young innocents giggled and begged for his interest with their eyes, married ladies flirted coyly, sometimes shrewdly offering their own invitations, which he refused, every one. The greatest lesson he'd learned in his thirty-four years was to never, under any circumstance, trust a married woman. Such faith in hidden, experienced charms would ultimately ruin a man. As it had nearly ruined him.

Groaning within, Sam had to wonder why his mind always wandered to his past at times like this.

Considering lifelong struggles he couldn't change did nothing but agitate his mind and body, on many levels. And an obvious agitation at a carefree event such as this wouldn't help him seduce a woman, which was ultimately his only goal for tonight. He swiftly needed a change of attitude or he'd be riding home alone.

"Alone again, eh?"

That wry comment, echoing his thoughts, came from Colin Ramsey, his longtime friend, occasional competitor where women were concerned, and the only man at the party who fairly equaled him in rank. Aside from that, there were no two men more opposite in every regard in all of England.

"And you're not, I've noticed," Sam replied snidely without looking at him. "I think you've been with every lady here tonight."

Colin chuckled. "I'm certain you mean only on the dance floor?"

"Naturally."

"Naturally. Then yes, I've danced with nearly every lady here tonight." He grunted. "My feet hurt."

"Try soaking them," Sam muttered.

"Ah," Colin remarked immediately. "That's what *you* do after a long night of waltzing?"

Sam fought the urge to snort. "Yes, that's what *I* do after a long night of waltzing."

Colin laughed again, glancing over his surroundings as he lifted his hand to take another full swallow of his drink. "You waltzing. On a frosty day in Hades," he added over the rim of his tumbler.

Sam ignored that and sipped his whiskey, noting how Lady Swan's daughter, Edna, didn't look at all like a beautiful, elegant bird, especially in the low-cut chiffon gown of pastel pink that exposed her thick neck. Then again, Edna, who stole glances in his direction and smiled prettily at him as she twirled with Lord Some-body-or-Other, wasn't all that *un*attractive. Sometimes in the future he might consider her a prospective wife, for she came from a good line, had a satisfactory face, and the general good health and roundness of hips to bear children easily. Producing an heir was really all his duty required, anyway. But in the last analysis, standard Englishwomen were one and the same to him, a blur of dainty expression, fair skin, and brown hair, and most of them bored him. He supposed at some point soon he would have to choose *somebody* to be his duchess, be-fore he died of one malady or another and his wealth and assets became his brother's. He would marry an angel of death before he allowed that to happen. But probably not sweet, rather ordinary Edna, and not anytime soon.

"She fancies you, you know," Colin said, interrupt-ing his thoughts.

Sam looked down at his friend, who stood only an inch or two shorter than his own extraordinary six feet three inches. Colin, who dressed only in expensive finery—tonight black and white silk—continued to gaze out across the dance floor, appearing totally at ease, as he always did under the scrutiny of the ton's roving eye. Sam almost voiced his disgust, for as long as he could remember he'd felt a certain mix of jealousy and admiration for Colin's easy charm, his confident, re-laxed nature and intuition where ladies were concerned. In comparison, he had never had an easy moment with a woman in his life.

"She fancies my money," he corrected.

"An obstacle of which you should be deeply proud," Colin retorted.

He said nothing to that.

"Yet you don't fancy her in the least I suppose," his friend added.

"Not in the least."

Colin took another drink from his glass. "I know her family has you on their short list of eligibles and she's got a handsome dowry—"

"What are you, her mother's bloody matchmaker?" He tipped his head in Edna Swan's direction. "You're not married; you court her."

"I don't need her dowry, either," Colin replied nonchalantly.

Again, Sam had no comment, nor did his friend expect a rebuttal. They'd been bantering back and forth about nothing whatsoever for years, which Sam found appealing in their friendship.

"Holy God, did you see that?"

Sam started, surprised by Colin's exclamation of shock. He gazed to his friend again to find the man staring across the ballroom toward the grand staircase, a landing just above the crowd designed to expose ladies in finery and mothers on the outlook.

"See what?" he asked, annoyed.

Colin grinned crookedly. "An angel in brilliant gold."

Sam focused on the stairs of marble, noticing only two ordinary girls in pink as they stepped onto the dance floor and into a whirl of pastel skirts. Nothing as unfashionable as gold. Or was gold in fashion these days? "I take it you saw a lady *you* want to marry?"

"Yes."

Such a blunt affirmation made him blink. His brows rose as he repeated, "Yes? You do know, don't you, that the word *marriage* implies a lifetime commitment, something you've thus far been loath to sample."

Colin ignored that fact completely, still mesmerized by the now-missing woman of his momentary blinding infatuation. "She's magnificent, but I lost her after she descended the staircase."

Sam grunted in satisfaction. "Pity. You'll likely never see her again."

Colin laughed. "Oh, I intend to see her again. It's only proper that we be introduced before the wedding, don't you think?"

It was, apparently a rhetorical question on his part, as Colin handed his empty tumbler to a nearby footman and walked away, quickly disappearing into the crowd.

"She's probably already married," Sam mumbled to himself, an affirmation of sorts that made him feel better. The most beautiful women, the most desirable women both in and out of bed, were always married. That judgment, over the years, had marred him. And on occasion saved him.

A pity indeed.

"Your grace?"

Sam turned his attention to his right to note with a trace of irritation that the Lady Ramona Greenfield had planted her statuesque figure beside him, a smile of genuine pleasure crossing her wide, thin lips.

"Lady Ramona, how are you this evening?" he asked appropriately, trying to keep a marked hesitation from his voice. There could only be one reason she'd sought him out this night.

"Your grace," she repeated, curtsying once as he took her hand and raised it to his lips, "I have some interesting news for you."

Sam sighed. The woman positively *lived* for match-making. "News?" was all he offered in response.

"More like an unusual opportunity, I suppose." She patted down stray, graying hair on the side of her head in feigned hesitation. "An introduction, more precisely, if I may be so bold. Although I must say this introduction may be a bit... unconventional."

The word "unconventional" made him frown fractionally. He had assumed such intrusion by Lady Ramona was in no doubt regarding Miss Edna Swan, and yet he couldn't imagine the shy, unassuming girl asking Lady Ramona to arrange an introduction. "Please go on," was all he could think of to say, his interest scratched.

The woman shifted from one foot to the other, gently pulling at the lace handkerchief wrapped loosely through her fingers. "Well, your grace, it seems there is a..." She leaned toward him and fairly mouthed, "*Frenchwoman*—who would like to make your acquaintance."

His body went perfectly still. For a second Sam felt his gut clench, his hand tighten around his tumbler of its own accord.

A Frenchwoman. How utterly uncanny considering his past—and beyond his patience, his time. There was nobody else on earth he would refuse with more gratification.

Giving Lady Ramona what he thought was his most charming smile, he replied with a slight nod, "I must thank you for the opportunity, but I don't think an introduction at this time would be appropriate, madam."

Such a response was rude; he knew that the moment her lips parted in a trifle gasp. And yet in his position she'd never question it, or repeat it in better circles.

But to his surprise, Lady Ramona didn't budge. Her face grew pink with discomfort and she fidgeted in her stays, but she remained determined in stance.

"Begging your pardon, your grace," she said, her voice lowered as she leaned toward him, "but this French-woman is ... different. She's quite insistent, and she is of exceptional quality, if I may say so."

He supposed at this point she had to say so. But such a description piqued his interest, as she knew it would. His brows rose. "Indeed."

Lady Ramona stood back again, smiling with satisfaction, relishing in the effect of her persuasion. "Yes, your grace. She asked for you by name."

Now *that* ensured an introduction. Sam changed his mind suddenly, deciding that meeting a Frenchwoman of "exceptional quality"—whatever that meant—would at the very least be an enticing addition to what had so far been a rather banal party.

After handing his half-empty tumbler to a passing footman, he smiled wryly and gave the lady a slight bow. "Then it would be my pleasure to meet her and be formally introduced."

Lady Ramona paused for only a second or two, her confidence obviously returned to her with the raising of her chin. She looked on the verge of adding something when another heavyset woman Sam didn't know interrupted them both, whispered in her ear, and scurried off.

Lady Ramona gave him one more slight curtsy. "If you will remain here, your grace, I shall be back momentarily."

"Then naturally I'll stay rooted to the spot in high anticipation," he replied.

For a moment she didn't know whether he meant that sarcastically and if she should respond, then obviously decided against comment. With a rather unsure smile, she turned and left him, disappearing into the crowd.

Sam rubbed his tired eyes, his impatience returning. His goal for tonight was to find a woman to seduce, not to become disenchanted and turned completely impotent by meeting a Frenchwoman, someone he'd dislike on principle and would *never* consider bedding no matter how sexually attractive she might be. With it would come too many painful memories of a past he longed to forget. Sometimes living up to his title proved so very fatiguing, no doubt furthering his continued bad luck where women were concerned. He needed to get this so-called meeting he'd reluctantly agreed to done quickly, then make the necessary excuses and take his leave in search of a more tempting venue.

Then he saw the angel in gold. No, not an angel as Colin had described, for she was surely the same creature his friend had seen earlier, but an exotic goddess of rare beauty and haunting blue eyes.

It had to be the glint of her shimmering gown that impressed him first, drawing immediate attention to her tall, shapely form, as it was certainly designed to do. The rich fabric sparkled in candlelight, beckoning him to gaze upon her outlined figure of stunning distinction—long, slender legs that rose to gently rounded hips, a narrowed waist and lifted breasts that would fill a man's hands—and then to a face that could only be described as one of pure, godly perfection.

He stared, enthralled, and for a timeless moment the vision rendered him dumbstruck.

She must have sensed his distraction, his surprise at the flawlessness of her beauty, for such women always could. Suddenly, as she neared him, one corner of her full, pink lips lifted into a knowing, wry, pleasure-filled smile. Of course she would offer him an amazing self-assurance, even defiance. She was French, after all. An intoxicating enchantress who used her assets. And she certainly had assets—of which he wanted no part.

Regaining his coolness, he clasped his hands behind his back, then purposely straightened his shoulders and stiffened, putting an invisible barrier between them. She stopped directly in front of him, next to Lady Ramona, who fairly preened with delight, all eyes in the vicinity focused on the three of them.

Sam mistrusted her immediately for no real reason he could define, and smelled her—pure vanilla and spice—the instant Lady Ramona began her introduction.

"My lord duke," the matchmaking busybody piped in gleefully above the din of the orchestra, "may I introduce the Lady Olivia Shea, formerly of Elmsboro, now of Paris. Lady Olivia, his grace, the Duke of Durham."

"Your grace," she murmured, with a curtsy, extending her gloved hand.

Her voice matched her appearance, an unusual, husky mix of sensuality, drama, and intrigue, carrying only a trace of an accent from her lips to his ears.

Sam reached out and wrapped his fingers around hers, tightening his grasp just enough to let her know that he'd be nothing to play with, that he remained the stronger of the two in this little rendezvous the Lady Olivia Shea had planned.

Aside from a slight narrowing of her eyes, she didn't appear to notice his attempt at superiority. Her skin felt warm beneath the satin of her gloves.

The music drew to a stop as he murmured, "Lady Olivia, I'm enchanted."

Lady Ramona clasped her palms together in front of her bosom. "Well, then, I'll leave you two to get acquainted."

He didn't look at her but offered her a nod. Lady Olivia said, "Thank you ever so, Lady Ramona."

The older woman hesitated, then cleared her throat to remind Sam that he still held to the beauty's fingers. A social faux pas under any circumstance, and naturally a matron at the ball would take it upon herself to save his reputation. He almost laughed at the thought, but instead released the Frenchwoman's hand as he should have seconds earlier. With that, Lady Ramona curtsied quickly and turned her attention to the crowd, waving to some other poor soul.

The music started up again, this time a waltz he didn't recognize. He certainly hoped Lady Olivia didn't expect him to ask her to dance. He loathed dancing. But at this point he wasn't even sure what to say to her.

She continued to stare at him, intently, as her hands

clutched a gold and ivory fan at her waist. Then she leaned toward him, her smile deepening as she whispered haughtily, "No more running, my darling. You can no longer escape me. I've found you."

She'd found him? Frenchwomen were certainly bold in their propositions. He remembered that from experience, and a certain coldness enveloped him.

Sam smirked and shoved his hands in his pockets. "I don't believe I've ever heard that sort of overture from a lady before," he drawled.

For the first time since their eyes had met, the Lady Olivia seemed uncertain. She blinked, straightening a bit as her smile faded. Then she raised her chin again in a measure of defiance.

"Why do you continue to play games with me?" she asked with more annoyance than confidence. "Can you not even acknowledge me? Is the crowd truly that important to your stellar reputation? You don't even look surprised."

It was Sam's turn to feel confused, though he did his best not to show it. "Surprised? I assure you, Lady Olivia, formerly of Elmsboro now of Paris, that very little about the French surprises me anymore." He lowered his voice and dropped his head slightly closer to hers. "And as for playing games, I gave that up long ago."

Her cheeks pinkened under the candlelight; her stunning blue eyes sparkled with a glint of ire. Sam didn't even know what the hell they were talking about, but what really irritated him was his desire to continue the conversation. He supposed he just liked looking at her.

"You've ruined me," she breathed, her voice and body suddenly hard with fierce anger.

Now he understood what they were talking about, and it enraged him. He fisted his hands in his pockets, careful not to draw attention to the two of them any more than she did just by being in the ballroom.

In an icy tenor he replied, "If you think to extort money from me by such a claim, I give you fair warning that no matter the boldness of your assertions, you will lose. My reputation is already floundered, my beautiful lady, and I have enough money to fight you to your grave."

She wanted to hit him. He could see it in her eyes, in the way her gaze traveled up and down his rigid body looking for the best place to strike, in the tightness of every muscle in her body. But she'd never do it here in front of society's elite, for she was far too refined. In some very strange manner, Sam found the entire thought a bit arousing, which thoroughly confounded him.

"Well, isn't this surprising?"

Sam jerked his head back, noticing that Colin stood at his side again, another drink in hand as he glanced from one of them to the other. Lady Olivia took a step back in apparent shock as well, flustered, it seemed, as she opened her fan and began swishing it in front of her breasts.

"You are truly the fairest of them all tonight," Colin said with a bow to her. "How on earth did I escape this introduction?"

Lady Olivia attempted a smile, curtsying briefly. "Good sir."

He reached for one of her hands and gently kissed the gloved fingers. "I am Colin Ramsey of Newark, though I see you've met my friend first. How the angels must be weeping."

She shifted her glance from one to the other, and Sam noted that she looked as unsettled by the interruption as he was, unsure what to do or say.

Sam suddenly felt confined, uncomfortable and hot in the muggy ballroom, wishing he could simply turn and walk away. But *she* had entered his very ordered realm of boredom with accusations and threats that disturbed him. His entire evening had shifted for the worse, and Colin was as charming as ever in his ignorance.

"Lady Olivia Shea," he fairly barked in introduction, "formerly of Elmsboro, now of Paris."

Colin tossed him a confused glance, then gazed back to the goddess in gold.

"So do you count yourself a Frenchwoman or an Englishwoman?" he asked.

"I am both," she offered, giving him a more genuine smile. "My late father was English, my late mother was from Paris." She pinched her lips together and shot Sam a seething look. "My *husband* is English."

God. A married Frenchwoman claiming he'd ruined her. Then again, maybe she would forget she'd accused him of improprieties after meeting Colin, London's most eligible gentleman of charm. Fat chance, that, with his luck.

"Husband?" Colin slapped his chest with his palm. "You wound me, dear lady."

Sam shifted from one foot to the other, his impatience growing, wishing he could tell Colin to get over it and go away.

Lady Olivia, however, had the decency to blush at his friend's ridiculous feigned infatuation. Or so it seemed to him. Maybe her heightened color was a product of the heat.

"Is your husband here tonight?" Colin continued jovially. "I would like to meet the man whose good fortune is so obviously beyond mine."

The Frenchwoman actually giggled—a melodious sound that rang in his ears of true innocence and joy. It totally unnerved him.

Then, in an instant of time, the Lady Olivia sighed and turned her attention back to him as she gave him a solid stare, her shy demeanor changing to one of pure smugness.

"Indeed, sir," she said without pause, grinning pretentiously, her gaze focused and intense. "This is my husband. Did he not tell you of me? I am married to Edmund."

It took hours, he thought, for her imperious and brazen announcement to invade his well-ordered, calculating mind; hours, it seemed, for him to comprehend the words she spoke and the central meaning behind them; hours for him to realize that in the slice of a second, this Frenchwoman of "exceptional quality" who stood before him had changed the course of his life.

Edmund. She thought he was Edmund.

The heat of the ballroom became thick and oppressive; the music a blaring cacophony. Expression controlled, he tightened his jaw, determined to remain composed even as his nostrils flared and his heart thudded suddenly from a dark, burning, surfacing rage.

She thought he was Edmund. She claimed to *know* the brother who nearly bankrupted him socially, stole the woman he loved, then left the country ten years ago, never to return.

This Frenchwoman had *married* Edmund. Or so she said.

Jesus.

She must have noticed his reaction, or perhaps rather his *inaction* to her bold affirmation, for at that moment she took a measured step back, watching him closely as her lips thinned.

"Did you think I wouldn't find you, my darling?" she asked haughtily, her shoulders rigid with indignation. "Did you think I wouldn't have the wherewithal to look? Or perhaps you just assumed I'd no longer have the funds to leave France after taking them from me so surreptitiously."

If Sam had been nonplussed by her beauty at first glance, he was veritably speechless now. There were so many questions rumbling through his mind. So many answers he would now be forced to obtain, answers that he really didn't want to know, least of all relating to her personally. But as his head began to clear, as his heartbeat began to slow, he realized that this woman was the key to finding Edmund, to finally learning what his nefarious brother had done when he'd left all those years ago.

Thankfully, Colin remained quiet, obviously understanding the shock and probably just as confused by the lady's pronouncements as he was. Yet he kept the slightest crooked grin on his mouth, no doubt enjoying this crazy turn of events, this spectacle, watching them both as he sipped his whiskey.

Sam ran his fingers through his hair, choosing

abruptly, and without *much* malicious intent, he decided, to play the game subtly, if not dastardly. He would deal with the deception later. Right now he wanted her in the palm of his hand, so to speak.

"You seem to have found me just fine, Olivia," he drawled, planting a wry smile on his mouth as he used her given name easily.

Colin chuckled. "Oh, what a tangled web we weave..."

Sam cast him a fast, silent warning. Then noting that nobody in their immediate surroundings appeared to be the least bit interested in their discussion, he reached out and clasped the Frenchwoman's arm.

"Dance with me," he whispered.

Her mouth dropped open a little at his daring, but she shut it again and smiled without humor. "I don't think so. I am here to confront you, Edmund, not to dance—"

"Confront me dancing, then," he interjected, pulling her against him before she could offer another protest.

She definitely didn't want to dance. Her body remained tight with anger, her cheeks flushed by either the warmth of the room or continued indignation, he couldn't be sure which.

Drawing her toward the center of the floor, he guided her into a steady rhythm, blending into the crowd that seemed to part for them. He supposed they made an appealing couple, both tall and dark, her clear, fair skin and blue, blue eyes contrasted by her nearly black hair and shimmering golden gown. No, he was quite sure it was simply her they stared at. He looked like an English nobleman; she looked...fabulous. The Lady Olivia Shea was undoubtedly the loveliest woman at the ball this night, possibly the loveliest woman he had encountered in years. And she knew him as Edmund. A profoundly uncomfortable turn of events, on every conceivable level.

"I see you've practiced," she said with some impudence and an obvious irritation at being forced to waltz with him.

I see my brother hasn't lost his touch for choosing sharp-tongued goddesses.

"What else is a man of my position to do, my darling Olivia?" he asked in reply, with all sincerity, observing that she danced quite well and followed his lead perfectly.

"Indeed. I didn't know you were a man of such a grand one, *your grace*," she fairly spat. "How convenient for you that you kept such intriguing information from me."

Sam tried not to smile. God, she was dazzling. "You didn't ask."

She almost gasped. "You're despicable."

He did smile at that. He couldn't help himself. "I've actually been called worse, but never by anyone quite so beautiful."

Such a softly spoken admittance—whether honest or facetious—seemed to captivate her, if only for a second, as her brow crinkled and she appeared at a loss for words. Then she lowered her gaze and scanned others in their vicinity.

Seething, she repeated, "I didn't come here to dance."

His lids narrowed as he smirked. "So you said. And yet you're marvelous at it. I could dance with you all evening."

Again she appeared to hesitate, failing faintly in her stride, her expression exposing a trace of confusion. Then she shook herself, blinking quickly and finding her pace once more.

Looking back into his eyes, she tightly clasped his shoulder with her gloved hand and glared at him directly. "Why are you doing this? I don't want you, your title, your name. And I especially don't want you to speak romantic words to me, as we both know they mean nothing. They never have."

He didn't respond to that, only watched her.

The music came to a halt and they slowed to a standstill.

Swiftly, she stepped away from him as if scorched by his very presence.

Once more glaring at him, chin raised, her fingers clutching her delicate fan at her breasts, she murmured, "I want my money returned to me, Edmund. And then I want our marriage annulled. The humiliation ends here, or so help me, by all that is holy, I will ruin *you*."

Although he did not take her threat seriously, he felt strangely troubled by her disclosure. Still, he wasn't all that surprised by it. If in fact this woman had known Edmund, everything she'd said tonight could very well be the truth. The Edmund he remembered would have readily ruined a young woman, would have easily taken her fortune and disappeared, even married her for it beforehand. Such had always been his very conniving nature. Yet at this point Sam had no information about anything regarding his long-lost brother, and for all he knew, this Frenchwoman could be part of some plot to extort money from him—with Edmund's help or without him. Just a mere knowledge of his and his brother's sordid past could be used against them for a prize, and Lady Olivia Shea, formerly of Elmsboro, now of Paris, possessed the smarts to do it. He'd learned that much in the last ten minutes.

For now he couldn't trust her, or any words she spoke from her beautiful, luscious pink lips. That was certain. But she was the first person in years to claim a recent, intimate relationship with Edmund, and such vital information, to him, was a value greater than a trunk filled with diamonds.

The music started again and the two of them edged toward the pillar to avoid the masses twirling in dance. Colin remained where he'd been standing, though he now laughed jovially as he spoke and flirted with three adoring ladies. Nothing ever changed—except that at this party Sam had the attention of the stunning Lady Olivia.

"Very well," he maintained matter-of-factly, his hands clasped behind him as he gazed into her eyes. "Since I have no desire to be ruined, I shall do my part." He paused, then teased, "If you do yours, Olivia."

She blinked. "My part? I have no part in this scheme."

He lifted his brows in innocence. "No? Then I'll take it upon myself to find one for you."

She was completely flustered now, her cheeks rosy again. He obviously infuriated her, and Sam wondered if his brother had done the same, feeling an odd satisfaction at the notion.

"My only concern is the House of Nivan, and you know it," she whispered a shade above the music. "Aside from that, there is nothing between us, you cowardly man."

Sam almost felt wounded. He had no idea what she meant by her "House of Nivan" comment, but if not for the fact that she assumed he was Edmund, her statement would have stung deeply.

Someone from the dance floor bumped into her, shoving her dangerously close to him. She didn't seem to notice or care; her penetrating gaze never wavered.

"Get your finances in order," she continued carefully, "and remember one thing..."

"Which one thing is that?" he asked softly.

She grabbed his arm boldly, clinging to him for support. "You'll never have this again."

Then on tiptoe, in the midst of a gathering of hundreds, she reached up and gently placed her warm lips on his, lingering there for the briefest few seconds before quickly trailing her tongue across his top lip and pulling away from him.

Sam swallowed, his body charged, his mind a sudden whirl of awareness, none of it good.

She toyed with him, using the expertise of the French, now smiling knowingly up to his face, her eyes gleaming with self-satisfied mischief.

He never moved, never acknowledged her action.

"You have one week, my darling *husband,* before I tell the world what you did to me."

With a lift of her skirts, the Lady Olivia Shea turned her back on him and disappeared into the crowd.

Sam stood rigidly still, ignoring the laugh from Colin, ignoring the stares of the appalled, one thought penetrating above all others:

With her lies danger...

Chapter 2

Olivia paced the bright scarlet carpeting of Lady Abethnot's pristine drawing room, fingers laced behind her, staring at the tiny green-stemmed red apples that dotted the wallpaper, waiting impatiently for Edmund to arrive as he said he would in his note to her this morning.

It had been three days since the ball. Three days for her to consider their rather heated conversation, their uncomfortable dance, that unconventional...kiss. If one could call it a kiss. She shivered at the memory of his warm touch, her boldness that, up until the moment of contact, had been totally unplanned.

He had most definitely changed in the last few months, and not just physically. True, his hair was quite short now, his skin not as deeply tanned, no doubt because he'd moved from sunny France to chilly London, and he'd dispensed of the jewelry and cologne, which surprised her most. But it was more than that. He *acted* different from the Edmund she remembered, and it had been just his unusual behavior of three days ago that confused her now, made her pause, forced her to think rationally about him for the first time since she left Paris two months ago.

Truthfully, she hadn't known Edmund very long before they'd married. But they seemed to take to each other easily, with an almost reckless abandonment, at least on her part, and she told herself at the time that getting to know each other better would be one of the joys of their married life. How naive she'd been! Edmund had never really loved *her,* he'd loved her money, as she had discovered upon visiting her bank shortly after he had abandoned her, her social prestige, her unique ability to run a challenging business from which he could profit by theft. And for all her smarts, she had been blinded by his appearance, his smooth and gracious behavior, his words of undying affection.

But never again. Never again would she allow herself to be taken by a man's good charm. Never again would she allow her intelligence, and especially her skills as a woman of industry, to be stolen and used by a professional liar. Her mother had instilled more common sense in her than that.

All of this had been in her thoughts constantly since he'd left her on their wedding night—until three nights ago at the ball when she'd met her husband again.

The moment she'd laid eyes on him she felt more than the intense pain of betrayal and humiliation she fully expected. She also recognized instantly that she was still very much attracted to him physically, something she thought would have passed naturally by this time. She knew she didn't love him anymore, but she certainly, to her irritation, felt drawn to him as a woman to a man. That was probably the greatest betrayal of all.

Still, the changes in him, though subtle, as she considered it carefully, confounded her the most. He'd become far more aloof, diffident even, as witnessed by his standing next to a pillar all evening instead of mingling. The Edmund she knew would have danced with every woman in attendance, from beginning to end, laughing his beautiful laugh, charming them into submission—as he'd done to her.

Olivia abruptly stopped pacing and stared at the large, velvet-draped window, now rain-splattered so that she could see nothing beyond the glass but the murky grayness of late afternoon. Lifting a square satin pillow off the sofa at her right, she began twirling it absentmindedly with her fingers, engaged in deep, confusing contemplation.

He wasn't her husband.

But that was nonsense. Of course he was.

Yet in some manner he…wasn't. Not entirely. Not like she remembered him, at the very least. Could a person change so much in a matter of months? Or had it all been an act? And he'd *never* mentioned that he was a duke. Good God, she'd married a man of such noble blood, and he never told her? Instead he resorted to stealing her inheritance?

He's not the Edmund I married…

A knock on the drawing room door startled her.

Before she summoned a reply, Lady Abethnot entered in a flurry of pale pink skirts and plump cheeks.

"Olivia," she remarked, a pleasant smile on her lips, "you have a guest. His grace, the Duke of Durham."

Lady Abethnot gestured with her arm, and he stepped around the woman to enter the room, tall and stately, dressed all too handsomely in a dark brown frock coat and trousers, expressionless save for his eyes, which glared at her like one who was ready to do battle with the devil.

"Madam," he murmured.

She curtsied. "Your grace."

"Well, then," Lady Abethnot cut in through a loud sigh. "I'll leave you to talk alone for a bit."

"Thank you," Olivia said with a smile to her hostess.

The lady smiled at her in return. "I'll only be in the next room should you choose to partake of refreshments. Call if you need me." With that she scurried out, leaving the door open a respectable crack as propriety demanded.

He didn't seem to notice Lady Abethnot's departure at all. He just stared hard at her. Her husband who was not her husband. In every way.

Olivia quashed a sudden burst of inappropriate laughter that threatened to escape from the absurdity of it all. For at that second she realized definitively that this man, identical to Edmund in every physical way, was *not* the man she married.

Instinctively, she threw the pillow at him before he could speak. He caught it in one hand, then tossed it onto the leather chaise beside him.

"Who are you?" she asked bitterly, breaking the silence between them.

Without pause or prevarication he replied, "I am Samson Carlisle, Duke of Durham. Edmund is my brother."

She managed to hide her surprise, clasping her hands behind her back. "Your twin."

"Yes."

That explained everything.

His gaze traveled slowly up and down the length of her body, for no reason she could think of, and his scrutiny made her shiver inside. He was certainly more arrogant than Edmund, and for a split second she also thought perhaps a bit more devastating in appearance.

"But you're obviously older," she said, watching him carefully.

He raised an eyebrow at that. "Only by three minutes, to be precise."

She chuckled from his distinct display of defensiveness, tipping her head to the side a fraction. "I meant no offense, your grace. However identical the two of you appear, you are the man with the title."

One corner of his mouth turned up snidely. "So I've been told by my brother, repeatedly."

"Ahh...I see." Now she understood. Jealousy on Edmund's part lay at the core. For all she knew of her husband, she didn't doubt it in the least.

Silence reigned for a moment or two, and she shifted uncomfortably from one foot to the other. To a great degree, this man surprised her. He didn't flirt, he didn't sit, he didn't even look around the well-decorated drawing room. He just stared at her, expressionless. Olivia wasn't sure what to do.

"I suppose I'm now your sister by marriage," she remarked, attempting to break the ice.

"So you say," he returned at once.

That insult took her aback. "So I say?" It was her turn to look him up and down. "Are you always so dour, sir?"

Clearly caught off guard by her audaciousness, he jerked his head back a little. Then he answered simply, "Usually. I'm nothing like Edmund."

"That's an understatement," she agreed with a grunt.

His eyes narrowed and he clasped his hands behind his back. "Knowing I'm nothing like Edmund, madam," he said gravely, "is the only reason I'm here today."

In some very strange manner, that remark, no doubt posed to be intimidating, warmed her instead, though she would never let such a weakness to his rather mundane comment show in expression or voice.

Smiling satisfactorily, she glanced down briefly to the sofa, running her fingertips gently along the cushioned back. "You look very much like him," she admitted pleasantly, "though it only took me ten minutes or so to realize how different you are in personality."

At long last he began to take a few steps into the drawing room. "I wouldn't know. I haven't seen or spoken to Edmund in nearly a decade."

She almost gasped. Her head shot up abruptly as she looked back into his eyes. "I suppose that's why he never mentioned he had a twin. I can only guess the two of you had some sort of falling out."

He didn't answer her immediately, though he did drop his gaze from her for the first time since entering Lady Abethnot's home, continuing to walk slowly toward her as he grumbled, "When did you meet him?"

His redirection of the path of their conversation didn't slip by her. Of course she wanted—needed—to know what actually happened to split them into warring enemies all those years ago. But she reined in her curiosity for now. With this turn of events she had more important things to consider. This man wasn't her husband, and Edmund had been the one to steal her money. Yesterday she thought she had answers; this afternoon she realized she could be as far as ever from getting her funds returned to her, or at least getting some sort of justice. And above everything else, she now had *this* man to contend with. What a nightmare.

Olivia felt a sudden jolt of nervousness as he neared her. Instead of answering his question, she asked instead, "Why did you lie to me about your identity at the ball?"

He snickered, the first sign from him of anything remotely resembling humor. "Because it was far too entertaining to watch you treat me, and think of me, as Edmund."

Incensed, Olivia couldn't think of a reasonable thing to say to that. She took a step away from him as he took one nearer. He moved fairly next to her now, so close that the hem of her rose-colored skirts brushed his dark, polished shoes. She stood her ground this time, though, determined not to let him see how confused he made her just by his presence. She had the distinct feeling the man used intimidation on purpose because of his incredible height and very masculine build. Edmund had never done that, but then Edmund got his way by flirting, not intimidating. She suddenly had to wonder if this man had ever flirted with a woman in his life.

"When did you meet my brother?" he asked again, more pointedly this time.

She blinked, then ran her palms down her tightly corseted waist. "Wouldn't you rather sit to discuss this?"

His brows drew together fractionally, indicating to her that he hadn't even thought about sitting.

"Very well," he said abruptly, turning and moving to the settee, "but my time is valuable, Lady Olivia."

"As is mine, your grace," she replied at once, her tone conveying a growing impatience. "I'm quite certain you won't stay a minute longer than is necessary."

Her twist of words amused him. She could tell by the droll look he tossed in her direction as he sat heavily on the bright red cushion, though he didn't comment. She gracefully lowered her body into a small parlor chair near the window, facing him directly across a tea table.

He waited for her to begin, and she didn't waste his time. "I met your brother at a soiree celebrating the birthday of our gracious Empress Eugenie. Of course she wasn't in attendance, but it was in her honor, and everyone who is *anyone* was there."

"Naturally," he drawled.

Olivia realized she was in danger of rambling, her nerves making her resemble a typical capricious miss rather than the intelligent lady she was raised to embody. She shifted her bottom in her chair so that she sat ever more regally, then clasped her palms together loosely in her lap, concentrating on keeping to the point. "Edmund is quite a charming man and he flattered me, your grace. I'm certain you're aware of his skills and his reputation as a rake. I was not entirely ignorant of his spurious adoration, you understand, but he also seemed quite fascinated by my work for the empress, and that impressed *me*—"

"Fascinated by your *work* for the empress?" he cut in as he crossed one leg over the other and stretched his arms wide across the back of the settee.

She tried very hard not to stare at the muscles of his chest as they instantly pressed against the whiteness of his tailored shirt, pulling the buttons taut. The man had a...healthy physique. Or so she suspected. She refused to look him over brazenly to be sure.

"Yes," she replied after clearing her throat. "I think it was the central reason I quickly became...enamored of him."

"What type of work do you do, Lady Olivia?" he asked, his amusement now coupled with a bit of genuine intrigue.

He didn't know. Which meant he hadn't checked what he could of her background after her appearance at the ball. For a few seconds she felt a tad insulted that he didn't seem concerned about her veiled threats of three days ago, but then not that many in London knew her now that she was grown and living in France. It did, however, give her an odd sense of satisfaction to inform him that "her work" had nothing to do with menial labor, nor was she talking about volunteering for one of Eugenie's good causes. In truth, she adored watching gentlemen squirm when she told them she ran a business for profit, and that she was quite successful at it.

"I'm the proprietor of my late stepfather's manufacturing company. In essence, I am the sole manager of the House of Nivan in Paris."

It took only seconds for her to realize he had no idea on earth what she was talking about. She'd wondered about that the night of the ball as well, when she'd mentioned Nivan and he'd given her a blank stare. She now understood why.

Sighing, she eased lightly into her stays and expounded. "The House of Nivan is a company that produces perfume, your grace, and is considered one of the best in all of France. We also make fragranced soaps, scents, and smelling salts, and ship our product all over the civilized world, as we've done for more than forty years."

If she'd surprised him with that announcement, he seemed as staid about it as she was proud. His brows drew together slightly and he glanced up and down her sitting form again, this time with calculation. That made her warm beneath her silk gown, her face flush with heat, but Olivia ignored it, hoping her cheeks weren't overly pink.

Finally he drew in a long, slow breath. "So, I'm assuming you—or rather your business—makes a perfume for the Empress Eugenie?"

"Exactly," she replied. "We serve the French elite along with three or four other good quality fragrance houses in France. However, the one the empress frequents is always considered the finest, even if it isn't actually so.

Until just recently, her choice for her fragrance purchases was the House of Nivan; she'd been with us for nearly a decade. And when she patronized us exclusively, she brought with her other fashionable clientele. Of course she is free to choose a different house at any time, if any one of them creates a scent she prefers, and so we try very hard to remain competitive. Because of your brother, your grace, my business has lost that competitive edge." She leaned forward a little, staring into his eyes intently. "I want that edge returned to me."

The duke adjusted his large body on the settee a bit, relaxing as he more or less analyzed her. "I'm impressed," he said at last.

Olivia blinked, unsure whether he meant that truthfully or sarcastically, or what it might be, exactly, that impressed him. He didn't seem at all interested in the art of creating fragrances, but he continued to watch her closely, as if expecting her to get to whatever it might be that she considered the point.

He began to drum his fingertips along the top of the settee. "I'm guessing Edmund stole funds from you that you insist are for keeping the princess adorned in fragrance?"

She crossed her arms over her breasts. "That's a bit simplistic. But yes, he stole much of the money I had saved to invest in the business after my mother's death two years ago. If I don't repay the debts I owe to keep running it, I will be forced to close the House of Nivan." She paused, then with a gentle lift of her chin added bitterly, "I believe Edmund used me for this purpose, and planned it from the day he met me."

The Duke of Durham remained silent for a long time

it seemed, watching her, his dark eyes narrowed in speculation. Then he leaned forward, elbows on knees, his hands clasped together in front of him. "How, exactly, did my brother manage to steal from you?"

She gazed at him as if he were daft. "He married me."

He snickered. "Yes, apparently, but I can't imagine a woman of your obvious intelligence and...business sense just giving him the money should he simply ask for it. I'm curious as to how he planned this."

His words and tone conveyed sincerity, and Olivia felt warm to her bones from such a compliment, though she was careful not to beam. She didn't think a man, aside from perhaps her father, had ever called her intelligent before. "Edmund took copies of our marriage documents and withdrew money from my bank as only a husband can, with the help of my banker, of course."

"I see," he replied, expressionless. "How awfully convenient."

Olivia wasn't sure if that comment annoyed her or not. "Is there some reason you don't believe me?"

He inhaled deeply again and sat back a little. "I have no reason *not* to believe you, Lady Olivia, because I know Edmund. I would never steal funds from my wife and then leave her, but he—the brother I remember—very well might. As I said before, Edmund and I are very different. Our personalities are as opposite as our appearance is similar."

She couldn't argue that. Standing side by side she wasn't certain she would be able to tell them apart.

"You don't wear a fragrance," she said aloud without thought, studying him.

He did look genuinely surprised by that unexpected comment. "I'd rather bathe. I loathe cologne."

Smiling, she countered, "In our modern society a person no longer wears a scent simply to hide offensive human odor, your grace. A man's choice of cologne tells much about his personality, his style, and he wears it to express that part of him."

He grunted at that. "You're saying I lack personality and style, madam?"

"Of course not," she scoffed. "You just haven't found the fragrance to match yours yet."

For the first time the Duke of Durham actually grinned at her, and the look, so magnificently handsome and balanced with charm, nearly melted her in her chair.

"As you have found yours?"

Olivia felt perspiration break out on the back of her neck, her upper lip, and she fought the urge to pat it. Why on earth did he seem so...cool? "I wear many fragrances," she replied neutrally. "I usually choose one to fit my mood."

"Ah. So I noticed."

"You noticed?" was all she could think of to say in response.

He shrugged as if his comment had meant nothing. "You smell different today." His expression turning grave once more, he added, "I'm very perceptive when I need to be, Lady Olivia."

That warning struck home, and with it an uncomfortable silence grew. For a moment or two he continued to watch her with keen eyes, and to her credit, she remained composed, forthright in her bearing, though certainly blushing terribly from the fact that he thought about how she *smelled*. She just prayed he wouldn't notice her embarrassment—even if he was as perceptive as he claimed to be.

Then at last he rubbed his chin with long fingers and stood again. She did the same, as gracefully as she could under the circumstances.

"I'll need to see the copies of your marriage documents," he said.

"Of course; I'll get them."

He pulled a face of surprise, and Olivia reined in a smile of satisfaction as she lifted her skirts and walked past him toward the small oak secretary near the window.

"I've had copies made. Edmund certainly has one. But this is the original document that I do need returned to me."

She glanced up to him and he smiled dryly. "You seem to have thought of everything, Lady Olivia."

"Yes," she replied at once, handing him a quilled pen. "I also need your signature, should you decide not to return this."

He walked up to stand very close beside her. She couldn't help it this time, she refused to drop her gaze from his, but she instinctively took a step back from his amazing height and overbearing stance.

"Of course, Lady Olivia," he consented, looking down to her flushed face, his tone deep and sincerely amused.

She forced herself not to fidget as she handed him the pen. "You'll note that the top paper states that I'm giving you my marriage certificate, to be returned to me after you've had adequate time to evaluate it."

He finally glanced down to the paper. Then taking the pen from her fingertips, he dipped it in ink and scribbled his signature on it.

"Thank you, your grace," she said after he slipped the pen back into the inkwell.

"It's been my pleasure to accommodate you, madam," he drawled, standing tall again and staring down at her.

Olivia couldn't take any more of the oppressive heat in Lady Abethnot's drawing room, or maybe it was just his oppressive closeness. It didn't matter; she was done with him for today.

Quickly, she gathered up the paperwork and handed him the appropriate certificate.

"Thank you, sir, for your promptness in this matter," she offered pleasantly.

"Of course," he replied without extrapolating.

For a discomfiting moment neither of them moved. Then he tilted his head to the side a fraction and asked, "What do you consider yourself, Lady Olivia, French or English?"

She pulled back in surprise, lacing her fingers together behind her. "I am both."

He continued to gaze into her eyes for several long seconds, then nodded vaguely. "Of course you are."

She had no idea how to take that, and he supplied no other explanation.

Another awkward moment passed. Then he took a small step away from her and bowed his head once.

"I shall be in touch with you within a matter of days, madam, at which time we will discuss what we're going to do about my wayward brother."

"Thank you, your grace."

He lowered his gaze down her form one final time and, she thought, paused far too long at her breasts. She didn't move.

"Good day, Lady Olivia," he said flatly before he turned on his heel and walked out of the drawing room.

Her heartbeat raced for a long time, it seemed, after she'd heard Lady Abethnot's front door close behind him. Then she collapsed into the settee without thought to wrinkling her billowing skirts, staring out the window at the sprinkling rain, only one thought in her mind:

He might prove more dangerous than Edmund...

Chapter 3

I am both.

   She'd said it the night of the ball, too, and he'd thought it just as ridiculous then. How could one be both French *and* English? It was true that one could be born of both, as in Lady Olivia's case—an English father and a French mother. But it was beyond his comprehension how a person could choose to be of both heritages. One was either French *or* English. Not both.

   She was a most annoying woman, in more ways than he could name, possessing a remarkably strong intellect for an Englishwoman of aristocratic background, coupled with a face and body that defied description. That bothered him most of all.

   Yet it shouldn't, he admonished himself, shifting his large frame in the carriage as he rode along Upper Rhine Street toward Colin's town house. That she still looked like the French goddess he'd seen in her the night of the ball was really not her *fault*. He'd hoped she'd be less appealing under the telling light of afternoon, but nothing about her, or her clothing, could be considered remotely ordinary. True, she wore much less formal attire today—a day gown in...blue? He couldn't remember. Even so it remained obvious how remarkable she looked in or out of clothes, making it extremely difficult for him to concentrate on anything she actually said. And he hated admitting that he was attracted to her—his brother's *wife,* for God's sake. What a nightmare this could turn out to be.

The morning had been stormy, gloomy and gray, but as evening approached the rain began to ease somewhat, allowing him to alight from his carriage at the front gate of Colin's home without getting drenched. He marched quickly to the tall black door and knocked hard, twice. After a long moment a silver-haired butler he'd never seen before answered and moved aside immediately for him to enter. Sam stifled a chuckle. Colin changed employees like he changed his drawers. He'd never seen the same servants twice, and each time he visited, he wondered if his friend rotated the help so much because of his clandestine work for the Crown. But then he didn't really care and he'd never thought to ask. Right now he had more important issues on his mind.

After walking swiftly through the parlor and down the entire length of the long, dimly lit hallway, Sam rapped twice on the door to Colin's spacious study, where he'd been told his friend awaited him, then opened it without waiting for reply. The warmth of the low burning fire struck him immediately, as did the strong odor of tobacco that encircled Colin's head as he sat behind his enormous oak desk.

Sir Walter Stemmons of Scotland Yard, a hard, broad-shouldered man with a pockmarked face and keen eyes that missed nothing, stood beside his friend, peering down to paperwork in which they were both obviously engrossed, until Colin glanced up and grinned dryly at him.

Sam snorted as he stepped inside, closing the door behind him. He knew what was coming.

"So, the damsel tie you down?" Colin asked with a flick of his head.

"Literally or figuratively?" he returned nonchalantly, walking toward a black leather chair beside the fireplace.

Sir Walter chuckled and stood upright, pulling down hard on his sleeves. "If my wife had any notion of the things bachelors discuss—"

"She'd tie you down?" Sam cut in.

"I'm deathly afraid so, yes," Sir Walter said with a nod and a crooked grin that made his features look remarkably young for his nearly sixty years. "Colin has been explaining your unusual dilemma, your grace. I'll be happy to help in any way I can, of course."

Sam nodded a silent thanks to the man as he sat heavily on the cushioned leather, leaning slightly to the side and stretching the opposite leg out in front of him. "It could get rather complicated, I'm afraid. I don't want to take too much of your time away from the Yard."

With a toss of his hand, Sir Walter balked at that and

leaned his hip against the edge of the desk. "I'm nearly retired at this point," he maintained, his voice gruffly proud. "My time is generally my own, meaning that I can take my own cases, and frankly, any threat to the peerage *is* my business."

Sam didn't know if he'd call Olivia Shea a threat to the peerage, unless one considered her striking appearance.

Dammit.

"She didn't seem very threatening to me," Colin said lightly.

He groaned inwardly and rubbed his tired eyes with his fingers and thumb. "She claims Edmund married her then disappeared, taking her fortune with him."

Sir Walter grunted. Colin let out a low whistle then mumbled, "Unbelievable."

Sam looked directly at the two men. "Really? I don't think so. This is Edmund we're discussing. I'd only be more surprised if he'd married and cheated a homely girl. But true to form, Olivia isn't homely in the least."

"No, not in the least," Colin repeated through a grin. He sat forward, forearms atop the papers and notes on his cluttered desk. "What did you bring me?"

"Her marriage license." Sam waved the paper in front of him but remained sitting, wanting to talk the situation through before he gave it to his friend to scrutinize.

Colin raised his brows. "Indeed. The original? She trusted you with it?"

His lips thinned into a line of annoyance. "She made me sign for it."

Both men chuckled, and Sam felt a certain flush creep up his neck.

"She's thought of everything, hasn't she?" Colin remarked.

Sam's eyes narrowed. "She's apparently something of a perfumer, and manages a business called the House of Nivan in Paris."

Sir Walter remained silent, kneading his chin with his fingers and thumb as he absorbed the information like a good detective would.

"Fascinating," Colin said seconds later, bemused. "And I gather she's come here looking for her wayward scoundrel of a husband but found you instead."

Sam tendered no response to that. Instead, he bluntly asked, "What did you think of her?"

Colin shrugged minutely. "She's amazing; well-spoken, well-dressed, stunning to look at."

He sighed. "Besides the physical."

Colin's chair creaked as he sat back fully and relaxed again. "I don't know."

"That doesn't help me," he said through a snort. "I need more of your first impression of the woman. Just...ideas, thoughts that come to mind, however seemingly insignificant."

After a long moment of a more serious contemplation, Colin expounded. "She's...clever, and obviously spirited. A woman of passions, which, I suppose, is typical of the French."

So very true, Sam thought, in *every* respect, which worried him, frankly.

"Under the right circumstances," Colin continued, "she might prove to be an engaging confidante; she seems genuinely quick with words and...sophisticated, probably due to her travels and apparently good upbringing. However, these are my impressions from only talking to her briefly, Sam."

"May I suggest she's probably also extremely organized?" Sir Walter piped in. He pushed himself away from the desk edge to stand straight again, crossing his arms over his chest as he began to pace to the side of it, staring down to the hardwood floor. "I realize I've never met her personally, but if she truly oversees a thriving perfume business—and I say thriving because if Edmund indeed stole her money, she had to have enough for him to spend the time devising this enormous scheme—then she can certainly plan and execute operations. She was clearly determined and independent enough to come to England on her own in search of her missing husband. Most ladies would never dream of such a thing."

"Organized, determined, independent. The worst qualities in a female," Sam said, wiping his palm down his face in feigned pain.

Sir Walter laughed. "I'm sure there are worse."

"Like stupidity," Colin interjected, his tone rather sober in light of the discussion. "It should be noted that if she *did* marry your brother, Sam, such an action was obviously unwise. She didn't seem at all dense to me, or shy. She's certainly sensual, but not obviously a frivolous romantic, so there's no telling what he might have told her, or how he might have charmed her, to get her to wed him." Colin drew a long breath and let it out slowly. "There's also the possibility that she devised this scheme all by herself after meeting Edmund and learning his twin brother is a wealthy man of the British nobility. I think she's probably that smart."

He'd thought so, too, and added, "It's also possible that she and Edmund are lovers, married or not, and that they're working together to extort money from me by playing on my sympathies for an abandoned female and my contempt for my brother." He gave the two men a sideways glance. "Her showing at the ball three nights ago might have been the first act in a very long play of wit and games and devious calculation. I don't know her, but I wouldn't put anything past Edmund. And she *is* half French."

"Doesn't that also make her half English?" Sir Walter asked carefully.

Sam chose not to respond to what he knew was a rhetorical question. Both Colin and a few he knew well at the Yard, Sir Walter included, were very much aware of his past relations with one particular Frenchwoman. Some scandals never died, however one tried to forget them, or however one's friends tried to put past mistakes in a positive light.

Colin drummed his fingertips on the top of a pile of tossed papers. "It doesn't help that she's beautiful also, does it?"

Tightening his jaw, he softly replied, "No, that doesn't help at all."

Silence droned for a few seconds. Then Colin said, "Let me see the document."

Sam stood warily and walked to the desk, holding the marriage license in his outstretched hand.

Colin reached for it gingerly, then lighting a lamp on his desk, he placed the paper beneath it and began to scrutinize it inch by inch.

Sir Walter stood behind his friend, staring down at

the document, his thick brows crinkled. Sam waited with as much patience as he could muster under the circumstances, trying not to ask Colin questions before he'd finished his evaluation. This was what he did for a living, and the man was quite possibly the greatest forger—and the greatest detector of forged documents—that had ever lived in England. He'd been caught at the age of twenty-four, sentenced to work for the Crown, and this he'd readily done for more than twelve years. But very few people knew of his work. To everybody outside a small circle of friends and colleagues, Colin was simply the dashing, but rather lazy, Duke of Newark who spent his time attending parties and flirting with the ladies. The fact that his line of work remained a tightly held secret was their government's greatest asset.

Colin started to chuckle and his head popped up. "This is marvelous."

Sam frowned and leaned over the desk. "How so?"

His friend leaned on the armrest of his rocker and tapped the document. "It's an *excellent* forgery. Well . . . it's not a forgery exactly, but it's not a legitimate license of marriage, either."

"What does that mean?" Sir Walter asked, peering closer.

"That the document is real, but it's been altered. Look here."

Sam turned his neck aslant to better view the area at the bottom right edge of the document where Colin ran the pad of his thumb over the indented seal.

"The document itself is legal, meaning this is the actual document used to record civil marriages in whichever parish they were married in the country of

France." Colin raised an old steel magnifying glass and analyzed the bottom right corner. "However, the seal height is off—it's pressed in too high. It's also got one or two tiny indentations on the bottom of it that aren't normally there."

"You've seen other marriage documents enough to know this?" Sam asked.

Colin shot him a quick, perplexed glance. "Of course."

He had nothing to say to that.

"And as I look at the entire document now enlarged," Colin continued, "there are letters printed off center, perhaps one-twentieth of an inch. See that?"

Sam squinted, staring hard where Colin traced the supposed falsity with a fingertip, yet saw nothing that appeared less than perfect. "No, I don't."

Colin didn't offer a clarification. Instead, he flipped the paper over for a second or two, then back again. Finally, he lifted the magnifying glass again and slowly followed the edges of the document, then moved in to the lettering, tracing each one attentively.

Moments later he straightened once more and tossed the counterfeit license of marriage on top of his own pile of paperwork. "I'd have to see a recent signature from Edmund to know if he actually signed this. But aside from that, this document is real, and it's been altered, making it a forgery, and a very expensive one. Of that I'm sure."

Silence prevailed for a second or two, then Sam said thoughtfully, "Meaning someone spent a lot of money to enact this scam. Do you know anyone who could do this kind of work?"

"Personally?" Colin frowned, shaking his head. "No, not offhand. But I'll think on it, check with some of my contacts if you'd like. It might take some time."

Unfortunately, time was a luxury Sam was afraid he might not have. He ran his fingers roughly through his hair. "Do what you can. It might help."

"So," Sir Walter chimed in, turning his back on them and rounding the desk to stare out the window, hands clasped behind him, "are they not married, then? Or would it still be a legal marriage if done in the eyes of the Church, regardless of the signed document? I would think so."

Sam's stomach suddenly clenched uncomfortably; it had been the one question he'd been hesitating to ask.

Colin thought about that for a moment. "I think so, too, but it would depend upon who performed the ceremony. The name on this document means nothing." He leaned forward to read the license. "Jean-Pierre Savant. I'm sure that's a very common name in France, and it could be entirely made up."

"Or it could be legitimate," Sam argued.

"Yes," Colin agreed. "And if the signature is that of a man of the cloth, ordained to perform marriages, then I'd have to say they're legally wed, regardless of the document, at least in the eyes of the Church. And remember, witnesses always count."

"But we must keep in mind," Sir Walter said, turning back to consider them, "that actors and even witnesses can be purchased. If she *is* married to Edmund, even if only in the eyes of the Church, her money is his. He's not then guilty of anything but abandonment."

Sam groaned, once more rubbing his eyes. "Which would leave her my responsibility."

Sir Walter let out a long, loud breath and shoved his hands in his pockets. "Probably. At least until an annulment is secured. Does she have family?"

Sam shook his head. "I've no idea. But I suppose the bright side is that she has no children from the union."

"You can't be sure of that," Colin remarked softly.

Sam thought about that for a moment. Then, turning away from the desk, he strode toward the fireplace, his gaze falling on the burning embers. "I just don't think so. She never mentioned a child, which would be the ultimate argument for my help, financial or otherwise." He shook his head minutely and clasped his hands behind his back. "I don't know how long they were married before he allegedly left, but if she had a child, I think she'd tell me for nothing more than just the sympathy." He paused, then added, "And she's also very...trim."

"Trim," Colin repeated almost pensively. "And spectacularly shapely, I should add."

Sam ignored that, closing his eyes briefly to chastise himself. He shouldn't have mentioned her figure. Her appearance was irrelevant as far as he was concerned. Or at least it should be.

With a deep inhale, he turned to face his friends once more, with stately bearing, his expression grave. "As I see it, gentlemen," he speculated, "there are two possibilities here. She's either telling the truth—as far as she knows it—and my brother married her under false pretenses and absconded with her...perfume fortune. Or she's lying and has come here to extort part of *my* fortune. Now, if she's actually telling the truth, and if Edmund actually took her money, they are either married or they are not. Either way, if she is being truthful about Edmund, then she probably believes they are. The only other scenario is that she and Edmund are in this together, in which case I could become the ultimate fool." Though the thought made him almost physically ill, he also noted that he lacked any real surprise. Edmund's manipulations had stopped shocking him years ago.

Sir Walter cleared his throat. "Well, to err on the side of caution is the prudent thing to do, of course. Until you understand the situation better, get to know her better, you can't trust anything more than what she tells you, and only take that at face value."

Sam nodded in complete agreement. The last thing he intended to do as far as Lady Olivia was concerned was to show her his hand, regardless of whether he bluffed.

"Want me to make a copy of the marriage document?" Colin offered, interrupting his thoughts.

"Can you do it quickly?" he asked, walking toward the two men again.

Colin lifted the forgery and gazed at it once more, front and back. "I suppose I can have a good copy done for you in a day or two."

"That will do," Sam said with appreciation. "I'll invite her to dinner or some such thing in a few days. That should give her time to wonder what I'm doing about her announcement."

"You don't trust her at all, do you," Colin stated rather than asked.

"Not for a minute," he returned at once, "and for other reasons besides the fact that she's a French-woman." Pacing in front of the desk, he noted for the first time that Colin had his study walls recently papered in a god-awful shade of brown. Not that it mattered. "Think of it this way," he continued, his voice direct as his impressions of the situation began to solidify. "If she's sincere, and truly believes she's legally married, I have the upper hand with the knowledge that she's been duped by my brother. If she's not sincere, she'll be forced to wonder how much I believe of her story, and whether I trust her or anything she says."

"She'll likely wonder that anyway," Sir Walter remarked.

"True," he acknowledged. He stopped pacing and gazed out the window to his left. "Which means my plan must be better than hers."

"What plan?" Then Colin sighed, leaning back heavily in his chair, lacing his fingers together behind his head. "Tell me you're not going to France."

"No, I *am* going to France."

"With *her*?"

Sam almost laughed at the priceless look of shock, even subtle envy, that Colin gave him.

"Of course." He leaned over his friend's desk, placing his palms flat on the scattering of paperwork. "Frankly, I don't care who she is—if she's only naive or lying with pleasure, or whether she's working with Edmund or looking for him as she says. I want to find my brother—"

"And Claudette?"

Sam immediately stood erect, his gut burning again

with a displaced anger and resentment he'd tried to hide for years.

"If she's with him, perhaps."

"For revenge," Colin bluntly said for him.

"To set things straight," he murmured in quick response, explaining nothing.

Colin slowly shook his head. Then sitting forward, forearms resting on the cluttered desktop, fingers interlocking, he gazed up at Sam's face, his tone underscored with warning. "Nothing has changed in all the years he's been gone. You know why he left, and although this beauty, who claims to be his wife, is part French—"

"And part English," he cut in.

Colin blinked innocently. "Now you're defending her?"

Sam didn't know whether to be angry or grateful to Colin for helping him keep things in perspective. "I know what I'm doing."

"Well then," Sir Walter added, rubbing his palms along his wide chest, "I'd be careful if I were you. From what you've described of the Lady Olivia, she doesn't strike me as a woman to be undermined. Especially if she's toying with *you*."

Sam nodded once, acknowledging the older man's advice with an uncomfortable sense of foreboding.

"So you'd use her for revenge," Colin maintained wryly.

Sam said nothing for a moment, then harshly whispered, "Opportunity."

The rain suddenly intensified again, pelting the large window behind the desk, interrupting their discourse with a reminder of outside realities.

Colin stood and stretched. "Let's eat, gentlemen. I've got a new cook and he's marvelous with a hen."

Back to realities indeed. "As are you, my friend."

Sir Walter snickered; Colin laughed outright. "And yet you seem to attract the ones of exceptional beauty."

"Who never belong to me," he quickly countered.

"There's always Edna Swan..."

He didn't like that option, either.

Chapter 4

Olivia knocked impatiently on the front door of number 2 Parson's Street, invitation in hand. She wasn't certain if this was the Duke of Durham's residence or only that of a friend with whom the man stayed while in the city. She'd learned from Lady Abethnot that the man spent most of the year secluded in his Cornish estate near Penzance. But he'd asked her here for dinner, in a hastily written note, to discuss their "mutual predicament"—whatever that was—and she had quickly consented to the summons. If dinner was to be served, all the better.

Her first impression of the outside of this rather large stone town house was one of amazement that a person could fairly "hide" a home of this size and elegant beauty in the middle of a busy city street. Granted, whoever owned the property lived in a very good neighborhood, but its deceptive appearance was no doubt caused by the manner in which the house stood back, well shaded by trees and sculpted shrubs that lined the cobblestone walkway from the edge of the drive, where she'd stepped from the cushioned coach he'd sent for her, to the gas-lighted entryway. The scents of spring were in the air, insects buzzing at the coming twilight, and she breathed deeply of the gentle fragrance of a wide variety of roses mixed with juniper and a tinge of leftover rainfall. Such intoxicating and refreshing scents would normally instill a moment of calm—if not for her extreme nervousness at seeing *him* again.

The door opened at that precise moment, startling her from her attempt at relaxing thoughts. She straightened her spine instinctively to acknowledge the butler, dressed formally in black on white, but before she could utter a sound or offer him her invitation, the man gave her a slight bow.

"Lady Olivia," he said with wide, thick lips that hardly moved. "His grace is waiting for you in the dining room."

"Thank you," she replied, walking into the town house as he stepped aside for her.

She wore no shawl, as the day had been quite warm, and so she handed him only her bonnet, then smoothed wayward strands of hair into the uptwisted curls loosely piled atop her head.

"This way, if you please," directed the butler, who still offered her no name of his own, as he turned and began to lead her down a dimly lit corridor.

Olivia didn't hesitate; she wasn't afraid in the least. Beside herself with nerves, perhaps, but definitely not afraid. She raised her chin, straightened her shoulders, and walked with confidence across a dark marble floor, expensive and covered with forest green and burgundy colored Persian rugs. The inside of the house awed her even more than the outside, decorated in various hues of gold, red, and bronze and containing a wealth, it seemed, of imported furniture and accessories, its style distinctively masculine. If there's one thing she knew already about the Duke of Durham, it was that he had exquisite taste and plenty of money—or his friends did. He smelled good, too, even without cologne, something she'd never considered about a man before. Every man she'd ever known had worn cologne, including Edmund.

She shook herself of such ridiculous thoughts. Why on earth she thought of the way he *smelled* at a time like this was beyond her imagination. Tonight she needed, above all things, to remain *focused*.

With her stolen company funds and the precarious future of Nivan front and center in her mind, Olivia immediately forced herself to concentrate on the meeting ahead as she walked into the dining room. The aroma of oranges and roasted game struck her at once, as did the pleasing atmosphere of thick burgundy carpet, painted walls of teal and brown, polished furniture in dark cherrywood, and the warmth of a slow burning fire.

Then she noticed him, and her heart actually skipped a beat or two—before it began to race with a tinge of discomfiture and a flair of uncertainty.

Focus, focus, focus.

The Duke of Durham stood next to the grate, one

elbow of his very tall frame resting on the thick, oak mantel, holding a half-filled glass of amber liquid between his long fingers, the other hand in the pocket of his trousers, which managed to push his frock coat away from his body. Her gaze naturally fell there first, to his expensive, white silk shirt pulled tautly over a strong, broad chest. His clothes—black over white— were expertly tailored to fit his unusually large body, his cravat the only piece of color to adorn him in a shade of emerald green, and of course everything he wore only spoke of quality. She now knew to expect nothing less from this man, and for the first time she began to wonder why Edmund felt the need to go to great lengths to steal her fortune when his brother had such a good one of his own. Then again, maybe that was just precisely why.

At last she glanced to his face, and thoughts of her husband instantly vanished. Although he looked like Edmund in mere physical appearance, the Duke of Durham was nothing like his brother in expression or bearing. Where Edmund was jovial and friendly, this man exuded power and intensity, a force to be regarded with the gravest of purpose. Both men were handsome beyond words, but where Edmund was flirtatious, this man certainly wasn't, in any manner.

He looked at her, his gaze suddenly locking with hers in a frank, marked intention to intimidate, radiating an energy of its own that almost startled her.

Olivia shivered within, pausing with rapid clarity of thought. He didn't trust her at all, she realized from that one, biting glare from his deeply brown eyes. He didn't trust her—and yet he asked her here tonight, which meant he believed that she knew his brother, whatever their relationship might be. She had hoped for more, but, at the very least, his obvious acceptance of her, however uncertain, was a start, she supposed.

Tensely, attempting to overcome her mounting anxiety by taking a deep breath, Olivia allowed her wide satin skirts to clear the doorway and fall gracefully around her as she stepped farther into the dining room, nodding once to the man whose gaze began to scan her very, very slowly from head to foot.

"Good evening, your grace," she said as pleasantly as she could, wanting to set a congenial tone, like a brother-to-sister discussion, though her voice sounded tight to her ears and her cheeks felt overly hot from his candid inspection of her person.

"Olivia," he drawled, making her very ordinary name sound far too...sensuous.

She squirmed a little in her stays and laced her fingers tightly together in front of her. "Thank you for the invitation to dinner."

One side of his mouth curled up. "It is the least I can do for the woman who claims to be married to my brother."

Claims? She'd given him the marriage license to inspect, for heaven sake. What more proof could he possibly need? And his obvious use of the word "woman" instead of "lady" piqued her even more. If he'd been any other man, she would have put him in his place. He wasn't stupid, and such careful usage implied that she lied. And *that* was an assault on her character. Watching him now solidified her argument that he wasn't to be trusted any more than he evidently trusted her.

Standing rigidly, her expression flat, she remarked, "My goodness, your grace, you are such a flatterer."

He blinked quickly, visibly surprised by such a comeback, and to her great amusement he looked genuinely confused. That made her smile in satisfaction. If he expected her to be like every other female he knew, intimidated and frightened into submission by his haughty...*dominion,* then he was in for a wickedly sad treat.

Gently lifting her skirts again, she sauntered toward him, her expression tepid despite her nerves. "Is this lovely home yours?" she asked, her tone as mundane as the question.

He took a swallow of his drink, his gaze never wavering from hers. "No. It belongs to a friend."

"Ah. Of course."

His brows drew together fractionally at that. He had no idea what she implied by that comment, but he refused to ask. Stubborn man. But then he *looked* stubborn.

"Would you like a sherry?" he offered flatly, pulling away from the fireplace at last.

"Please," she replied, stopping short as she approached him.

With a final glance down her form, he turned and walked to a large, polished sidebar behind the dining table that was already set beautifully for two in burgundy lace and white Sèvres china.

"Is he also Edmund's friend?"

"He was."

She watched him reach for a decanter, lift the top and begin to pour a small amount of amber liquid into a sherry glass. The man certainly wasn't gifted in the art of conversation. "What is his name?"

He didn't answer for a moment as he put the crystal decanter back in its place. Then he turned and moved toward her again, her drink in his outstretched hand. "Colin Ramsey, the gentleman you met at the ball, but I don't suppose Edmund ever mentioned him or you would have acknowledged that."

She frowned minutely as she accepted refreshment from him, mindful not to touch his fingers as she did so. "No, Edmund never mentioned anyone in England save you, and even then you were only the vague older brother whom he said remained jealous of his good fortune. I just assumed you were old and married, living in the country and caring for a brood." She paused, then added almost insolently, "He never said you were a twin."

"And you didn't find that rather odd?" he asked seconds later.

"That you aren't old and married, or the part about being a twin?"

He snorted, then took a sip of his drink, his gaze lingering on her. "That he didn't want to discuss me."

"Yes, of course I found that odd," she admitted honestly. "But the few times I asked about his family and former friends, he gave me a quick answer, then changed the subject jovially enough for me not to really concern myself with what I now think was evasiveness."

"It no doubt was," he remarked wryly. "When one is running from something, or someone, he usually doesn't want it discussed."

She took a sip of very tasteful sherry, desperate to have questions answered but not wanting to appear too anxious. "Well, since he at least mentioned you, I suppose I'm relieved to know he wasn't running from you."

The man's dark eyes narrowed significantly, and Olivia had to admit she felt rather proud to have irritated him. He wasn't certain if her words were spoken facetiously, or if she really had no idea how Edmund despised his brother, and she was glad to have the upper hand, at least in one regard.

After a long moment he took a step closer to her so that he stood near enough for her to notice the stubble on his firm jawline. In any other gentleman she would have been annoyed that he hadn't bothered to shave again for dinner. In this man it seemed almost... distinguished. In an alluring sort of way.

"Am I that fearful, Lady Olivia?"

She shook herself, annoyed that she'd let her thoughts stray.

Focus!

"Fearful?" She held her shoulders back rigidly. "Fearful of what?"

He laughed. A solid, deep laugh of honest enjoyment.

It startled Olivia so much she almost dropped her sherry. The Duke of Durham was positively gorgeous when he laughed.

Moments later, his amusement subsiding, he gazed forcefully into her eyes and murmured, "In the past, madam, I've been more fearful to bold ladies who've learned I've discovered their lies, however small." He leaned toward her slightly and lowered his voice. "Or however extravagant."

It took several seconds before she could react to such a telling statement. Then grinning purposefully, she said, "I'm so glad to know you'll continue to be your charming self with me, then."

He tried not to smile again, but failed halfheartedly, and she couldn't help noticing the small dimple in his right cheek—a facial feature Edmund surprisingly lacked. Suddenly she was enjoying their bantering. She cocked her head in his direction as if they shared a secret. "But just to guard myself, your grace, who are these bold ladies?"

Without pause, his smile hardened into a line of sharp bitterness. "Frenchwomen, Lady Olivia. I've never met one I trusted."

He wasn't enjoying her any longer. And in fact, with the look of sheer contempt etched into his countenance from just that one, innocent question, she realized he would never trust her, or even like her because of her duel heritage. She wished she knew the reason behind his animosity, though it wouldn't make one slight bit of difference in any relationship they might have. She didn't care much for him, either. Arrogant ass.

With a snicker, Olivia took another sip of sherry and turned away from him, fairly gliding across the carpeted floor toward the far end of the dining table, knowing instinctively that his gaze followed her every move. Reaching out with a delicate touch, she slid her fingertips along the hard, polished surface then rubbed them gingerly on a lace napkin. "So, in using such... refined logic, I suppose you think that at least half the time you'll not know if I'm telling you the truth. Pity that."

He didn't immediately respond, as she thought he might if for no other reason than to avoid an increase in the awkwardness between them. Finally, after a few lingering seconds of silence, she glanced back at him through lowered lashes, noting with a kind of odd pleasure that he seemed to be scrutinizing every bit of her—from the dark curls that framed her face and sat dressed with pearls on top of her head, to the line of her jaw and the curve of her bosom, to the intricate details of her expensive, scarlet satin evening gown. And he liked what he saw. As a woman, she knew that instinctively.

Olivia felt a sudden twist of knots in her stomach, a flicker of something undefined creep under her skin. She'd never felt such a charged response, this sort of... *knowingness,* with Edmund. The feeling startled her as much as it confused her, since not only was this man standing across the room, but just seconds ago she'd come to realize how much he didn't like her, wouldn't trust her, and resented her entering his obviously well-ordered life.

"You certainly know how to tease a man, don't you, Lady Olivia?" he murmured in a husky timbre, the intensity of his words slicing into her thoughts.

She raised her brows fractionally, trying her best to control the moment by keeping it civil and pleasant. "Tease? In what manner am I teasing you, sir?"

His dark eyes narrowed, and in one quick motion he finished off his drink, placing the empty glass on the fireplace mantel. Very slowly he said, "I didn't necessarily mean you were teasing *me,* madam, at least not right now, or with intention." He clasped his hands behind his back and began to stroll toward her, eyeing the carpet as he spoke with some contemplation. "I mean, rather, that everything about you—your refined, haughty look, your elegance, your obvious...glamour— is molded with perfection and triggered into action by desire on the part of a man, *any* man." He glanced back into her eyes as he moved to her side once more. "Whether you created this image yourself or were molded into such a stunning creature by God is unknown, and probably irrelevant." He lowered his voice to a deep, hard whisper to add, "You're a product of beauty, Olivia, just like the perfume you market, and naturally I'm very impressed by it, as you no doubt intended me to be. But a product is still a product. I won't be deceived by it."

Deceived? Did he think she was trying to *deceive* him? His insults—regardless of the fact that he mixed them with compliments—inflamed her. He had intentionally cut into everything she was as a woman, defining her mere *appearance* as something to actually be *wary* of. Olivia couldn't remember a time when she'd been accused so despicably by a gentleman. Still, she refused to move away from him, to succumb to his overbearing nature by cowering, or to react as he likely expected and slap his enigmatic, handsome face. No, she was better than he assumed her to be, and she intended to prove it to him. He expected her to be frivolous and narcissistic, as he seemed to think all Frenchwomen were, but instead she would show him restraint with balance.

Eyes flashing defiance as they penetrated his, she placed her sherry on the tabletop beside her and tightly laced her fingers together in front of her. "Thank you for your gracious compliments, sir," she said with feigned sweetness. "I'm so glad you appreciate my efforts to look my best when in the company of others."

His cheek twitched once, but he offered nothing in reply.

Thoroughly smug, she smiled to add, "But as you know, products can be bought and sold, *I* cannot. Remember that."

Seconds ticked by in brutal slowness as he stared down at her boldly, and for the briefest of moments she feared he might dismiss her—or grab her and shake her senseless.

"Did you love my brother?"

That quietly asked question certainly came out of nowhere, and frankly startled her. Eyes widening, she pulled back from him a little, still unnerved by his proximity and enraged by his audacity, and finding it extremely difficult to understand his sudden change in subject. "I beg your pardon?"

His lip twitched with a very tiny, knowing grin. "I asked you if you loved my brother. We've had three conversations about him now, about the fact that he married you and stole your fortune, about your desire to find him at any cost, but not once have you mentioned a love for him." He shrugged one shoulder. "I'm intensely curious."

Olivia could feel her face turning scarlet under his scrutiny, probably the same shade as her gown. After a solid inhale, she maintained, "Of course I did."

For seconds the Duke of Durham simply stared into her eyes, his features hard, his expression unreadable as he apparently gauged her rather staid response, perhaps even hoping for more, which she wasn't about to offer. Particulars were none of his business.

And then, beyond her wildest imaginings, he did the unthinkable. He grasped her chin with one strong hand, and as he lifted it, he brought his lips down to hers—not in a crush of passion, but in a simple connection, a subtle touch of tenderness that defied the moment of exasperation between them.

It took Olivia what felt like days for her to come to the realization that he was actually kissing her. Momentarily stunned, she tried to shake her head free of his, groaning in protest as she drew her hands up and pressed them forcefully against his silk dinner jacket, attempting to shove him away. He reacted by placing one of his large palms on the back of her head and holding her steadily against him as he strengthened the bond of his mouth on hers, lightly caressing her lips until she had no choice but to succumb.

She did, with a fading measure of reluctance and a whirlwind of emotions suddenly swimming through her, making her legs weak and her body come alive beneath her corset. He radiated warmth, smelled divine, and tasted...heavenly. Pure magic. And then, just as she felt ready to melt into his arms and open completely to his urging, he gently released her, slowly pushing her face away from his, though managing to graze the pad of a finger or two across her lips as he did so.

Olivia gasped for breath and, after a moment, opened

her eyes, staring at the fine threading of his waistcoat as she remained careful not to look up at him.

Oh, God, he had *kissed* her. On purpose. And he...he was a marvelous kisser.

Immediately, guilt and regret flooded her senses and she took a step away from his powerful physique. "Are you insane?" she whispered.

He inhaled deeply. "Momentarily," he admitted in a husky murmur.

"You had no right to do that," she said, her voice low and shaky. "I am married to your brother."

"And I have every right to challenge your purpose in bringing that fact to my attention, madam."

Her head shot up with intention to verbally attack his character. Instead, for the first time, she became aware of just how affected he'd been by their embrace. She swallowed, unnerved by his flushed face, his labored breathing, the intensity of his heated gaze as it clung to hers. Just the knowledge that he'd been physically stimulated by the simple touch of her lips to his confused her.

"How on earth was *kissing* me a challenge?" she asked in whispered fury.

Without hesitation, he said, "You're attracted to me."
Just as you're attracted to me.

"You *are* insane. And a cad," was all she managed to enunciate, her fluster limiting her ability to rationally consider a profound reply to a statement so laughable if it weren't so disturbing.

He almost smirked, shoving his hands in his pockets. "You're not the first Frenchwoman to tell me that."

She placed her palm on her heated cheek. "I'm certain I'm not the only *Englishwoman* to tell you that, either."

He didn't respond, just looked her up and down again very slowly, his features hard and distrusting. After a moment of waiting for something—anything from him—Olivia took another step back and turned, shifting her gaze to the loosely drawn drapes, the pads of her fingers on her lips as if to block them from his scrutiny.

After seconds of unbearable awkwardness, at least on her part, he thankfully walked away from her, toward the dining room door, and pulled on the thick bronze rope to ring the bell for service. Three footmen entered almost at once, their hands filled with food on silver trays, which they began laying atop the oak buffet against the far wall, never glancing at either of them as they worked silently and professionally.

Olivia wasn't certain if she felt grateful for the interruption or annoyed by the sudden presence of others, regardless of the fact that servants were supposed to be invisible. In her experience they gossiped, though at this point she decided a trifle gossip was the least of her concerns.

Suddenly the butler entered and began speaking with the duke in muted tones. Olivia took the opportunity of his distraction to try to compose herself, inhaling a few deep breaths and straightening her skirts with calming hands, willing her speeding heart to still.

Her brother-in-law stood handsomely tall and stately, now seemingly unaffected by their brief encounter as he continued to offer instruction, she assumed, to the butler, who nodded in obedience. At last their conversation ended and the servants all departed without a glance in her direction, closing the door quietly behind them, leaving the two of them alone once again to dine casually on obviously exquisite fare, serving themselves and conversing as if nothing at all had just happened. Ridiculous notion.

He looked at her openly again, rubbing his jaw with his fingers and thumb. "Shall we eat, dearest sister?"

Olivia fairly rolled her eyes. Could his sarcasm be any more blatant?

She smiled sweetly, though she no longer felt like eating. "Of course, your grace."

With a tepid smile, he motioned to the steaming buffet with his hand. "Please. We have much to discuss."

He wanted a discussion now? God in heaven, the Duke of Durham had just *kissed* her. No explanation, no warning, and she had liked it. She had liked it terribly—enough to make any conversation they might have extremely uncomfortable, at least for her. It occurred to her suddenly that such a despicably pleasurable action might have been planned from the beginning to disconcert her, thereby giving him the advantage in any discussion they might have. If that was the case, the poor, arrogant man would be in for a true challenge of female proportions. He just had no idea who he was dealing with, and that would serve *her* purpose.

With a sweep of her skirts and a polite nod, Olivia grinned and walked elegantly to the waiting food.

He couldn't possibly be more angry with himself for taking advantage of her like that, for using the situation to his benefit by confronting her not with words, but with overt lust. And yet he still wasn't convinced she'd been all that surprised. She had come into his life, after all, and certainly with her own plans of attack. Yet tonight she had surprised him. Instead of storming out of the house, or breaking into tears, or even just slapping his face like any other woman might, she'd managed instead to remain composed, sitting across from him now, eating orange duckling and chestnut stuffing with grace and charm after a shockingly simple kiss that even *she* knew had numbed them both. The Lady Olivia Shea was different, an astute female, one who apparently enjoyed matching wits with the gentlemen in her life, and Sam wasn't sure if he approved of her unusual nature or not. Not that his feelings were relevant in the least at this point.

"How is your dinner, Olivia?" he asked pleasantly.

She glanced up from across the table as she delicately piled stuffing on her fork with her knife. "Delicious, thank you. And how is yours, your grace?"

He grunted at her stilted demeanor. "Perfect."

She smiled agreeably and sliced once more into her roasted game. "You'll have to mention to your friend that he's employed a marvelous cook. Is he here this evening?"

Sam had to shake himself from actually cursing aloud. Such a pointless and banal conversation. "Let's discuss that rather enticing kiss we shared instead."

He watched her hesitate for only a fraction of a second, her fork halfway to her mouth. Then, without looking at him, she lowered it and remarked, "If we're going to talk about something besides the weather and the food, I'd rather discuss Edmund and what you're going to do to help me get my funds returned to me." She sat back and patted her mouth gently with her napkin. "I've been away from Nivan too long as it is, your grace; I need to return home soon to oversee my business. Though being a man of inherited wealth you may not completely understand that."

Although she impressed him with her ability to appear self-possessed and focused on her task in light of his somewhat improper suggestion, Sam nevertheless felt insulted from nothing more than the simple smile on her pretty pink mouth. Oddly enough, her feigned confidence both disgusted and aroused him.

Shifting his chair, he placed his own knife and fork on his plate and relaxed against the cushion, resting his elbows on the armrests as he eyed her carefully. "I have a proposition for you, Olivia."

She raised her wineglass to her mouth, swallowed a sip, and licked her lips. "A proposition for retrieving my money, I'm assuming," she said rather than asked, lowering her glass back to the table.

This time her pleasant assurance absolutely *did* annoy him, though he refused to let her have the satisfaction of knowing it. Instead, he nodded slowly, pursing his lips in apparent thought. "Perhaps, although I'm not certain you'll be so smug with yourself after hearing my thoughts."

Her mouth dropped open a bit, then closed again to form a tight line. "I am not smug, but that's beside the point, your grace. Frankly, what you think of me is irrelevant."

"The point is," he explained, darkening his voice

with intensity as he sat forward, "what we think of each other is less important than what we can do for each other in this matter, Olivia."

Her smile gradually faded as she cocked her head to eye him carefully. "What we can do for each other?"

He cleared his throat, raising his wineglass and studying her over the top of it. "You need my help, and after considering all the options, I've decided to help you."

After a long moment, she maintained, "I need my funds returned to me, which is my primary concern. You seem to enjoy sidestepping that issue, but the fact that you are my husband's brother makes you responsible for his deceit. I believe I've been more than clear in this matter."

"Oh, you have," he replied, drawing the glass to his mouth. After a swallow, he added, "But I have specific reasons for finding my brother, and you're the first person in years who's claimed to recently see him and spend time in his company."

Her eyes flashed in irritation. "Actually, I recently married him."

He almost grinned. Her comment fed directly into his merging thoughts. "Yes, you did, and strangely enough, I'm beginning to believe your claims."

She straightened in her chair and folded her hands in her lap. "Should I thank you?" she asked sarcastically, and obviously perturbed.

He did smile then, in anticipation, though as much as he wanted to answer, he managed to brush over that question. "I propose that we look for Edmund together, Lady Olivia, in France."

She didn't reply at once, just watched him dubiously. Then very slowly she asked, "How do you suggest we do that exactly? Where would we start, and who would chaperone us on this quest? And why France? Since he's stolen from me, one can only assume he's left the country."

Sam drew in a long breath, relishing this moment even as his pulse began to beat in his temple from pure anticipation. "I think we should start in Paris because that's where he was last seen. We can trace his movements, visit those he knew, those with whom he socialized. If he was involved with other people in this scheme to swindle you of your fortune, we'll catch them off guard."

She huffed. "Who on earth would be so despicable?"

He shrugged nonchalantly. "I've no idea. But the best place to find out, the best place to start looking, is in Paris."

She thought about that for a while. "I assumed he'd return here, to his home, his family."

"Edmund would never return to England," he replied sharply.

Her brows rose. "How do you know this, sir?"

He adjusted his large form in his chair, not yet ready to reveal too much about his past when he didn't yet trust much of what she said. "Suffice it to say I know how my brother thinks."

She almost snorted. "Yes, well, I thought I did, too."

His eyes narrowed as he watched her. Then he murmured, "We'll go to France, start there anyway, to see if anyone reveals his whereabouts because they'll think I'm him."

"What do you mean they'll think you're him?" she asked with slowly building suspicion.

"You are married to a man who is my *twin,* Olivia," he murmured gravely, stressing that point to hit home. The side of his mouth curled up. "Whoever he's involved with will certainly be shocked to see me with you after he's swindled you of your fortune. It'll stir the bees' nest hopefully, and in turn draw out some information." He paused, then added matter-of-factly, "Unless you have a better idea."

It seemed to take a long time for her to understand his so-called proposition, to come to terms with exactly what it was he suggested they do. And then, instead of becoming indignant or shocked, her mouth turned up in amusement.

"You're serious," she murmured.

He took another sip of wine to prolong his answering. "Oh, I'm very serious, which is why I kissed you. If I am to pose as Edmund, you and I will have to act like we're married." After a pause, he added, "There's an attraction between us, so it shouldn't be too difficult."

She stilled, her features going flat, though her eyes widened with incredulity. Sam waited, enjoying the moment immensely.

"I'm...speechless," she whispered seconds later.

He lifted his fork again and speared a bite of what remained of his orange duck. "Speechlessness is good in a woman, I think."

"You're despicable to even suggest that we—" She coughed, then swallowed. "—that we—"

She couldn't finish voicing her thoughts. He remained silent, drawing her fears out as long as he could, for absolutely no other reason than the fact that he enjoyed watching her face flush and her body squirm from the mere thought of the two of them becoming intimate. And he knew she was thinking about just such an act now, as she blinked quickly, then looked away uncomfortably, then reached for her wineglass and finished off the contents in two unladylike swallows.

Sam placed his elbows on his armrests and tented his fingers in front of him, giving her time to visualize everything, relishing the feel of his own body reacting as it should from the idea of seeing her spread out on the sheets and beckoning with her sultry blue eyes for him to take her. Of course that would never happen if she still loved Edmund, and the two of them were in fact legally married, but it was a marvelous thought nonetheless.

At last she shook her head as if to clear such disturbing thoughts from her mind, then smiled matter-of-factly and looked at him directly. "Of course we cannot—"

He raised his brows. "Cannot?"

She never moved her gaze. "We cannot be indiscreet, your grace."

He had to admire her boldness, even if her comment could mean any number of things. "Of course not, Lady Olivia. You are my responsibility as my sister by marriage and I take that very seriously."

She relaxed in her chair minutely, nearly smiling with a measure of relief. "I've no doubt." Seconds later she admitted, "Aside from a few details to be worked out, it sounds like a decent start, considering what little information we have. When do we leave?"

Sam tried not to appear stunned at her sudden approval of his plan. It struck him then that under different circumstances he might actually like this woman and all her mischievous charm and apparent intelligence. Her indescribable physical beauty would only be an added bonus. He couldn't say that about any other lady he knew. In fact, as he considered it now, he'd never known a woman who came in such a tightly wrapped package of fascinating glamour, power, and smarts. And this one belonged to his brother. If it weren't so laughable, it would have infuriated him.

"We leave Saturday after next," he replied, a bit too harshly, turning his attention back to his food with a forceful fork.

Again she paused, likely trying to assess his change in mood. He only wished he could tell her how uncomfortable she made *him* under the circumstances, but to do so would be admitting an inappropriate lust. He'd rather just come across as mad.

"Thank you ever so, your grace," she retorted, her sarcasm all but slicing the air as she lifted her fork as well. "You've been more than generous."

He didn't glance up as they began to eat again in silence. She didn't understand his animosity, and frankly, he wanted it to stay that way. The less they liked each other, the easier, and faster, this trip would be.

At least that was his hope.

Chapter 5

⌒⌒⌒

The Parisian sunset spread out as a vast display of brilliant color, hues of orange and gold made darker by the smoky haze that rose above tall buildings lining Rue Gabrielle, where Olivia now alighted from their private coach to stand beside her brother-in-law, the most irritating, most stubborn, most...masculine Duke of Durham. Of the three words that best described him, the last was the most exact, though he was also vain and arrogant and serious to a fault.

Their journey from London, across the Channel and into Paris, had been uneventful and rather fast as far as trips go. Although just being in his presence made her nervous, a feeling she'd never experienced with Edmund, he hadn't spoken much to her aside from the necessary, although she did think he stared at her far too often, his lingering gaze only serving to intensify her agitation. They'd endured each other's company, talking when appropriate, and spending nights in separate quarters when they had to rest. Now, after entering Paris, the ruse would begin and she'd need to pretend to be his wife, a deception that both excited and appalled her.

They'd arrived only a short while ago, and already the doubts were gnawing at her for agreeing to such an improper scheme, yet now there was no turning back. And as she stepped onto the curb at the Nivan storefront, even the concierge referred to him as her husband, without appearing surprised to see her again with the man he assumed was Edmund after weeks away. The duke played his part well, speaking to the man for a moment in French, assuring that their luggage and trunks would be arriving shortly and ordering them to be taken to their apartments upstairs. His word use and accent were excellent. She hadn't considered that he'd know the language, though she shouldn't have been surprised that he would be properly educated as one of the aristocracy. Edmund spoke French, but then, he'd lived in the country for years.

"Which way, madam?" the duke leaned over to murmur in her ear.

The feel of his warm breath on her lobe made her shiver even in the late spring heat and stagnant city air. "Inside," she snapped, as if that were a remarkably stupid question for him to ask.

She could positively feel him smirking behind her, which she ignored as she lifted her skirts and walked toward the front doors, held open by a footman for her to enter without a pause in her stride.

The familiar scents of lavender and spices filled her nostrils, immediately cutting out the odors of horses and street fare. At last she was home, back in friendly territory, a realization that proved to instantly soothe her for the first time in weeks.

"Madame Carlisle, you have returned!"

Olivia grinned as Normand Paquette, her assistant and longtime friend and advisor, made his way out from behind the sales counter, arms extended.

"Normand, it's so good to be home," she said as he grasped her shoulders and gently kissed both cheeks.

"*Oui,* such a dreadful trip north took too long," he added, his mouth turned down into a clearly forced frown.

She squeezed his upper arms with gloved fingers. "How is everything? Did the shipment of sandalwood finally arrive? Is Madame Gauthier still unsure about her choice for—"

The duke cleared his throat behind them. Olivia turned sharply, still holding Normand by the arms. "Uh, forgive me, darling," she stressed for his benefit. "You remember Monsieur Paquette, my assistant?"

Normand bowed his head slightly. "Monsieur Carlisle, welcome home."

Olivia could feel the duke move to stand directly behind her, and for a second she thought he might grasp her shoulders in possessive display. She instinctively dropped her hold of Normand as if he'd caught fire.

"Monsieur Paquette," her faux husband acknowledged, his tone deep and formal. "We meet again."

"Normand, please," the Frenchman insisted, smiling

matter-of-factly. "No need for such formality between us. Your wife has been greatly missed. Nivan is very fortunate to have her returned to us."

It was altogether telling for her assistant to remind them of her absence in this way. He wasn't rude, exactly, but then Normand was never rude. Yet the man had never trusted, or even liked, Edmund, and she noticed a tension in the air that wasn't there a moment ago. She took it upon herself to ignore it and press on.

"Monsieur Carlisle and I will retire to our apartments first, Normand. Tomorrow you and I will discuss business and gossip over tea," she said with a grin.

Normand laughed and leaned forward to kiss her again on one cheek. "So good to see you, Olivia. Please, get rest. I let Madame Allard know yesterday of your arrival this evening so she would tidy up and have a bit of food awaiting you."

Madame Allard was her part-time housekeeper and cook, who normally worked only short days but helped her tremendously with household matters when she was busy with the business. Olivia managed a sigh of relief that she'd gotten word in time to make up the spare bed with clean sheets. In her mind, that was more important than food at this point.

"*Merci,* Normand. I will see you in the morning."

He moved out of the way to let them pass, and the duke took her elbow as she escorted them past the display cases and two sales girls with watchful eyes, whom Olivia didn't recall ever meeting. But then sales girls came and went, and Normand was usually the one to hire them, or dismiss them if their work suffered.

Nearing the back of the building, Olivia led the duke through the small and richly decorated private salon, where elegant ladies took tea or wine while discussing the newest scents, then raised her skirts with both hands to climb the circular staircase beyond it, freshly painted in stark white and carpeted in rich red brocade. It led up to the third floor apartments where she lived when in Paris.

The duke followed silently, standing closely behind her while she pulled the key from her velvet reticule and inserted it into the lock of her private quarters. With a quick turn to the right it gave way easily, and she entered at once, her brother-in-law following without hesitation.

Striding into the parlor on her left, Olivia closed her eyes and breathed deeply, feeling a certain tension leave her body as she warmed to the accustomed smells and sounds of home.

"Leave the door open a crack for the footmen to bring in our baggage," she said as she began pulling on the fingers of her gloves.

"I'm not a servant, madam."

She whirled around in surprise, her skirts thrashing his legs as he fairly towered over her. "I—I didn't mean to imply that you were, your grace," she stated with firm resolve, still clutching her gloves.

He stared down at her, his mouth turned up at one corner, his eyes showing a trace of irritation. "This may be your home, Olivia, but I am in charge of the operation, remember that."

She blinked, her sudden good feeling of returned contentment melting away like snow on warm skin with one solid glance up and down his rigid body. "The 'operation'? What operation?"

He drew in a deep breath and clasped his hands behind his back, his gaze never leaving her face. "Let us be clear about this, dearest sister," he clarified, his tone low and grave. "You may be back at Nivan and in your former relaxed and prosperous environment, but you're not here to return to your daily routine, happy and in control of all that surrounds you. I'm with you this time, for a singular purpose, for as long as it takes to complete our mission."

Exasperated, she hissed, "I know that!"

"Do you?"

"Yes," she insisted forcefully, suddenly angry that he spoke to her as if she were a five-year-old. "I know what we've come to France for, sir, but let's be realistic. You use words like 'operation' and 'mission' as if this journey to find your brother is some kind of formalized...military action. It's not. This is about my livelihood, about commitment and the man I married, regardless of your concerns." She straightened her shoulders in a show of dignity, pulling at her gloves again and fairly ripping them from her hands. "Perhaps you should think less about yourself and more about exactly why you're here in the first place."

He didn't say anything for a moment or two, just watched her with calculating, almost ruthless eyes. Then, in a quiet murmur, he asked, "Has it not occurred to you that instead of concern for *my* desires, I've come all this way because I'm thinking of you?"

That confused her totally, as she had no idea how to answer a question that clearly held several possible meanings beneath its innocence. Instinctively she took a step away from his overbearingly male stature, feeling a rising heat within from his uncomfortable closeness.

Before she lost the nerve, she crossed her arms over her breasts and replied succinctly, "Perhaps thinking of me *is* a concern for your desires, your grace, since you seem to enjoy spending an obscene amount of time staring at my face and person."

He couldn't believe she said that. She could see it in the small, immediate jarring of his head, the way his eyes lit with incredulity and widened a fraction. For a slice of a second her cleverness in stumping him infused her with pure satisfaction—until he stepped toward her and grasped the edges of her long silk gloves, still clutched in her hands, and used them to slowly draw her against him.

"Your face and form are the most exquisite I have ever seen in my life, Olivia Shea, no doubt sculpted to perfection by the gods," he said in a coarse whisper. "You are, indeed, a package of beauty that defies description, and I can't help but be aware of it every time I lay eyes on you, which I'm fairly confident you actually enjoy."

It was her turn to be shocked; heat suffused her neck and cheeks. "How dare you suggest—"

He jerked her harder against him, effectively cutting her off, his legs draped by her skirts, his body so close his chest rubbed against her bare arms, now molded to her breasts. She couldn't move, mesmerized by his uncanny ability to deprive her of words or action.

"I have learned that not only is desire both sweet *and* bitter, it is almost always mutual." His jaw hardened, his eyelids narrowed. "Your mere presence may tempt me, my Lady Olivia, but I promise you now, you will never, *ever* win me."

Win him?

His warm, moist breath captured stray curls on her cheek, making them tickle her skin, and for countless seconds she couldn't comprehend anything logically except the fact that he smelled heavenly and felt… warm. Like a man.

"This is not a competition, your grace," she breathed through clenched teeth, capturing his gaze with one of defiance as he gradually pulled away from her.

The hard planes of his face relaxed minutely; he cocked his head to one side, loosening his grip on her gloves. Calmly, he replied, "I'm beginning to think it might be, at least from your perspective."

A sharp rap at the door startled them both, interrupting the sudden awkwardness of their extreme closeness. Olivia took a quick step back and away from him as he released her without reluctance.

"Madame, your baggage," the building concierge said after clearing his throat.

Flustered, she averted her gaze to the Frenchman. "*Merci,* Antoine," she replied, breezing past the duke in noble fashion. "Please place my trunks in my private quarters, and my husband's in the guest room."

If the concierge thought her request odd, he didn't show it. Immediately he began to do as she ordered, utilizing two footmen to carry their belongings to their respective rooms. She felt more than noticed the duke turn away from her and move to the parlor window that looked west toward the darkening sky.

Moments later and without another word, Antoine and the footmen departed, closing the door solidly behind them. Alone once again, the awkward silence droned.

"You're going to have to stop calling me 'your grace.'"

Through a long, full breath, she turned to face him, her pulse quickening as she watched him reach up to loosen his tie and unbutton the top of his shirt. Even Edmund hadn't undressed in front of her, and the picture of this man doing it stirred her, warming her to the bone. She forced the indecent thoughts he provoked from her mind, matching his movement by lifting her hands to tidy tendrils of hair that had escaped her plaits.

"Just a moment ago," she retorted, attempting to keep the conversation focused, "you forbade me to treat you as a servant."

He tossed her a wry grin, resting his palms on the windowsill behind him. "There is an in-between, Olivia."

His casualness made her mad for no reason she could fathom. "Oh? Shall I call you Edmund, then?"

"When we're around others, yes. When we're alone like this, I prefer Sam." He waited, then added a bit more gently, "It is my Christian name."

In all this time that she'd known him, which, all things considered, wasn't actually that long, his Christian name had never once crossed her mind. She now recalled that he'd mentioned it at their first private meeting, but only in passing. Odd that she hadn't considered him a separate individual before now. Always, he seemed to be a replica, or more precisely, a variation, of her husband, not a completely different man. A man with his own unique experiences, his own hopes and dreams and disappointments.

Averting her gaze, Olivia moved to her small pine secretary, lifting a stack of notes and cards resting on top that had come by post during her absence. "I imagine Sam is short for Samuel?" she asked, sifting through them with little concentration.

"No, Samson," he replied.

She frowned, realizing she'd missed Madame Le-Blanc's annual spring soiree while she'd been gone, a party that usually drummed up plenty of business for the coming summer scents.

"Then I suppose for this little adventure I shall play your Delilah," she remarked, half jesting.

With quiet intensity he murmured, "Is that your goal? To seduce me?"

Olivia fumbled with the stack of mail in her hands, dropping several note cards onto the thick teal carpeting at her feet. She tossed him a fast glance, her cheeks flushing hotly from the sudden notion of what he thought she meant by such a simple statement. Or was he just trying to shock her? Of course *he* didn't appear at all fazed.

He watched her gather her correspondence loosely in her hands and place it all back on her secretary in a jumbled heap, not moving to help, and no doubt enjoying every second of her discomfiture. Olivia decided not to give him the satisfaction of thinking he could unsettle her every time he opened his mouth to offer a snide comment or question.

After smoothing her skirts, she faced him once more with grim posture and what she hoped was a haughty little smile upon her mouth.

"Sam..." she started, clearing her throat and lacing her fingers behind her back. "I *meant* that I will thoroughly enjoy playing Delilah to your Samson for every crafty, underhanded, or manipulative thing we must do to find my husband and return my funds to me." She narrowed her eyes in defiance, hoping he understood that she could not be used. "I will do my part and act superbly, but seduction? Never. You and I will never be lovers."

He continued to eye her speculatively from across the room, then crossed his arms over his chest, his brows pinched in contemplation. "Isn't that what Samson said to Delilah? And just look where it got him." He snickered, one side of his mouth turned up acridly. "Be aware, Olivia; I am not so drawn to you—or any woman—that I will risk losing my own fortune, or more importantly, my life or my sanity, and I never intend to be."

Her jaw dropped open a fraction. Ironically, she couldn't remember if either Samson or Delilah said such a thing at all, or who seduced whom first; her biblical knowledge was lacking. But that hardly mattered. She knew what lay between herself and the Duke of Durham. He didn't like her, didn't trust her, and he toyed with her purposely to get her to react in the negative every time they conversed in private. What kind of man did that to a woman he didn't know?

A cynical one.

Someone hurt you badly, too.

Such a thoughtful revelation about his hidden character surprised her. She had absolutely no intention of becoming close to this man, physically or emotionally, and she didn't particularly want to ponder the idea. They didn't need to like or enjoy each other, but they absolutely needed to get along. Her livelihood depended on their mutual cooperation.

Sighing, Olivia surrendered and replied, "Perhaps, your grace—"

"Sam."

"Of course. I forgot." Planting what she hoped looked like a genuine smile on her lips, she nodded once, in acquiescence. "Perhaps, Sam, you and I are not as different in pasts and in future needs as we might think."

He raised a brow at that, though offered no comment.

She dropped her arms to her sides and took a step toward him. "What I mean is that regardless of how we view each other, and where our trusts lay, I propose that we tame our differences, combine our common experiences, and try to work together."

Olivia smugly decided her suggestion was quite satisfactory and would no doubt be agreed upon immediately, perhaps with even a shake of hands to signify an agreement of sorts.

He apparently didn't take it that way at all.

The Duke of Durham stood upright once more, staring down at her, though his expression seemed more guarded than angry.

"We're very different, Lady Olivia," he grumbled quietly, his face and body tight with a haunted weariness he couldn't hide. "But that shouldn't, and won't, matter, so there's no use dwelling on it. For now, I'm exhausted, in no mood for dinner, and would like to retire." He strode past her and toward the guest bedroom where the footman had deposited his trunk and personal items. Without glancing back in her direction, he added over his shoulder, "We'll start looking for my brother in the morning." He shut the door behind him, turning the lock with a click.

Olivia just stood there for a minute or two, staring at the newly painted oak, open-mouthed and suddenly deflated. The sky wasn't even completely dark yet and he had gone to bed—no thought to eating, no thought of getting to know each other better, no thought to an evening of planning their next move together. No thought to her whatsoever.

The brute.

For the very first time, she felt a strange flicker of elation that she had been fortunate enough to meet Edmund first, and marry him instead.

Chapter 6

He couldn't sleep. It had been hours—or at least it seemed that way—since he'd settled down between the cool sheets and laid his head on the feather pillow, attempting to drown his memories and current irritations in a sea of street noise and a grumbling stomach. He'd been an idiot to announce that he didn't want dinner, that he just wanted to go to bed. He was famished, and tired, true, but not sleepy, especially with her in the next room.

He was too wound up to doze off. Nerves on edge, he'd tried to relax, but the longer he tried, the more he just stared at the ceiling, picturing his brother, always angry with him; Claudette, the beautiful woman who had come between them and altered their futures; and a host of past thoughts and feelings that merged together to interfere with peaceful slumber. And then there was his brother's new wife, invariably in the background, sliding into every scene of remembrance to annoy and provoke him with her stunning image, her haughty smile and determined mind full of mischief, enticing him by her mere sudden—and completely undesired—existence.

Two weeks ago, Sam recalled, he had been bored; bored with his tedious work at the estate; bored with the ladies he knew who encircled him, or more accurately his title and wealth, like vultures in waiting; bored with what had become an otherwise mundane life. Now, of course, he'd moved beyond boredom to a whole new realm of irritation, to reservation regarding his immediate future, to a measured restlessness, and yes, a seemingly endless state of physical arousal.

Sam groaned and turned onto his side, staring at filtered streetlight that spotted the darkened wall of the small guest bedroom. Her well-maintained and expensive apartments lay in the bustling business district, though in a respectful and clean part of town, he'd noticed. He didn't particularly enjoy the noise and quick-paced dirtiness of the city—any city—and he certainly wasn't pleased to be in this one. Although she'd decorated her home in lovely fashion, he supposed, all pastels and flowers that resembled the particular style of the day, he refused to consider becoming comfortable here.

But *here* wasn't the problem. *She* was.

For the first time in his life he felt totally perplexed by a woman. He didn't know what to think of her, how to interpret her moods and objectives, how much to trust her decisions, actions, and words. Because of his uncharacteristic lack of knowledge where she was concerned, he didn't act when he was with her, he *re*acted, and that, he'd realized over the course of the evening, could not only be a mistake but a danger to their still proper relationship. Normally, Sam considered himself a cool and even-tempered individual, controlled and self-possessed almost to a fault. But somehow, in only a few short days together, the Lady Olivia seemed to bring out the strangest responses in him, though he was, gratefully, fairly able to hide the affects. Or at least he thought so.

She vexed him with her feisty attitude; she made him want to shake her to rid her of the streak of defiant determination she possessed. And embarrassingly enough, the simple notion that such a beautiful creature married his brother made him inexplicably mad. Just mad. The most vivid memory of his childhood remained the fact that Edmund always seemed to win, in every competition in which they were both engaged. Sam rationally knew that many of his brother's achievements over his were related to the duty that came with his title, and that all of his memories were tempered by age and immaturity. Still, *he* wasn't allowed to roam free of responsibility, and never had been; Edmund not only had the opportunity, he took it with pleasure, and always had. In a manner, Sam supposed he was envious. *He* had obligations where Edmund had money, time, and choices. *He* would be required to marry a suitable woman regardless of her looks and intelligence, where Edmund could marry as he wished. Sam realized then that the old streak of jealousy toward his brother had returned in full force to slap him in the face. Not only had Edmund married a smart, remarkably beautiful woman, he had married very, very well. The Lady Olivia Shea, daughter of the late Earl of Elmsboro, had been an excellent catch.

But were they married? It would be the last great mystery until they found his brother and learned the truth of the man's deception. The only thing Sam was sure about was that Olivia truly thought they were. After spending only a few days with her, she'd managed to convince him of her belief that she was Edmund's wife, regardless of the circumstance in which she now found herself. And that, he considered with a dismay that shocked him, put the greatest damper on their relationship, whatever it might be, and his growing desire to have her.

Sam sighed and squeezed his eyes shut, turning onto his back again and pushing the sheets down to the edge of the bed with his bare feet, his body growing hot and uncomfortable in the suddenly stuffy room. Lying there quietly, his arms supporting his head beneath the pillows, he envisioned her nude form, curled up on a soft layer of white feathers and red rose petals, gazing at him with passion-filled eyes as her long black hair fell loosely around her shoulders, the ends curling around pink nipples that stood out and beckoned him to taste. Slowly, she offered him a stirring smile and reached out with an open palm, her long, shapely legs gradually lengthening to give him full frontal view of her exquisitely curved form. She invited him by reaching down and stroking her thigh with a perfectly manicured nail, back and forth, her fingertips brushing ever so gently against the thick black curls between her legs as she slowly opened her knees for his pleasure...

Sam's chest tightened as his body grew hard with desire once again. Had he been so long without a woman that his mind no longer worked to discriminate between those he could and couldn't possibly ever have? To those he shouldn't even desire because of a past that had changed him?

No, this went beyond such choice, such simple lust. This was strictly about her. *She* did this to him, and she probably didn't even realize it, which made it all the worse—or maybe more exciting? But God, what he wouldn't give right now to have her open the door to her guest room, walk to his side, and reach out and touch his hot, rigid flesh with a warm soft hand. His release from her stroking would be bliss beyond words.

Oh, yes, Olivia... Make me—

Sam's eyes popped open and he slowly raised himself up on his elbows, shaking his mind clear, his ears suddenly attuned to the tiniest sounds coming from beyond his room. And then he heard it again—a creak of the floor and a wooden chair briefly scraped across it.

She was awake, like him. And thinking of him as he was of her? Probably not. He'd never known a woman to fantasize about a man that way, or admit to lusty thoughts. And while everything in his well-ordered and intelligent mind told Sam to lie back down, close his eyes again, and *finish* his erotic vision, his impulses got the better of him.

Throwing his legs over the side of the bed, he waited only a moment or two for his erection to die a slow and painful death, then reached for his trousers and a linen pullover shirt, deciding it would be best for both of them if he were at least decently covered. He could only hope she'd be wearing nothing but a silken, sheer chemise.

Sam stood by the door for a few seconds, listening. Hearing nothing, he opened it cautiously and stepped out into the dimly lit hallway.

Since he'd stubbornly marched off to bed earlier in the evening, he hadn't taken the time to observe the layout of her home, though he had seen the parlor, now straight ahead of him, and assumed the dining room and kitchen were to his left, where he now noticed a faint sliver of light coming from under a swing door.

Sam walked silently toward it, reached out with the palm of one hand and opened it.

The movement obviously caught her by surprise. He heard her slight gasp before he saw her.

She sat at the end of the table, her vivid blue eyes wide with uncertainty, clearly startled by his presence as she held a mug of what he assumed to be tea in mid-movement to her lips.

"Your grace—"

"Sam," he cut in, annoyed that she continued to ignore his request to call him by his given name. But he supposed that was natural given her upbringing and the circumstance in which they found themselves. "Am I disturbing you?" he asked casually, walking a few paces into the room.

Her ambivalence toward him, given their quarrel a few hours earlier, showed on her face, but to his mollification, she overcame it at once.

"Of course not, please come in," she said pleasantly, lowering the mug to the tabletop.

Sam glanced quickly around the small room, noting how her kitchen lacked the embellishment and charm of the rest of her apartments. It remained small, functional he supposed, and tidy. Everything about Olivia Shea, he decided, spoke of fastidiousness above all description. But a kitchen wouldn't be a place to receive guests, and so little had been spent on its design. Aside from a small stove, it consisted of only a wash basin and a few small cupboards, everything but the stove painted a glossy white. A square serving bowl of apples and plums sat next to a brightly burning oil lamp in the center of the table, its shiny fruit the only color to adorn the room. If it weren't for her glossy black hair, now falling free to her shoulders and behind her back, and of course those stunning blue eyes, even she would melt into the background. Indeed, she looked absolutely *nothing* like the gorgeous, erotic creature in his fantasy of just a few minutes ago, as she—unfortunately— wasn't wearing the flimsy chemise he'd envisioned, but a stark white cotton nightgown buttoned to her chin and covering her arms to her knuckles. Sam had to admit, though, that the appeal she naturally possessed remained in all its innocent glory even now.

"You seem to be studying me," she said in a curious light, her head tilted to one side.

He smiled and readily pulled out the chair opposite her, sitting heavily then leaning back to stretch his legs out, crossing one ankle over the other. "Not at all."

He knew she waited for more of an explanation, but she didn't pry. She was too properly bred for that, though he thought he might have seen a flicker of annoyance cross her features.

"Did I awaken you?" she asked after a pause and a sip from her mug.

He drew in a deep breath and folded his hands over his stomach. "Actually, I hadn't been able to fall asleep."

She frowned faintly, her gaze traveling the length of his body, taking in all that she could see from above and beside the tabletop.

Sam supposed he looked completely disheveled and inappropriate in his untucked shirt and bare feet. Still, she didn't seem to judge him and his attire, only notice it.

"I'm sorry about that," she said, raising her mug again and taking another sip or two. "I know if one is not accustomed to it, the city lights and noise can seem quite blaring, even when tired."

"The city isn't the problem. Although I spend much of my time on my estate in Cornwall, I also live part of the year in London proper." He smiled again. "No, if I'm tired, I can sleep through anything."

"I see." She caressed the side of the mug with her fingers. "So if you weren't tired, why did you so readily retire this evening?"

The awkwardness of the question caught him off guard, and in a manner troubled him. If they were to succeed in their scheme to find his brother, they needed to get along, and get along on various intimate levels, regardless of his self-preserving lack of trust in her. She was smart enough to detect dishonesty in his answer.

Sitting forward and laying his arm flat on the table, Sam eyed her directly. "In truth, madam, your presence—or the presence of any woman—sometimes makes me...uncomfortable." He hesitated, then decided to add, "The gentle sex and I have never mixed all that well in casual company."

"I see."

Strangely, to his annoyance, she didn't look all that surprised.

"So you excused yourself for bed hours early and without dinner or a late supper to...get away from me?"

He adjusted his body in his chair. "Perhaps."

She chuckled very softly. "Dearest brother, I didn't think I was all that frightful to a man of your stature."

Sam discerned an odd, restless tension envelop them both, not because she teased him for his supposed cowardice, but because she called him brother. The more he thought about it, the less he liked her thinking of him in that regard, especially since the more he knew her, the more he thought of her sexually.

"What are you drinking?" he asked in a purposeful attempt to change the subject. If she was surprised by the turn of conversation, she didn't show it.

"Warm milk and honey, actually. It helps me fall asleep when I'm having trouble doing so. Would you like a cup?"

"Uh, no thank you," he replied, pulling a face. "Sounds positively awful."

She smiled. "Didn't your mother ever suggest it when you couldn't sleep?"

He smirked. "I didn't really know my mother."

The look on her face was very telling, though he couldn't decide if she was shocked or appalled.

"Didn't know her?" She tipped her head to one side

speculatively. "Edmund said he left for the Continent before she passed on and that business kept him from attending her funeral."

"She died seven years ago," he confirmed. Shrugging, he amended, "But I'm sure you're aware that in my world I wouldn't have interacted much with my mother. Instead, I knew my nanny, then my governess, my personal valet, my riding instructor, my music instructor, various tutors...shall I go on?"

To his strange delight, her expression fell flat and her forehead creased in frown.

"No, I understand," she admitted softly, sinking a little into her chair. "Although Edmund said he had a very loving childhood, with wonderful memories of his parents—"

"Edmund lied," he cut in through a snort.

She blinked. "Lied...Of course."

He regretted his utterance almost at once as he watched her falter, her body shudder as if trying to repudiate such a thought. Then she clasped her upper arms with her palms and hugged herself, lowering her gaze to the tabletop.

He cleared his throat, feeling rather subdued by her despondency over another confirmation regarding his deceitful, cheating, brother. "You have to understand that Edmund and I certainly have different perceptions of our childhoods."

She offered him a tentative smile again, looking back into his eyes. "I've no doubt. Siblings always seem to."

"True," he continued. "However, we were raised exactly the same way, with the same disciplines that provided us with nearly identical opportunities. The only difference in our upbringing is that, in the end, more was expected of me."

"Because of your birth order," she interjected.

He nodded and lifted one of the bright red apples out of the bowl in the center of the table, studying it without thought as he twirled it around slowly in his hands. "Even today Edmund has freedoms I never had and never will, including the luxury to do as he pleases. But my brother resented the fact that because I was born three minutes before him, by a stroke of luck, whether ill or good, I will always receive opportunities and fortune he could never have. This is one of the key reasons he left a decade ago."

"And yet he managed to marry first," she remarked after a long pause of consideration.

His brows drew together. "Yes." He wasn't sure if he dare add that Edmund had no obligation to marry and had never wanted to, at least not when he'd last seen his brother.

"Why aren't you married, Sam? That would, naturally, be your greatest duty to fulfill."

Such a personal question took him by surprise. It was the first time she seemed more curious about him and his life and motives than she did Edmund's, which, frankly, both bothered and pleased him.

"Unlike my brother," he started, replacing the apple with great care in its rightful place in the fruit bowl, "I've not yet met a lovely heiress to fulfill my marital...expectations."

For a split second he thought she might actually laugh. She blinked and rubbed her lips together, then sat forward and placed her arms on the table, palms down, her mug just beneath her chin.

"For a man bound to his duty, your grace, I'm amazed that you can afford to be so picky when a bride had to have been chosen for you years ago. Are you telling me there are no eligible ladies of gentle breeding who are willing to succumb to your good charms?"

He didn't know whether to snap back in irritation or chuckle from her ingenuity. But he felt certain that Olivia Shea was purposely teasing him, the first step in a more relaxed stand between them.

"A bride was chosen for me, the very lovely Lady Rowena Downsbury, daughter of the Earl of Layton. But alas, in the end she did the unthinkable and eloped with an American sea captain, sailing to the United States five weeks before our wedding."

"How positively scandalous," she murmured, her wide eyes sparkling from a combination of lamplight and awe.

He grinned dryly, drumming his fingertips on the tabletop to reply, "You've absolutely no idea."

She said nothing for another minute, absorbing the details, it seemed. Then her smile faded a little. "I suppose that must have hurt you. Emotionally, I mean."

He frowned fractionally and tilted his head to the side. "Hurt me? No. I only wish she'd left sooner, saving me the money I'd spent on wedding and honeymoon arrangements. Of course in the end her father lost the most and remained the angriest."

"Naturally."

Sam straightened when her sarcasm hit home, though he had to wonder if she took aim at him or her father.

"I was not in love with Rowena," he explained, then wished at once he could take that ridiculous statement back.

She smiled fractionally. "I wouldn't have thought that you were. Marriage isn't about love, especially in our class." She folded her hands in her lap. "I've learned my lesson well, your grace. Never trust a man who says he is in love with you."

Such an announcement irked him irrationally—and indescribably. "I suppose Edmund told you he was."

"In love with me?"

"Did he?"

She eyed him directly, lashes narrowed as if she studied him to evaluate his trust. Or deception.

"I have been wooed by many men, your grace," she replied evenly, returning to a bit of formality between them. "Most of them desired either my...innocence, or my inheritance, for nefarious purposes. Fortunately, until I met Edmund, I was blessed with a keen mind where men are concerned and was quite able to resist them."

"But not Edmund."

She thought about that for a second or two. "Edmund was different."

"You mean he behaved differently?" he prodded with growing interest.

"Yes, in a manner of speaking." She frowned. "He didn't...he didn't react to my appearance like other gentlemen, which, I admit, had me a little perplexed in the beginning. I suppose it appealed to my vanity to make him notice me."

That truly shocked him. "You're telling me, madam, that he didn't take notice of your unusual beauty?"

His frankness made her blush. He could see the pinkness fill her cheeks even in lamplight, and the look was striking, affecting him again at a base level, which he tried hard to ignore.

After rubbing her nose with the back of her hand and brushing her palms across her lap, she shifted uncomfortably in her chair, crossing one leg over the other. "Not exactly." She hesitated, then continued. "Edmund told me he thought I looked lovely on many occasions, but it's more complex than that. He took a rather...peculiar interest in me. He seemed to thoroughly enjoy my company, and liked to be seen with me socially. But he—" She shrugged and shook her head. "It's very hard to explain."

He nodded, then urged, "And yet I really need to know."

She wasn't sure if she believed him. He could sense it, see it in her wavering gaze. But his persuading seemed to work.

"He took little interest in my family, my past, but he cared immensely about my abilities as a businesswoman and my work at Nivan," she carried on slowly, voice lowered. "He seemed very proud of me, my appearance, my accomplishments. But he...he didn't think of me..."

She paused once more, fidgeting with her hands in her lap.

Sam waited, finding her embarrassment altogether charming and enjoying the moment far more than he knew he should. And he was, quite frankly, fascinated by this revelation.

Her lashes fluttered downward; she couldn't look at him.

"Although Edmund *said* he loved me, and that he married me for love, he never seemed to discover... passion with me. There was nothing remotely passionate about our relationship. I admit that after a while that bothered me."

For the first time in years Sam sat motionless, stumped beyond words. "I see," was the only response he could think of.

After another slight hesitation, she looked up again, directly at him, breathing deeply for confidence. "You have to understand, sir, that when I met your brother, and he reacted as a gentleman should in all ways, I found it refreshing. I was...drawn to him because he seemed to genuinely...*like* me. There was something different, something...friendly about the marriage that appealed to me."

Now he understood. Sort of. "It sounds very much like a marriage of convenience."

"With all things considered, sir, marriage to your brother wasn't—and hasn't been—all that convenient."

That quick comeback amused him. "No, I suppose not."

After a moment of silence her brows drew together in reflection. "Edmund said he loved me, and I believed him. But since he's left I've come to realize that it's more accurate to say he liked me, but he loved only what he loved *about* me. Does that make sense?"

Only to a woman. "Not exactly," he replied.

She expelled an irritated sigh and rubbed her forehead at her temples with both hands. "What I mean is, Edmund loved—wanted—what he loved about me— my wealth, my appearance, my intelligence, my social standing, my contacts in the community. Maybe even the power of Nivan as a business patronized by the empress. But in the end, even though Edmund found me enjoyable to be with, he never loved what I truly am. He never loved *me*. I only wish I had realized that before I spoke my vows."

His chair creaked under him as Sam sat forward, elbows on knees, and clasped his hands together in front of him. "He used you, Olivia."

She sat straighter in her seat, eyeing him defiantly. "That's putting it rather simplistically."

He shrugged. "And yet, in a word, that's exactly what he did. Married you for everything but you."

For the first time since he'd met her, she seemed on the verge of tears, blinking excessively and gazing at the ceiling for a few long seconds. Frankly, he loathed it when a woman cried, and yet this time it almost seemed appropriate. It was a defining moment, because in that instant he decided he felt something for her beyond the extremes of irritation and lust. She had roused a compassion in him that he didn't think he'd experienced for a woman before, although rationally he admitted to himself that such a feeling came from the fact that she was now his responsibility. At least he hoped that's where it came from. Then again, she could be playing him for a fool; most women tried to. Being compassionate certainly didn't mean letting his guard down where she was concerned.

She cleared her throat and shook her hair back again. "Most people of our class marry for those reasons, your grace. This is nothing new. I was, and am, prepared to experience a solid marriage without romantic notions or love. I don't need that to be satisfied."

"Yes, but most ladies who marry for convenience, or arrangement, get something in return for the lack of romantic interest from their husbands. Whether there is love or not, they gain satisfaction from the stability of the union, from their children, family, social causes related to the marriage. My brother apparently left you with nothing, and that not only seems unfair, it's deceitful."

Instead of breaking down, as he expected any other lady might have, she tipped her head to the side a fraction and gazed at him thoughtfully for a moment or two, eyes narrowed and just a trace of a smile appearing on her lips.

"Apparently?" she repeated very softly.

"Yes," he murmured.

He hadn't wanted her to catch that inference. But at this point he couldn't lie about the skepticism that remained regarding her disclosures about his brother. Whether *he* liked her or not, he wasn't about to completely believe her without proof. For all he knew, she and Edmund were in this together as co-conspirators, though the more acquainted he and Olivia became, the less he thought it likely. Still, he wasn't about to let her know that yet.

She continued to eye him expectantly for a few seconds longer, seemingly waiting for him to explain. When at last she must have realized that he had no intention of doing so, she offered him a knowing nod or two and wearily stood. They'd reached an impasse.

"I have brandy, if you'd prefer that," she offered softly.

He slowly pushed his fingers through his hair. "Prefer that?"

"To the warm milk." She swallowed. "To help you sleep."

Awkward silence reigned, though Sam could hardly say the room, or the apartment, was quiet, given the variances of city noise—laughter, drunken singing, and the like—drifting in from the street below. Yet that hardly mattered when not only her scrutiny but her sweetness captured him suddenly, drawing him in, enveloping him in an unanticipated, static charge of total awareness.

Her eyes widened and she gripped her empty mug between her palms.

She feels it too...

"No thank you," he whispered, slowly raising himself and moving forward a step to stand in front of her. "I'm sure I'll doze off eventually."

He gazed down to her face, noting the smoothness of her complexion, the hesitancy in her eyes, her pulse beating rapidly in her temple.

Edmund might lose.

It was a stunning, explosive idea, and the satisfaction he felt at that moment, coupled with a myriad of confusing possibilities, overwhelmed him.

Edmund had taken Claudette. And here his brother's wife stood before him, sweet and innocent and uncommonly beautiful, fighting the urge to be seduced.

But would such a game work if Edmund didn't want her?

"Are you off to bed, then?" she asked, interrupting his thoughts with a delicate crease in her forehead.

He shook himself back to the moment. "I am, Lady Olivia," he replied with a slight, formal nod.

Her lips pulled back into a gentle smile. "Livi."

She had mesmerizing lips. "Pardon?"

"Those who know me best call me Livi," she said softly.

They simply looked at each other for a few seconds more, then she withdrew first by leaning over to extinguish the lamp, offering him a fast but captivating view of the movement of bare breasts beneath her cotton nightgown.

God, how could Edmund not want her?

"Good night, Livi."

In total darkness she replied in whisper, "Sleep well, Sam."

He turned away from her and left the kitchen, walking silently back to the guest room by pale moonlight through shuttered windows, aroused and uncomfortable, his mind on only one thing:

Edmund has already lost.

Chapter 7

I t was a lovely day for a tour, at least seasonally speaking. The predawn showers had given way to brilliant sunshine and dewy fresh air, promising a day of warmth to bathe the bustling city. Of course, she had slept fitfully after their rather friendly discussion of the night before, tossing and turning between the sheets, her mind racing, filled with the continuous, confusing, and positively...indecent thoughts of him. So much for enjoying springtime. And the warm milk obviously hadn't worked.

Her personal maid, Marie-Nicole, Normand's youngest daughter at fifteen, had arrived at precisely seven o'clock, as she did every morning, to help her with her toilette and the donning of her dress, today's choice being a modest yellow chiffon day gown with a raised, square neckline of white lace and puffed half sleeves.

After braiding her hair into two loops and lifting them to fasten daintily on top of her head with mother-of-pearl combs, Marie-Nicole departed, leaving her alone to face the Duke of Durham.

He walked beside her now as they left her apartments for the boutique where she would be giving him a basic understanding of the history and necessity of perfume and its industry. Theirs had been a rather fast breakfast, more silence than awkwardness between them, both taking coffee, fruit, and cheese but keeping conversation to a minimum. Olivia supposed they were both a bit uncomfortable after the shared verbal intimacy of the night before, though perhaps it was more accurate to describe him as distracted.

In truth, she had enjoyed their time together last evening. He hadn't seemed to notice her bedtime wear, which, under the circumstance, wasn't exactly indecent since her nightgown covered her from chin to toe. He, on the other hand, held her captivated by his casual attire and somewhat more open demeanor. She had never been in the presence of a man half dressed before, even her husband. Then again, her brother-in-law hadn't been exactly exposed, either. He'd worn trousers and a shirt, but his feet were bare, and she could scarcely avoid staring at his magnificent chest, where a trace of dark hair had escaped the low vee at his neck. She only hoped he hadn't noticed her preoccupation with his person. He hadn't seemed to, anyway, at least not until the very end of the conversation when that shiver of . . . *something* passed between them.

She'd never experienced such an odd feeling with any other man before last night, and that's what troubled her the most, she supposed. It had been truly distinctive, unique even, and the funniest thing to her was the fact that nothing had actually *happened.*

He stood slightly behind her now as they descended the steps into the salon, her awareness of him just as keen as it had ever been, making her wish she'd brought her fan. If nothing else, it would have given her something to do with her hands.

The plan, as they'd discussed over breakfast, would be to take some time this morning to acquaint him with the various aspects of Nivan, and the perfume industry in general, much of which Edmund already knew. Later they would sit over tea and discuss the next course of action.

Olivia fairly breezed into the storefront from the salon, inhaling the marvelous fragrances of the day, recognizing the Oriental subgroups immediately as the scents of the season. This was the work she adored, and she'd been gone from her passion too long.

Normand seemed busy assisting two elegant ladies near the front display table, giving her ample time to begin the tutoring before he interrupted them.

"Do you recognize the scent in the air?" she asked to start the discussion, controlling her nerves by forcing a pleasant smile upon her mouth as she gazed up to him.

"I remember the spice," he replied rather blandly. "You wore it."

That quick answer took her aback. Not only because it came so fast, but more so because he recalled a vague scent she'd only worn in his presence once.

Without pause in her stride, she confirmed, "Correct. It's the scent of the spring."

"The scent of the spring?"

"Yes. Every year new scents are developed here in France, and in Italy and the Asian world, which we import. They're different combinations, really, of the classics, although some can be entirely original. Some ladies, and even gentlemen, choose a new scent each year, some even each season."

He said nothing to that as she walked to the center of the boutique to stand next to a round, glass case filled with perfume jars, or *flacons*, pomanders, potpourri bowls, and sachets. Placing her palms on top, her back to Normand and the ladies to keep them from discerning any part of their conversation, she eyed him directly across the case.

"Perfume, and its industry, are as old as the ancient world. I won't bore you with details on the distillation process; however, you should know basics because Edmund does."

He folded his arms across his chest, circling the glass case to move closer. That flustered her, imposed on her thoughts, and she made a turn to move. He quickly reached out and placed his open hand gently over her knuckles.

"Don't," he murmured. "They're watching, and we are married, after all."

"Of course," she replied, though the warmth of his palm on her bare skin made her markedly hot of a sudden.

She drew a full breath to continue, deciding to just get to the point. "There are six essential fragrances of time, your grace—"

"Sam," he whispered.

He truly possessed a knack for distracting her, though she wasn't exactly sure why. Lifting her lips in a half smile, she returned, "Edmund."

"They can't hear us, Olivia."

She shot a brief glance over her shoulder, finding Normand and the ladies engaged in rapt conversation. Of course he was right. "That's irrelevant."

His brows rose and he nodded once. "If it makes you more comfortable."

More comfortable? She couldn't be less comfortable at the moment. Instead of admittance, however, she brushed over that concern and returned to her original dialogue.

"As I said, there are six basic fragrances that have been used over time. What I'd like to do is explain them to you in a little detail, giving you a chance to sample each one."

"I don't think I need to sample them," he remarked.

She noted the trace of exasperation in his voice but chose to ignore it. "You'll need to choose a fragrance."

He exhaled a fast breath, finally drawing his hand away. "Why?"

She frowned, momentarily disconcerted. "So you'll smell like Edmund."

He practically gaped at her, and she could feel the heat suffuse her cheeks as she realized what she'd said and that he was on the verge of breaking out into laughter.

"And, um, what if I'd rather not *smell* like my brother?" he asked, a trace of annoyed amusement coloring his tone.

Olivia momentarily closed her eyes and wiped a

palm across her brow. "This isn't an option, sir, you'll need a scent. Edmund always wore fragrance, and someone would notice if you didn't."

He glanced around the boutique as he shoved his hands in the pockets of his day jacket. "Then choose something original. Something you'd like *me* to wear, Olivia."

His voice had lowered to a rough murmur, especially when he said her name, and she felt her insides melt in the most peculiar manner. "But you—"

"Am my own man," he articulated in deep whisper.

She blinked quickly, her lips parting in a rebuttal that never came. He kept his eyes locked with hers, clearly waiting for her to acknowledge his statement of fact, which of course was already obvious to her. Or submit to him in some feminine fashion. And yet the only thing she could think of at that moment was that he had the most amazing eyes—dark as chocolate, surrounded by thick black lashes. Odd that she couldn't recall if Edmund's eyes were the same shade, or how they appeared when he looked at her; Edmund always seemed to be smiling. But this man's eyes penetrated hers as if he were trying to read her mind, or force her into submission. She felt as confused suddenly as she had when he'd first kissed her back in London.

He waited, without any notice of her discomfort, and after a second or two Olivia shook herself from such reckless thoughts and drew a deep breath for confidence.

"I think," she said after clearing her throat, "what we'll do to reach an agreement is create something unique, for you, for the season."

His brows rose again, his mouth tipped up in a trace of amusement. She ignored the fact that he'd more or less suggested the same thing.

She began running the pads of her fingers along the top of the glass case. "I realize you don't like to wear cologne—"

"I never wear cologne," he corrected, watching her.

She ignored his interruption with a half smile. "And so I think I'll choose a newer scent for you, create one of my own, and that way nobody will know when you're posing as Edmund. He chooses new scents frequently."

He snorted, and almost—almost—rolled his eyes. She didn't know whether to chuckle or scold him.

"I'll do this for you, *Sam,* so that you don't have to *smell* like him."

He smiled wryly. "I'll just smell like—"

"Yourself."

"In a perfume factory."

It was Olivia's turn to roll her eyes. "Give me some credit. I do know what I'm doing."

"I've no doubt," he drawled.

"May I continue?"

"Please," he returned a bit too sarcastically.

She nodded to him once. "As I was saying, there are six basic fragrance types that have been used over time. First we have frankincense, a warm, balsamic scent from Arabia, originally used as incense and enjoyed very much in the ancient world by many of the Caesars, Alexander the Great, even Queen Hatshepsut. Eventually it became a favorite perfume in China, and later in Renaissance Italy.

"Next is rose, the most widely used and enjoyed scent from around the world, from ancient Greeks, Romans, and later Parisians. It's particularly enjoyed by English ladies, and was one of Queen Elizabeth's favorites.

"Third is sandalwood-jasmine, a marvelous botanical array imported originally from India and Kashmir. Sandalwood exudes a very warm, sensual odor, and jasmine an abundant floral appeal that's been much attributed to the growth of perfumery during the Renaissance.

"Fourth, we have orange blossom, a very delicious, sweet scent from East Asia, a floral aroma that we use as the primary ingredient in eau de cologne, which I'll get to in a moment."

He let out a long exhale, as a sign of impatience, she was certain. She ignored it.

"Next is spice, the main ingredient of the fragrance you smell drifting through Nivan at this time." She broke her instruction for a moment, leaning over the glass top to whisper, "We always fill sachets with the scent of the season and place them everywhere in the store— under pillows and cushions in the salon, behind counters, sofas, under the desks and in the drawers, and even in waste bins. It works beautifully by challenging the customer to ask about it. Then we can introduce it as something new and exciting that all of Paris is talking about and that each lady positively *needs* in her fragrance collection. It makes very good business sense."

Her brother-in-law hadn't commented at all since she began her essence introduction, though he did cross his arms over his chest with that, continuing to gaze at her, his expression bland but his eyes seemingly enraptured by her oration. She didn't know if that was good or bad. But she wanted to get this done. Normand would interrupt them shortly; she could count on it.

She patted the back of her hair into place, just for something to do, she supposed, and finished quickly.

"Well, in any case, spice comes primarily from both the Near and Far East, and tends to be a mixture of ginger, cloves, nutmeg, and cinnamon, in various combinations, and sometimes mixed with other scents."

"It's the scent of the season," he drawled, leaning his hip on the edge of the glass.

Olivia started, quite surprised that he'd offered something to the conversation. "Yes, exactly." She wished she could decipher his manner, read his thoughts from his rather staid expression. Certainly he had to find this at least *remotely* interesting. Edmund did. Then again, he wasn't Edmund, and every minute in his presence, she grew more keenly aware of that fact.

"There is only one more, your grace," she said matter-of-factly, then felt a bit subdued when he didn't correct her for using his more formal designation.

She straightened, and continued. "Finally there is eau de cologne, a French favorite originating from the Farina family in 1709, and which, I might add, adorned the wrists and filled the sachets of Madame du Barry." She shrugged. "And of course it's well known that Napoleon preferred it."

"Of course," he agreed.

She hesitated, uncertain if he mocked her, though in

the end deciding it hardly mattered. The point was that he needed to know the basics.

"Now," she carried on, tipping her head to the side and eyeing him thoughtfully, "Edmund tended to prefer eau de cologne, or a mixture of orange blossom and sandalwood with a trace of spice. For you, however, I think—"

"I refuse to smell like a flower," he said.

Did he think she knew nothing? She grinned. "No roses for you, then?"

He didn't smile in return. "No."

She sighed at his emphatic stance. "Well, I think I can do something with a mix of frankincense and spice, perhaps adding a touch of musk, but be aware, *darling,* you are going to have to wear it."

His eyelids narrowed a fraction, whether in annoyance or daring, she couldn't be sure, and she had to wonder if it was because she'd ordered him, or the fact that she called him by an endearment. Maybe he just didn't like having no choice in the matter. If nothing else, Samson Carlisle, Duke of Durham, remained a man in charge. She knew that instinctively. And it was going to be a long day.

One of the ladies in the shop suddenly laughed uproariously, sharply slicing into their engrossed tête-à-tête. Olivia and the duke both looked around toward the sound, noting that the bigger, and louder, of the two women had leaned forward to whisper something to Normand, at which time the man slapped his palm against his ruffled shirt and chuckled, shaking his head as if these ladies were the most marvelously entertaining creatures to ever step foot in Nivan. Of course they'd never know he charmed them all. It was one of the reasons Nivan sold so well.

Wearily, she returned her attention to Sam and said, "Perhaps it's time we experimented with a few samples."

If it weren't for her—the glamourous perfection that was her face, the excitement in her features as she spoke of work she adored, the slight sway of her hips and curve of her breasts beneath her flattering yet totally conservative day gown, and yes, even the subtle scent she exuded—Sam thought he might burst into tears of absolute boredom. In truth he couldn't care any less about perfume and its history except where the information applied to Edmund and his relationship with his so-called wife. But being a man of intelligent mind, he realized he needed to listen to her explanations and to attempt to absorb at least some of it.

Actually, the more he listened, the more he found himself absorbed by her. She fascinated him in a manner he couldn't exactly understand. She took her work very seriously—too seriously, some might say, considering her sex—but he found that almost...alluring. She obviously had a deeply felt passion for perfume, its history, its function in society, its processing, which he certainly didn't care to hear about in detail, and she clearly possessed an astute business sense not usually found in females. Frankly, he was coming to admire her, and as Sam recalled now, he didn't think he'd ever—in his life—admired a woman for anything other than how she looked on his arm or in his bed. A strange sensation, indeed.

Olivia motioned for him to follow her to an ornately carved, white-painted desk, behind which stood a series of white wooden shelves attached to a wall, papered in textured red velvet. Golden tassels hung from the corners of the shelves to add ornateness to the look and to frame all the little bottles, dozens of them, some made simply of glass, clear and colored, some ceramic, some painted elaborately, some even appearing to be inlaid with gold or jewels, though whether real or paste, he couldn't tell. From the clientele, however, he assumed at least some of them were real. And the bottles, he guessed, contained all the various scents du jour. He groaned inwardly, hoping to God she wouldn't make him sniff them all. He supposed he should just be thankful his friends weren't here to witness this.

"Please be seated," she said pleasantly, motioning for him to lower his large frame onto the tiny red velveteen chair in front of the desk. He did so without comment, only to wonder how French ladies with big bottoms and large hoops managed it. Then again, it was obviously not here for comfort but for appearances, as was the entire shop's decoration.

Olivia expertly moved her skirts to the side and sat gracefully in the same style chair behind the desk, opposite him, scooting it forward a little so she could rest her wrists on the edge.

"Now," she began, "this is where we sample fragrances."

"You're not going to make me smell all of those, are you?" he asked, motioning to the rows of fancy containers with a nod of his head.

Her brow creased for a second or two, then she

turned to view the bottles behind her. "Those?" She looked back at him. "Those are empty. We sell those to complement the distinctive fragrance created for each individual."

"Oh," he mumbled, unable to think of a better reply. He felt utterly ridiculous.

"That way," she continued, "each lady, or gentleman, can not only choose a unique scent, but carry it in a personally selected *flacon*—the French word for flask, or for our purposes, perfume bottle—original only to the House of Nivan. All the good houses do the same."

Sam wiped a palm across the back of his neck, feeling uncomfortably warm. He looked at her again, noting how relaxed she seemed in her domain, sitting beautifully upright in her velveteen chair. And he had to give her high credit for not making him feel stupid.

"I see," he remarked.

She gave him a genuine smile of pleasure, not one of derision or haughtiness, and it boosted his opinion of her another level.

"Now," she started once more, "I have a few"—she leaned to her side and pulled a small drawer out from beneath the desktop—"samples here. At least enough to give you an idea of what we offer in the basic scents I was telling you about a few minutes ago."

She gingerly placed a small wooden tray in front of him. Inside, in compact, specially designed inserts, lay a row of miniature square glass jars, approximately one inch by one inch, labeled with each individual scent. With nimble fingers she lifted one out of the tray and carefully pulled off a corklike top.

"This is sandalwood." She waved it two or three times under his nose. "You can easily detect the warmth in it, but it's not necessarily sweet—until you add the floral of the jasmine. That boosts the full-bodied, botanical essence of the fragrance."

What did she want him to say? What a lovely odor? It smelled like perfume. Thankfully, she put the cork back in and replaced it, choosing another bottle before he could comment.

"Now, this is the scent again when combined with jasmine." She pulled the cork and offered it to him. "Smell the difference? It's sweeter, more feminine in color, a bit rounder in its essence."

Rounder in its essence? He had absolutely no idea what that meant, but he could detect the scent of flowers. At least that was progress. He nodded, sat back again and waited for the next bottle.

"This is orange blossom," she continued in eagerness, "and one of my personal favorites, especially mixed with the right amount of spice."

He could definitely smell the orange, though he had trouble imagining a "spicy orange" scent that someone would actually want to wear on his or her person. He did, however, notice that a few stray curls had escaped her plaits to fall over her shoulder, nestling between the uplifted curve of her breasts, sticking to her dewy skin. The view distracted him from his scent lesson.

". . . of Edmund's favorites, eau de cologne."

She'd said something as she stuck another bottle under his nose, and he dutifully took a whiff to satisfy her. Immediately he pulled back. "I don't like that one at all."

"No? Very well, then," she replied without judgment, replacing the cork and putting it back in the tray.

"Especially if it was Edmund's favorite," he added with sly intent, resting his elbow on the padded arm and interlocking his fingers in his lap.

She peeked up through her lashes, offering him a crooked grin. "Or Napoleon's?"

"Precisely."

"Ahh."

Sam wished he knew what she was thinking beneath her professional facade, but he wasn't about to ask. She'd moved on, still smiling, lifting another bottle. He was beginning to find their interaction almost on the verge of being enjoyable. Amazing—spending time with a woman outside of bed and enjoying it.

"Next we have spice, one of my personal preferences actually, as it carries a very clean base and isn't overly sweet; it can stand alone as a scent of its own."

She held it out for him and he dutifully breathed in. "I detect the cloves," he said almost without thinking. Didn't she say it was made from cloves? She must have, because her eyes lit up and she nodded once to him.

"Very good, Sam."

He felt strangely proud for impressing her.

"Spice can be worn by both gentlemen and ladies. With a bit of mixture from other scents, it can be made sweeter, or darker and more masculine with a touch of musk. That's what I think I'll do for you."

"Good. Perfect," he said quickly.

She returned the bottle to its slot, then pushed the tray to the side and placed her arms on the desk, crossing one over the other as she gazed at him directly.

"Bored, are you?" she asked with narrowed eyes and a wry smile.

"Of course not."

"Liar," she teased.

He could only shrug.

She reached for the samples to put them away. "Then to save time I won't bother with the rose, since I presume you know what that smells like."

"It's my sister's favorite," he said with a smirk and a shake of his head. "One always knows Elise has entered a room simply by the smell. Wears it in excess, in my opinion, but then she's never bothered with my opinion."

Olivia stilled, her hand holding the tray in midair as she stared at him, her features going slack from what appeared to be sheer surprise.

"So, choosing a new fragrance today, Monsieur Carlisle?" Normand strode around the glass display case as he neared them at last. "Something for the spring?"

The interruption startled her and, for some unknown reason, totally irritated him. Sam straightened in his chair and nodded once to the man while she resumed her task of placing the tray of samples back in its drawer.

"I suppose it is time if we are to attend a social function or two in the coming days," Olivia replied, her good-natured pose returning as she raised her face so Normand could give her a peck on both cheeks. "But my dear husband is being rather selective today."

"Is he?"

"As always." She gave an exaggerated sigh. "Though I think we've decided on a blend that will work."

The Frenchman stood to regard him from behind Olivia's chair, his hands clutching the back of it, fingers next to her shoulders. "And your choice, monsieur?"

"A spice base, naturally," he answered in perfect French, smiling congenially, as he thought Edmund would, noting how annoyed he felt for no apparent reason. "It is the scent of the season, is it not?"

"Oh, indeed, indeed."

He studied Normand as sunlight from the window cast a bright stream upon his middle-aged face. Sam didn't think women would find the man handsome, but he had a charming disposition—real or fabricated—that ladies no doubt enjoyed. He presented himself in a nonconfrontational light, even soft and pleasing, probably a necessity in the perfume industry, where women were the prime consumers.

But something about the Frenchman disturbed him, and Sam couldn't put his finger on why, or even what it was, exactly. He had keen dark eyes, deeply set, a large, bulbous nose, a receding hairline, and almost no chin at all, though the thickness of his neck tended to disguise that particular lack. He wasn't exactly fat, but he carried a heaviness around the middle that made him look healthily fed.

No, it wasn't the man's rather ordinary appearance that unsettled him, but something else, something he couldn't define, and he supposed his inability to do so bothered him the most. And he seemed almost possessive of Olivia. That annoyed him, too. Sam had to wonder what Edmund would have thought about that, or if his brother had even noticed.

"Well, I suppose we should get some luncheon,

darling," Olivia chimed in after a brief but uncomfortable pause. She started to rise and Normand automatically took her elbow to help her.

Sam stood immediately and, without clear thought, reached out and grasped one of her hands. In his best commanding voice, he said, "Shall we find an outdoor café, Livi? Please excuse us, Normand."

She hesitated for a slice of a second, a frown gracing her face as she glanced at him.

"Of course," Normand returned, dropping her elbow at once.

The man's smile never faltered, though Sam had the distinct impression he had become suddenly watchful, thoughtful. His brows creased slightly and he backed up a step so Olivia could move out from behind the desk. She lifted her skirts, and without a glance to either one of them, sauntered toward the storefront.

"It's a lovely day, darling. I'm starved," she declared, her voice oddly taut with cheerfulness.

"Normand," Sam acknowledged, then turned and headed to Olivia's side, where she waited for him, face turned to stare through the glass to the bustling street beyond. He took her elbow, as the Frenchman had done, but he held her closer to him as he opened the door and ushered her through, knowing without looking that Normand still kept his observant gaze locked on their backs as they strode out into the open air.

Chapter 8

Normand had a secret. A marvelous secret. A very, *very* big and potentially lucrative secret. And what a joy it would be to tease the countess with it—just tease, of course, because he didn't want to give *everything* away and allow her more control over their scheme than she already had. He wanted to be in charge for a change. And, *mon Dieu,* this bit of news had simply fallen in his lap.

His face upturned into his first genuine grin in weeks, Normand rang the bell to the Countess Renier's suite on the top floor of the Hotel d' Empress. She stayed only here while visiting Paris and, as far as he knew, she hadn't yet returned to the country since the last time he spoke with her more than three weeks ago.

Seconds later the door cracked open, then widened

when her butler, Rene, recognized him, ushering him inside with a wide palm and a formal sway of his arm.

"Madame is at her toilette, Monsieur Paquette, though I'm sure she'll see you if you prefer to wait?"

Prefer to wait? He'd wait till the second coming of Christ to see the look on her face when he revealed his news. Life couldn't get much better than this.

"I'll wait," he said bluntly to the tall, graying gentleman. "I'd like coffee."

"Of course," Rene replied properly. "Right this way."

Normand followed the stout older man into the countess's parlor, a cluttered room she'd grossly over-decorated in a floral display of bright pink and rose red. Although the countess still retained her beauty after so many years, and took care with her person so that she graced the air with sophisticated elegance in all she wore and did, her living establishments, both here and in the country, nauseated him each time he was forced to sit and gossip in such garish glory.

Today she'd cracked the windows to allow the breeze to enter, and had placed bright red roses in a crystal vase on the tea table, obviously expecting to entertain this afternoon. Furniture crowded the rather small area, as she'd added another bright pink velveteen set-tee since his last visit. It was totally unnecessary, in his opinion, and no doubt meant to complement the one overstuffed sofa, covered with the largest, ugliest embroidered red roses he had ever seen, that now sat in the center of the room. Various floral and landscape paintings adorned all four walls, compromising nearly every inch of available space, all framed in the same brilliant shade of gold as the thick-corded tassels that gently retained red velveteen drapes, all of which purposely gathered by at least a yard on the plush pink carpeting.

Normand sat as usual in one of the pink and white striped wing chairs that faced the sofa, tapping his fingertips together with impatience. Rene returned in only a minute or two, silently placed a silver tray on the tea table in front of him, then lifted the pot and poured the aromatic hot brew into one of the two rose-painted china cups, before he bowed stiffly and turned to make his exit. Normand helped himself, adding sugar and milk to his taste. He realized, of course, that the countess would make him wait; that was just her style. The woman never awakened before noon, and took nearly two hours with her toilette, a fact Normand knew only because he had the audacity to call on her at eleven once and was curtly informed that madame was still asleep and *never* greeted callers before three.

Well, he was here today, long before three, because once they'd started working together—if one could use that word to describe their particular collaboration—he'd been entitled to privileges others weren't, especially when he had vital information, as he did now.

But this afternoon's wait proved to be longer than usual. Contemplating a third cup of coffee, which he ultimately decided against because asking to use her private washroom would prove to be an embarrassment, he reached into his left jacket pocket and removed the golden timepiece his grandmother had given him. Half past one. He'd been here nearly forty-five minutes. Annoying that, but then it occurred to him that the lovely countess would be more angry at herself for making him wait when she learned the crucial nature of his visit. He had to stop himself from rubbing his hands together in glee.

Finally, footsteps clapped across the floor in the entryway behind him. He placed his cup and saucer back on the silver tray and stood abruptly, turning toward the doorway and brushing down the jacket of his morning suit just as Rene reentered the parlor and formally announced the countess with flair, as if he were a bloody dignitary instead of a simple perfume shopkeeper. Then again, he thought proudly, neither Nivan nor its management would ever be described as simple by anyone who frequented the establishment.

Normand clutched his perspiring palms behind him, shoulders erect with confidence, his expression gently grave to the level he wanted to portray as the Countess Renier de Chartes breezed into the room as if floating on a gust of scented, warm air, her usual haughty smile planted perfectly across her painted red mouth. Indeed, she looked beautiful as always, primped, colored, and scented appropriately for a spring afternoon of entertaining.

Normand bopped up on his heels, then his toes, concentrating on his bearing, his countenance, and especially his hands behind him so he didn't annoy her; the countess had informed him last time they were together that he spoke too much with his hands. In general, he disliked her, mostly for the air of superiority with which she never failed to smother him. But then she held the reins in their very unusual relationship and nothing could be done about that hard fact. At least for now.

"Normand," she said, nodding curtly once as she walked to his side, her tone and expression pleasant.

He bowed, then took the creamed and manicured hand she offered him, lifting it to his lips for a gentle peck.

"Madame Comtesse, you are ravishing this afternoon, as always."

"Merci," she replied with a tip of her forehead.

He stood back. "I have news."

"Oh? Then sit, sit." She gestured to the chair, giving him permission to return to it.

Normand lowered his body onto the cushion again, though he remained erect, his shoulders tight with anticipation.

The countess followed suit, sitting gracefully on the sofa opposite him, fussing with her wide silk skirts until they lay just perfectly around her ankles, then folding her hands in her lap to give him her undivided attention at last.

"Now, dearest Normand," she said through an exaggerated sigh, "what is this...news you have for me?"

With polite control he managed to paste a discerning smile on his mouth, pausing just long enough to collect his thoughts—and make *her* wait for a change.

Clearing his throat, he locked his gaze with hers and murmured, "I had an interesting visit with Monsieur Carlisle this morning, at Nivan."

For seconds she seemed confused, her penciled brows drawing together minutely. Then she relaxed against the sofa cushion and raised her chin a little in a show of contention.

"You are mistaken. Edmund is in Grasse," she replied, her tone authoritative as it cooled a shade. "I received a note from him just three days ago and he never mentioned returning. At least not so soon."

Normand hadn't thought of that and he almost kicked himself for never considering they'd be in constant communication. Still, this might work to his advantage if she even remotely doubted her dear Edmund's intentions.

He leaned back as she had done, placing his elbows on the armrests and tenting his fingers together in front of him. "Pardon, madame, but I am not mistaken. Edmund is here, in Paris, at Nivan. He returned yesterday, with Olivia." He paused, strictly for effect, then shrugged one shoulder and added, "She evidently found him."

"And what?" the countess snapped immediately. "Forced him to return with her?"

"I have no idea," he said. And he didn't. But he knew there was more to the man's return, or at least he suspected more, than he would tell the woman sitting across from him. Withholding a bit gave him an advantage that he would most surely be able to use in the coming days.

He could see her try to grapple with the information, debating whether to believe or disbelieve his word; whether to dismiss him immediately or probe him for answers; whether she should leave at once and go to Edmund, catching him unawares and drilling him about his unexpected return with Olivia, or bide her time, consider her options, think things through as an intelligent, cultured lady, and one who would not be intimidated.

Evidently culture won.

"Well, what did he say to you?" she prodded moments later.

He let out a long exhale, almost giddy in his desire to ruffle her preening feathers. "Very little. I only spent a few minutes with the happy couple in the boutique this morning as Monsieur Carlisle chose a new spring fragrance."

She smiled wryly. "Happy?"

This was the opening he wanted. He frowned purposely, nodding. And then with thoughtfulness in his voice, murmured, "Actually, as I think about it now, I wouldn't call it happy, exactly. More like..." He gazed briefly to the gilded, meretricious ceiling, then back into her eyes. "It appeared as if they've found some new... understanding in each other. Or perhaps *of* each other."

She clearly had no idea what he meant.

"An understanding," she repeated, looking at him as if he had the brain of a bug and obviously couldn't explain himself.

Normand knew he would enjoy reliving this moment for the rest of his life. "Something between them has changed. They couldn't take their eyes off each other." He licked his lips and added poignantly, "Or more precisely, he couldn't take his eyes off her."

The countess never moved, never broke her expression, never even appeared to blink. She just stared at him as a minute passed by in utter silence. He waited, unsure what to anticipate in reaction from her, though he knew she had absorbed and processed the information, all its facets and ultimate implications.

"I thought you should know," he said, his voice low and deliberately solemn.

At last she breathed deeply, her red lips widening into a smile, though he knew it was false because of the tightness in her jaw—and the fact that her eyes remained hard, focused and calculating.

"However interesting this news is, Normand, I have trouble believing darling little Olivia, pretty though she is, would capture Edmund's interest. If not before their wedding, why now?" She shook her head as if to convince herself of the absurdity of such an insinuation. "No, what you're...suggesting is impossible."

He tapped his fingertips together and tipped his head toward her once. "I'm sure you're right, Madame Comtesse."

"Of course I'm right," she retorted, her exasperation showing beneath her crisp demeanor.

"And yet," Normand continued, "they stayed the night together in her apartments."

That enraged her; he watched her bite down tightly even as her perfectly powdered face flushed rosy to the roots of her shiny and expertly plaited blond hair. Yet he couldn't be certain if she'd become suddenly furious because of the delicate information he'd provided, or the fact that he'd had the audacity to say such a thing to her knowing how she felt about Edmund. Her reaction pleased him, though, and that was enough.

"I'm not stupid, Normand," she said in warning, challenging him with her fixed glare.

He slapped a hand on his chest, looking at her in feigned shock. "It would never occur to me to think such a thing. I am only here to inform you of what I know."

"Which obviously isn't very much," she countered.

A ridiculous comment since he was the one who'd come to her today with what they both knew was incredible news. But in his usual sagacious manner he bit his tongue and ignored that rude remark.

She reached for the china pot to pour herself what now had to be cold coffee. Normand watched her stir in two teaspoons of sugar, and he could swear her hands were shaking. Seeing the Countess Renier unnerved was a novel and remarkably satisfying experience.

"So what do you suppose we do about it?" she asked seconds later.

The question surprised him. She made a habit of never asking him his opinion about anything that didn't have to do with a new scent for her sachets. And he couldn't recall a time when she'd quizzed him for actual advice. At that moment Normand realized just how alarmed she really was.

Leaning forward in his chair, he folded his hands in front of him and rested his elbows on his knees. "I would think, Madame Comtesse, that if he arrived here without your knowledge, he's hiding something."

"Nonsense," she blurted, though she set her coffee cup and saucer on the tray with a clatter.

"Nevertheless, he *is* here, with his *wife,* who apparently thinks they're truly married, and you were not informed." He paused again, watching her reaction closely. "Something is amiss."

She swallowed hard and reached for her cup again, holding it without drinking.

"We all knew she went looking for him," he continued, tone lowered. "Did it not occur to you that she would look in Grasse?"

"Of course it occurred to me," she maintained, gently frowning as she dropped her gaze to what remained of the liquid inside and ran her thumb across the rim of her saucer. "But I never imagined that Edmund would respond to her sudden, unexpected appearance by following her back here. What would be the purpose?"

It was the most honest and open admittance she'd ever said in front of him. Her mind was obviously churning with possibilities, none of them positive, or she would have been able to maintain her air of sophisticated impudence much better than she was right now.

"I really don't know," he answered, rubbing his palms together in front of him. "But I do think we should try to find out why he hasn't contacted you. There could be a very good reason—"

"I'm sure there is," she cut in, her imperious air returning at once. "But I want you to say nothing to him. For now."

"Naturally," he acquiesced with a smile. "I didn't even let on that I suspected anything was odd about his return, and he never gave me reason to question his intentions."

"I'm sure he didn't. He's too smart for that," she returned, placing her half-filled cup of cold coffee back on the silver tray again.

Normand tried not to show the intense anger that immediately suffused him from her calculated insult to his intelligence—or rather, his intuitiveness, which was working just fine, thank you very much. And someday, somehow, he would use it against her. That day couldn't come soon enough, either.

"I think you should confront them together," he maintained, his throat tight. "See what he says when she's by his side, and how she reacts to him. You'll learn more that way than by simply sending for him and meeting him privately."

She drew in a breath deep enough to lift her shoulders and ample bosom, smiling at him again, her haughty composure returned as if she'd never carried a fraction of doubt.

"I've already thought of that, Normand," she informed him, brushing her fingertips across her lap. "I shall be attending the engagement gala on Saturday night for the Comtesse Brillon. Olivia will be there, and if her *husband* is in town, he'll certainly escort her."

Normand knew this was true. The Countess Brillon remained one of Nivan's wealthiest and devoted clients. Olivia would certainly have been invited, and as she was back in town, she would attend, no question.

"But she'll expect to see you there, and so will Edmund," he offered cautiously.

Her smile deepened. "What can he do, or reveal, in a crowd of people?" She shrugged and waved a hand to dismiss his concern. "They cannot hide from me forever. And if they're not in attendance, *then* I will know something is amiss. I cannot draw conclusions about this new...development strictly from your word and assessment."

She was correct, as usual, and Normand felt another slice of anger rip through him. Condescending bitch.

Abruptly, she rose, a sure sign of dismissal, and

Normand had no choice but to stand as well, noting, oddly enough, how her blond hair and lime green day gown looked strangely ugly in a room filled with garish pink and rose red. He wouldn't be able to blend a scent for her right now if he tried.

"I shall be on my way," he said, a formal smile planted on his mouth.

"Of course, dear Normand."

He stared down at the coffee service, rubbing his cheek with his palm, wavering for the first time that afternoon, then deciding she'd made him mad enough already. He'd just play her tit for tat.

"You know," he said quietly, "there is always the possibility that Edmund was able to get the money already, and that he thinks the House of Govance is within reach." He neglected to add that her dear, darling Edmund might be keeping the funds, and the benefits provided by the young heiress he attempted to swindle this time, to himself. A reasonable deduction if one were to assume the man had returned to Paris without notifying her.

But he didn't need to mention that aspect. He glanced back to her face, recognizing a returning fury in the glare she offered him—after he noticed the briefest hesitation. Again he stopped himself from basking in the triumph. She hadn't thought of that.

Her lovely blue eyes narrowed; her suspicion and irritation became a sudden, palpable force. "You've spoken quite above yourself for one day, Normand," she warned quietly, her smile dissolved.

He acknowledged her by nodding once. "I apologize. My only intention was to inform you of my thoughts and—"

"And you've informed me. Thank you. Now I'm tired and think I shall lie down."

Tired? Apparently she'd had an exhausting toilette.

She held out her hand for him to kiss, and he obliged her, dropping a quick peck on her knuckles before standing back, his arms to his sides. "Well, then, should I hear anything else—"

"You'll come and tell me at once, I know," she finished for him, lifting her skirts and moving gracefully toward the parlor door. "Thank you, Normand. Rene will see you out."

He stood where he was for a few seconds longer, listening to her departing footsteps, clutching his hands into fists without intention. But as he walked to the door, where the dutiful Rene suddenly appeared and stood without expression, holding his bowler hat for him upon his exit, Normand got the last laugh within himself. For, my goodness, if she had been a little kinder, a little more accommodating financially, he might have told her everything. As it was, he'd give a year's salary to be able to attend the Comtesse de Brillon's engagement party Saturday next, when the imperious, calculating woman who thought she remained in control came face-to-face not with her dearest Edmund, but with the brother—one Samson Carlisle, Duke of Durham. The last person on earth she would ever expect to see in France, or would ever want to see again.

Normand stepped off the garden pathway and onto the bustling street, pausing near a flower vendor's cart, where he closed his eyes and inhaled deeply of the fresh, sweet scent, then lifted his face to the sun.

It really was a beautiful day.

Chapter 9

Olivia adored parties under almost any circumstance. Gala events invariably provided a prime atmosphere to meet and be seen, whereby she could easily and profitably promote Nivan and the newest scents of the season. And of course they were fun. This evening's affair, however, would undoubtedly prove to be like nothing she'd ever experienced before. Not only would she be playacting in front of acquaintances, patrons, and the elite, she'd be playacting alongside the most unnerving man she'd ever known in her life.

Their last few days together had been interesting. They'd shared several conversations, mostly of a casual nature, though she was able to clarify the one thing he'd said that truly shocked her: he had a sister. Or more accurately, he and Edmund had a sister, the existence of whom her husband had deliberately kept from her. After days of troubled thought, she still couldn't understand why. She'd mentioned as much to Sam, and it was his interpretation that Edmund had simply not wanted to share much of his personal past. It frustrated her to no end, but she had to admit at last that the more she knew Sam, the more her husband appeared to be a lying, cheating scoundrel who wanted only her money. That she felt humiliated, duped, and yes, stupid to fall for such a schemer, was an understatement. All along, she supposed, since Edmund had left, she'd been hoping she was wrong.

Aside from revealing that his twenty-seven-year-old sister Elise had married an influential landowner, lived in the country, and cared for her four children, Sam had been mostly remote in his thoughts, not revealing much of himself nor asking anything of her while she went about her work in the boutique. But he refused to leave her side, and his constant attention had started to annoy her, not because he did or said anything particularly irritating, but because his mere presence was so distracting.

He still didn't trust her. She knew that instinctively, and by the manner in which he refused to take his eyes off of her person, as if he were waiting for her to inadvertently expose prevarications in her actions, words, and deeds. But she'd done nothing to make him suspicious of her motives, and between them these last few days, they'd been able to find some measure of companionship, she supposed. Tonight, however, would be a remarkable event. Many of those at the party would assume he was Edmund, question him, perhaps revealing important information regarding his brother that

Olivia didn't know. Their performance to discover the truth to Edmund's whereabouts was about to begin. At least that was their hope.

Sam remained close to her side now, as they descended from their hired coach and began to walk in silence toward the large front doors of the Countess Louise Brillon's fabulous estate located several miles to the west of Paris. Olivia's nervousness escalated with each step they took along the cobblestone path that wound through freshly cut grass, colorful rosebushes, and thick bougainvillea, all trimmed to perfection and emanating an enticing floral aroma. The night air tingled with anticipation and warmth, the starlit sky only barely discernible above the bright illumination of the house as laughter, music, and conversation boomed louder with every closing pace.

She'd dressed in one of her finest evening gowns, an expensive creation of elaborately embroidered scarlet and gold satin, tightly corseted, with wide hoops and a low, square neckline that amply lifted her bosom but hid most of her cleavage beneath a sheer line of golden lace. Embroidered flowers were sewn into the hem and three-quarter sleeves, matching the detail in the ivory fan she carried. To complement the look, she'd donned large ruby earrings, a coordinating pendant, and pinned her hair up loosely in curls.

Sam had stared at her intently, taking in every aspect of her appearance with a most calculated inspection when she finally presented herself to him in her apartments before they left. He approved, she knew, though he'd said nothing in particular regarding her choice of gown or overall appearance. He, however, looked positively magnificent in formal evening attire. He'd donned an expertly fashioned suit in pitch-black, only made more striking by the white, frilled silk shirt, silk trimmed collar and revers, and double-breasted waistcoat that outlined his muscled chest and torso. In retrospect, she didn't think Edmund had ever looked so handsome. In part, Sam's hair distinguished him, as it was shorter than her husband's and combed back from his face, providing a perfect view of his chiseled features, dark brown eyes, and ever-contemplative expression. That worried her, too, because Edmund always conveyed a jovial mood, especially in public. Out of necessity, if their plan were to work, she'd have to remind Sam to do the same.

She had been to the countess's home on several occasions, most having to do with the lady's lavish taste in perfume and her desire to try the latest scents in the comfort of her newly decorated parlor. Olivia always obliged the woman, partly because she liked her, but also because she had been one of Nivan's best customers and her influence among French noblewomen roused continued interest in the boutique. The Countess Brillon rivaled the Empress Eugenie in purchases. These two women probably bought the most expensive perfumes, sachets, bath salts, soaps, and oils, and in the greatest quantities, than the rest of their clientele combined.

Tonight, Olivia noticed immediately how the countess had beautified the inside of her estate for the party, adding an embellishment of gold and teal ribbons around floral arrangements and tablecloths that matched perfectly with her Renaissance Revival–style furnishings and rich, colorful Oriental carpeting.

Guests had been arriving for some time when she and Sam finally stepped into the great ballroom. Through a haze of smoke and laughter, the smell of food and strong cologne, she spotted the countess and her betrothed, near the bottom of the staircase as they greeted the elite of Paris upon arrival.

Sam gently grasped her elbow as he guided her toward the queue in an effort to make quick introductions before melding into the crowd. She followed as directed, though it now occurred to her that this deception could be far more difficult than they'd envisioned when they went about planning it. In the last few days she had given Sam a general outline of who would be here, the usual and unusual personality quirks and appearance of those with whom they would likely need to converse. And yet the distinguished, incredibly handsome man who now stood beside her, cool and resolved, didn't behave at all like her husband. The guests here tonight would know him as Edmund, but the more she knew of him personally, the easier it was to recognize the differences between the two. They were identical in appearance, but nearly total opposites in every other respect. Sam needed to demonstrate considerable acting skills or suspicions would certainly be raised and the gossip would begin. Olivia only prayed they'd be able to simply blend in without much notice or speculation.

She learned at once that it was not to be. The moment the two of them stood at the top of the red carpeted stairs leading down to the ballroom, already alive with dance and conversation, the air seemed to still around them. Heads turned and whispers began, heard even above the six-piece orchestra now playing a Chopin waltz in excellent form, as the atmosphere suddenly tensed with anticipation.

"They've noticed us," she said in a whisper, clutching her closed fan at her waist.

He continued to clasp her elbow solidly as he glanced down at her face. "They've noticed *you,* and all the gaping men are envious that I have you on my arm." Reflectively, he added, "I only wish my friends were here to witness this moment."

"Friends?"

He fairly snorted, directing his attention back toward the crowd as they moved down the stairs. "Yes, Olivia, scandalous though my past may be, I still have friends."

She blinked, a bit taken aback by the annoyance in his tone and the intriguing mention of a scandal he had kept from her. Then again, he could simply be referring to his brother's shameful antics. But more important, she had never intended to insult him and needed him to understand that.

"Of course you have friends," she scoffed, lowering her voice as she leaned into him. "I met one of them, remember? Besides, I would never presume otherwise."

"No?" he asked without looking at her.

She had the impression his mind was elsewhere as they paused and he scanned the Countess Brillon's guests from two steps above the ballroom floor. She, however, was more interested in keeping his attention on her and their conversation for the moment.

"What scandal could be so great that you would lose your friends?"

He jerked his head around to stare down at her face, his brows furrowed as he studied her.

She waited, watching him, knowing they would shortly be introduced to the countess. "What scandal?" she asked again seconds later, hoping she didn't sound too urgent.

Suddenly he dropped his gaze to her breasts, letting it linger long enough for her to feel the heat. Then he lifted it again to her eyes. "You look beautiful tonight, Livi," he murmured, his expression softening. "The scandal is that my brother ruined a lady so magnificent in every regard. Edmund is a fool."

Her face flushed warm as her mouth went dry. The heat she felt only moments ago now turned to fire, radiating between them, causing her heartbeat to still before suddenly racing with an odd form of excitement, even anticipation. He'd flattered her as he'd flustered her, and somewhere in the dark recesses of her mind it occurred to her that not only had he done so intentionally, he'd done so with perfect honesty. She realized at that moment that she'd never been courted by any man who'd made her feel like the Duke of Durham did with a simple look, a word or two. It took her seconds to curb her desire to lean up and kiss him, here in the ballroom, in front of everyone. A shameful thought in every respect.

His mouth curved once more into a trace of a knowing smile. "You smell good, too." Then he turned and guided her down the final steps and toward their hostess.

Olivia shook herself internally, attempting to regain her composure quickly. "Cad," she leaned into him to whisper.

He actually chuckled but offered nothing else. And then, as if it were the most natural thing in the world, he swept her around and presented her as his wife to the Countess Brillon with a flair and the expertise of an inspired actor. His interpretation of Edmund was more than perfect. It was positively brilliant.

"Olivia, darling!" Louise Brillon exclaimed as she reached out with gloved arms to embrace her as a guest, bestowing a breezy kiss to each cheek before pulling back to gaze at her. "I'm so pleased you've returned. And you've brought your distinguished husband with you. What a marvelous surprise."

Sam gently grasped the lady's extended hand and bowed deeply as he lifted it to his lips. "Madame Comtesse, you are positively radiant tonight," he said, grinning broadly. "I give you my heartfelt congratulations on your upcoming nuptials. How happy you must be."

Olivia watched as the countess, dressed beautifully in a gown of royal blue satin and white lace flounces, fairly preened, clutching her betrothed's upper arm. "He is a gem," she replied with heartfelt warmth. "May I introduce Monsieur Antonio Salana, my future husband."

And so she and Sam became briefly acquainted with the wealthy Italian exporter who was to become the Countess Brillon's third husband, a man of distinguished heritage twice her age, who undoubtedly possessed the wealth she expected from a marital union.

"Please, enjoy yourselves this evening," the man said in French before turning his attention to the next guest in the queue.

"Oh, and Olivia, darling," the countess added as they

took a step toward the dance floor, "your aunt should be here shortly. I know she was thrilled to learn you were back in town and with your husband." She placed her gloved palm on Olivia's shoulder. "And of course we all know she would never miss one of my parties."

Olivia groaned within. She very much disliked her late stepfather's sister, a woman who enjoyed her drink as much as she coveted what was left of Olivia's family inheritance. But then duty required that she pretend just the opposite, and she would never mention her disdain to anyone socially.

"How wonderful," she replied brightly. "I shall look forward to seeing her, Madame Comtesse." She glanced up to Sam, who was looking at her with a peculiar lift of his brows. "Shall we get some champagne, darling?"

He nodded once, smiling with an abundance of charm, as Edmund would. "Of course. And then, we dance."

Olivia placed a hand on his slightly raised arm and together they worked their way through the throngs of guests toward the far east wall where large oblong windows stood open, allowing the nighttime breeze to offer a bit of relief to the stuffy ballroom. Footmen in crimson livery stood beneath them, dishing out plates of hors d'oeuvres and pouring a never-ending supply of champagne. Sam led her toward the corner, where he reached for two freshly filled crystal flutes from a silver tray, handing one to her.

Olivia took a sip or two to calm her nerves, savoring the taste that was nothing short of delicious. He, however, just held his glass, watching her closely, acting as if there were no one else in the ballroom.

"Who is your aunt?" he asked after a moment.

She was afraid he'd want to know. "My late stepfather's sister. A nuisance of a lady who enjoys her wine and gentlemen too much for comment." She sighed. "You'll certainly meet her tonight, and"—she looked him up and down—"she'll very much like you."

He raised his brows, smiling wryly. "Oh? Then I shall enjoy getting to know her."

She almost snorted. "No you won't. On that you can trust me."

He chuckled again, and Olivia decided she thoroughly adored it when he laughed.

Tipping his head to the side, he asked, "So why do you expect her to like me in particular?"

She closed her eyes and pinched her lips together briefly. He was intentionally baiting her, but she supposed she couldn't keep it from him. He would know soon enough. After another long sip of champagne, she replied lightly, "Because she blatantly flirted with my husband in the company of anyone, including me."

Such an admission embarrassed her, and Olivia turned her gaze to the north wall of the ballroom, staring without interest at the row of elegantly carved giltwood mirrors that reflected an array of color and the brightness of a thousand candles.

"I want to dance with you," he said after a moment, his tone deep and almost caressing.

Relieved that he'd changed the subject, she planted a smile on her lips and inhaled fully as she once again looked up at his face. "You know I'd enjoy that."

The intensity of his gaze captured hers. "As would I, Livi."

She shivered inside from the silky smooth way he said her name, from the odd way he looked at her, as if they shared an intimate secret that was theirs alone and always would be. But it also reminded her of their shared interest in the ball this night, their sole reason for being here.

She took a step forward, closing the distance between them, holding her fan in one hand, the stem of her champagne flute in the other. He didn't move, didn't take his eyes off her.

"I have to tell you something that I probably should have told you before now," she said, her voice carrying just above the din of the party, of the orchestra, which now began playing a minuet. "As much as I…enjoy hearing you call me Livi, Edmund refused to do so, and everybody knew it." She cleared her throat. "You called me that in front of Normand the other day, though I doubt he would have noticed such a discrepancy since he wasn't around Edmund all that terribly much. But you probably shouldn't use the name when we're around others. Just to be safe."

He didn't react much, she observed, which meant he didn't understand or perhaps was simply trying to. She shifted from one foot to the other, starting to feel uncomfortably warm beneath her agonizingly tight stays, then took another sip of her champagne.

"You should have told me this before," he replied seconds later.

She exhaled a fast breath. "I know. It's just that I…" She swallowed. "I—"

"Enjoy it when I call you that," he finished for her, repeating her own acknowledgment.

The uncomfortable heat rose to her face, and she opened her fan for the first time that evening, gently swishing it in front of her. "Yes, I admit I do. It's what my mother called me, my father, very close friends. Edmund simply didn't like it. But when you say it, it's..." She glanced around to see if anyone watched the awkward moment between them, noting with relief that the ballroom guests carried on as if they weren't even present in the room. "I don't know. I can't explain it."

"I can. It's intimate."

Her eyes shot back to his face. Shaking her head, she explained, "No, it's simply more...informal, familial, and where you and I are...relations, it only makes sense that you would use it."

He smirked. "But it's also more intimate, and *I* like it. For that reason."

"I think I would like to dance now," she said, forcing a pleasant smile.

"However," he continued, ignoring her subject change, "per your gracious request, I will refrain from calling you Livi when we are in the company of others. Just as from this moment on you will never again—anywhere—call me 'brother.'"

That completely confused her. He was her brother by law.

"Agreed?" he prodded.

She bit her bottom lip, then acquiesced. "Agreed."

"And," he added, lowering his voice and stepping close enough to her that her skirts draped his legs and his head angled above hers, "when we are in any intimate situation where I shall be able to call you Livi, you will call me Sam. Not 'brother,' not 'sir,' not 'your grace,' and *never* Edmund. Just Sam.'"

She couldn't help but gape at him.

"Unless," he amended with a shrug, stepping back a bit, "you'd prefer to call me by some other endearment, in which case I would be most...pleased."

An endearment? *Pleased?*

Suddenly he smiled—a breathtakingly gorgeous smile that made her knees weaken.

"Let's dance, my beautiful Lady Olivia," he said in a near whisper.

Without giving her an opportunity to object or comment further, he took her champagne glass and placed it along with his, which he hadn't touched, on a buffet table two steps to his right. Then he offered her his arm and she placed her palm on it without thought.

He moved toward the center of the ballroom floor as she closed her fan. Then she was in his arms and twirling to the sound of an expertly played and beautiful waltz.

Vaguely, she became aware of others watching them, and she supposed they had to make a striking pair, especially with his enormous height, which, thankfully, she matched without feeling too overwhelmed. He kept his eyes on her, leading her perfectly in time to the music. He was a marvelous dancer, and again the differences between this man and her husband became apparent. Edmund could dance as well as anyone, but Sam remained focused, seemingly absorbed in her; Edmund's mind often seemed to be elsewhere, as if he'd rather be mingling. The more she knew this man, the more her relationship with her husband troubled her.

"Tell me of your family," he murmured, lowering his mouth to her ear.

She pulled back a bit in surprise. "My family?"

He smirked. "Let's just say I'm more interested in your past than the perfume flavor of the season."

She grinned. "They're not *flavors,* dear man, they're *scents.*"

"Ah. Yes, of course."

He twirled her in time to the music, though Olivia noticed that he was gradually moving them toward the balcony doors, for which she was quite glad. She desperately needed the breeze.

"Well then, since we're discussing it, which scent are you wearing tonight?" he asked moments later.

She realized he couldn't care any less, but thankful for the mundane topic, she yielded to his desire to know. "I'm wearing a vanilla-based spice with just a hint of citrus for color."

"Hmm. Sounds edible."

She giggled, throwing her head back a little, and with that he pulled her tighter against him, her torso in contact with his so that her hoops pushed out behind her. Being so close was positively indecent, and yet she refused to back away from his powerful embrace. She simply didn't want to move.

"Tell me, darling Olivia, do you...bathe in these fragrances as well?" he asked huskily.

She blinked at him, shocked that he would imagine such a thing, smacking his shoulder lightly with her fan. "That, good *husband,* is certainly none of your business," she returned altogether too coyly, utterly enjoying his company, a grin still upon her lips. "And

I refuse to allow you to nibble at my skin to find out."

It took her seconds to realize what she'd said, and then it hit her with the force of a windstorm. She stiffened against him, her eyes widening with concern. She'd gone too far.

"I'm sorry—"

"Just dance with me, Olivia," he cut in, his tone thoughtful, even remote.

His smile had faded as well but he didn't loosen his grip. If anything he held her tighter against him, his gaze traveling across her face, her hair and shoulders, then pausing briefly at her lips before returning to meet her eyes once more. He felt unbelievably powerful in her arms, his muscles large and solid, harder than she'd imagined, his facial features defined and ruggedly handsome. Irresistible. Such observations made her remarkably breathless.

They slowed their movements to a standstill as the waltz ended only minutes later, though she couldn't bring herself to pull away from him. Not yet. She inhaled deeply to calm her speeding heartbeat as she continued to hold him in her grasp, as she felt his arm behind her at her waist, her gloved palm in his as he held it against his chest, noting how he'd worn the fragrance she'd selected for him and that it suited him divinely.

"Would you like some air?" he asked, interrupting her thoughts of him with a delicate hint of reality.

Immediately, she took a step away from him, her cheeks flushed, her body hot, her senses heightened to levels she didn't at all comprehend. He released her and she blinked quickly, lowering her gaze to her gown, fluffing her skirts, more for something to do to escape the awkwardness she felt than for any other reason.

Then, as if the lights had been dimmed for hours and were suddenly raised to blaring extremes, she realized they stood on the parquet floor surrounded by party guests who attempted to dance around them.

"Shall we walk, darling?" she asked, her mind whirling even as she lifted her shoulders to express a regal composure never lost, squeezing her fan at her bodice with both hands.

She could have sworn he wanted to laugh. She saw it in his eyes.

"To the balcony, Lady Olivia?" he asked with consummate charm.

Her senses gradually returning, she gave him a tight smile. "Wonderful." Lowering her voice, she added, "My aunt will be here shortly—she always makes a grand entrance—and I would prefer to delay your introduction as long as possible." It was a weak excuse, but he seemed to believe it.

He smiled, a truly engaging smile full of genuine humor. "Afraid I might not live up to a husband's expectations?"

She took his arm and they turned toward the large French doors in the distance. "I refuse to even answer that."

He laughed aloud as he escorted her to open air.

Chapter 10

Sam had no idea what the hell was wrong with him, though he hoped a walk in the outside air would clear his head enough to enlighten him. After a week of suffering periods of complete boredom saved only by Olivia's vibrant personality and desire to keep him engrossed in the day-to-day operations of Nivan, for which he possessed almost no interest at all, he was truly looking forward to this night where he could begin to do *something*, or at the very least learn something that would lead him to Edmund. He should be speaking to those who knew his brother, both socially and professionally as the husband of Nivan's proprietor, gauging their reactions, their responses, hoping for a slip of the tongue. Not dancing. He loathed dancing, which made his desire to waltz with her even more suspect in his mind. Instead of being rational and taking this night seriously, he'd thus far behaved like a schoolboy with an infatuation to match the best of them. And considering his experience with women, and the fact that he now neared the age of thirty-five, he really did know better. Even now he should be inside, mingling, talking, even separating from Olivia for a good portion of the evening to learn what he could without her interference, innocent though it might be.

But he had to admit that his brother's wife had left him speechless on more than one occasion these last few hours. First when she stood before him in her apartments, dressed to elegant perfection, stunning him with a profound beauty enhanced by a poise unmatched; next when she laughed at something he said as if she truly enjoyed him; and of course nothing could compare to the rush of sensations he felt when she mentioned the notion of him nibbling at her skin. He tried very hard to rid himself of the vision of her coming to him dripping wet from a scented bath, then letting him taste her warm, soft body over every curve and under every delectable hidden inch of her.

But what disturbed him most of all was the way she clung to him when they danced, the way she fit so splendidly in his arms, the way she looked at him, her eyes full of confusion and desire, probably all beyond her awareness, or so he preferred to think. He wasn't used to a woman being at one moment innocent *and* inviting, especially when he'd never met a woman who didn't want something from him. It occurred to him that Olivia might want him, or more correctly *need* him, in her attempt to find Edmund and save her business, but only in a strictly naive, *brotherly* relationship. No wonder she felt confused.

The warm night air caressed his skin, helping him relax, to come to terms with this new awareness, to bring his mind back to the reality at hand. She walked silently beside him now after stopping twice, very briefly, to speak to couples she knew socially as they exited the ballroom. He'd followed her lead and acted exactly as Edmund would have, and he had to give her credit for helping him along by saying, "You remember Monsieur Levesque, don't you, darling?" or "I think we had dinner at Madame Valois's estate last September, isn't that right?" To which he replied with all of Edmund's false charm, "Of course, Madame Valois, and aren't you looking as lovely as ever." Yes, quite the actor, he was. He just wished he didn't have to pretend to be the brother who had ruined his reputation and stolen his lover all those years ago. And now he had Olivia on his arm, Edmund's wife, or so *she* believed. God, what to do with her—

"What are you thinking?"

She'd asked the question softly, her voice cutting into his irritating reflections as she paused by the balcony's edge to glance up at his face, brushing a lock of breeze-blown hair from her forehead with gloved fingers.

He leaned against the iron railing, resting his elbows on top, clasping his hands together as he turned his head to regard her. "I'm thinking I'm a marvelous actor. I should work on the stage."

She laughed quietly, rotating her body so that she, too, faced the floral array and grassy hillside that stretched out for miles to the east toward the rising moon. "In some very perverse way it is fun, isn't it? Pretending to be married to sniff out your brother, and what might remain of my inheritance." She inhaled deeply and lowered her gaze to the fountain, lit up by torchlight and gurgling just beneath the balcony. "We'll probably need to socialize more if we're to learn anything at all tonight."

He thought they'd learned a lot already, though not a bit of it had to do with Edmund. "I think I'm up to the challenge," he maintained, rubbing his palms together in front of him.

"Are you," she stated rather than asked, a note of amusement creeping into her voice again. "Even so," she carried on affably, "I don't think you should leave Durham for a life with a traveling company."

He slapped his hand against his chest in feigned shock. "Madam, you wound me. You think I lack talent?"

"Oh, I know you're quite talented." She gave him a sideways peek, grinning slyly. "I only mean that your . . . best talents obviously lay elsewhere."

"Indeed, they do," he agreed, watching her closely.

After a brief pause, she relaxed into her stays and looked away, her face half hidden in shadow. "I think your best talents are in teasing unsuspecting ladies."

Her keenness intrigued as much as it surprised him. "I'll have you know, Olivia Shea, formerly of Elmsboro, that I have never, in all my years, been accused of teasing a woman in any flattering manner. I've been accused of being far too serious to entertain them, or of ignoring them altogether. But never flattery." He very slowly moved closer to her, feeling her skirts brush against his shins. "So I suppose, in that regard, you are my first."

"Your first?" She smiled, but didn't look at him. "I rather doubt that, Sam. I'm sure you attract the ladies no matter what you say or do. Your personality is far too magnetic. That's the tease, and where your individual charm lies."

Sam couldn't recall a time when a compliment warmed him as this one did, and she'd said it as if it were merely a passing thought. "I'm very different from Edmund," he murmured, feeling an urgent need to stress what they both knew was obvious.

She nodded, turning to meet his gaze again, her own expression thoughtful. "Yes, but Edmund is like most gentlemen—pretentiously charming in the hope of favors, jovial even when they're not feeling that way inside, complimentary not because they want to share their appreciation, but because they want something in return. The sad thing is, it's all selfishly false." She ran her index finger back and forth along the top of the railing. "The one thing I admire most about you, Sam, is that you're honest. You may be serious to a fault, but that in itself is charming because it's genuine. If there are ladies who don't understand it, or sense that peculiar charm in you, then it's they who have lost."

Her voice had taken on a contemplative quality, but he had no doubt that she believed what she said, and he couldn't begin to consider a reply. In truth, he found her insight beyond flattering. She was the first woman he'd ever known who made him feel appreciated for who he was as a man.

She remained quiet for several long moments, and he stood beside her in companionable silence. Music from the ballroom drifted outside through the many open windows; occasionally, animated voices or laughter could be heard in the distance. But the two of them were essentially alone, a move he'd planned, choosing a spot as far away from the French doors as he could reasonably lead her.

"You asked about my family," she said at last.

"I did," he replied, reveling, oddly enough, in the shared intimacy and her desire to open up to him.

"Well, let's see," she began. "I am an only child. I knew my mother much better than my father, but then I was a girl, you know, and he didn't think we had much in common."

Sam wasn't the least surprised, but decided against mentioning that fact. He remained silent, allowing her to continue at her own pace.

She turned her fan around in her hands, staring at it, smiling vaguely at her memories. "When my father died seven years ago, my mother—a Frenchwoman by birth who has extended family here—decided she wanted to return to France. Immediately we were on a ship and back in Paris. It was soon after our return that she met Monsieur Jean-Francois Nivan."

"The owner of the boutique," he said for clarification.

She nodded. "Yes, and it had been in his family for three generations. He was a good man, a good stepfather and provider, I suppose, and my mother did care for him, though he was nearly twice her age and in ailing health. But their marriage offered security for both of us. At his death, my mother became Nivan's proprietor, but as much as she appreciated the social atmosphere the boutique provided, she had no sense for business. When she died two years ago, I took control, making it profitable again and expanding our name across France. This is precisely why the Princess Eugenie buys solely from us now, though thanks to your brother, I'm afraid that could change."

"How did your mother die?" he asked after a moment.

She sighed softly. "She came down with a nasty bout of influenza. At least that's what her physician said."

"And that left you alone."

She tipped her head to the side. "Not exactly alone. I do have family here, though they're scattered about France." Frowning, she added, "My closest relation is my aunt, and several cousins of Monsieur Nivan's who live and work in Grasse, which has become the center of the worldwide perfume industry in recent years. And I do see them on occasion since I travel there at least twice a year to keep myself abreast of the latest scents and new information within the industry." She lowered her voice to just above a whisper. "I've been using my inheritance to build our name. Edmund took that from me, and to be perfectly honest with you, Sam, the more I know you, and learn of my husband's secrets and ill intentions toward me from the start, the harder it is to keep from hating him."

As he watched her struggle internally with a hurt deeply felt, caused solely by his coward of a brother, Sam felt his own anger toward Edmund flame anew. The more he grew to know Olivia, the more he grew to believe she truly was the innocent in all of this. His logical caution toward her, God help him, was starting to dissipate.

"So I suppose you're also curious as to why I remain in charge of the business?"

He wasn't thinking any such thing at the moment, but he brushed over that. "It is unusual for a lady of your means and social position to be...working, shall we say."

She smiled again. "My stepfather's brother, Robert, was the beneficiary, and to this day he still owns it, though he lives in Grasse as well. He's very confident in my abilities, and as I adore the work, I'm very dedicated to keeping Nivan one of the top-selling perfume boutiques in all of France."

"Which might be at risk because you married Edmund," he interjected softly.

She inhaled deeply, lifting her face to the moonlight as she closed her eyes. "Edmund never understood my dedication. To him, Nivan is a simple store that sells perfumery to spoiled ladies. But he only thought that because he didn't care to understand the trade, and he certainly never understood *me*." She opened her eyes again and pivoted slightly to look at him. "Nivan has been the only true joy in my life. Knowing every detail of my business, every eccentricity of each loyal patron, and ultimately using that knowledge to operate the shop superbly, has been my greatest personal accomplishment. Nivan, and I, are known throughout France for being the best at what, and how, we sell. Nothing in my world compares to that achievement. Certainly not my marriage, though at one time I confess that I'd hoped it might."

Sam remained silent for a few moments, admiring her commitment even as he sensed a gnawing, confusing frustration within him for his own lack of dedication to anything in his life aside from running his estate as expected. For the first time since they'd met, he realized what a truly unusual woman stood before him. He'd never known another like her. Not only was Edmund a fool for abusing the gift he'd been given, he'd been heartlessly cruel in stealing that very innocence that, combined with her astute personality, made her unique.

"Olivia?" he murmured, his tone deep and soft.

With resolve, she stood fully upright once more, straightening her shoulders and clutching her fan in front of her. "I'm sorry if I carried on. Would you like to go back into the party now?"

He shook his head slowly, then reached out and took hold of her chin with his finger and thumb.

She tensed, her eyes growing large as they reflected the moonlight in their dark depths. "We should mingle. We—We're not learning much out here alone."

Her voice caught and he could swear she faintly trembled. She knew what was coming, sensed his desire, and he marveled in it because she made absolutely no attempt to pull away.

"I think we're learning plenty," he whispered huskily. Then he lowered his head with agonizing control and gently covered her mouth with his.

Sam wasn't sure what to expect in her reaction, but they both knew immediately that this kiss was far different from the first one they'd shared in England. Instead of being shocked by the contact, or squirming for release, she remained very, very still, allowing him to begin an exploration of her lips with just a soft brush of his. And he took his time, knowing she would need to be coaxed into responding, waiting to embrace her until she realized how deeply he wanted to go.

It took many long moments, it seemed, for her to begin answering the urgency in his touch. When at last he felt her start to succumb, he gradually lowered one arm and wrapped it around her back, palm splayed across her spine, pulling her gently nearer to him. She leaned into his body then, giving herself to the feel of it as her head tilted to one side and she began to kiss him back.

And she was a marvelous kisser. Or maybe he imagined as much because it had been ages since he'd been kissed by a woman who wanted him as much as he did her. He could hear his heart beating loudly in his temples, feel the rush of blood course through his veins, sense her uncertainty even as she dropped her fan to the ground at her side without notice. Then she reached up and wrapped her arms around his neck.

Growing confident in his effort, Sam placed his free palm high on her waist. She sighed, pushing her fingers into his hair, lightly caressing. He felt her breasts against his chest, their fullness taunting him with his ever increasing desire to touch, to let her realize the affect she had on him, to show her the extent of his need. His kiss grew ever bolder as he drew his tongue across her upper lip, then pressed his mouth against hers again, demanding, beckoning, tasting, savoring.

She moaned softly and let herself go, giving in to the moment as she drew her palm to his face, stroking his cheek with her thumb. And he followed her lead, holding her firmly against him, moving one hand to her hair, entwining his fingers in the softness while daringly allowing his other hand to drift ever so slowly toward the soft curve of her breast. He couldn't, wouldn't, touch her there yet. Not yet. Not until she made it clear that she needed it.

Her breath came as fast as his, quickened by the rising heat between them, and finally he pulled away a fraction and lowered his lips to her chin, to her throat and jawline, kissing, teasing, brushing her soft and delicate skin with his lips. She panted in his arms, holding his head firmly, lifting her face skyward to allow him access.

Her eagerness became clear. With reckless abandon, he raised his hand to cup her breast over her gown, the decorative golden lace grazing his palm as he lingered there, unmoving.

She moaned again, this time with an unquestionable desire to be touched, and as his lips found hers once more, his fingers at last dipped below the lace to caress the top slope of one soft mound of enticing flesh. She didn't even appear to notice. She clung to him, tasting him, and he held her, his muscles taut, his mind and body losing control with each passing second.

And then before he knew what was happening, she started pulling away, very faintly, bringing her arm down from around his neck to grasp the hand he still held at her breast.

It took all that was in him to allow her to remove his fingers from her forbidden softness, his head reeling, his skin on fire, his heart pounding in his chest. It seemed like hours before he realized she had taken a step back and now held his hand between both of her own, placing small kisses on his knuckles, running his fingertips back and forth across her cheek, her lips.

At last he opened his eyes to look down at her, and Sam knew immediately that this would be a defining moment in his life. Never had a woman treated him so tenderly during a spell of such raging desire between them. To say he felt awkward was an understatement. She was shaking, breathing as heavily as he, and yet she caressed him as if he were delicate and rare, even cherished.

Slowly, senses returning, Sam once again became aware of where they were, where they stood, of the music and gaiety surrounding them, of the smell of the warm, night air mingled with the arousing scent of her skin, which seemed to cling to him even now.

Her eyes remained closed, but he could almost feel the flush of desire still emanating from her. With one quick motion he reached for her, placing his palms on her shoulders and pulling her against him. She followed his lead in silence as he tucked her head beneath his neck with one hand, her cheek against his chest, wrapping his other arm around her to hold her close.

God, there had to be something wrong with him. He'd never before felt protective of a woman he'd just passionately kissed, never before experienced such a hunger within for a pleasure he shouldn't have. She confused him as she surprised him, giving herself to him, not as a lustful woman, but as one in desperate need of passion, of feeling desired. He still tasted the sweetness of her lips on his, still reeled from her unique feel, her scent that lingered, the charge of their attraction sizzling in the air around him.

He held her until her breathing slowed, until her trembling stopped, wondering with irritation and a trace of desperation where the hell they would, or should, go from here.

"I think there's something wrong with me."

Her soft, husky whisper of apprehension that matched his own warmed his heart. "There's nothing wrong with you, Livi," he said quietly, smiling to himself.

She stayed still for another moment or two, staring out to the moonlit night. He leaned over and kissed the top of her head, inhaling the scent of vanilla and spice that he knew he would forever associate with her and her unforgettable beauty. Then finally, gradually, she placed her palms on his chest and pushed herself away from him.

He stood upright, his hands at his sides, though he never moved his gaze from her. She couldn't bring herself to look at him, though, and he allowed her a few seconds to collect her thoughts.

"This—This wasn't right," she whispered. Drawing a deep breath, she tried again. "This wasn't right, it was—"

"Perfect," he finished for her.

She shook her head as she loosely covered her mouth with her fingers. "I'm married, Sam."

He swallowed with aggravated emotion from the shame she expressed in her desperate need to convince him of something that nagged him to his bones.

"What you had with my brother was never a

marriage," he maintained after a long pause, shoving his hands into the pockets of his evening jacket.

"That's irrelevant."

Not bloody likely. "We have a job to do, Olivia," he said with an insistence that surprised him. "Until we find Edmund, we take each day as it comes."

For the first time since they'd kissed, she raised her lashes and gazed up at his face. His insides gnawed at him as he noticed the glassy covering of tears she was trying very hard not to suffer. As much as he wanted to reach for her this very second, to take her in his arms again and shield her from hurt and bewilderment both he and his brother had caused, he didn't dare. Her emotions were volatile from their unconventional and explosive attraction—as were his.

"It'll be all right," he soothed, reaching up to skim her hairline with his fingertips. "Everything will unfold as it should."

For several long moments she continued to stare at him with wide, troubled eyes. And then, with resolve, she visibly shook herself and straightened. "I'm sorry this happened."

He grinned wryly. "No you're not, and neither am I. We both knew it was coming."

"It won't happen again."

That made him want to laugh. Instead, he said, "Whatever the lady wants."

She peeked at him sideways. "I enjoyed it, though."

He couldn't believe she admitted that. So much for his abating arousal. "As did I." His expression, his voice, grew serious. "I don't think I've ever enjoyed a kiss more. I mean that, Livi."

She inhaled sharply, shakily, then whispered, "Why?"

He hadn't expected her to ask, and he certainly wasn't prepared to respond. But somehow the truth revealed itself. "I've never known a woman like you. In everything you do and say, even how you kiss, you're unique."

With a trace of a smile to her lips, she looked at him and breathed, "I would have said exactly the same about you, Sam. I've never known another man like you."

He couldn't stop himself from asking, "Even Edmund?"

She didn't hesitate to reply. "Especially Edmund."

A rush of odd sensations engulfed him in waves. He'd never been thought of as uniquely different from his brother by anyone. That the first would be Olivia proved to be the irony of the ages.

"We should get back to the party," she said through a long sigh.

"Damn the party."

She grinned, a slow grin that widened with each passing second.

"My goodness, there you are. How did the two of you find your way out here?"

Olivia took a quick step away from him, turning toward the shadowed figure of a well-coiffed woman who stood watching them in the distance. But it was the voice that had startled them.

Her voice.

Sam felt his blood turn to a river of ice, drowning out all but a paralyzing shock. A peculiar unreality set in and his heart began to thud in his chest; his body broke out into a freezing sweat.

"You...uh...seemed to have dropped your fan, darling."

Olivia recovered herself quickly. "Oh. So I have." She reached down to retrieve it. "My husband and I were just talking, Aunt Claudette."

"Of course you were. What else would you be doing out here all alone?" the older woman replied.

And then she stepped closer to them, and the image he'd tried to shove forcefully from his thoughts, his memories, his past, came back with clarity to slap him hard in the face.

Jesus.

"The night is beautiful, Aunt, and Edmund and I—"

"Were talking by moonlight. Yes, so you said. How lovely."

Sam couldn't move. He stood frozen to the spot, reliving a nightmare that was only just beginning anew.

Claudette. Jesus, holy God in heaven. Edmund, what have you done?

Olivia moved toward her, grasping her shoulders and offering a peck to each cheek. "It's wonderful to see you," she said brightly. "Edmund, the Countess Renier has arrived."

She'd said that for his benefit, to inform him of her aunt's title, which told him only that Olivia was even now completely oblivious to the depth of his brother's deception.

Claudette looked beyond her, and Sam could feel the woman's intense gaze upon him, sensed a rush of emotion from her, none of it pleasant.

Jesus.

"I see you've found your husband," Claudette

quipped, moving closer so the rising moon finally cast a dim light upon her features. And then she placed her palms on his cheeks and gave him a fast kiss to the mouth. "Edmund, dear, I'm so glad you're home. Olivia has missed you terribly."

For a split second Sam had no idea what to do. Then his mind kicked into action, and as much as he despised the pretense, he became his brother once more. "I was afraid you might not make it tonight," he said, grinning devilishly, "but then Olivia and I know you far too well." He paused, then added, "Don't we, Claudette?"

She gazed up to his face for a moment, her brow pinched into a delicate frown. "Indeed, you do."

An uncomfortable moment reigned supreme. The tension in the air fairly crackled, threatening to match the tautness of every muscle in his body. He squeezed his hands into fists at his sides and then flexed them again. Olivia watched him, certainly concerned by his lack of charming conversation, and yet she could never know the difficulty it took for him to remain where he stood and not leave the scene without another thought or word to either of them. As shameful as it was to consider it, he had to take note of the fact that beneath all the deception he witnessed at this moment, he still hadn't completely discounted the fact that Olivia could be part of it. She could lust after him, kiss him with perfection, and still deceive him. He'd learned that lesson years ago, strangely enough from her deceitful aunt Claudette. He had trouble believing the intimate time they'd just shared could be anything less than a real display of feeling on her part, but there remained a chance that the three of them were playing him for a fool—and underhandedly vying for his money.

Still, if she truly were innocent at the hands of two very cruel people, she deserved justice, and there was no better person to give it to her than the brother of the man who set her up for ruin.

He cleared his throat and nodded once, lifting his arm toward the woman who had betrayed him all those years ago.

"Well. Dearest Aunt, now that you have arrived to grace us with your lovely company, it would be my utmost pleasure if you'd consent to dancing with me."

He could feel Olivia's stunned gaze fall upon him, and because of his confusion over this incredible turn of events, he couldn't even look at her. That, he decided, troubled him most of all.

Claudette beamed at the suggestion and placed her well-manicured palm on his jacket sleeve. "It would be *my* pleasure, dearest nephew." Leading him away, she added over her shoulder, "Perhaps you could use the time to freshen yourself, Olivia. You seem a bit palled. I'll take it from here and keep your husband entertained for a while."

And then Claudette, ever in control, led him down the balcony path toward the French doors and into the ballroom, Olivia following closely behind, her gaze burning a hole in his back.

Chapter 11

The shock of seeing her again was beginning to wear off; a good thing, as he needed to remain focused to keep the pretense alive. Claudette hadn't yet realized his identity, or at least he didn't think she had. But there was no telling how long the ruse could last. True, he hadn't seen her in a decade, though beyond the undeniable fact of her intelligence, she was cunning and manipulative by nature, expecting insincerity in others, and she prided herself on finding it. Now, as she clung to his arm, her blond hair piled high on her head and brushing against his chin, her perfume invaded his nostrils with the pungent scent of roses.

Roses. Claudette always wore roses, and it would remain the scent he'd forever identify with her. The odor fairly nauseated him now, especially when coupled with the thick fog of smoke and stuffy heat that permeated the ballroom. The crowd had grown, slowing their progress toward the dance floor, but she would expect him to socialize with her, pretend with her. And with so much at stake, he decided he needed to be more than convincing. He needed to *be* Edmund tonight.

"You smell wonderful," he leaned over to whisper in her ear.

She tipped her head up and gave him a knowing smile. "Darling, Edmund. Ever the flatterer."

"Only when it's warranted," he admitted with an ease and a natural grin that almost astonished him.

She laughed. "Let's dance, darling. We have much to discuss."

Her jovial attitude expressed a mood he knew she didn't feel. It had been years, but he could still read her temperament like a book. She was livid at his appearance tonight, and jealous of Olivia, which he found both oddly amusing and suspicious. That she still carried on some sort of relationship with his brother was obvious, though the extent or limit of that relationship was anyone's guess.

Finally they reached the center of the ballroom floor, and without a word or hesitation, he turned and swept the woman who was once his lover, the woman who had caused such a scandal in his life all those years ago, into his arms. It took her no time to come to the point.

With a false smile planted firmly on her painted mouth, she stared at him directly. "Why are you back in Paris? You can't possibly be finished with the Govance heiress."

He wished he knew who the "Govance heiress" was, and where she lived. But Claudette's question did tell him that Edmund had been sent from the city to do her bidding, and probably to woo another unsuspecting female of her fortune. No surprise in that, really.

"Olivia found me," he replied lightly. "I couldn't very well say I wasn't done with our...endeavor, shall we say."

She expelled a short puff of air that lifted the wisps of hair on her forehead. "So what did you tell her? She had to have been furious with you."

He smiled wryly. "I told her very little, actually."

"What *exactly* did you *say*?"

She kept a rigid smile on her face even as she cut him with her biting tone. The one thing he remembered about Claudette was that she always, invariably, needed to be in control. That she acted so irritated by his evasiveness, not to mention his totally unexpected return without her knowledge, meant it was tearing her up inside. He could feel her anger by the way she dug her painted nails into his well-protected shoulder and gripped his hand to the point of pain.

He chuckled as if she'd said something deviously amusing, for the benefit of those dancing around them, hoping to God he'd be able to make this explanation believable. "I told her *exactly* that being the foolish man I am, I gambled away most of the money and was terrified of returning to her. I told her that such a weakness was part of my upbringing, and that I still adore her. And then I asked her to forgive me."

Claudette snorted most unbecomingly, and for the first time her face crinkled in distaste. Amazingly, after all this time, he still thought of her as a beautiful woman, only now he wasn't the least bit attracted to her charms.

"Did she believe you?"

He winked at her, then murmured, "I'm here, aren't I?"

She continued to gaze up at his face, her eyes narrowed in challenging suspicion.

"Is she still in love with you?" she asked, her voice controlled even as a trace of unsureness seeped through the question just barely heard above the din.

Sam felt his heart thumping hard in his chest. He wanted to lash out at her, to tell her with great enjoyment that Olivia, her dearest niece, couldn't possibly be in love with her so-called husband and kiss *him* the way she just did. Oddly enough, it was that sudden realization that made him feel remarkably calm inside, elated even, and with that he offered her a genuine grin.

"I believe so, Madame Comtesse. But then, isn't that what you want?"

For a few seconds, as he circled her around the parquet floor with expert ease in time to the waltz, she didn't answer, though Sam knew her mind churned with ideas and worries. She looked older, the fine lines on her face more pronounced, even glaring under bright light. Still, her cosmetic application suited her and did manage to hide some of the telling signs of age. But then maybe he was jaded in his critical eye. To the oblivious onlooker, she'd no doubt appear the beautiful, buxom blond woman with the face of an angel. Just as he'd seen her the day she first walked into his life.

"I didn't like the fact that you returned without telling me, darling," she cooed at last, her words slicing into his thoughts.

He frowned, stroking her back with his fingertips. "Of course. I'm deeply sorry about that."

"Why didn't you tell me?"

The famous Claudette whine. He certainly hadn't missed that in all these years. Inhaling a long, full breath, he replied, "Because Olivia hasn't left my side since our return, and I couldn't very well tell her I was going to visit you. That would have certainly raised her suspicions."

She sighed, slowing her footsteps as the music selection played so expertly by the orchestra came to a close. "So what, pray tell, were you doing outside on the balcony with my lovely niece just now, Edmund? You seemed to be involved in a fairly...intimate conversation." She very slowly took the arm he offered to lead her toward a buffet table. "It almost seemed as if something's changed between the two of you."

That's the understatement of the century. "Oh, I don't think so. We'd danced and she felt warm so I escorted her outside for some air. Why do you ask?" It felt good to put her on the defense for once.

She squeezed his arm, eyeing him through half-closed lashes as she accepted a full champagne glass from him. "I'm jealous, darling."

He chuckled, noting how the tension eased from his rigid spine. Jealous, indeed. *Only if it interferes with your calculated plans.* He leaned over and whispered for her benefit alone, "Cunning witch."

She laughed. "You've no idea."

Sam stared her squarely in the eye. "Oh, but I know you very well, don't I, dearest *Aunt*?"

Claudette blinked quickly several times, hesitating

as her smile faded, then quickly swallowed the contents of her champagne flute before reaching for another. Sam stood his ground, waiting, unfazed, though wishing he could be more direct with her without raising her leeriness.

At last she stepped closer to him, turning him with a palm to his elbow so they faced away from the crowd and toward the open windows. "I heard you were sleeping with her, in her apartments," she murmured. Then through a sigh of exasperation, she added, "I thought we had an agreement, Edmund."

He could only begin to imagine what that agreement might be, but more important, it now became apparent that he and Olivia were being watched by someone reporting to her. That rattled him a bit even if he wasn't all that surprised.

"Edmund?"

He shrugged, then admitted, "I am sleeping in her guest room for now." *For now.* He couldn't help but smile at the scintillating idea of changing that circumstance. "I don't think she's up to a more intimate companionship."

She seemed to physically relax beside him. Then, with the first genuine tone of distress, she asserted, "You simply cannot consummate your relationship with her, Edmund. We've talked about the consequences before, and I think they're even more vital now that you've returned. Olivia will want you to bed her, but you must be firm in your resolve. Are we still in agreement over this issue?"

Sam felt as if he'd been kicked in the gut, knocking the wind from him with the force of a thousand horses.

His brother had never bedded Olivia. Or at least

Claudette believed he hadn't. Was Edmund that stupid? Or that smart? It would make sense to keep the option of annulment open, for both of them, should they present their marriage license as legitimate, and in that regard Edmund had done Olivia a tremendous favor. If one could call it that. It could also be that his love for Claudette kept him faithful to her, though Sam doubted that idea simply out of past experience. Or maybe his brother just wanted to avoid the risk of getting Olivia with child, a possibility that seemed far more likely. As far as Claudette was concerned, perhaps she didn't want them to consummate their faux marriage because of her familial care for her niece, or she was against it for personal reasons, and in Sam's mind, the latter made more sense. The most surprising part for him was that Edmund didn't want to sleep with the woman who truly believed they were married. She would have given herself to him gladly; if not for pleasure, then for duty. It had to be Edmund who had retreated from the intimacy. Edmund and Claudette were in this together. Always, Edmund and Claudette.

Still, once again he couldn't rid himself entirely of the nagging notion that Olivia was involved in the deception and the three of them were playing him for money and ultimate ruin. There remained the chance that Olivia had told her aunt who he was before tonight's event. His caution regarding his brother and Claudette had always led him to consider the worst of possibilities. And it bothered him tremendously that he didn't yet know Olivia well enough to trust her. She had kissed him passionately, but could she act that well? He simply didn't know.

Jesus. What the hell do I believe?

His incredulity regarding the million and one implications of this development must have shown in his
expression.

"I see that I've shocked you," Claudette said with a
crooked, unflattering lift of her lips. "I'd hoped to. I
realize you never wanted to make love to her before,
but seeing you outside...well..." She grabbed her pink
satin skirts and shook them out. "I suppose I just let my
imagination run away with me."

Sam felt fairly certain she didn't see them kissing
and hadn't heard a word they shared, or her reaction
would have been far more hysterical.

"You know I don't want her," he said quietly, finding
it difficult not to choke on the words, "but pretenses
must be kept."

"Of course they must." Her eyes brightened and she
finished off the contents of her second flute in three
large swallows. "My goodness, but you look like you
need some champagne as well, darling," she said fondly
with a gentle pat to his cheek. Then she leaned up on
her tiptoes and whispered in his ear, "I'm staying in the
second floor guest room, at the corner of the east wing.
I'll see you there later." And then without waiting for
his reply, she backed away from him.

"Well, I'm sure your lovely wife is missing you by
now, Edmund, and I must mingle." She smoothed the
back of her hair. "We'll have a lovely chat another time.
I'd adore hearing more about your recent travels." With
a lift of her skirts, she turned on her heels and left him.

Sam stared at her departing back until she disappeared into the crowd. Then, in sudden desperation, he
went looking for a whiskey.

Chapter 12

Olivia had never felt so utterly confused in all of her life. This had been a night to remember, and for so many reasons beyond sharing an absolutely divine kiss with someone she should never have even *dreamt* of kissing. To desire him as a man, in his own right, was simply wrong, probably in a thousand ways she had yet to consider. He held an undeniable, ruthless, and perfectly delicious spell over her that she couldn't seem to overcome no matter how hard she tried, though it didn't help to admit to herself that thus far she'd hardly been trying to avoid his advances, be they physical or not. How in heaven's name could she have these...*feelings* for the brother of her husband? Why, oh *why,* did he keep pursuing her as if there were no consequences to his actions? Being together as they were tonight went far beyond friendly companionship, though she realized with some rationale that he wasn't completely at fault for the indiscretion. She'd responded to him as no lady should, at least outside the privacy of the marital bedchamber. But above it all, more than every consideration, they both had to realize they had absolutely no future together romantically. Their attraction to each other needed to end, and end now. She just wasn't so sure how to do it.

She'd tried not to watch as he danced with her aunt, and she'd scolded herself more than once for being utterly unable to control herself to that end, following them with her eyes while she stood talking to two of Nivan's patrons in front of a buffet table. They looked agreeable in each other's arms, but she did note a certain hardness in Sam's posture and expression that he hadn't exhibited with her. True, Claudette's interruption on the balcony had startled them both, but he'd more than shocked her when he asked her aunt to dance, particularly after the intimate moment they'd only just shared. She hadn't expected him to leave her so abruptly after she'd mentioned Claudette's obvious appreciation of her husband's charms. But then maybe that was why Sam seemed interested in her. Olivia only wished she hadn't felt that same tinge of jealousy settle in the pit of her stomach when she saw them together. She shouldn't feel jealousy of any kind where Sam was concerned, and that irked her most of all, she decided. But apparently, and of course most importantly, the ruse still worked. Claudette didn't appear to suspect he wasn't Edmund, as Olivia had feared from the beginning.

Now they rode together in silence back to Nivan,

Sam sitting across from her, eyes closed, though she knew he wasn't sleeping. He hadn't said as much as two words to her since they'd left the party. She hadn't wanted to leave, and they hadn't originally planned to, but he insisted, telling her only that it was imperative that she not see her aunt again this evening. He refused to tell her why, or what he and Claudette had discussed during their few minutes together, and it irritated her that he remained silent even now that they were alone. She wanted answers and she was starting to tire of waiting for him to speak.

"Why were you so anxious for us to leave the ball, Sam?" she asked as their hired coach exited the lane on the Brillon estate and turned toward town.

He only grunted, keeping his eyes closed. "We'll talk about it back at Nivan."

Exhaling a fast breath, she prodded, "Did you learn something you're keeping from me? What did you discuss with my aunt?"

"Olivia, be a little patient."

His tone had an edge to it that she didn't think she'd heard from him before. His evasiveness and decision to make her wait made her mad though. They'd planned on staying the night at the estate, and yet no sooner had he finished the waltz with her aunt, he found her, a double whiskey in his hand, and practically forced her out the door, swallowing the remains of his drink in a few large gulps. That surprised her, too, for he seemed more disturbed than the event should have made him. Truth be told, she was positively dying to know what Claudette had said to him to get him so upset—or what she'd done.

"Are you feeling light-headed from the drink?" she asked softly.

He smirked. "I didn't have enough."

She wasn't certain if he meant he didn't have enough to feel the alcohol, or he didn't have enough to calm his nerves after the excitement of the evening. She could only see vague lines on his face as the inside of the coach cast them in shadow, the only light being reflections from a fairly bright moon and a few street lamps they passed along the way.

Olivia adjusted her skirts, smoothing them out over her thighs, then opened her fan and brushed the edges with a gloved fingertip.

"Stop fidgeting," he said brusquely.

That annoyed her even more. "I'm sorry, sir, but with everything that's happened tonight, you expect me to be calm? You won't even tell me what Claudette—"

"We'll discuss it when we get home." He lifted his eyelids a fraction, just enough for her to tell he was looking at her. "Right now I need to think, so why don't you relax."

Relax? How could she possibly do that? When he closed his eyes again, she gave him an exaggerated, and not too ladylike, snort, then decided quizzing him further would only make him angry with her, in which case she'd risk his continued silence when they reached her apartments. That in mind, she scooted down into the cushion and leaned back to rest her head on the seat, just as he had, closing her own eyes for the remainder of the long ride home.

She must have dozed because it seemed like only seconds later when she felt the coach slow its progress as it pulled up in front of the boutique. Blinking quickly to clear her head, she sat upright, as Sam did across from her, then clutched her skirts with one hand and took the driver's with the other as he helped her descend the steps to the street below.

Sam followed without a word as she pulled the key to the building from a pocket in her gown, then led the way through the darkened store, up the stairs, and down the hall to her home. Once inside, she immediately walked to her pine secretary, lit a gas lamp, then turned to him, crossing her arms over her breasts.

"Are you ready for a discussion now?" She supposed that sounded a bit curt if not downright rude, but she was as tired as she was angry at the moment and didn't care how he gauged her mood.

He took his time closing the door softly and securing the lock. Then he faced her, shoving his fingers harshly through his hair, fatigue obvious in his narrowed eyes, on the hardness of his features.

"I suggest you change first," he remarked coolly, his voice and movements controlled as he began to remove his evening jacket.

She stood where she was, her spine rigid. "Change? Change into what?"

His expression darkened with annoyance. "Into something more comfortable."

"I'm perfectly comfortable now."

"No, you're not, and neither am I." He started walking toward the guest room. "Meet me in the kitchen when you're ready."

Olivia hated it when a man ordered her to do something she didn't want to do. Trouble was, tonight he was right. She'd been wearing a corset, tightly drawn, for several hours, which didn't help her temperament at all. And changing would also give her time to collect her thoughts, as she obviously hadn't done so on the ride home.

It took her a good twenty minutes, since she had no one to help her with her gown, jewelry, and hair pins, but when at last she entered the kitchen, her robe tied securely around her waist, her hair brushed to a shine to fall down her back, she found him sitting in the chair he'd occupied the first night they talked, though he'd turned it outward so he could lean his head against the wall.

She walked around his outstretched legs, noting that he'd not so much changed as simply removed his outer-wear and tie so that he now wore only his trousers and ruffled shirt, unbuttoned at the neck and cuffs, which he'd rolled up nearly to his elbows. She supposed, for a man, he was comfortable enough without being inde-cent in the company of a lady who was not his wife.

She moved to the opposite chair and sat, watching him, folding her hands together on the tabletop to indi-cate she wanted honesty, and now.

He remained silent for a moment, staring not at her, but straight ahead, at the clock she'd placed beside the stove.

Finally, she broke the tension. "It's after two."

He didn't acknowledge that fact. Instead, he replied, "You must be feeling refreshed since you slept all the way home."

She sighed. "I wouldn't say I slept. I was thinking with my eyes closed, just as you were."

He turned his head a little, eyeing her with a smirk on his mouth. "You snore, Olivia."

She fairly gaped at him. "I most certainly do not snore!"

"But I will say," he carried on, ignoring her exclamation, "it's a very dainty, feminine snore. One that suits a beautiful and enticing woman like you."

He said it quite casually, as if they'd met in the middle of the blessed night to mundanely discuss the quality of tea and the merits of its trade. He seemed to enjoy catching her off guard, which, under the circumstances of the evening, made her uncomfortable now that they sat alone together in her home. Better to ignore his teasing remark and get to the point at hand.

"Will you please tell me why you were so anxious to leave?" she asked forthrightly. "And don't say it's because I looked palled."

He almost smiled. "That was rather rude of her."

She lifted her shoulders lightly in shrug. "I'm embarrassed to say that kind of remark is fairly standard for my aunt Claudette, especially where I am concerned."

He placed a forearm flat on the table as his eyes roved over her face. "She's just jealous."

She knit her brows in puzzlement. "Jealous? I sincerely doubt that. She's quite the beauty, my aunt, and everyone knows it. Including her."

"Indeed."

She shifted her body in her chair, a bit irritated that he didn't argue with her—or tell her outright that she was lovelier, as her husband would have done without thought. But then maybe he didn't think so, and that, she had to admit, troubled her in the most inappropriate way.

"Did Edmund think she was beautiful?" he asked seconds later.

She tilted her head a little to the side. "I would guess so. He never said what he thought of her, actually. Now that I think about it, that does seem strange."

"How so?"

He seemed genuinely curious, and so, through a soft exhaled breath, she admitted, "Claudette was physically attracted to Edmund, which I think you must know by now, though I daresay she never did anything completely improper in the company of others. She is my aunt, after all, and is well-bred and generally respectful." That might be giving her too much credit, but when he said nothing in reply, she continued. "It was obvious to everyone that Edmund seemed to enjoy a certain... rapport with her, but he never, that I recall, mentioned his thoughts or feelings about her one way or the other. At least not to me."

After a long moment of silence he murmured, "I see."

She didn't think he did, but Claudette was irrelevant to their conversation. If Sam had suspicions about Edmund romancing her aunt, Edmund would be in Paris to do just that, and Olivia believed almost certainly that he wasn't. Again, she wanted to get back to what happened tonight.

"Are you going to tell me why you practically dragged me from the ball?"

He studied her by lamplight, his expression one of grim contemplation. Then at last, his tone deep and laced with gentleness, he replied, "Because your aunt expected me to meet her in her bedchamber later. I wasn't interested, and didn't want to be there when she discovered that."

She stilled, her mind and body going numb as a strange feeling of dread mixed with absolute incredulity washed over her.

"My aunt—" She couldn't even repeat it. Such a thought, such an *idea,* went beyond the incredible to the despicable. "That's impossible," she managed to choke out in a whisper, gradually lowering her gaze.

He inhaled deeply, turning in the chair so he fully faced her, clasping his hands together in front of him, arms outstretched on the tabletop. "I'm sorry."

"Maybe you misunderstood her," she broached, mouth dry, suddenly freezing in the stuffy kitchen. She pulled her robe tighter around her, hugging herself.

"I didn't misunderstand, Olivia."

No, she supposed he wouldn't, being a man. And it wasn't as if she doubted Claudette could have posed such a suggestion. Still…Her eyes shot back to his face. "Did she really believe you were Edmund?"

Without hesitation he asserted, "Yes. She did."

Olivia shivered, drawing her shoulders up as she squeezed her arms into her body, blinking hard in an attempt to keep herself from breaking down into a crying fit in front of him. The idea that Edmund might have been…involved with her aunt made her nauseated, physically ill.

"But that doesn't make sense," she murmured, her voice shaky. "Edmund never showed any interest in her at all, at least not when I was around the two of them."

Sam said nothing, just continued to watch her, and it took her nearly a minute to realize he didn't need to respond. She grasped the implication of her own words at last—her husband showed no interest in her aunt when they were all *together.*

"It's quite possible," she mumbled after licking her lips, "that he rebuffed her. She's been known to be a bit...aggressive when it comes to what she wants."

He waited, then said, "When you think about everything my brother has done to you, do you believe that?"

His voice had a certain edge of irritation to it, as if he desperately wanted her to understand but couldn't simply explain it all. She needed to grasp the details, focus on what Edmund did, what he said, what her aunt's personality was like. When she considered it like that—the quick marriage at his insistence, the wedding night that was not a wedding night, his nefarious scheme of stealing her inheritance—she could come up with no other conclusion than the one Sam implied.

She couldn't control it any longer; her eyes filled with tears. "How could he betray me like that?" A bolt of sheer anger sliced through her. "You clearly know him better than I, Sam," she charged, her gaze burning into his. "Are you suggesting he planned to marry me and steal my fortune, all with the help of my *aunt*?"

He stayed silent for a few moments, regarding her with narrowed eyes. Then he ran one palm harshly down his face. "Olivia, I think there's a lot more to this entire situation than you're aware of."

She sneered. "That's painfully obvious. I don't even pretend to know *anything* anymore." With that, she stood abruptly, her arms wrapped snugly around her as she began to pace the kitchen floor. She didn't look at him, though she felt his eyes on her, watching her actions, probably trying to determine what was going through her mind. At last she stopped in front of the sink, staring into the basin, seeing nothing.

"So, unlike your brother, you weren't the least bit interested in her invitation?" she asked, her voice just a shade above a whisper.

"If this is about me," he replied slowly, "then no. I wasn't the least bit interested."

"Why?" she breathed.

The silence in the room boomed thick and intense. Finally, he murmured, "I think you've been hurt enough, Olivia."

It wasn't much of a response, but then what did she expect? Undying devotion? In truth, she shouldn't have asked him that. *Nothing* of this situation was about him, and who he chose to romance was entirely none of her business, even if it was a relation of hers. And yet she couldn't deny the way her spirits lifted a little from his candor, and his caring.

"Are you going to tell me what you think about your brother's whereabouts? What you think is going on?" she asked, her tone riddled with a quiet, steady anger.

She heard him inhale deeply again, and she drummed up the courage to lift her head and turn, facing him once more. The light from the lamp cast shadows on each handsome feature, reflecting in his dark eyes as they remained fixed on her, on his thick, shiny hair that fell loosely across his brow, his hardened jaw and grimly set lips. His sheer attractiveness made her insides flutter even as she waited for him to answer the most grave of questions, her posture determined, her stare haunted, pleading for the truth.

After a long moment he said, "I will tell you what I think, if you'll be honest with me in return."

She hadn't expected that. "Honest about what?"

He tipped his head to the side a fraction. "We'll get to that. First, what exactly is Govance?"

She frowned, shaking her head negligibly in confusion. "Where did you hear of Govance?"

"Claudette mentioned it."

That seemed rather odd to her, as neither her aunt nor Edmund had anything to do with other houses. She leaned back against the sink edge, her arms folded in front of her. "Govance is a large and well-respected house of fragrance, though they cater to the wider industry, primarily Asian trade. They only have one small shop in Paris, but—why?"

He remained quiet for a moment or two, regarding her. Then, "Who is its heiress?"

Her mind began to race, her thoughts quickening. "The *heiress* of Govance? That's probably Brigitte Marcotte. She's the granddaughter of the owner."

He looked down at his fingers, tapping them together in front of him. "How old is she?"

Olivia began to see where his questions were leading, only to feel a greater bewilderment coupled with fearful anticipation. "I don't know her exact age," she said, "but she's probably nineteen or twenty by now. I haven't seen her in about five years."

He sat up a little. "She doesn't live here?"

"No, she lives in Grasse, where the world fragrance market—" Her eyes widened; she slowly lowered her arms to her sides as the pieces began falling into place. "You think Edmund..."

"Is in Grasse, wooing the unsuspecting Brigitte of her fortune," he finished for her. "Just as he did you."

She tried very hard to concentrate, to digest the implication, to grasp what such an incredible assumption could mean. "But if you learned that from Claudette, then—then she knows where he is, where he's been all this time. She's part of the deception."

"Edmund is deceitful and clever in his own right, but he couldn't possibly know interested parties in the perfume business. I think," he admitted austerely, "that not only does your aunt intend to reap the benefits, she probably planned the whole thing, including his marriage to you."

Olivia no longer wanted to cry, she wanted to hit something. She suddenly couldn't breathe, couldn't comprehend such utter disregard for decency, couldn't believe the people she loved, who she thought loved *her,* would betray her entire future for money. She gulped for air, spinning around to stare out the window, then turning back again, arms flailing at her sides as she began to move about the kitchen in semicircles, unseeing, feeling everything in utter shock.

He must have realized the depth of her stupefaction, for he stood at once, his chair sliding back with a loud skid across the wooden floor, and walked quickly toward her.

"Claudette—" She swallowed, then ran all ten fingers

through her hair until it pulled behind her. "Claudette introduced me to him, wanted me to marry him. *Urged* me to marry him," she spat in a whispered jumble.

"Olivia," Sam said soothingly, placing his palms gently on her shoulders to hold her still.

She couldn't stand the touch, needed air. Immediately, she brushed his arms aside and walked swiftly to the opposite wall, staring down to all the lovely little porcelain teapots she'd collected over the years, now sitting daintily on her pantry shelf. She fought the strong desire to smash them to little bits of shard.

It was all becoming clear—the lies, the shrewdness, the artful deceit. And the whys.

"Claudette wanted to take charge of Nivan when Jean-Francois died," she disclosed bitterly, "because she knew my mother was inept at management and everyone else lived in Grasse. And she was right." She shivered. "But Claudette would have surely embezzled every penny if she had control, running Nivan to insolvency, and everybody—*everybody*—knew it. That's why even her brother, Robert Nivan, denied her the opportunity, and gave the boutique to me to manage." She tossed Sam a biting look over her shoulder. "So it appears that when she couldn't have what she wanted, she set her own niece up for ruin with the help of a charming, spectacular-looking, *cunning* man."

"We'll get your money back," he said tightly.

A caustic laugh bubbled up in her throat. "My money? Do you think this is all about my inheritance?" She pivoted quickly to confront him. "What about my dignity, my feelings? What about being used? Even *you* said that, Sam. He used me. *They* used me."

Crossing his arms over his chest, he simply looked at her, his body tense, his expression taut. "I know. And I'm sorry," he admitted with quiet intensity. "But you're going to have to trust me."

"Trust you?" Standing tall, glaring at him, she asked, "Tell me, your grace, why did you kiss me tonight?"

That question clearly stunned him. His mouth dropped open minutely as he looked her up and down. Then gritting his teeth, he narrowed his eyes and began to walk slowly toward her.

"I believe we kissed each other, madam, though I can't fathom what that marvelous moment of passion has to do with this conversation."

She shook her head defiantly, ignoring the tingle of exhilaration that surged through her from his choice of words. "It has everything to do with it," she maintained, her voice shaky even as she attempted to stick to the point. "You kissed me, and purposely kissing a married woman like that hardly engenders trust. Do you kiss all the married ladies you know?"

"Married," he repeated in a dark whisper.

She stood her ground, her back to the wall, her palm gripping the edge of the pantry of teapots, noting with only the slightest hesitation that his tone had grown as cold as his countenance.

"What if I said to you that I don't believe you're legally married to my brother?"

She sneered. "I'd say you've lost your mind. Or you're a magnificent liar, trying to confuse me into falling for your charms, just as Edmund did."

His cheek twitched; he stepped closer. "Is that why

you think I kissed you tonight? To make you fall for me?" He gave her a sarcastic smile. "Believe me, sweet, I don't need to present lies to a woman to attract her interest."

She couldn't think of a response, as such a statement was very likely true. "Then why did you?"

"Tell me, darling, beautiful Lady Olivia," he asked in deep murmur, ignoring her question, "did Edmund ever make love to you?"

She gasped, appalled into silence as he moved nearer to her—so close he now towered over her, his eyes like shiny, hard marbles, reflecting lamp light and oozing anger.

"Did he?" he whispered again. "And I don't mean make love with words of flattery, but make love as a husband makes love to a wife, physically, in the marriage bed."

She blinked quickly, as terrified of his bearing at the moment as she was of the heat suddenly radiating between them. "The intimacy I shared with Edmund has nothing to do with this conversation," she managed to choke out.

That didn't deter him in the least. "You opened the door with your question about our kiss," he whispered huskily, "and your concerns about trust. Perhaps I worry about trusting you. Answer me, and answer me honestly."

He still hadn't touched her, but he couldn't get any closer without doing so. Olivia felt her knees go weak. "I'm going to bed."

"Answer me first."

"No."

His dark brows rose minutely. "No, Edmund didn't make love to you as a husband should?"

Tears filled her eyes again, though this time they emerged from pure frustration. "You're despicable."

"I've been called worse," he acknowledged flatly. "Did Edmund make love to you?"

Why did he keep asking her that? "He's my husband," she seethed, clenching her hands into fists. "What do you think?"

He pulled back a little, just enough to give him room to lower his gaze and blatantly ogle her, making her feel naked and exposed for his view.

"I think that any woman who smells like you do, and looks like you do, and kisses like you do, is missing what she needs most from a husband."

Fury inflamed her and she drew her hand up to slap him hard. But instead of making contact with his cheek, he reacted just as quickly, grabbing her wrist in midair and holding it tightly.

"Did—he—make—love to you, Livi?" he breathed, daring her to defy him.

A tear rolled down her cheek but she refused to cower, to give in to a weaker emotion. Through clenched teeth she whispered, "No."

He seemed to stagger from that admission, as if he never expected it, sucking in a sharp, quick breath as he eased his grip on her wrist and took a half step back. She watched his expression falter in a matter of seconds, changing from stony determination to a sort of odd disbelief. And then he exhaled a long, warm sigh that touched her skin and made her shiver from the inside out.

"He left me on my wedding night," she continued, her voice breaking from the memory. "He kissed me as you kissed me, and then humiliated me, just as you're doing now." With a negligible lift of her chin, she recklessly asserted, "You're just like him."

That instantly transformed his aggravation with her to a rage of the purest kind, as she knew it would. But instead of releasing her in disgust as she expected him to do, he placed his free hand flat on her bare chest, just beneath the base of her throat, shoving her back against the wall before she could blink.

"I am *nothing* like Edmund, Olivia, and you know it," he charged, his low timbre thick with warning. "*I* would never, and *will* never, leave you devastated and wanting for anything. I have more honor than that."

Something inside of her melted—from the veracity laced through his words, from the depth of urgency in his eyes—and with that awareness, she started to shake, her tears flowing without regard.

Through a soft sob, barely heard, she said, "I know…"

Her gentle submission gave him a second of pause. And then the look he gave her promptly changed from absolute fury to a raw, fiery hunger. His mouth clamped down on hers, hard and fast and consuming, covering the scream that welled up inside her from a contact so unexpected—but so desperately needed.

He kissed her with a pent-up longing that went beyond all reason, his tongue invading, searching, searing,

begging for response. She whimpered, trying to draw
breath as he pushed his entire body up against her, pinning her to the wall. She felt every rigid muscle of his
powerful form, every ounce of his incredible strength
drawing her in, enveloping her, shielding her from escape should she try.

He groaned low in his chest, and the sound of it, the
sound of desire in its purest form, inflamed her in a
manner she'd never felt before.

Tears stained her cheeks as she began to kiss him
back, greedily, without clear thought, her body, her
mind and modest intentions invaded and conquered by
a yearning as great as his. She placed a palm on his
shoulder, but with a savagery she didn't at all understand or expect, he grabbed both of her wrists in his
large left hand and raised them above her head, securing them against the wall while he continued his delicious assault on her mouth, overwhelming her with a
perfectly rapturous torment.

He lowered his free hand and she vaguely became
aware of him fumbling with the tie on her robe. She
squirmed a little in protest, but he ignored it, persistent
in his longing to arouse the depths of her passion, his
kissing relentless as he suddenly grasped her tongue
and sucked it.

Olivia felt her nerves ignite, her body tingle through
every tremor that whipped through her, her whimper-
ing a din from a world of instantaneous pleasure. And
then he covered her breast over her sheer cotton nightgown and she could no longer stand.

He sensed her weakness, held firm to her wrists as
he shoved his knee between her legs to help support

her. She moaned low and long when he began flicking his thumb across her nipple, encouraging him with a lust she could no longer control.

At last he pulled away from her mouth and she leaned her head back, gasping for breath, her eyes tightly shut. He kissed her cheek, her chin, and neck as his palm and nails caressed her breasts, one after the other, with arduous determination.

She panted; he responded in kind, his breath hot and heavy and rapid against her neck, her cheeks and ear. He gently bit her lobe, and with a low, throaty moan she instinctively rubbed herself against his thigh, encouraging him with the uncontrollable response. He inhaled sharply, squeezing her nipples, rubbing them with his thumb, expertly caressing her with one strong hand.

"God, Livi," he said in a pained, muffled voice against her ear. "Let me give you what you need. Let *me*..."

She jerked against him, her short, little mewls echoing through the bare, dark kitchen in a wordless plea for fulfilment. He took her mouth again, hungrily, forcefully, granting her desire. And then he dropped his hand from her breast and reached down, pulling at the hem of her nightgown, lifting it handful by handful, tugging until it gave way from between their legs. Then, as no man had ever done before, he traced a line of exquisite fire up one bare thigh until he reached the point of his desire, her hidden pleasure.

Olivia squirmed against him, suddenly afraid, and yet wanting his touch beyond all sanity. When at last she felt his fingers graze her intimate mound of hair, a flicker of shame shot through her, only to pass quickly into oblivion as he slipped between her delicate folds and began stroking her slowly, gently, her wetness coating his fingers.

He pulled his mouth away from hers. "Feel me here," he whispered, his voice hoarse, ragged, against her cheek. "This is what you need."

His movements summoned exquisite sensations within her, pushing her beyond hearing anything but the pounding of her heart. Eyes squeezed shut, she moaned quietly, pressing herself against his fingers, her head shoved back, letting him take the full weight of her arms above her.

With deliberate slowness he caressed her, slipping one finger inside of her and then out again, and then picking up the pace to meet her demand, resting his cheek against hers, his forehead on the wall, kissing her ear, brushing his nose in her hair. She met his rhythm, panting, her mind screaming for him to stop, beseeching him to probe deeper and give her everything.

Suddenly her body tensed against him. He moved his mouth to hers, sensing her fulfillment, driving one finger inside of her as she thrust against the others.

"Oh no," she breathed against his lips, "Oh, no…"

"Yes," he answered with urgency. "Let me feel you come."

Her eyes shot open. "No…"

He pulled back to watch her, his teeth clenched, his gaze melding with hers. "Oh, yes…"

It hit her then, a shockwave of forbidden ecstasy that exploded deep within, making her cry out, causing her body to shudder through each crest of intense pleasure, through each measured pulse that squeezed his finger and left her breathless.

She gasped. "Sam—"

"I'm right here," he whispered gruffly, soothingly, "watching, feeling everything."

She squeezed her eyes shut, unable to look at him, unable to comprehend what she'd just done with him, what he'd done to her. He continued to touch her, keeping the sensation alive and tingling, his fingers moving faintly, almost lovingly, as he seemed to relish in the hot, slick moisture that now poured out of her with each easing ripple of gratification.

Finally she stilled, forcing herself to calm as he slowly released her wrists so she could lower her arms to her sides. He continued to hold her pinned against the wall with his body, and for the first time Olivia became acutely aware of his rigid need pressed against her stomach. She tried to ignore it as she kept her eyes tightly closed, as she attempted to slow her breathing, her racing heart, tried to come to terms with what had just happened.

Neither of them said anything for a few seconds, though she could feel the tenseness and heat emanating from his body, knew he was attempting to remain in control as he once again leaned in to rest his forehead on the wall, his flushed cheek grazing hers. She moved one knee toward his thigh, uncomfortable with his hand still between her legs, and at last he withdrew, allowing her nightgown to fall in a bunch to the floor.

Mortification overwhelmed her as her mind gradually

cleared and she realized what he'd just done to her—and how wantonly she'd reacted to his touch.

"Don't," he said weakly, sensing her sudden desire to flee. "Don't go yet."

Olivia couldn't speak, didn't want to, but she remained perfectly still as he asked, unsure what to do, what he expected from her at this moment.

His breathing continued to come in rasps, but he'd edged his body sideways enough to allow her to inhale deeply and steadily, which in turn kept her from shaking.

Emotions she couldn't at all understand raced through her mind—a thousand and one of them that trapped her, made her feel at the same time vulnerable and alone, cherished and admired, afraid and devastated, and more than anything, charged with an almost paralyzing wonder.

He shouldn't have done this, and in a way she hated him for taking advantage of her. She hated him almost as much as she trusted him, needed him, and everything he did for her.

She couldn't help the tears this time. They welled up in her eyes even as she kept them tightly shut—tears of frustration, anger, hurt, even longing for unfulfilled dreams. He could have taken her, had wanted to be with her intimately, and yet he hadn't forced her to do anything but betray her own body. And at this moment, still embraced by him, still recovering from a blissful turmoil, she despised him as much as she wanted him again, in every way.

At last, in a husky murmur, he broke the silence. "You asked me why I kissed you tonight."

She shook her head minutely, incapable of responding.

"Livi," he whispered, rubbing the tip of his nose along her ear, "I kissed you because everything about you begs me to."

"No," she breathed.

He inhaled fully, and gradually pulled away from her, though even with her eyes closed she could feel the heat of his gaze on her face. And then she felt his fingertips gently glide along her brow, down one cheek, wiping away her tears.

"You're so soft, so beautiful," he whispered in a gruff, faraway voice. "Please—"

But she'd already moved to the side, quickly, knocking the pantry with her hip and rattling her beautiful porcelain teapots as she skirted past him toward the door, away from the shame and confusion, leaving him alone in the silent, dimly lit kitchen.

Chapter 13

Claudette paced the floor in her parlor, absolutely furious. *Furious.* Never had Edmund treated her with such disdain as he had last night. Oh, she supposed he'd been himself when they danced, if not a bit aloof, which she assumed had to do with her finding him returned to Paris without notification, just like a naughty puppy with his tail between his legs. But to disregard an open invitation to her room went far beyond anything he'd ever done before. In all the years she'd known him, he'd never denied her the pleasures of the bedroom. Discovering, after a thorough search of the ballroom at one o'clock in the morning, that he'd left with his *wife* at just past midnight had completely enraged her. She couldn't sleep, couldn't eat, and had arrived back at her suite just before eight that morning, surprising her entire staff with her untimely appearance as they all stared at her with open mouths.

True, she undoubtedly looked a fright, as her expertly pinned coiffure had come loose during her coach ride home, and she still wore her ball gown, now wrinkled. But then she had every right to be upset! First she learns that Edmund returned to Paris unannounced, and then she finds the two of them alone on the *balcony,* of all places, sharing their own little tête-à-tête as if there were no one else on earth! If she had never been jealous of Olivia before last night, nothing compared to the surge of emotions that coursed through her upon finding Edmund beside her, bodies nearly touching, heads tipped together as they engaged in intimate discussion. She'd *never* seen Edmund so clearly enraptured by anything Olivia had to say, and the second she came upon them by moonlight, she fought the urge to rip the little minx to shreds with her perfectly painted nails. Or better yet, walk to Edmund's side and kiss him soundly in front of Olivia's pretty, innocent eyes, laying claim to him, letting her know at last that the man she thought she married was, in point of fact, already taken and had been for years. But, alas, good breeding reigned and she'd restrained herself to the best of her ability, reminding herself with gleeful satisfaction that Edmund might be pretending with Olivia, but it would be *her* bed he'd be lying in come dawn. His ignoring her demand for a late-night sexual interlude had been the final blow.

Now, after what she could only view as a purposeful, spiteful avoidance of her, she didn't know what to do. She needed to talk to him, to learn exactly how much had been accomplished in Grasse before Olivia

found him, and then just exactly what transpired between the two of them in the days leading up to last
evening's fiasco. His explanation of staying in his faux
wife's good graces and returning to Paris with her made
sense, and yet...it didn't. Edmund never did anything
without her consent, or at the very least informing her,
especially something as vital and delicate as this. More
importantly, she knew, just *knew,* that he couldn't possibly be finished courting the Govance heiress.

After hours of careful consideration, she decided she
had no choice but to confront him at Nivan, where he
likely was at the moment, curled up in her bed. God,
she didn't know what to do without telling Olivia everything, without admitting her part in this incredible
fraud. Oh, she wanted to, but then what? Where would
that leave her? Very probably imprisoned, a situation in
which she simply refused to find herself. Still, Olivia
would need to prove fault on her part, and Olivia certainly still believed that she and Edmund were married
or she wouldn't have been so cordial last night, or quite
so attached to him.

But for now she could think of only one thing to do,
and that was to see Edmund and make certain he hadn't
decided on his own to bed darling, little Olivia. And
the only way she could be sure of that was to catch
them off guard, together, in her niece's apartments.

That resolution in mind, she grabbed her parasol
from the coatrack by the front door and swiftly headed
for Nivan.

The storefront looked deceptively vacant upon her
arrival. Normand stood at his usual post by the front

display case, tallying receipts or some other such business. He looked up when the door opened, then fairly gaped at her, as surprised as her staff, apparently, at seeing her wide-awake and moving about the city before luncheon.

Planting a smug smile on her face, she said, "I'm here to visit the happy couple."

He immediately clamped his mouth shut and closed the black receipt book. After glancing around quickly to make certain they were alone, he walked out from behind the glass case and came toward her.

"Madame Comtesse, how lovely you look today," he said, honoring her presence with a slight bow.

She scoffed, knowing she looked horrendous from lack of sleep and no morning toilette, though she had no time to argue his ridiculous comment. Closing her parasol with some fuss, she replied, "I know my way to her apartments, Normand."

"Oh, of course, madame," he muttered, popping up onto his toes, his hands clasped behind him. "But you'll not find her there, I'm afraid."

Claudette started, staring at him. "I beg your pardon?"

He gave her a half shrug. "She isn't here. When I arrived this morning, Madame Carlisle was on her way out."

"Out?" Her eyes narrowed with malicious intent. "Out to do what? Where?"

He frowned deeply. "I've no idea, though she was quite plainly in a hurry. And she had baggage brought down and carried a large valise."

Claudette's brows drew together. "*Baggage?* And

what time was that, dear Normand?" she asked too sweetly.

"Oh, about... nine or so."

"Nine," she repeated flatly. When he offered nothing else, she asked, exasperated, "So her husband is upstairs alone?"

He shook his head. "No, actually, he left just after she did."

She missed him? No longer wishing to hide her annoyance, she threw her hands wide, knocking the glass display case with her parasol. "Well, don't make me wait, where did they go?"

He gaped at her in feigned shock, then placed one palm wide on his expensive linen shirt. "Madame Comtesse, surely you realize it is not my place to ask."

Claudette felt her face flush with renewed anger. She could think of no greater satisfaction than to strangle the information out of him. Little ant. But before she dared begin a tirade of vile comments, the door behind her swung wide as two large ladies entered, clearly a mother and daughter, talking and laughing between them, disrupting her delicate interrogation.

Normand applied a charming expression to his face and quickly turned his attention to them. "Madame et Mademoiselle Tanquay. How wonderful to see you this bright morning. I will be with you shortly."

She didn't have time for this. "Normand—"

"Madame Comtesse," he interrupted, rotating back to her, "may I speak with you for a moment in the salon?"

Claudette's mouth opened a fraction in surprise, then she caught herself and smiled satisfactorily, realizing that he finally might actually have some useful information to share. "Of course," she replied, lifting her chin and straightening her shoulders, then turning her back on him to lead the way.

He followed closely behind her, and as soon as they entered the semiprivate sitting room, she turned on him again, her bearing composed, her expression hard with impatience. "What do you have for me, Normand?" she demanded curtly.

He took his time, rubbing his jaw with his palm as he glanced over his shoulder, peeking around the partially drawn red drapes to check on his customers, now engrossed in the little sachets of various scents on the shelf behind the display case as they sniffed and chattered.

Claudette waited, her irritation growing, knowing his reluctance to engage her was purposeful as he made her anticipate the information—for which he would no doubt expect a reward. She truly despised him.

At last, he gave her his full attention. "I know something..." he drawled, his voice lowered.

"Of course you do," she snapped. "You couldn't possibly think I'd step back into this ugly red salon for champagne and seasonal scent sampling with you."

That snide remark didn't daunt him at all. Smiling pleasantly, he said, "I'll need to be compensated, naturally."

Normand the ant. So predictable. "What is it?"

He crossed his arms over his chest and took a step closer to her. "I particularly like that diamond bracelet you're wearing."

She followed his gaze to her left wrist where, in all its glory, dangled twenty karats of exquisite stones, purchased for her by her first husband some fifteen years ago. It was by far her best piece of jewelry, worn to only the finest occasions, as last night's ball was supposed to be. His suggestion, his apparent belief that she'd even *consider* giving it to him, appalled her beyond description.

"You can't be serious," she seethed in astonishment. "You have clearly lost your mind, Normand, if you think I'd stand here and give you diamonds—*these* diamonds—for little bits of old news."

He sighed with exaggeration, shaking his head as he glanced down to the tips of his shiny black shoes, rubbing one back and forth across the carpet.

"I think, madame, that I might reconsider if I were you. The...uh...information that I alone possess is quite probably worth it." He looked back into her eyes. "At least to you."

For the first time since she'd known the man, he actually gave her pause. She didn't think she'd ever seen him so arrogant, so sure that he held her under his command, at least for the moment.

"What is your point, Normand?" she asked very carefully, making it clear by her gravely soft voice and rigid stance that she wasn't to be toyed with any longer.

He tossed a look over his shoulder again, stalling. Then he leaned toward her and murmured, "I believe I'd like the bracelet first."

She absolutely could not believe his audacity. Tipping her head to the side, she sneered. "Tell me where they are, where they went, and I'll consider it."

He snickered and scratched his side whiskers. "Oh, Madame Comtesse, I know so much more than that."

Again he'd startled her, and she blinked quickly,

looking him up and down, her features contorted in disbelieving disgust.

"The bracelet?" he said again, holding his hand out, palm up.

She wanted to kill him—but not before she found out what details he actually held; his self-satisfied grin alone expressed the urgency about what he knew, which in itself told her much. He never would have demanded anything of such great personal value to her without good reason. Normand might be a sorry little bastard, but he wasn't stupid.

Tossing her parasol on the velveteen sofa behind her, she practically ripped the diamonds from her wrist. "You know I'll get it back," she warned with a scathing glare. "I'll have you arrested for theft."

"Oh, no, I don't think so," he countered at once, amiably. "I'll have it picked apart and sold in pieces before noon. I have...acquaintances, shall we say, who do that. For a small fee, of course."

She hated him. She really did. Nostrils flaring, her face tight with rage, she threw the bracelet at him hard, hitting him in the chest, where he caught it easily with one hand.

"Tell me," she demanded through clenched teeth, squeezing her hands into fists at her sides.

He waited, purposely defying her as he raised the jewels up for inspection, each diamond reflecting rays of sunlight from a nearby window as he twisted it around with his thumb and forefinger.

"Normand, I swear to you—"

He snapped his palm over the bracelet and grinned. "Perhaps you'd like to sit."

She leaned into him. "Tell me now, you little toad, or so help me I'll stab you in the throat with my parasol and leave you here to bleed to death on this ugly red carpet."

That threat didn't even make him blink. He continued to smile at her as he said matter-of-factly, "I'd be willing to bet this lovely piece of jewelry that they're both on their way to Grasse."

She gasped, gaping at him. "That's *it*?"

"Noooo..."

Claudette was ready to explode, her temper made worse because he knew it.

"Now think, Madame Comtesse," he continued very quietly, his eyes narrowing as he shoved his hands in the pockets of his morning suit. "Why do you think they'd travel to Grasse?"

Something troubling started gnawing at her, deep in her gut, making her waver, a notion as yet undefined. "Why do *you* think they're going there, Normand?" she returned, her voice deadly tight.

He inhaled deeply and bopped up on his toes again. "I think they're on their way to confront the man they believe is Olivia's husband who is now in the process of attempting to swindle Brigitte Marcotte of Govance."

Claudette just stared at him, then shook her head in tiny movements, thoroughly confused. And then, like a clap of nearby thunder, the truth sliced through her and she jumped back from him, wide-eyed and stunned beyond all thought, caught up in a storm of pure disbelief.

"Oh, my God," she whispered as the room started to spin before her.

With an agreeable air, Normand asked, "Would you like to sit now?"

She couldn't breathe, couldn't speak. Her legs gave way beneath her and she tripped on the hem of her skirt as she backed up a step, falling onto the sofa, her derriere plopping down on her expensive parasol without notice.

It took several long, painful seconds for her to come to terms with such a staggering and potentially perilous development. She just stared at the carpeting, shaking as she began to perspire from head to foot, began to understand what had taken place without her knowledge, without her insight, began to understand what would soon be happening in Grasse, as she sat here blindly ignorant, piecing together the horrible truth.

Samson was here. Sam had come to France, secretly, at *Olivia's* bidding, or maybe even with her. She had gone in search of her wayward husband, not in Grasse as assumed, but in England, alone, and had come home with Sam instead.

Samson and Olivia.

Holy Mother of God.

Her gaze slowly drifted up to Normand, who stood exactly as he had before, bopping up and down on his toes, a smug little grin on his despicable mouth.

"You knew," she whispered.

He shrugged. "I guessed."

Never had she felt such a mixture of base emotions pass through her in a moment's time—confusion, frustration, fear, and pure rage. Mostly rage, directed at herself for being so completely dense to the facts staring her straight in the face for the last several days.

She should have guessed the ruse as Normand had, and faster. She should have *known*. All the telltale signs were there—Sam's excellent dancing, his shorter hair, when Edmund was so vain about keeping it a certain length, his aloofness toward her even as she flirted, then her witnessing the shared intimate moment between him and her niece on the balcony. God, and she'd invited him to her room! No wonder he fled. She no doubt looked a fool to everybody, and Samson had certainly enjoyed her idiocy most of all.

"When?" she managed to croak out. "How did you know?"

"Monsieur? Le parfum, s'il vous plaît?"

Normand whirled around at the interruption, as startled by the two ladies behind him as she was.

An irrational fury seized her. "He's engaged," she articulated, her deep, anger-filled voice penetrating the walls.

Both women gawked at her. Then Normand stepped in to resurrect the encounter. "Give me just a moment, ladies, please? Choose any scent or item you like and for your patience I will honor you both by subtracting half of the sale price."

They didn't exactly thank him for his generosity, but they didn't flee, either. Claudette ignored them as they hesitated for a few seconds, then turned and walked back toward the display cases, whispering between them.

Normand looked down at her again, his expression flat with annoyance, eyes narrowed.

She ignored that, too. "How did you guess?" she asked again, her sensibilities starting to return.

He sighed. "First, because he called her Livi—"

"Edmund despises names of endearment," she cut in, clutching her rumpled skirt with both hands.

"Yes. I *know*," Normand maintained, his tone cool. "That drew my suspicions immediately. But there was also something a bit more . . . subtle between them."

"What?" she pressed, brows furrowed.

He grinned slyly, enjoying the moment for all it was worth. "There was the way he stared at her."

"*Stared* at her?"

Gleefully, he leaned toward her and divulged, "I'd say he's enthralled by her. As Olivia is by him."

She felt heat suffuse her face, sweat bead on her upper lip, her heart begin to race.

This cannot be happening.

For the first time in her life Claudette thought she might actually faint. The red salon seemed to whirl around her in a crimson eddy, nauseating her, making her feel dizzy in the stuffy heat, in her suddenly squeezing stays and heavy, drooping gown.

She closed her eyes, inhaling as deeply as she could, then again, attempting to focus, to gain control of her senses and thoughts, to come to terms with everything this unexpected revelation could mean for her, and even for Edmund. For both of them as a couple. Everything had changed, and she needed to concentrate, to make some wise decisions now that Sam was involved and Olivia no doubt knew much of their scheme, if not all of it. Everything had changed, and she couldn't possibly consider her options here, with the little ant leering at her.

With great aplomb she raised her lashes to gaze at Normand once more. He still watched her, though more with careful curiosity than with his former impertinence. She smiled at him wryly, her confidence returning. Then she slowly stood to meet the level of his bold gaze with her own, smoothing her skirts, and then her hair off her forehead, still beaded with perspiration.

"Well," she said blandly, "I suppose I'll need to prepare for a trip to Grasse."

He smirked, bouncing up again on his toes. "I'm sure Monsieur Carlisle will be pleased to see you."

She raised a brow. "I'm sure that he will."

"And I have patrons who need my attention," he carried on. "Then I'll see someone about selling the diamonds."

He'd said that out of pure spite, reminding her again what it cost her to be given details putting her one step ahead of them all. Frankly, it was a small price to pay for the edge—Samson and dear, sweet, little Olivia weren't aware of what she knew.

Claudette reached behind her and grabbed her parasol. Then in two steps she was upon him. "Enjoy the money you make from my bracelet, Normand. I'm sure you'll spend it wisely."

He nodded once. "I'm sure that I will, Madame Comtesse. I wish you a safe and fruitful journey."

With great joy, she rammed her parasol onto the top of his shoe, pressing down hard on his toes. "You're a bastard, Normand."

And then she moved past him, ignoring his sharp intake of breath and reddening face as she strode with head held high through Nivan and out the front door.

Chapter 14

The last thing Sam wanted to do was travel to Grasse. Jesus, the Mediterranean coast in June? It was hot enough already, and the sweltering heat of southern France would likely kill him. But that's where his brother had taken up residence, and he wasn't about to allow Olivia to travel there by herself, which, by default, made his feelings in the matter moot.

He had been waiting for Olivia, listening for her that early morning following their night of unexpected passion, knowing she might attempt to leave without him and head for Grasse alone. And when she tried to do exactly that, he was ready, following her out the door of Nivan and grasping her arm before she reached her waiting carriage.

Naturally, she'd been furious with him for discovering her intent to leave Paris in pursuit of Edmund herself, but he also realized the fault that made her want to run out on him lay entirely at his feet. He shouldn't have kissed her, coaxed her to climax without her intention, without any consideration of the consequences, especially her feelings. And to take her against her kitchen *wall,* no less. God, what was he thinking? She'd bewitched him, enveloped him in some mysterious ... power. A power she alone possessed, for in all of his good-for-nothing life of past relationships, he didn't think any woman had made him feel the conflicting and unconventional things he felt for Olivia—the untempered lust, the aggravation, the need to tame and seduce and protect. Not even Claudette.

He simply couldn't get her out of his mind, hadn't been able to do so for even a minute since the night of their first meeting in England, a moment that now seemed a lifetime ago. But in every way he could imagine, she entranced and surprised him—her intelligence and unusually keen sense for business; her sweet, engaging laugh; her single-minded determination; and yes, even her innocence. And to make matters between them even more difficult, she truly had to be the most physically goddamned beautiful woman he'd ever seen or personally known. More than anything, though, she confused him to the point of irrationality, and not only was irrationality under any circumstance unlike him, his irrational actions concerning Olivia bothered him more than all the other factors combined.

He'd wanted her so badly the night of the ball, and in response to his urgent and inexplicable need to touch her, she had become desperate for him, even though she denied it. He knew the fairer sex and their responses too well, and he didn't think he'd been with a woman before who had been so ready and wet, had come so fast from his simple stroking. She'd nearly driven him over the edge, and certainly she could feel his response to her climax afterward, when he moved up against her so she could know what she did to him physically.

But was she a virgin? He still had to wonder. She'd reacted to his touch, but that didn't necessarily mean she possessed any real experience. Yet just because she hadn't lain with Edmund didn't mean she hadn't been bedded before, either. She was French, after all, nearly twenty-five years old, and every Frenchwoman he'd ever known had been rather promiscuous. But then maybe he was jaded by his past, which sometimes came back to overwhelm him, and haunt him, as it did by bringing Claudette into his life again after all these years.

Now at last they were nearly to Grasse, the final leg of their journey through Provence to the town of their destination, alone in their hired coach, for which he'd had to pay a pretty penny to ensure a private ride. Their trip thus far had been slow going, as it had rained lightly but steadily since they'd left the city and entered the countryside, only to return to full sunshine yesterday when they traveled through the Gorges Du Loup and passed through field after field of aroma-rich lavender.

He sensed they'd both begun to feel a building anxiousness this morning after a breakfast of tea and brioche, realizing they were almost there. That wasn't to say Olivia was speaking to him, for in fact she refused to utter a word unless she found it positively necessary to do so. He'd allowed her separate quarters when they stopped for the evening, but only after threatening to hunt her down if she left without his knowledge in the middle of the night. He'd been fairly confident in her compliance, as they were traveling to the same place for a singular purpose, and in many respects she needed him, which probably made her all the angrier.

He watched her now as she sat across from him on the padded coach seat, her ivory fan clutched in her hands as they rested on her lap, her eyes closed from the bouncing and steady movement of the ride. Today she'd coiled her plaited hair on top of her head and donned a typical day gown in bright aqua silk, her first opportunity to wear something other than the dark blue traveling gown that she'd insisted was quite comfortable even when buttoned to the neck. Not that it hadn't flattered her figure even then, as Sam decided he could appreciate every one of her attributes no matter what she wore. But of course today was different since they would very soon be confronting the man who had ruined her financially, the man who looked just like him but differed in every other way, and she evidently wanted to look her best and most confident. Her aqua gown, cut squarely and low across her bosom, enhanced her figure, her flushed cheeks and vivid blue eyes, and had to keep her cooler now that the summer heat had returned on the final day of their trip.

She hadn't said much at all to him today, and altogether refused to address their intimate encounter of the other night. There wasn't much to discuss on that end, he supposed, though he hoped she thought about it as often as he did. But now that they neared Grasse, they needed to communicate, needed to exchange ideas and organize their plans. They needed to agree and get along. With that in mind, Sam decided it was time to break the ice and get down to business.

"What are you going to say to my brother when you see him?"

Her eyelashes fluttered open. "I don't know," she replied with only the slightest hesitation. "I'm not sure how to confront him yet."

Considering her determination and general assertiveness, that surprised him. "Would you like me to confront him first?"

"No," she answered curtly.

He leaned his head back against the cushion, holding her gaze. "You can't stay angry with me forever, Olivia."

That certainly got her attention. Her cheeks pinkened as her jaw tightened. "I'm not angry, I'm tired."

"I see." He interlocked his fingers in front of him. "Well, since you're not angry with me, would you like to discuss what happened between us the other night?"

For a moment or two she said nothing. Then she closed her eyes again. "I've already forgotten the incident."

The incident? Sam had to press his lips together to keep from chuckling. "You know, *I* haven't forgotten it, Olivia," he drawled. "I keep reliving it every second of every day." He knew he was baiting her, but for some odd reason he wanted her to know exactly how she affected him in a purely sexual way.

Her nostrils flared in indignation, and then she raised her lashes once more and glared at him. "If I were to relive it, as you say you do," she revealed huskily, "I would be betraying my husband. And even as much as

I despise what he's done to me, I took vows that I intend to honor. It seems the only thing I have left is my word."

That response surprised him. He wasn't used to faithfulness in marriage, or any relationship, and so it hadn't occurred to him that she could be so upset over some perceived weakness of the flesh. Now he understood how deeply his lovemaking had bothered her, and in a way, he admired her for her devotion—as much as it perturbed him that she could so quickly dismiss what they'd shared.

They stared at each other for several long seconds, indecision weighing on every breath he took. And then he decided to hell with the doubts, he wanted her to know the truth, and she needed to be told, before they faced his brother.

"Olivia," he started, sitting up a little as he ran his fingers through his hair, "I have something to tell you that you're not going to like."

She fairly snorted. "I don't know if I can stand any more surprises from you, your grace."

"Stop calling me that," he charged, his own irritation seeping into his tone. "I think we've gone far beyond formalities, don't you?"

She glanced out the window to the lavender-coated hillside, then back again, her features resolute. "I really don't want to play games anymore, Sam."

"I don't either," he returned softly, stretching his legs out in the coach so his feet pushed under the hem of her gown. "No more games. And no more lies."

She tapped her fan on her lap, eyelids narrowed in wariness. "Are you telling me you've lied to me?"

Sam detected the slightest trace of hurt wrapped around her question, and it warmed him within. He smiled vaguely. "No, I've never lied to you, Livi, but I have withheld information."

Her brows gently furrowed and she looked him up and down cautiously. "What information?"

He sighed, then said, "Important, even key information. And it's going to upset you."

She swallowed hard, but otherwise remained rigid in her bearing, no doubt bracing herself for more turmoil. He wished there were a good, easy way to explain everything he knew about her marriage, but he couldn't think of one. Drawing a long, deep breath, he decided to just aim for sincerity.

"I'm going to tell you something, Olivia, and no matter how it makes you feel, I want you to know that it's the truth as I know it."

He waited for her to say something, but she just looked at him.

He leaned forward and put his elbows on his knees, folding his hands together in front of him. "Remember Colin Ramsey, the man you met at the ball in London?"

She tipped her head to the side a fraction. "Yes, of course I do. He's quite difficult to forget."

Sam didn't know if that was good or bad, though the stab of jealousy piercing his chest annoyed him. Colin, the ladies' man—gregarious, charming, flirtatious. Everything he wasn't.

"You liked him, did you?" he asked, regretting the stupid and irrelevant question the moment the words left his mouth.

She smiled wryly. "He's very handsome."

Handsome? That's it? What he'd wanted to hear was that she would never be interested in a man like him, but there was no way on earth he'd ask her to expound on her description of his friend.

He nodded, deciding it best to just move on. "What I'm about to tell you stays between us, do you understand?"

After a long pause, she maintained, "You're going to tell me he's involved in something illicit?"

Without hesitation he murmured, "Yes."

She frowned as she opened her fan, swishing it very slowly in front of her face. "I can't imagine what your friend's...activities have to do with me, sir."

Her continued formality was starting to irritate him. "Livi, love, so help me God, if you call me 'sir' or 'your grace' again when we are alone like this, in private, I'm going to grab you and kiss the living breath out of you."

Her fan stopped moving in midair as her mouth dropped open a little. Then she gritted her teeth and inhaled sharply. "Do not call me 'love,'" she articulated, fanning herself again. "I am not your love, and such informality between us is improper."

Again she'd said something he hadn't anticipated, and her instant and bold denouncement stung him far more than he would have expected. Very softly he replied, "You're certainly not Edmund's love, Olivia, and that's what I want to discuss."

She blinked, unsure, then once more turned her attention to the view outside. "You're talking in circles, Sam."

"So I am, I suppose," he acknowledged through a

sigh. He watched her, noting her rigid posture, the tension emanating from her stoic expression. This was going to hurt her deeply, but he could see no other way to get around the revelation than to just reveal the facts as he knew them. "Let me get to the point."

"Please," she said curtly.

He tapped his fingers together in front of him. "Colin Ramsey is a British agent."

It took seconds for that bit of news to sink in. Then slowly she pulled her gaze from the window, her brows tightly furrowed, gaping at him as if he were completely insane. He continued before she could mention her disbelief.

Gravely, he said, "He specializes in forgery, in forged documents, that he both creates and deciphers for the government. He's very, very good at what he does, is very experienced, and for his unique services they pay him well. He's never been known to fail in detecting a fraudulent work." He paused, watching her closely, then asked, "Do you understand?"

She remained silent for a moment, studying him intently, though she no longer looked annoyed, she looked edgy, twisting her fan in her hands.

Finally, she murmured, "What does he have to do with me?"

Sam had no idea how to put it delicately, so he simply revealed, "I had him review and analyze the marriage license you gave me."

She shook her head a little, uncertain of his words and the meaning behind them. "But I gave you the original," she returned, her tone low and controlled. "Not the copy. If he thought it was a forgery, then he's mistaken."

"He's not mistaken," he said gently. "The marriage document you and Edmund signed, the *original* document, isn't legal."

She stilled, her eyes opening wide with incredulity. "That's not possible." She drew a shaky breath. "I spoke vows; I was married by a priest—"

"Olivia," he cut in, his voice deeply solemn, "I suspect you spoke those vows in front of a hired actor."

He couldn't take his eyes off her. She blinked quickly, her features expressing shock coupled with confusion, suspicion coupled with anguish. He'd expected the heartache, and so felt the uncanny need to experience it with her. Edmund had hurt her profoundly, and that in itself made him despise his brother anew.

"I—I can't believe you," she whispered after a moment, her eyes brimming with tears she desperately tried not to shed in front of him.

"Tell me," he urged after a long, deep breath, "was Edmund eager to announce your nuptials to Society?"

The question surprised her, and she hesitated before answering. "No. Because we'd married so quickly after our first introduction, he told me it would be better to wait and I agreed with him."

"I see. So it might well be that outside of your Parisian circles people still don't know about your supposed marriage."

"Probably not."

He ran a palm harshly down his face. "I would suggest he's posing as a bachelor. Why do you think he's in Grasse, courting another unsuspecting heiress? Because he *can*. Why do you think he didn't bed you on your wedding night? Because taking you would not only complicate his plan of continued detachment from you emotionally, he could impregnate you, a risk he would never take because he *expected,* from the moment you met each other, to leave you. He had no intention of chancing the obstacle of an unwanted child, which, in a very sick way, was probably the most honorable thing he's ever done in his life." He paused for a few seconds, then said fervently, "Every fact in this sordid scheme indicates that you're not married to Edmund, Olivia. And as much as that realization cheers me personally, I would never lie to you about this. *Never.*"

It took her several long minutes, it seemed, to come to terms with his pronouncement, his explanations and rationale, and what they meant to her and her relationship with his brother. She lowered her lashes and stared at her lap, her body very still, her breathing steady, nearly silent. At last she whispered, *"Why?"*

She couldn't understand the insult, the reason for the deception, any more than he could. "Edmund is a deceitful bastard, and always has been. There's no other explanation of why he does the things he does beyond his own personal selfishness."

She looked up again, her face pale, features slack, her watery gaze melding with his as she contemplated the lies, searched for answers. "And my aunt knew of this, planned it with him."

"Yes," he replied, fighting the urge to reach over and touch her, knowing if he tried, she'd rebuff him quickly. "I'm sure of it."

Finally she straightened her shoulders and shook herself, rubbing her eyes with one thumb and forefinger then wiping a cheek with her palm. "Do you—"

She cleared her throat, squeezed her fan with both hands. "Do you think they're lovers?"

Sam felt his insides twist in knots. She stared at her lap, unable to look at him, exuding a sweetness that melted his heart. "Olivia..."

She snickered bitterly. "You do, don't you?"

Sitting back on the seat cushion, with keen tenderness he admitted, "I think they've been lovers for years."

She shook her head, then leaned her temple against the side of the coach, staring out at the passing landscape.

He had no idea what to say to her, and so he remained quiet as well, resting his head on the cushion behind him, noting how the day had passed quickly and they were very near the outskirts of the town. They had to find a place to stay the night, gather their thoughts, make a plan of action, and later face the enemy that was his brother.

"Why didn't you tell me this before, Sam?"

He turned his head to look at her again. She remained as she had before, gazing out the window. After a few long seconds of thought he replied, "I didn't know if you were lying to me, if you and Edmund had planned this scheme together to swindle me of some of *my* inheritance." He drew in a full breath, then added hesitatingly, "I didn't know if I could trust you."

She shook her head. "What makes you think you can trust me now?"

"I don't know," he replied at once. "I really don't know why I trust you, but I do. And that's the most honest answer I can give you."

She shifted her body in her seat, eyeing him askance. "I hate you for not telling me until now," she whispered, a dark anger penetrating her voice.

He felt like a worm. Expelling a slow breath, he said, "I know. I'm sorry."

She just watched him, caressing the smooth ivory of her fan back and forth with her fingertips, her expression guarded. Then to his complete shock, she placed her fan on the cushion next to her and raised her body off the moving coach seat to cross over to his side, sliding herself in next to him, her gown spilling over his legs. She scrutinized every feature of his face, his chest, and shoulders. And then she reached out, wrapping her arms around his neck to hug him tightly, tucking her face under his chin.

"I hate you, Sam," she whispered up to his earlobe. She kissed his jawline once before cradling herself against him. "I hate you—but I need you so badly. God help me, but you're the only person I trust in the world."

A curious sense of unreality enveloped him, clouding his sensible, thinking mind with a fine mist of bewildering feelings he couldn't at all comprehend, or tame. He had no idea what to say, what she expected him to do, if anything. She smelled like heaven, felt so soft, and for the first time that he could recall, he relished in the closeness of a woman without the slightest sexual intent. He twisted his body in the seat a little so he could wrap his arms around her and hold her with ease.

She relaxed her grip a little, and after a few moments of silence she murmured, "Thank you."

Sam ached to kiss her right here in the coach, to caress her fears away, her anger and anguish, to explore every bit of emotion she brought out in him, to show her how he cared about her and her future.

As if reading his thoughts, she suddenly, and without warning, leaned up and placed her lips on his, gingerly, not moving but just lightly touching him. He felt her longing, her loneliness, in that one brush of warmth, and a nearly inaudible growl rolled in his throat. But he didn't move, didn't push for more, knowing the time for passion would come later. Every doubt about his need of her, his desire to be a part of her, became instantly clear, had in fact vanished the moment she confessed her trust in him. He would wait for her, but there was no longer a question that she would be his.

Gradually, she pulled away and sat up, withdrawing her arms from around him and relaxing them in her lap. Her gaze roved over his face, pausing at his lips, his hair and eyes, her forehead crinkled with a trace of curiosity—or puzzlement.

"I know what you're thinking," she said at last.

He smiled to himself, knowing fully well she had no idea at all. "You do?"

She nodded slowly, eyes narrowed in careful thought. "You want to pretend, to make Edmund think you and I are married."

Truthfully, he hadn't thought of that at all, and for a moment he wondered what good it would do. But pretending to be married to her would certainly add to the confusion, and it might make for a very satisfying time. Actually, it might be the best way to confront his brother and catch him off guard.

"Can you act that well, Lady Olivia?" he drawled teasingly.

She swiftly left his side to sit across from him once again, eyeing him mischievously, a sly grin playing across her mouth as she smoothed her skirt back into place. Then she tipped her shoulders toward him, allowing him a scant view of her cleavage. "I won't even have to, my darling man," she murmured huskily. "I think you're enraptured already."

He smirked. "You're very good."

"Only of necessity," she replied, sitting back for a final time, lifting her fan again and opening it.

He closed his eyes, leaning his head against the cushion.

"Sam?" she whispered seconds later.

"Hmm?"

She paused, then softly admitted, "I really don't hate you at all."

He grinned, peeking at her through half-open lashes. "I know. I don't hate you, either, Livi."

Chapter 15

Although their families had always been rather close, Olivia hadn't seen Brigitte Marcotte in years, and yet she had no trouble spotting the woman the moment she walked into the dining room of Grasse's Maison de la Fleur, the hotel in which she and Sam had taken up residence two days ago. Against Sam's better judgment, she had wanted to meet Brigitte alone somewhere in the town where Edmund wouldn't likely appear to interrupt them, and as she and Sam had inquired upon their arrival, he wasn't staying at the hotel. Olivia felt more than ready to confront him, but she decided it might be better to let the Govance heiress know exactly what kind of deceitful man Edmund was, realizing that Brigitte might have already lost her heart to the cad, making their encounter this afternoon uncomfortable. Even so, Olivia decided she had no choice but to enlighten the woman.

Originally, Sam had wanted the two of them to con-front Edmund first, to surprise him with their unex-pected presence, relaying the information they had regarding his nefarious behavior and the shocking news about his underhanded relationship with Claudette. But after a day and a half of quietly inquiring in the town, they learned nothing about him or his whereabouts. They knew he was here, but decided he had to be stay-ing at the Govance estate, which, Olivia mused, could make their situation far more complicated if he'd be-come close with the family. The only way to be certain was to talk to Brigitte.

So yesterday Olivia had sent a note, inviting Brigitte to tea at the hotel today at four. The dining room matched the ambience of the town, with its small dis-plays of local artwork, petite handcrafted vases of freshly cut flowers on every white, Provincial-style ta-ble. She had chosen one next to the window, near the back of the room, where they could share their words in private, unsure how Brigitte would take the news that the charming, handsome man who courted her cared only for her fortune.

Now, as Brigitte entered the establishment, Olivia stood, catching the woman's eye immediately. She waved a hand and Brigitte smiled and began to walk toward her.

Although now nearly twenty, the young Govance heiress hadn't changed much in the few years since Olivia had last seen her. She had always been a rather tall, lanky child, blond with fair skin and a trace of freckles across her nose. Now she simply looked older—still thin, but she'd plaited her long hair atop her head, and her face, though never what one would call engaging or beautiful, had taken on a soft femininity that Olivia found attractive, even pretty. She no longer bounded like a child, but walked gracefully toward her in a day gown of deep lavender and wide hoops that added to her slight figure and fair coloring rather than detracting from them.

Olivia returned the smile as the woman approached the table. "Brigitte, how good it is to see you after all these years," she said with genuine delight.

"I can't believe it!" Brigitte grasped her shoulders with both hands, her lavender reticule dangling from a gloved wrist as she leaned in to drop a peck on both cheeks. "Getting your note was such a surprise."

Olivia gestured to the opposite chair, then sat again in her own. Immediately, their *garçon* brought them tea for two, as she'd ordered, and two individual plates of delicious smelling *tarte aux myrtilles,* placing them on the table between them, then excusing himself with a nod.

"I'm sure it must have been a surprise, as I haven't been to Grasse since Monsieur Nivan died," Olivia started, wanting to get to the point before she lost the nerve. "But I do have a reason for being here today."

Brigitte took no time in helping herself to tea, quickly pouring hers into her delicate, gold inlaid china cup and adding two teaspoons of sugar, which she stirred with dainty fingers.

"Oh, I expected as much," the younger woman replied as she turned her concentration to her blueberry tart. "I gather you've invited me here today to discuss Edmund?"

Olivia nearly fell off her chair. As she'd told Sam, Edmund had wanted to keep their marriage arrangements discreet. And yet Brigitte clearly knew of her acquaintance with the man, and that he was the reason for her unexpected visit to the south of France.

Brigitte seemed to anticipate her astonishment. Her mouth turned up into a crooked grin of self-satisfaction as she met Olivia's gaze and leaned back casually in her chair.

"Edmund told me all about your romantic debacle," she disclosed pleasantly. "I certainly hope you haven't come all this way in the hopes of stealing him back from me, because frankly I don't think he'd be interested."

Olivia must have been gaping at the woman, for she suddenly laughed, tossing her head back and then shaking it.

"I see I've startled you with that news," Brigitte said, cutting into her tart again, "but yes, Edmund told me all about what happened between you."

Olivia's mouth had gone dry and she reached for the cream to pour a dash into her full cup of tea. Finding her voice at last, she replied, "What exactly did he tell you, Brigitte?"

The woman shrugged as she swallowed a mouthful of blueberries. Then she placed her spoon on her plate, patted her lips with her lace napkin, and folded her hands in her lap, staring across the table with her head tipped to the side, her expression thoughtful. "He told me that he thought he was in love with you, but after you broke his heart, he realized otherwise." Cheerfully, she added, "But all the better for me. I hope you haven't come to Grasse thinking to win back his devotion."

Olivia noted that it was the second time she'd mentioned the notion of her wanting to regain Edmund's affections, leading her to believe it might be a concern for Brigitte. But then Brigitte, as she remembered her, had always been a bit skittish.

Recovering herself, Olivia took a sip from her china cup, finding the flavor weak by her standards but deciding that hardly mattered when her entire plan of saving the poor Govance heiress had just been tossed out the window.

"I don't have any intention of wooing him back," she admitted, a bit too sternly. Then deciding it best to just get to the point, the truth, she finally asked, "What exactly did Edmund say about our relationship, about his marrying me?"

That struck a nerve, as Brigitte's gray-blue eyes narrowed and her lips thinned to a flat, unbecoming line. "He told me how you so callously left him days before the wedding, breaking his heart, which I'm grateful to say I've been able to heal with my constant devotion."

This totally unforeseen development positively stunned Olivia into speechlessness. She never imagined that Edmund would be so devious in not only courting an innocent lady on false pretenses, but adding to the story with outright lies to further his disgusting plan. It appeared he'd thought of everything, even the fact that his first faux wife might catch up to him by coming to Grasse to "save" the unsuspecting heiress. The only advantage she seemed to have left was the fact that Edmund couldn't possibly ever consider that she'd bring Sam. That would be his greatest shock of all, and suddenly Olivia couldn't wait to witness their meeting face-to-face.

Her tea forgotten, Olivia leaned back in her chair as well, eyeing the woman speculatively. "Brigitte, you're not going to like hearing this, but Edmund lied to you. He lied to both of us—"

"Nonsense," she cut in sharply with a toss of her hand. "He has no reason to lie." Suddenly she sat forward, resting her palms on the edge of the table, the smooth lines of her face hardening, her cheeks glowing bright pink. "You may not like hearing *this,* Olivia, but Edmund loves me, and I don't intend to throw him aside because you make false claims about him. He has proposed, and I have accepted, and we're to be married in a month." Slowly she relaxed again into her seat. "Now, if you've come here to win back his love, you have my blessing to try. But any devious scheme you might arrange won't work. I can promise you that. He's the most devoted man I've ever known, and he's still quite angry at you for what you did to him."

Olivia felt a swell of intense anger and frustration flow through her, appeased only by her knowledge that the woman sitting across from her would soon feel the anguish she had, and didn't deserve it, either.

With graceful self-restraint, she asked, "Did he tell you about his brother? That he also has a sister?"

Brigitte blinked, then frowned, seemingly taken aback by the question. "Of course."

Olivia wasn't altogether certain she believed her. Her answer seemed a touch too defensive, though at this point she didn't think Brigitte would admit it even if she had no knowledge of Edmund's siblings.

She leaned forward once more, her voice lowered in admonishment. "Brigitte, I . . . believe that Edmund is after your inheritance, everything that will be rightfully yours when your *grand-père* dies—"

Brigitte abruptly stood, glaring at her, her lips contorted into a crooked smirk. "Say what you will, Olivia, but I know Edmund—have known him for months. He cannot be such a great actor that he can completely fool me, *and* my family, with a professed love he doesn't feel."

Oh, yes he can. She fisted her hands in her lap. "He did it to me."

Brigitte closed her eyes and shook her head. After a full inhale, she opened them again, staring down through tear-glazed eyes, her spine rigid, voice controlled.

"You know, Olivia, I may not be as beautiful as you, as graceful or alluring, but I am ready to marry a man you chose not to marry yourself. Perhaps he doesn't love me as he loved you, but for me that's irrelevant. He's devoted to me, to Govance and my family, and he will make a good husband, just as I know I'll make him a good wife."

Olivia simply had no idea what to say, how to react to such determination, such blind infatuation. Brigitte was headstrong and clearly entranced by Edmund's handsomeness, his charm, which she understood all too well. It had worked on her, and she had been utterly fooled by a devious blackguard. Would *she* have listened to Brigitte if he'd courted and cheated her first in Grasse, leaving her on their wedding night, then come to Paris to set his nefarious pursuits on her as the heiress of Nivan? Very likely not—because Edmund was just that good at seducing a woman with false love. For the first time, Olivia felt she'd been wrong to meet Brigitte ahead of time, though truthfully there was no way for her to know just how far Edmund had dug his talons into this innocent woman's neck.

"I'm sorry," she conveyed through a sigh, reaching up to place a palm on the other woman's arm. "I—I didn't want to upset you. That was never my intention." Deciding this was the moment for her ploy to be revealed, she maintained, "Of course, if Edmund is your choice, I wish you only years of happiness. Besides, my feelings for him are moot. I am married to someone else."

Brigitte physically slumped into her stays, her features going slack in sheer relief that she couldn't begin to hide. "I'm sorry, too, Olivia. I'm sorry that you chose to leave him heartbroken, but because you did, he eventually found me, and I am happy." She inhaled deeply and tried to smile. "And, because I am so sure of Edmund's devotion, I cordially invite you to attend our engagement gathering, this Friday evening at seven, followed by our engagement ball Saturday night."

Olivia's brows rose as her heart began to race. This would be the perfect opportunity for enlightenment, for all of them. "I'd be delighted," she replied, hoping she didn't sound too enthusiastic.

"Friday's affair will be small, allowing for few local acquaintances," Brigitte carried on, the pace of her words quickening with her excitement. "Saturday's ball will, naturally, be the event of the Season. Nearly every Govance patron and the local elite will be in attendance." She clutched her reticule to her waist with both hands. "Grand-père has always adored you and your mother, Olivia, and I'm sure he'd want to see you again after all these years. He would never forgive me if he learned you were in Grasse and weren't invited."

Olivia slowly stood to meet the younger woman's gaze. Cautiously, she asked, "Does he know about Edmund and me?"

"Grand-père? *Non,*" Brigitte answered defiantly, seemingly surprised at the question. "I have no reason to tell him, and if you do, it will only make you look selfish and spiteful."

That was very likely true. Olivia clasped her hands behind her back. "Then I sincerely look forward to attending both of your engagement parties." Her voice caught in her throat. "May I, um, bring my husband?"

Brigitte brightened considerably at the notion. "Please, of course. I'm sure Edmund would enjoy meeting him."

You have no idea . . . "Good," she said, smiling in return. Then, with purpose, she rubbed her jaw with her fingers, her brows furrowed in thought. "May I suggest you don't mention my visit to him?"

"To Edmund? He's in Nice, making arrangements for our honeymoon, and won't be returning until Friday. And besides," she fairly retorted, "I wouldn't dream of it. I wouldn't want to upset him days before our big celebration."

Which, Olivia realized, meant Brigitte absolutely had doubts about her betrothed and his past. Perhaps that was for the best, as the entire sordid truth was to reveal itself at the party this weekend. And, she decided, the revelation would be better before the wedding than after.

"I will see you Friday, then," she said.

Brigitte leaned in and dutifully kissed her cheeks. "On Friday, dear Olivia. And *merci* for the tea."

She turned on her heel, made ready for her departure, then paused, glancing back over her shoulder. "Why did you come to Grasse? Certainly you wouldn't have come all the way here just to confront Edmund and me when you've married another man."

She grinned. "It was time to visit Govance, to see for myself which fragrances you've chosen for the season. I only heard of your engagement when my husband and I arrived."

That seemed to satisfy the woman. She raised her chin minutely, almost triumphantly. "It *has* been the talk of the town."

And then with a wave, she pivoted around and fairly waltzed from the dining room.

Chapter 16

By mutual agreement they'd decided that she alone would attend tonight's party. After much discussion, she and Sam had come to the conclusion that it would be better for her to see Brigitte and Edmund together, in the company of others, so she could view his reaction to her arrival, could witness his relationship with Brigitte and her family, and do so in a place where she would be perfectly safe and unlikely to arouse his verbal ire. He couldn't exactly expose her as his "former wife" or victim around the Govance family and those she knew in the business who would no doubt be in attendance. Edmund couldn't do anything to her, or say anything revealing, and yet his reaction to her presence would be telling indeed. So they'd decided to startle him, to confuse and shock him. Tonight would be the tease; tomorrow night the full confrontation.

She had no greater desire than to see Edmund squirm in front of his family-to-be. She yearned, more than anything, to waltz up to the man, act as if she were only there for Brigitte, and see what he'd do. The satisfaction to come was going to be enormous.

And so, donning an evening gown of scarlet satin with short puffed sleeves and a low scooped neckline, her best ruby earrings, and curling her hair atop her head, Olivia left Sam at the hotel, promising she would go to the party, make her appearance, her excuses, and return quickly as he'd insisted, then met her hired coach at seven o'clock.

Tonight she felt edgy, her heart thumping double-time, her nerves on end. In the three days since meeting Brigitte for tea, she'd dealt with an odd mix of emotions rumbling through her, not all of them good. She and Sam hadn't said much to each other, had more or less kept to themselves, and it seemed his mood had darkened as well. She'd taken a day to visit the Govance boutique in the center of town, then their warehouse, learning what she could about their newest scents and expectations for the coming season and year. Sam had declined to accompany her, which she took for nothing more than a lack of interest on his part. At least she hoped that's all it was. She had, however, found it difficult to concentrate on her business, as her mind wandered constantly to him, to facing Edmund and the coming weekend. They shared the same hotel suite but slept in separate bedchambers, and he hadn't been much for words, she assumed, because he was doing his own planning on just how he would finally reveal himself to the brother he hadn't seen in a decade.

Olivia didn't understand the animosity Sam held for Edmund, and Sam had been tight-lipped about the cause, or causes, as the case might be. She hadn't pressed him to reveal his thoughts, but her curiosity had started to get the better of her now that they were so close to the confrontation. To that end, she could hardly wait till all was revealed.

They hadn't devised much of a plan of action beyond general ideas, though they agreed to continue the pretense of being a married couple, mostly because they were sharing the same hotel suite and those in Grasse who knew her would question her decency, if not her sanity for doing so, without being properly wed. In a manner, she would be looking out for her business, and at this point in her life Nivan mattered to her more than anything else. The only thing that worried her was what would become of her reputation once they all learned the truth, which, she was afraid, would happen eventually. But she couldn't think about that now. All that mattered tonight was facing the man who'd tried to destroy her.

Her ride to the Govance estate went quickly, and she soon found herself alighting the brown brick steps to the high house proper, its dark beige colors, now lit up by torchlight, blending into the floral-splashed hillside and vineyards beyond. Two footmen in formal livery stood by the large, wooden front door to greet arriving guests, acknowledging her only with a nod as they opened it for her to enter.

Olivia hadn't been to the estate in several years, but her first thought as she stood in the entryway, now completely lamplit, brightened for the coming party, was how nothing had changed. Three stories in height, the inside, decorated in muted shades of tan, gold, and purple, complemented lavender hillsides and outdoor landscaping, as well as the bronze *d'ore* chandeliers, wrought-iron wall sconces, and an array of floral tapestries and area rugs scattered throughout the first-floor rooms.

She carried only a ruby-colored reticule and her gold-inlaid ivory fan and so had nothing to leave with the butler when he led her toward the drawing room where guests would first meet for hors d'oeuvres and champagne.

Drawing a deep breath to calm herself, she knew the moment for revelation now belonged to her, and so with great aplomb she straightened her spine, shoulders back, and walked in. Immediately, she became aware of a lull in conversation as several people, most of whom she knew, were hushed by her surprising arrival.

Her eyes darted about the scene for her first look at the man whom she'd once thought to be her husband. She soon grew disappointed, though, to note he wasn't yet among the crowd. Neither was Brigitte, which left her to mingle with family and acquaintants, the majority of whom worked in the perfume industry for the House of Govance, until the two guests of honor made their respective appearances.

Olivia smiled as her eyes fell on Ives-Francois Marcotte, Brigitte's late mother's father, the patriarch of the Govance estate and fortune, and the only surviving member of the family outside of Brigitte's father, who lived in Belgium with his second wife and their children.

He spotted her at once as she began to walk toward him, his eyes lighting up with his grin as he moved away from the cold grate, from his conversation with a gentleman she didn't know, to meet her halfway.

"Grand-père Marcotte," she said with genuine warmth, reaching up on her toes to kiss his cheeks. "How good it is to see you."

"Ah, Olivia," he remarked, grasping her shoulders and holding her at arm's length to view her up and down. "You look just like your mother did twenty-five years ago, and just as beautiful."

"You look wonderful, too, and just as handsome as ever." And he did, she thought, considering he had to be nearing the age of seventy-five or so, his hair still thick but now totally white, his brilliant blue eyes exuding intelligence and rigorous health.

He grinned, shaking his head. "I'm an old man, but I suppose my daily walks through the hills keep me breathing and content."

"As does good wine?" she hinted with a sly curve of her lips.

Chuckling, he replied, "But of course. One should never live life without good wine."

She gently patted his hand, which still rested on her shoulder. "Then I have no doubt that you'll be living and breathing for another thirty years."

"God willing, dear child, God willing." He dropped his arms to his sides. "I'm sure you know most of the guests here. Tonight is just a small gathering to introduce Monsieur Carlisle to friends, but tomorrow is the ball, as I assume Brigitte told you. She was quite happily surprised to see you after all these years, so I do hope you intend to come for that as well."

Olivia had to wonder if Brigitte also mentioned that

she'd been very well acquainted with his granddaughter's betrothed, or that she was now married, but decided not to remark on either for now. "I wouldn't miss it, Grand-père Marcotte." She glanced around the room. "And where is Brigitte?"

He stuffed his hands in the pockets of his charcoal gray evening jacket. "Oh, I think she is still dressing; you know how ladies are."

She laughed lightly, nodding once. "Indeed I do."

"But Monsieur Carlisle is here...somewhere." He looked around the room as well. "Brigitte says you've met him?"

It was a question, not a statement, and she felt compelled to simply play along with the answer she'd practiced. "Yes, of course. He's well acquainted with my aunt Claudette."

His thick white brows lifted with apparent surprise. "He didn't mention the Comtesse Renier, but I suppose that makes sense, especially since he knows you from his travels in Paris."

"I'm sure that's how they became acquainted."

"And how is Nivan faring?" he asked, lowering his voice.

She lightly shrugged, thankful for the change in subject. "We're doing very well, I suppose. Thank goodness for Normand and his keen sense for business. He's helped us keep the important patronage of many of the elites, including the Empress Eugenie."

"Ah, very good, very good." He leaned over, his aged eyes sparkling. "She's such a fastidious lady when it comes to fragrance, isn't she? But of course you never heard that from me."

Olivia laughed good-naturedly. "Never!"

He pulled back a little, catching the eye of someone over her shoulder. "I should socialize, my dear. But please, Olivia, while you're in Grasse, step over to the shop and sample some of our newest collections from Asia. I'd certainly like your opinion."

Or to sell me some, she thought with a grin. "I've already done that, Grand-père Marcotte, and I've decided to sample some things to be sent to Nivan later in the year, as the Season warrants."

"Wonderful," he replied, quite pleased. He took her gloved hands in his and held them gently. "It's so good to see you, Olivia. Enjoy the party, won't you?"

More than you could ever possibly know. "I'm sure I shall."

"Good."

And with that, he released her hands, patted her cheek, and took his leave.

Standing alone near the fireplace by the south wall, Olivia turned to face the center of the drawing room, searching for her first glimpse of Edmund, admitting to herself that although she felt more than ready to see him again, she'd never been more nervous in her life. She noticed several people whom she knew by name or reputation, and after exchanging pleasantries with two ladies who purchased perfume in Grasse for their local Paris boutique, she made her way toward the opposite end of the room, by the doorway that led to the adjoining dining hall, standing next to a walnut carved *buffet de chasse,* which put her in a far better position to view both entrances at once.

Too wound up to eat, she instead chose one of a

dozen filled champagne flutes sitting on the marble buffet top, taking three or four quick swallows to help keep her anxiety in check. Although Sam had agreed to their so-called plan of attack, she realized he still had misgivings about allowing her to attend alone tonight. He hadn't said as much, but she knew his facial expressions well now, witnessed his reluctance in the tightened planes of his face, in a gaze that sharply focused on her as she left him standing in front of the hotel on her quest to meet Edmund before he did. Even now at the party, attempting to concentrate on the coming moment she'd envisioned for months, she couldn't keep her mind off the brother who distracted her with a look, a kiss, a touch, couldn't quite push from her mind the memory of the way he'd made her body respond that night in her kitchen, a momentous event that had been terribly inappropriate on his part, horribly immoral on hers, and totally, inexplicably... heaven.

Sam. Sam. Sam...

Abruptly, she stood erect, heart racing, her keen eyes suddenly focusing on the subject of her anger and all her sorrowful regrets. From the dining hall doorway she spotted the snake of her mission, standing as tall and stately as ever in all his handsome glory, gazing down to a beaming Brigitte whose ten manicured fingers curled around his elbow as she clung tightly to his arm.

Olivia's mouth went dry as she backed up a step or two, nestling herself between the buffet and a large lady with wide hoops, taking a few seconds to catch her breath and observe the cad before he noticed her.

Tonight he wore an evening suit in rich navy, a sky blue waistcoat and white silk shirt, and navy and white striped cravat. He'd kept his hair the length she remembered, but he'd trimmed it behind the ears and combed it back off his face, as Sam did.

It occurred to her that although the two men were physically identical, Sam had a far more overbearing presence than did his younger brother, possibly due to being raised by birth order expectations, but more likely out of different personality traits. Sam always looked staggeringly handsome and aloof; Edmund always looked jovial and…sly. Sly and happy, she supposed, exactly as he appeared now, smiling down to his betrothed.

Brigitte gazed up to his face lovingly as applause and conversation broke out among the party guests by their arrival together. The bride-to-be seemed radiant, and obviously not at all worried about who might be in attendance to ruin the evening. Edmund, too, seemed positively free of concern, which either meant Brigitte had kept her word about not telling him of their meeting at tea, or he simply didn't care, so sure of his lady's devotion and his own plan of attack.

Brigitte's *grand-père* made a quick introduction, offered a toast of good wishes, then the couple began mingling as party guests turned back to their smaller groups of laughter and discussion, sampling champagne and hors d'oeuvres. Olivia scrutinized the two of them from her position in the corner, noting how Brigitte had chosen to wear an evening gown of sky-blue satin and white lace flounces to harmonize with Edmund's attire. She carried herself with ease in medium-wide hoops, her hair parted in the middle with two long, blond plaits wrapped up in circles around her ears. She wore little jewelry and no cosmetics that Olivia could see, and yet she looked rather beautiful, even glowing, no doubt due to the excitement of the evening and her wedding to come.

For a second or two Olivia felt a tinge of guilt at her desire to intrude on such an eventful occasion—until she reminded herself why she'd come in the first place, and how much this man had hurt her and intended to dupe Brigitte in exactly the same manner. With such resolution deeply set, she decided it was time to approach the happy couple and offer her congratulations.

Gathering every bit of strength and wisdom she possessed, she placed what remained of her drink on the walnut sideboard to her right, then lifted her skirts and walked with confidence toward Edmund, who now stood in the center of the drawing room, champagne in hand.

Brigitte noticed her first, looking her up and down, her expression overflowing with assessment. Then she pulled at Edmund's sleeve until he turned away from his discussion with two older gentlemen and leaned over so she could whisper in his ear. Suddenly, his head popped up and he cast his eyes upon her for the first time.

It was, indeed, a priceless moment. Edmund's typical, calculated smile vanished, his face physically paled, as he gazed upon her striding nonchalantly in his direction. And the only thing running through her mind at the moment was that she wished—oh, how she *wished*!—Sam was here to see this.

With a smile of pure, untempered satisfaction, she

walked up to them, her reticule and fan in her left hand as she held out the other for Brigitte to take.

"Dearest, Brigitte, you look positively radiant tonight," she said brightly as she leaned in to lightly kiss her cheeks. Then she stood back and placed her attention on Edmund the Snake.

Brigitte was the first to speak. "Darling, you remember the Lady Olivia Shea, from the House of Nivan."

Edmund blinked as if momentarily confounded, eyeing her from head to foot, clearly trying to come to terms with the fact that she actually stood in front of him, composed, polite, and inviting him to react first. She reached out with her hand, palm down, offering him her knuckles.

"Good evening, Monsieur Carlisle," she said, greeting him amiably with an innocent smile.

At last he recovered himself, realizing, she supposed, that he'd do well to acknowledge her and that she wasn't going to immediately embarrass him or start a rant.

"Of course. Lady Olivia." He cleared his throat as he grasped her fingers and raised her knuckles to his lips. "You look...well."

His hand felt cold and clammy, his panic certainly making him sweat. She grinned, prizing this moment of awkwardness for him. "It's lovely to see you again, and under such...incredible circumstances."

His smile flattened as his brows furrowed minutely. "Indeed. I had no idea that you were acquainted with the Marcottes, or the House of Govance."

Lying snake. "Well, how marvelous for all of us, *non*?" She opened her fan and began swishing it lightly in front of her. "Of course you know that my aunt Claudette has family in Grasse, though it's true I haven't been here personally in years. How fortunate that I'm able to attend this occasion in celebration of your upcoming marriage."

Watching her suspiciously, a pert little smile still smugly displayed on her mouth, Brigitte asked rather boldly, "And where is *your* husband, Olivia? I thought he was going to join you tonight."

Timed perfectly, such a shocking revelation couldn't have stunned Edmund more. His body jerked back a fraction as his face began to redden.

Without allowing him the ability to chime in, she returned without pause, "I'm afraid he's feeling a bit under the weather today, though he does send his best."

"I'm so sorry," Brigitte replied with only a trace of feeling, rubbing her palm up and down Edmund's sleeve.

She sighed. "Yes, well, you know, it's been so hot here."

Brigitte shook her head. "Oh, unusually so."

"And of course, being from England, he's not used to so much constant sunshine."

"True," the younger woman agreed with slightly furrowed brows. "I don't think it's rained in a week or more."

She carried on with the pleasantries. "Not since we've been here, I'm afraid."

Edmund's eyes had narrowed noticeably as they bored into hers. "You've married," he stated bluntly.

He sounded positively ridiculous to her, as if he were

digesting the information with infinite slowness. "Yes," she answered simply, directing her attention to him.

"And to an Englishman, darling, just like you," Brigitte added, gently squeezing his arm, which she had yet to release.

"Yes, come to think of it, he is rather like you, monsieur," she thoroughly enjoyed repeating, tilting her head as she scrutinized him from head to foot. "Though I do think he's taller, if only by a quarter of an inch or so."

"But he couldn't possibly be as handsome," Brigitte fairly purred, gazing up to his face.

Edmund smiled down at his betrothed—a particularly false smile, in her opinion, but then he had to be fuming right now, his mind racing with comments and questions he couldn't possibly ask. Olivia didn't think she could savor the moment more.

"Oh, but of course *I* think he's just as handsome," she countered, drawing her view back to Brigitte as she closed her fan again, holding it in front of her with both hands. "But then isn't that what all wives think of their own husbands?"

"Oh, *oui*," Brigitte concurred.

"So I suppose you and your husband are staying at the Maison de la Fleur?" Edmund asked, his tone cool, assessing.

"Oh, naturally," she replied with an innocent flair, deciding he'd find out if he wanted to, regardless of whether she told him. "We believe it's the nicest place in Grasse, and I didn't want to intrude on extended family when we arrived without notice."

"Naturally," he repeated, studying her intently. Then, with a sly lift of his lips, he asked, "Since he's from

England, perhaps I know him. What, may I ask, is his name?"

Olivia scolded herself for not previously considering that he might inquire about the man, even if it was a stupid question, considering he hadn't been to his native country in years and couldn't possibly know even a fraction of the population. But more to the point, if she mentioned Sam's name, Edmund would come to them tonight, at the hotel, and confront them there, which she absolutely did not want to happen when they weren't prepared for it. No, she wanted full revelation tomorrow night, at the ball, for all to witness.

Without a second thought she murmured, "His name is John. John Andrews. He's a banker from London."

His brows rose minutely as he scrutinized every inch of her, searching for hidden lies. "A banker?" he replied.

She beamed, thoroughly proud of herself for her ingenuity. "Yes, actually. He's helping me sort through my finances."

She could have sworn Edmund snorted.

Brigitte gaped at her. "Nivan is having financial difficulties?" she asked, her first question of genuine interest.

She scoffed, waving her hand in dismissal. "Oh, no, no, of course not. Our sales have been most appropriate for the year so far." She shot a quick glance at Edmund then looked back to Brigitte. "No, really, Monsieur Andrews has just been a gem in helping me restructure my *personal* inheritance. It seems," she added through a snicker, dropping her voice, "that by examination of the paperwork, I've apparently . . . lost some of it."

"Oh, I see," Brigitte murmured seconds later, her voice growing distant.

Edmund, body taut, face expressionless except for his flaring nostrils, looked as if he were ready to jump out of his skin. Or lunge for her throat. His innocent bride-to-be seemed completely oblivious to his posture of fury, though she now frowned, probably realizing that by touching on the subject of inheritances, Olivia risked exposing her belief that Edmund was after the Govance fortune through marriage. Although thrilled with her performance thus far, Olivia wasn't ready for a clash of wills, or a rush of tears.

Quickly, she brushed it all aside with a shake of her head and a light shrug. "I suppose keeping track of one's fortune just shouldn't be placed in the hands of ladies. Or at least that's what my husband says."

Edmund had no reply to that, but his face had hardened to stone; Brigitte simply nodded.

"Well, I suppose I shouldn't keep you two any longer," she said breezily, glancing around the room. "Goodness, so many people are here to celebrate and I'm taking all of your time." She looked back at them, smiling. "Perhaps we'll get a chance to chat later."

Brigitte brightened with obvious relief. "Yes, I suppose we should mingle, shouldn't we, darling?"

At that perfect moment, two older ladies Olivia didn't personally know interrupted the three of them with hugs and good wishes, and she backed up a step to allow them space.

With a final, meaningful look into Edmund's cold eyes, Olivia turned her back to him and walked toward the buffet table for another glass of champagne, this one sorely needed as she shivered within and her hands began to shake.

Her next responsibility would be to quickly take her leave, to make her excuses and head back to the safety of Sam's strong arms and the solid walls of the Maison de la Fleur. She felt exposed here, certain Edmund would keep a sharp eye on her, perhaps confront her if given opportunity, though she couldn't think of a reason he could draw upon to leave Brigitte's side for any length of time to speak to her privately.

Reaching for a flute of champagne from the buffet, her mind a whirl, nerves raw, she had no warning that he was upon her until he abruptly clutched her arm with enough strength and motion to splatter a measure of the pale liquid down the skirt of her evening gown and onto the plush floral carpeting at her feet.

Shocked, she couldn't move, and because they were in the corner of the room, they were turned away from everyone.

From behind, he leaned toward her and said in a low, rigid voice, "You will meet me tomorrow morning at ten, in the hotel's garden arbor. Be there alone. We need to talk, Olivia."

Before she could utter a response, he backed away, moving so quickly that by the time she spun around, he'd disappeared into the crowd of jovial guests, who carried on, enjoying the party atmosphere, taking no apparent notice of her or their few seconds together.

Olivia breathed deeply, more angry than scared, though she realized she needed to leave at once. Downing one large gulp of champagne, she placed her near empty flute on the buffet, then held her shaking hands together in front of her as she went looking for Grand-père Marcotte to bid him *au revoir* for the night.

Sam had been more or less pacing the floor of the hotel's foyer since the moment she left, worried more than he thought he'd be, though knowing the plan they'd devised would serve their purpose perfectly and that she would certainly be safe in the company of others. Still, he couldn't help but feel perturbed that he wasn't with her to watch her in action, to see the look on Edmund's face when he noticed her for the first time. He would simply have to wait for the details, and since it had now been more than two hours since her departure, his patience had started thinning.

He'd all but decided that since darkness had fallen he could comfortably wait inside, when he saw her coach pull up in front of the hotel and the driver alight from his perch to open her door.

Sam rushed to the coach, and the moment she caught his eye, she beamed, stopping him in his tracks.

"You're certainly anxious," she noted, grinning with a satisfaction she couldn't hide.

He clasped his hands behind his back, watching her with interest as she sauntered up to him. "I have nothing better to do than wait on you, Lady Olivia."

"As it should be," she remarked slyly.

She looked beautiful, glowing with a rosy vibrance that hadn't been there when she'd left. "Well?" he asked with raised brows after a long moment of silence on her part.

Then she squealed and practically jumped into his arms. "Oh, my God, Sam, it was magnificent! Simply

magnificent!" she said with a burst of delight, hugging
him tightly, her face tucked into his neck.

Sam was so stunned by her behavior, her act of fa-
miliarity, that he momentarily couldn't respond. And
then, as if it were the most natural thing in the world, he
closed his arms around her, holding her securely against
him, lifting her feet off the ground as she laughed in his
arms and kissed his neck with tiny pecks.

She enchanted him, smelling faintly of wine and
flowers, her hair silky soft against his cheek as he took
that moment in time—just one selfish moment—to savor the feel of her subtle curves, to relish the touch of
her lips on his skin, to drown in the innocence of her
laughter. Her happiness intoxicated him, and when at
last he felt her gingerly push her palms against his
shoulders in an effort to be released, it occurred to him
how lonely his world would be without her.

With keen reservation, he loosened his grip and lowered her to the ground.

She backed up a pace, grinning at him, her gaze taking in all of his face. "I have to tell you everything, but
let's go inside."

"A very good idea," he replied genially, his hands
resting on her waist.

She grasped one of them, and without thought or
additional word, practically pulled him along, hand in
hand, all the way up to the third floor.

Their suite provided modest accommodations, con-
sisting of two separate sleeping chambers and a center
room between them, its flowered papered walls enclos-
ing only one cherrywood, floral sofa and a matching
but simple table with two accompanying chairs. She

stood near the table, on top of which rested a lamp that she'd lit upon entrance, pulling her earrings from her lobes and then tossing them, along with her fan and reticule, on the wooden surface.

She faced him, her smile never fading. "It was magnificent."

Crossing his arms over his chest, he replied, "So you said."

"He was shocked, utterly shocked." She clasped her hands together in front of her. "Oh, my, but it was *fun,* Sam."

He moved to the sofa and sat heavily, extending his legs out in front of him, his arms folded across his stomach, gazing at her with amusement. "Had a good time, did you?"

"A *marvelous* time." She pulled out a chair and lowered her body daintily into the seat, spreading her red gown out around her ankles. "He went pale when he first laid eyes on me. Then after a few moments of speaking with him and Brigitte, he grew extremely angry, though he managed to hide it with greater ability than he hid his astonishment. His reaction was better than anything you could imagine, and the best part was, he couldn't say a word without revealing himself to his betrothed because she never left his side. He was all mine to handle." She held her palm to her mouth for a few seconds, giggling. "I told him I was married to a Mr. John Andrews, a banker from England, who was helping me with my personal finances because I'd *misplaced* some of my inheritance." She dropped her arms to her lap. "Oh, my God, Sam, I wish you'd been there to see it. The moment was *priceless.*"

Her exhilaration was contagious, and he found himself chuckling, leaning his head back against the sofa's frame. "I'd wish I'd been there just to see you in action, sweet. It took all my strength not to ride out there and watch."

She cocked her head to the side, smiling at him. "I thought about you the entire time."

That softly spoken revelation tied his stomach in knots, even as it warmed him from the inside out. "I hope so," he muttered, realizing with reluctance that she probably didn't mean it the way he wanted her to.

"I kept thinking what a night we would have had confronting him together," she continued, "with poor Brigitte on his arm, completely taken with the man, clinging to him as if I were going to steal him right from under her nose." She scoffed quite dramatically, rolling her eyes. "What an absurd notion."

Now he just wanted to kiss her senseless. "Did anything else happen? Did he say anything specifically about Nivan or your money?"

She squirmed a little, fussing with her skirt, her brows furrowed. "No, nothing specific, but then he really couldn't. I think I confused him more than anything, especially since I didn't act at all like a broken-hearted victim. But at one point Brigitte and I talked about the differences between Edmund and my husband." She eyed him impishly, her broad grin returning. "I told them both that not only was my husband taller by a quarter of an inch, he was certainly just as handsome."

Sam didn't think he could take much more of her disclosure without picking her up and making love to her right there on the carpet, uncertainties and unknowns be damned. The fact that she even noticed that one of the only differences between Edmund and himself was his own minutely greater height mattered to him more than she could ever know.

"How long did you speak to him?" he asked, searching for every detail lest she forget.

She shrugged a shoulder, thinking. "Well, not long, maybe five minutes, which was a good thing, probably. There were about...oh...three dozen people or so, all there to congratulate him, so I couldn't take up too much of his time. But he never said a word about you—Oh! I did mention Aunt Claudette's name, though only in passing." She leaned forward, eyes sparkling. "I would have adored hearing him talk about her, but the truth is, Sam, what I enjoyed most about the evening was knowing he *couldn't* comment on anything I said. He could do nothing but squirm, hoping I didn't reveal too much to his darling Brigitte."

She amazed him—her cleverness, her charm, her extraordinary beauty, inside and out. At that moment Sam decided that the stupidest thing Edmund had ever done in his life was to let this remarkable woman slip through his fingers.

"How did you feel about him, Olivia?" he asked with a great degree of hesitation, sitting forward to rest his elbows on his knees.

Perplexed, she asked in reply, "How did I feel about him? In what way?"

He rubbed his hands together in front of him, choosing his words carefully. "You've told me how you felt confronting him tonight, that you were solely in charge of the moment, but you also once told me you loved him. I'm curious to know if those feelings returned to you. Were you jealous of his devotion to Brigitte?" He paused, then piercing her gaze with his own, he asked directly, "Are you still in love with him?"

She just sat there, staring at him without expression, for minutes—or so it seemed to him. Then she abruptly stood. "Edmund is a fool," she maintained, voice low with certainty. "I could never love a fool."

He placed his palms on his knees, pushing himself up to stand beside her, overflowing with a relief he had yet to fully understand. "You know, Olivia, I was just thinking exactly the same thing."

Her eyes narrowed as she placed her hands on her hips. "You were?"

He took a step toward her, close enough to tower over her, gazing down at her face. "I was."

Slowly, she began to shake her head, her countenance returning to one of joyous anticipation. "Tomorrow night will be a complete unveiling, Sam, for everyone, and I can't *wait* to walk into that ball on your arm."

"I can't either," he murmured softly, controlling his urge to touch her.

For several seconds they stared at each other silently, a thickening tension enveloping them that he knew she could positively feel. Her eyes widened with sudden realization; her mouth opened a fraction as she licked her lips with uncertainty. And then she broke the spell by taking a step back.

"I—I think I'm ready to retire," she said.

The gnawing he felt in his gut, the outright desire he

couldn't assuage, very nearly overcame him. If she only knew what she did to him.

"Turn around," he ordered, his tone a bit sharper than he'd intended.

She shook herself, puzzled. "I—I don't—"

"So I can unbutton your gown," he explained softly.

He'd helped her this afternoon with that part of her dressing, only because she had no maid and, he supposed, she'd decided with her corset and petticoats she was covered enough for decency. Emergencies required unusual circumstances and all that. But now she seemed reluctant to allow him to help her.

He reached out and ran his fingers down her cheek. "It's all right, Olivia. Let me unbutton your gown and you can go to bed."

After only a second or two of indecision, and without further remark, she lowered her lashes and turned around for him to do as he insisted.

Meticulously, he started at the top, near her shoulder blades, his fingers brushing her skin, feeling warm gooseflesh rise to his touch as he began to unfasten each one, moving down her back and over her corset with ease until he reached her waist. Then he grasped her upper arms and turned her to face him once more.

The look she gave him this time struck him hard. Her eyes were full of acceptance, understanding, trust, and a shade of pure devotion.

Clutching her gown at her bosom to keep it from slipping, she placed her free hand on his cheek and said huskily, "Thank you, Sam. For everything."

He lifted her chin with his fingers. "I would do

anything for you," he whispered gravely, the intensity in his gaze full of hidden meanings and hopes.

She swallowed. "Good night, Sam."

He sighed within. "Good night, Livi."

Without a second glance, she turned once more and headed toward her room, closing the door softly behind her.

Chapter 17

This morning, for the first time since she set eyes on Sam all those weeks ago, she'd deliberately lied to him. She didn't just withhold the fact that she would be meeting Edmund alone in the hotel's garden at ten, which she had also done last night, but had made up a reasonable explanation for her absence so she could get away. Strangely enough, doing so made her feel just like the snake she was leaving him to meet. But she couldn't think of another way to get around his constant presence. If Sam had any inkling of her plan, he'd not permit her to go, or worse, insist on accompanying her, which would leave her, ultimately, unable to confront Edmund the way she wanted to.

So, during a breakfast of coffee and baguettes smothered with sweet lemon marmalade in the hotel dining room, she'd casually broached the topic of her immediate plans, stressing the need to leave a few minutes before ten for an appointment in fragrance sampling at one of the Govance boutiques. He'd eyed her suspiciously from across the small table, in silent speculation, she supposed, before he relented. In a quick thought on her part, she asked him if he'd like to escort her, knowing he'd refuse if it meant smelling perfume again, even though she carefully stressed that they would be completely different scents from those he'd sampled at Nivan. She grew nervous when he didn't immediately refuse, and for a second or two she wondered if he were able to detect her deceit—until he said he'd rather wait in his room and read last week's newspaper.

The sky had been overcast all morning, and by the time she said her good-byes to him and stepped outside onto the pavement at ten minutes to ten, it had turned quite dark with the promise of a thunderstorm to come.

Quickly, she made her way down the sidewalk, purposely passing the dining room windows without glancing inside in the hopes that Sam might see her taking the route toward the boutique three blocks away, though as soon as she reached the end of the street, she made a fast turn and headed around the building.

The Maison de la Fleur had been built in a U shape, with the flower garden placed directly in the center so patrons of the hotel could easily access the lawn path from the main floor foyer as well as view the beauty from their rooms above.

Because she had to traverse the long way around to the backside of the tan stone building, by the time she reached the garden gate that faced the center of the hotel, she knew it had to be just after their appointed meeting time. The white wrought-iron gate that protected the enclosure pushed aside easily with only minimal squeaking, and she hastily stepped into the alcove and onto the gravel path.

The sky continued to darken, the breeze picking up with the coming storm, and Olivia shivered, wrapping her arms around her, suddenly chilled wearing only a lavender silk day gown with its short puffed sleeves.

She took in her surroundings, not exactly afraid but growing more instinctively cautious by the second, then swiftly started down the path in the direction of the centrally located arbor, scarcely noticing all the elaborately trimmed bushes and small beds of well-tended, sweet-scented flowers in a variety of colors.

The area proved to be quite private, and it occurred to her that should anyone witness the two of them together, they would only appear to be involved in a romantic tryst, certainly nothing new to the French. Unless, of course, he intended to harm her.

Olivia immediately disregarded that thought entirely. Edmund might be a charming rogue of the most calculating kind, but he wasn't a danger, of that she was certain. Nevertheless, the simple notion that he might, in some way, attempt to hurt her physically, put her on edge as she quietly traversed the path, her senses sharpened, her nervousness growing with each step, until at last the arbor came into view.

A sudden gust of wind blew strands of her hair across her cheeks and eyes, and she cursed her less-than-brilliant idea of wearing only one thin ribbon to tie it back at her nape. She paused for a moment to brush it aside, and that's when she caught her first glimpse of him.

Her stomach muscles coiled into knots as she watched him, standing with ease inside the white latticework structure, his upper torso and head hidden from view by thick, blooming bougainvilleas clinging to divider trellises. He seemed relaxed as he leaned his hip against the low fencing, one ankle crossed over the other, his arms crossed over his chest.

With a deep breath for confidence, Olivia straightened, shoulders back as she clasped her hands behind her and strolled nonchalantly to the front of the three short steps, stopping for a moment so he could witness her determination in her lifted chin, her vague smile.

"Edmund," she drawled.

He stared directly into her eyes, his fierce gaze signifying his desire to intimidate. She tried very hard to ignore it.

"Olivia," he returned, his tone low and icy.

Slowly, she climbed the three steps into the arbor proper, moving to her left, opposite him, her back to the latticework fencing. "So we meet again," she said amiably.

"Indeed." He waited, then asked, "Why did you come to Grasse?"

She rubbed the toe of her shoe along the wooden floorboard, a certain thrill circulating through her because she'd anticipated this moment for months. Raising her lashes, she glared at him. "I want my inheritance returned at once. You remember my fortune, Edmund, the one you so callously stole from me?"

He was silent for a long while, simply watching her, it seemed, his head cocked to the side a little, his eyelids thinned, jaw rigidly set. And then he lowered his arms and stood erect as he began a leisurely stroll in her direction.

Olivia held her ground, though her smile had faded. "You're not going to kill me, are you?" she muttered rather sarcastically.

His lips curled up into a derisive smile. "You're as brash as ever."

"One needs to be brash when one has been stomped on by a lying scoundrel," she maintained, her pent-up anger seeping into her tone.

He reached up and scratched his jaw, his gaze ever watchful, still striding in her direction, though moving so slowly it was almost imperceptible.

"Where is your husband?" he asked matter-of-factly.

"Waiting for me just outside the main gate," she replied at once. "For my protection, you know, should I scream."

He actually chuckled, shaking his head as he did so. "Now who is the liar?"

Olivia swallowed her growing fear, though she'd absentmindedly reached behind her to latch on to the edge of the wooden fence butting up against her backside. With a lift of one brow, she singsonged, "You'll never know for certain, I suppose."

He stood about two feet away from her now, bearing down on her with his immense height, arms to his sides, his expression ruthless. "What is it you expect me to do, Olivia? Hand you over a bag of coins?"

She glared at him, leaning toward him to charge, "I expect you to give me every cent you stole, preferably in a bank note. And don't even *begin* to tell me you've spent it all on my aunt Claudette."

That snide remark truly seemed to stun him. His features went briefly slack and his eyes widened a fraction as his gaze roved over her entire form. Then he sneered. "Aren't you quite the tart."

He was obviously trying to shock her, even scare her. But she had waited far too long for this encounter to allow a little intimidation on his part to force her into retreat.

Pulling back a little, she lightly shrugged and said, "If I'm a tart, then I'm a very clever one, aren't I? And I'm certain you appreciate that since you've obviously known quite a few tarts in your day."

Olivia had never been so bold in front of him, and the minute shake of his head and faintly furrowed brows exposed his amazement.

With a snort of absolute disgust, she pushed herself away from the railing and began to walk a slow circle around him, fingers interlocked behind her, looking him up and down as if he were nothing better than a cockroach.

"What did you think I'd do when you left me? Cry in my pillow and accept my loss? Perhaps go to my aunt and cry on her shoulder while you listened and laughed at my naiveté in the next room?"

She stopped moving as she now stood behind him, in the center of the arbor, crossing her arms over her breasts as she watched him turn to meet her gaze, his features hardened with his tightly controlled rage.

"What exactly did you expect, Edmund?" she spat as her own anger grew. "Did it never occur to you that I'd pursue you? Did you think I'd just settle for the fact that a lying, betraying bastard pretended to marry me for my fortune, stole everything I'd worked for at Nivan, and then walked out on me during what I thought was my wedding night?" She snickered with loathing. "Really, Edmund, can you actually be that *stupid*?"

He'd fisted his hands at his sides, so tightly his knuckles whitened, but he didn't say a word for several long, intense moments of uncertainty on her part. Then in a low, haunting voice, he warned, "Be careful, Olivia."

Since she'd been boasting of her intelligence, she decided she'd be wise to heed his advice. He looked on the verge of explosion, his face red, his eyes glassy with a tightly controlled fury.

Drawing a long breath, she pivoted around and took three steps to the edge of the arbor, farther away from him, then eyed him again askance, thoughtfully.

"Are you planning to swindle Brigitte in the same manner?" she asked coolly, though truthfully not expecting him to admit it outright. He didn't disappoint.

"How did you learn our marriage wasn't real?" he asked, nostrils flaring, ignoring her question altogether.

"Didn't we just cover that?" She smirked, then enunciated, "I'm *smart,* Edmund."

He didn't do or say anything for almost a minute, just leered at her, his mind racing to put the pieces together. And then suddenly his tactics changed completely. Opening his fists, he stretched out his fingers then raked all ten of them through his hair, just like Sam did, and for a second or two it caught her off guard.

He started pacing in front of her, his head down, a trace of a smile creeping across his mouth. "So you want your funds returned to you," he said rather than asked, his tone taking on a lighter quality.

Although her fear of him had abated somewhat, he'd thoroughly aroused her suspicions with such a repetitive comment. She knew him better than he thought.

"And you want something in exchange," she remarked, a thought that sprung up out of nowhere but made perfect sense where Edmund was concerned.

He actually chuckled, crossing his arms over his chest as he paused in his stride and turned to face her directly. "I will return every penny posthaste if..."

He purposely baited her, trying to be charming. Just like the Edmund of old. "If?"

"If you swear to me you'll never mention any of this to anyone, especially Brigitte."

What he suggested was positively outrageous and unscrupulous, and if she complied, it would make her as deceitful as he. Yet that's what he wanted—to put her in a position where she'd be just as accountable for her actions. Her silence in exchange for her inheritance. And considering how much Nivan mattered to her, he fully believed that he held her tightly in the palm of his sneaky, oily hand.

"You think I would actually stoop to your despicable level and allow that woman to be robbed of not only her future but her dignity?" she asked, with more hesitation in her voice than she desired.

"I love Brigitte," he said matter-of-factly, "and I would never hurt her."

She shook her head, eyes narrowing. "Don't make me laugh, Edmund. You don't know the meaning of the word."

He shrugged. "Just because she's not as beautiful as you are, Olivia, doesn't mean I don't have feelings for her."

She couldn't believe his gall. "You're despicable."

He ignored that, taking a step toward her. "I've already bedded her," he disclosed rather casually. "I'm sure you don't want to see her reputation ruined."

A loud clap of distant thunder startled her—almost as much as his unbelievable revelation. "That's impossible," she blurted as a gust of wind blew her hair in her face again. She brushed it away quickly without thought. "Brigitte would never allow you to take such advantage before the wedding."

He shook his head negligibly, his features distorted by a disgust he refused to hide. "No, unlike you, Olivia, she isn't cold and insensitive to her future husband's needs."

She gasped as he stepped closer, staring down to her stunned face.

"I'm sure you don't want to see her ruined," he repeated for emphasis, his tone dark and admonishing, "and so I'm *suggesting* to you that you keep your pert little mouth shut about everything you know. In return, I will have a bank draft sent to you at Nivan within the week."

Olivia stared at him, hugging herself from the moist chill in the air, enraged at his audacity yet at this point totally unafraid of him. "You are such a loathsome creature."

His gaze drifted over her face. "Only to those who don't know me well, and you never really got to know me, Olivia."

She glanced down his frame, then up again. "Could you possibly be any more arrogant?"

He offered her his familiar, charming smile, placing

his palm gently on her cheek. "Oh, I can be so much more."

She quickly shoved his arm aside. "You don't fool me or frighten me, Edmund. I know exactly what you are."

His congenial nature eroded before her eyes. Leaning very close, lids thinned, face taut, he murmured, "I'm certain your... *banker* of a husband can't provide for you, or Nivan, the way your inheritance can. And of course if you're lying to me and you really aren't married, as I'm more inclined to believe, because..." he sneered, "I'm smart, too, then you absolutely need your funds returned to you. Think about that, Olivia."

Keeping his cold gaze locked with hers, he slowly backed away. "I'll never bother you again," he continued, his voice low, expression grave, "as long as *you* never mention any of this to Brigitte or anyone else." He paused, watching her closely, then added, "Do we have an agreement between us?"

He knew what she had to say, and yet he had no idea that she and Sam were one step ahead of him this time.

"Yes," she spat in a whisper.

"Good," he said pleasantly. He brushed his palms down his shirt and the front of his trousers. "I'll leave you then, since it appears it's going to rain." He turned, and with a wave over his shoulder, he remarked, "*Au revoir* until tonight."

She had such trouble containing a squeal of triumph until he was well out of view. And then as thick water droplets began to fall upon her cheeks, Olivia fairly waltzed from the arbor.

Until tonight, indeed.

Chapter 18

~~~∞~~~

Sam was enraged beyond anything he'd ever felt before. Enraged at her deceit and the great risk she took in meeting Edmund alone in a secluded alcove without his protection, enraged that he hadn't chosen to follow her when he found her excuse to visit a perfume boutique for the third time in as many days entirely suspect, and mostly enraged at himself for feeling the most absurd, irrational jealousy he'd ever experienced.

He'd noticed her immediately as he stared out the window of their suite, his second-floor room facing the garden and its center arbor. He couldn't miss her lavender gown among the greenery, and it had only taken seconds for his confusion to turn to shock when he laid eyes on his brother for the first time in a decade—close to her, baiting her, touching her with his hand. True, she'd batted it away, but the contact, the whispered words, the notion that they were together again, this time without his knowledge because she'd lied to him, left him shaken and, unbelievably, immensely scared of losing her.

He'd stunned her when he grabbed her arm the minute she returned from her little tryst and walked into the foyer, disregarding her surprise as he practically dragged her back to their suite without uttering a single word. She hadn't bothered to protest, probably because she felt guilty, but more so because she'd have to be asleep not to detect the depth of his anger at her.

It wasn't even eleven in the morning, but the second he saw her with Edmund, he'd made a final, everlasting decision. He was going to take her to bed. Right now.

He latched the door behind him quickly, then moved at once, past her, to close the open windows and lock them as well. The sky had darkened to almost black, the rainfall growing heavier by the minute, which would prove the perfect atmosphere for an afternoon of lovemaking. Inhaling a deep breath to calm the tension within him, he pivoted around to face her.

Fuming mad, her face flushed with indignation, she stood beside the floral sofa, glowering at him with hot defiance, hands on her hips as she struck a pose to intimidate him. He almost laughed.

"What are you doing?" she asked suspiciously.

He gazed into her eyes for a second or two, then began unbuttoning his shirt. "I'm going to make love to you."

She gasped, stepping back until her legs hit the edge of the sofa, her eyes widening to bright circles of complete mortification. "Absolutely not!"

"Oh, yes," he drawled, beginning a slow saunter in her direction, turning his attention to his cuffs.

To her credit, she didn't scream or try to run, which told him how shocked she was by his pronouncement—or just how badly she needed him, regardless of whether she realized it yet.

She scooted back along the edge of the sofa, away from him. "I—I refuse to give myself to anyone other than my husband."

A reasonable argument, he decided, but it didn't deter him in the least. "No more games, Olivia," he said decisively.

She looked him up and down as he approached, her gaze lingering on his exposed chest as she clutched her hands at her breasts in a growing panic she couldn't hide. "You're insane," she whispered with thick enunciation.

"Yes, I probably am," he agreed, a smirk on his mouth. "I'm insanely crazy about you."

She blinked, startled. "I'll scream," she muttered shakily.

He slowly shook his head. "No, you won't."

Thinking fast, she asserted, "You told me our first day in Paris that we would never be—"

"I lied," he enunciated.

He stood directly before her now, her back against the door, her eyes shining pools of consternation, of worry and longing she probably didn't even understand.

"It's time, Livi," he murmured, his tone gravelly and filled with conviction.

"You—" She licked her lips. "You wouldn't dare force me."

He didn't know if he should laugh or be insulted. Pressing his thumb lightly on her mouth, he whispered, "I know you don't believe I would. But it doesn't matter because I won't have to." He rubbed the tip across her lips, back and forth. "You want me just as much."

She started trembling. "You don't know what I want," she whispered.

That gnawed at him, tearing at that very minute part of him that made him fear she'd rather still be with Edmund.

In a dark, choked voice, he leaned over to whisper against her lips, "I'm not going to lose you now."

And then he kissed her, not gently, but with a strong, quick need, disregarding her immediate response because he knew it wouldn't last.

She squirmed against him initially, then tried to push him away with her palms to his chest.

He'd had enough. Without a word, he broke away from the kiss, took one look at the desire she tried to hide in her pinkened cheeks, the depths of her eyes, then leaned over and hoisted her onto his shoulder like a sack of grain.

"What the devil are you doing?" she wailed, shoving her palms into his back and pushing up hard in a fruitless attempt to free herself.

He ignored her meager desire to resist him, veering the two of them swiftly and with little effort toward his bedroom. Closing the door behind him with a shove from his foot, he walked straight to the bed, dumping her in a pile of lace and lavender silk atop the bright purple and green quilted coverlet.

He gazed down to her, watching with some amusement as she blew loosened hair from her mouth and brushed it off her cheek with her fingertips. "This is entirely inappropriate," she sputtered, though she made no attempt whatsoever to move.

"In what way?" he goaded, suppressing a grin.

She stared at him as if he were daft. "It's *daylight,* you idiot man," she said through clenched teeth.

"Good." He pursed his lips to keep from teasing her about her wickedly adorable innocence, kicking off his shoes then grasping his shirt as he pulled it from his shoulders and down his arms. "I want to see every delectable inch of you, so my timing couldn't be better."

She gasped, her mouth dropping open in absolute shock.

Very slowly, keeping his gaze locked with hers, he placed one knee on the bed, then his palms, gradually starting to inch toward her.

She reacted at once, pushing herself into the layer of thick pillows that rested against the wrought-iron headboard. "Do not come any closer to me, Samson. I'm warning you."

He said nothing to that, just gave her a sly grin as he straddled her feet, pinning her to the spot with his knees atop her wide skirts.

"Sam, please, you're not being rational," she said matter-of-factly, attempting to reason with him.

He grasped one foot and pulled at her soft leather shoe until it came free, then he dropped it to the floor and worked on the other. "You know what, Livi? I don't think I've ever been more rational in my entire life."

She shook her head in small, brisk movements, trying again to push herself farther back into the pillows. "This isn't right," she argued, though her voice quivered as it began to dawn on her that he couldn't be thwarted.

Discarding her other shoe, he very slowly began to run his palms over the arches of her silk-stockinged feet, to her ankles, caressing in circles, pausing only seconds before he grew bolder and pushed his fingers up and under her gown, his gaze never wavering.

"What—What are you doing?"

"I'm taking your clothes off," he murmured.

"Oh, no you're not."

He grinned again. "Now who's not being rational?"

She said nothing to that, just stared at him, mortified.

He caressed her calves with his palms. "Are you wearing a corset?"

"That's none of your business!"

"I'll assume that means no."

She hadn't made any attempt to flee, hadn't fought him physically at all, but she would undoubtedly try his patience every step of the way. An effort, he mused, that would prove highly rewarding.

Leaning over, he gently kissed her stockinged toes, laying tiny pecks on the tips of each one, then the bottom of each foot.

"You can't do that," she barked out, trying to pull her legs under her gown, which she couldn't possibly manage because he held them firmly with his palms.

Sam had only been with one other virgin, at the age of seventeen, and she had seduced him. This time—a far more meaningful time—he would have to be the initiator, a role he would savor minute by minute, demanding every bit of stamina he possessed to make him last until he slid himself inside of her.

"Even your stockings are scented," he murmured, his lips grazing the balls of her feet.

She just continued to stare at him with wide, dazed eyes. "That's because I keep them in a drawer of lilac-scented sachets and—"

"Stop talking, Olivia," he ordered in a whisper, his palms skimming her shins, his lips brushing her toes. And then he raised himself over her, his knees straddling her hips, and took her mouth with his.

She didn't protest this time. Instead, she didn't move, didn't respond, hoping, he supposed, that he would find her cold and undesirable. Instead, it made him all the more anxious to win her compliance, her heart and mind.

He coaxed her softly into giving in to him, indulging the taste of her lips, the soft scent of spice on her skin, the supple feel of her body beneath his that he just barely touched with his bare chest. He kissed her over and over, tempting her with a promise of things to come, gently giving, never pushing, never insisting she respond, until finally he felt her ease into the bed as she started to relax.

He pulled back enough to view her face, now flushed a dewy pink, her lips red and moist, her eyes shimmering from a gradually expanding desire.

Keeping his gaze joined with hers, he shifted to his side a little and reached up to pull a lacy lavender sleeve from her shoulder.

"Sam..."

It was her last great effort, and he had to give her credit for trying so hard.

"Shh…" He leaned over and placed his lips on the warm, silky skin at her collarbone, sweeping them back and forth. "You're so soft…"

"Please…" she whispered achingly.

And at that moment she gave in to him.

He lifted his head from her shoulder and took her mouth with his once more, kissing her deeply, feeling her open for him and reciprocate at last as she allowed him to taste her sweetness, his tongue invading her moist, hot mouth, probing, flicking across hers and then grasping it to gently suck. He moved his palm slowly across her bared shoulder to her neck, his fingertips caressing in feathery strokes, his thumb grazing her jaw.

His kiss intensified as his need grew, as he felt her respond to him with her own great longing, her breath coming quickly in short gasps. Lightly, he began to move his palm, crossing from her throat to her collarbone to her chest, and then lower still until he slipped it beneath the neckline of her gown, her chemise, and then closed it over one full, concealed breast.

She gasped against him, the slight sound from her mouth only fueling the fire within him, intensifying his determination. He began to knead her flesh beneath the fabric, flicking his thumb across her hardened nipple, then the pads of his fingers in slow, small circles.

She squirmed a little, not out of protest this time, but a need and a yearning for him to do more.

At last he pulled his lips away from hers, lifting himself a little to look down at her face.

Her eyes were closed, her breathing coming in rasps, her cheeks flushed with color. He continued to caress her breast, watching her closely, wallowing in her response.

"Livi…"

Her lashes fluttered as she lifted them, meeting his gaze with one of a growing, raging desire.

He raised his hand to her face and touched her cheek. "I'm going to undress you."

The slightest hesitation crossed her features, and then she nodded negligibly, closing her eyes again.

He reached up to untie the simple lavender ribbon that pulled her hair neatly from her forehead and temples. It came free with ease, and then he ran his fingers through the silken tresses to loosen them so that her beautiful black hair cascaded around the smoothness of her face and neck.

Hoisting himself up on one elbow, Sam took hold of her shoulder and nudged her gently. "Turn on your side," he directed with tenderness.

Silently, she complied, rotating her body so her back was to him and he could work through the six buttons that held the bodice of her silken dress together.

He promptly unfastened each one, then pushed his hand inside the fabric, caressing her bare back just above the edge of her cotton chemise with soft, wispy strokes from his fingertips.

She sighed long and low from the pleasure, the gentle tease, encouraging him in his pursuit. Lowering his mouth to her skin, he kissed her up and down, brushing his lips and the tip of his nose back and forth, exhaling warm, moist air that made gooseflesh rise. Then with perfect calculation, he gradually ran his tongue up her spine from the lowest point until he reached her neck.

She moaned quietly, entranced by the feel, and at last he shoved his hand beneath the top of her gown and pushed it over her shoulder, down the front of her chest, until his palm covered the bare flesh of her breast.

He groaned, his face in her hair, inhaling the scent of her, flicking his tongue across her earlobe, leaving soft kisses on her neck and cheek as he began to knead her, to glide his fingertips over her taut nipple, pinching it gently then circling it slowly with his palm.

"Sam..." she murmured in aching sweetness.

"I've never felt anything as soft as you are," he replied breathlessly in her ear. "Let me love you..."

A soft, throaty moan escaped her, and then she rotated back to face him, her gaze meeting his, searching, their beautiful blue depths pleading with him to fulfill every hope, her greatest desire.

She swallowed harshly, trembling, her expression bathed in an ocean of tender, sensuous emotion as she raised her hand and touched his face, her palm on his cheek, the tip of her thumb brushing against his lips.

He briefly closed his eyes to savor the feel of her devotion. Then very slowly he raised his lashes and focused on her carefully as he moved his hand so the back of it pushed against the top of her gown, lowering it inch by inch.

Her intense gaze never strayed. Her breathing quickened as her cheeks flushed with color anew when at last he grasped the neckline of her gown and chemise and pulled them down, first releasing one arm, then the other, until she lay exposed to him, nude to the waist.

He took in every part of her, from her tapered throat to her trim belly, his gaze fixed with hunger on her tight, rosy nipples, the tiny mole at the base of her right breast.

She remained still, watching him, yearning for his touch. Then with great restraint, and only a second's hesitation, he lowered his mouth to one round peak, taking her nipple into his mouth.

She inhaled sharply, quivering, running her fingers through his hair to hold his head steadily against her.

He sucked her delicate flesh with care, flicked his tongue over the tight, hot tip, listening for her reaction, then feeling a sudden rush of his own desire as she whimpered and began to move against him.

He quickened his pace, gliding his tongue across her chest, to explore, to inhale the scent of her skin, to taste and feel and show her how much he needed to bask in her pleasure.

She gasped, moaning in satisfaction, and he gave as she begged with her body, taunting her with every caress, every brush of his tongue, every gentle squeeze of his palm, until her legs became restless beneath her skirts and she began to move her hips.

With her instinctive response for more, he shifted his body slightly so he could at last leave a trail of fine kisses down her stomach, pausing only once to flick his tongue over the tiny mole beneath her breast, stopping only when he reached her navel.

She whimpered, needing more, and finally he grasped the edge of her gown and chemise and started tugging them together over her hips.

Glancing at her face, he noticed her eyes squeezed

shut, the back of one soft hand laying across her mouth as she mentally made herself ready for him to take in the beauty of her nude form.

She lifted her hips to guide him in his efforts as he ever so cautiously pulled at her gown until it gave way over the last restraint and released the most intimate part of her feminine curves for his view.

Sam swallowed harshly to control himself, his breathing and pounding heart.

He'd seen the naked female form many times in his adult life, but nothing in his past compared, or prepared him, for the vision he gazed upon now.

She was nothing short of breathtaking, from her silky, long black hair, to her round, aroused breasts, tapered waist, matted black curls between her legs, that part of her he so desperately wanted to kiss, to tease, to bury himself in, body and mind, never to depart.

He inhaled a deep, shaky breath, desperate to stroke her there, to build the passion within her over and over again. At that defining moment Sam realized he could never leave something so perfect, so precious, to be explored by anyone else.

Suddenly, she seemed to realize he'd paused in his lovemaking, and she instinctively lowered her arm to her breasts in a meager attempt to cover herself. He smiled, filled with an odd sense of serenity from the innocent gesture. And then he pulled the last bit of her clothing from her long, trim legs and tossed them on the floor beside the bed.

She still hadn't opened her eyes, her shyness enchanting him even as he desired nothing more than her eagerness. But that would come later.

Moving up alongside her again, he leaned over to kiss her lips, her face and neck, his hand returning to her breasts, caressing with care should the passion in her start to ebb.

"Olivia," he breathed against the soft skin of her face, "you are so much more than I dreamed..."

She whimpered again and he pulled back a little to stare down at her, one hand still teasing her breast, the other now resting at the edge of her forehead, his thumb tracing a line across her eyebrow. She still hadn't looked at him, and he noticed with a sharp pull to his gut that her lashes were laced with tiny tear droplets.

"Don't cry," he whispered, suddenly worried his attempt at seduction would fail.

She shook her head minutely. "I can't help it," she replied, squeezing her eyes even tighter. "I want you so much, but I'm so scared."

The sublime astonishment he felt at that second would forever be etched in his memory.

Jesus, God.

With a shudder, he pulled his hand from her breast and placed his fingertips on her lips, watching her in wonder as she kissed them.

She'd confessed a fear of him, of the coming sexual act. And his greatest, overwhelming fear at that moment was that he was falling in love with her.

Jesus...

A powerful eruption of emotions rushed through him, startling him beyond comprehension. And then he leaned over and kissed her lashes, one at a time, saving him from divulging his feelings for her when he didn't understand them completely himself.

She responded to the touch, drawing a deep breath before wrapping her free arm around his neck to hold him close.

He moved lower to take her mouth again with his, kissing her deeply, with every ounce of passion he possessed, giving her everything inside of him, showing her what she so desperately yearned to feel.

And then without reservation he lowered his hand to the curls between her legs, his fingers sliding through them toward the hidden paradise within.

Her legs tightened by instinct. "Shh...open for me, sweetheart," he whispered against her mouth.

She answered his request, very slowly relaxing her knees, and before she could change her mind, he glided his fingers into the soft, warm folds, his chest tightening when she sighed and whispered his name, arching her hips to take him deeper.

Her slick wetness coated him. Sam ground his teeth and steadied his breathing to control himself, to stay his own release before he could manage to take his trousers off and satisfy her.

She started panting as he began to stroke her, moving her hips, matching his rhythm perfectly in search of surrender. And she would climax quickly. She was just so wet, so ready.

"Livi, love, you know I'm going to enter you, don't you?" he asked, his lips against her ear, his tongue sucking the lobe, hoping to God he wouldn't have to explain the act before he did it.

She nodded and whispered, "Yes..."

Relief flooded him, coupled with encouragement and a hot new wave of desire.

He continued to stroke her, very slowly, coaxing her into short quick breaths and soft whimpers as he swiftly lifted his hips and fumbled with the buttons of his trousers, loosening them and pushing them down his legs faster than he ever had before. He kicked them from his feet, then scooted up to her again, lying beside her at last, as exposed as she.

Her body felt so warm next to his, her desire near its peak as he leaned over to kiss her breasts again, to suck and caress and taunt, as he continued to stroke her, slipping briefly inside of her, then out again, as he rotated his fingers on the nub of her pleasure until she nearly cried out.

Finally, and in one rapid motion, he crossed one leg over hers so the tip of his rigid erection rested against her hip.

She gasped, jerking a little when she felt it, but he held her closely, wanting her to experience the depth of his need, to grow used to the feel of his intimate touch.

And then with a speed that defied his craving for prolonged arousal, he pulled his fingers from between her legs and lifted himself over her, taking her mouth with his in hot frenzy, his tongue invading her sweetness, searching, sucking, his breathing now as erratic as hers. He nudged her thigh with his knee until she spread her legs wide to allow him access, then he placed his hips between them, steadying his body above hers with his forearms flat on the pillow beside her head.

He cupped her cheeks with his palms, teasing her lips with his, her eyelashes and nose with soft pecks. Then he slowly raised his head to gaze down at her face.

"Look at me, Livi," he urged in a breathless whisper.

She did as he bid her, her stunning blue eyes, glazed by desire, meeting his again for a final time before he would begin the invasion of her hot, tight sweetness and make her his own.

"Don't be afraid," he pleaded in a whisper, his voice raspy and thick.

She nodded negligibly, inhaling a shaky breath, her hands on his shoulders as she mindlessly skimmed his neck with her fingertips.

And with that, he placed the hard tip of his erection at the wet, hot center of her femininity, pausing for a second or two to steady himself.

"Sam," she whispered, closing her eyes, leaning up to kiss him.

Her sweet, gentle acceptance was all he needed. Very slowly, he began to push himself into her, stopping at once when she tensed, her body going rigid with a gasp from her lips.

He stilled, sensing the discomfort. Waiting for her to relax, he continued to kiss her, not with frenzy, but a tender grazing of his lips to hers, pulling himself out a little to reach down and grasp one of her knees, lifting her leg to make his entrance easier.

She pushed her fingers through his hair, kissed him back through every soft moan, through every whimper of building need.

"Relax, Livi, love," he murmured against her mouth, his voice strained with a losing effort to hold back.

She tried, he knew, to do as he asked, easing the tightness she felt in her hips and legs.

He began to slide into her once more, this time going deeper, feeling the moist hot walls inside of her give way to make room for him. It hurt her, he knew, and it pained him almost as much to know there was absolutely no way to avoid it. Silent tears streamed down her cheeks, touching his lips as he kept them locked with hers, coaxing her along with him as he entered her, then pulled back, entered ever farther, going deeper with each stroke, taking him to the brink of oblivion.

"You feel so good..." he said through a strained whisper, his body tense as he tried his very best to restrain an immediate climax of his own.

She whimpered, arching her back when, for a final time, he entered her as deeply as he could then ceased all movement, giving her a few seconds to adjust to the fullness as the pain gradually eased.

She would never fully know just how much he treasured this moment between them, what it felt like for him to be inside of a woman for the first time in ten long years. The sensation overwhelmed him, and he swallowed hard and squeezed his eyes shut to control his emotions, to rejoice in the exquisite power she held over him without her awareness.

She kissed him then, his cheeks and brow, his lips and jaw, and the sweetness emanating from her expressed everything she couldn't yet say to him in words, revealed just how much she'd longed for this moment, to feel him inside her for the very first time.

"God, Livi—"

"Give me everything..." she breathed against his skin.

He choked back a sob of pure ecstasy, gritting his teeth as he pulled out of her a little, putting his full weight on one arm so he could lift his body just enough to reach down between them to stroke her again with his fingers.

She arched her hips against him, her nails digging into his shoulders, the muscles inside of her urging him on as they bathed him in hot, wet sweetness.

She began to relax, to whimper, her head leaning back hard against the pillows as she turned herself over to the pleasure, as he stroked her steadily, increasing the pace, bringing her ever closer to her peak of fulfillment.

He remained motionless inside of her, knowing that if he thrust into her even once he'd lose himself and his determination to watch her come first, to escape in her release, to share it with her. His body broke out in perspiration as he tightened his jaw, concentrating on her and what she needed.

She writhed beneath him, urging him on, her fingers clinging to his shoulders as he stared down to her beautiful face, feeling everything, sensing her moment of climax as it neared.

Suddenly she gasped and jerked once. Her eyes flew open and she looked at him.

"Yes, my love...Come for me..."

And then she screamed, cutting into his skin with her nails, arching into him as she cascaded over the edge.

He didn't even have to move. Each wave of her pleasure, each pulse from within as she tightly encased him, took him instantly to the brink of paradise.

Sam stared at the beauty that was her, that was *his*—and then it hit him hard.

He exploded inside of her, his head falling back as he grunted through clenched teeth with each thrust he could no longer control, through the intensity of an ultimate satisfaction that shook his body, that merged his heart with hers as a sharing of one, in a rush of pure joy that fulfilled his every dream.

Chapter 19

Olivia opened her eyes, her mind foggy at first, unsure where she was for a moment as she gazed to the little bits of fruit and pinecones that adorned the wallpaper in his bedroom. *His* bedroom.

Oh, my God, what have I done?

She groaned inwardly, covering her eyes with a palm, wondering what in heaven's name she could possibly say to him as the memory of what they'd done came flooding back in all its shocking delight.

They must have both dozed off, for she now became aware of his naked form lying beside her, his head nestled in her neck, his warm, steady breathing brushing her skin as he draped both his arm across her belly, just under her breasts, and his calf over one of her legs.

She supposed she could hardly move without

disturbing him, though her instinct was to jump out of
bed and run far away from here, decently clothed of
course.

But then maybe he didn't expect her to do or say
anything. Maybe he'd simply get up, get dressed, and
then they could go on as they had before, never mentioning this…mishap again. Though she didn't think
Sam would consider making love to her a "mishap"
any more than she did.

Even as her mind whirled with a million uncertainties, she decided that what they'd shared had been the
most painful, and the most wonderful, exciting…glo-
rious experience of her life.

He was simply amazing. Amazing, giving, gentle,
and he'd treated her as if he truly cherished her and her
thoughts and feelings. Never had another man treated
her like Sam did, especially Edmund.

"What are you thinking?" he asked without moving,
his tone lazy and utterly content.

She supposed she had to speak to him even if she did
feel overwhelmed with embarrassment. Shaking her
head, she lowered her hand from her eyes to lay it on
the side of the bed. "It's not important."

He chuckled softly, the sound reverberating in his
chest, which lay next to hers.

"Olivia, do you know how many men ask that question while dreaming of that exact response from a
woman?"

That thoroughly confused her. "I don't understand
you."

He lifted his head a little so he could look at her,
though she kept her gaze fixed on the ceiling.

"Most women never stop talking," he said through a grunt. "All they want to do is explain things."

She laughed in spite of wanting to. "That's ridiculous."

"No it's not, and you're quite aware of it, being an absolutely perfect specimen of the fairer sex."

She couldn't stop grinning, closing her eyes as she decided he not only had a very keen understanding of females, he felt wonderful beside her.

"So," he asked again, leaning up on his elbow to gaze down to her face, "what were you thinking?"

She sighed, lifting her lashes once more to look at him at last, her heart melting from his amused expression, from his tousled hair and gorgeous dark eyes. "What do you think?" she returned softly.

He shook his head at her obstinance, a sly grin lifting one side of his mouth. "You were thinking what a marvelous lover I am."

She gaped at him, feeling the heat of embarrassment rising to her cheeks. "That's absurd."

He lifted a shoulder in a shrug, his eyes sparkling with wicked humor. "No it's not. It's normal."

She stared at him with feigned annoyance. "If you must know, I thought you were perfectly…adequate."

He pulled back a little, brows furrowed, looking at her as if she were insane. "Adequate? *Adequate?*"

She shrugged lightly. "You obviously think you're marvelous, so what does my opinion matter?"

She teased him, of course, and he knew it.

He slowly shook his head, glancing down her nude form. "Then I suppose I'll just have to be better the next time."

He couldn't possibly be serious. "Sam," she started very gravely, her voice taking on a somber note, "we can't ever do this again. It's—wrong."

To her complete shock, he chuckled, moving his free hand from beneath her breast to trace a trail across her belly, forcing a shiver from her as gooseflesh rose to his touch.

"Oh, Olivia...I have so many things to teach you, the first of which is to never, ever, ever say that to a man." He looked deeply into her eyes. "It only makes him desperate, and more determined."

She giggled despite her reluctance to appear anything but decisive.

He grinned, then fell back against the bed, lying flat beside her, staring at the ceiling. "What I'd really like to know is what the hell you were doing outside alone with Edmund."

That caught her completely off guard. Sighing, she said, "If I tell you, do you promise never to force me into your bed again?"

He laughed outright, irritating her a little because he didn't seem to take their predicament at all seriously.

He peeked at her sideways. "I swear I'll never force you into my bed. Now I want details."

She sighed, knowing without doubt that he was being sneaky—he didn't exactly force her today and yet he'd managed to get her unclothed and practically begging for him when it was the last thing on earth she'd intended to do.

She turned on her side to view him better, resting her head in her palm but keeping her free hand decently between them, partially covering her breasts.

"He wanted to meet me. He approached me at the party and more or less insisted I be there, at the arbor, at ten."

He watched her, his earlier amusement all but gone. "You should have told me."

Which really meant, she surmised at once, that he'd been hurt by her lie.

"I know. I'm sorry."

He groaned in irritation, then ran his fingers through his hair. "I don't think he'd ever hurt you physically, but meeting him alone like that, after just catching him by surprise the night before, was the wrong thing to do, Olivia."

That statement, and its implication of tenderness and worry, warmed her to her bones. With a vague smile on her lips, she reached out and ran a finger across his eyebrow. "Were you jealous?" she asked in a sly murmur.

His eyes narrowed as a trace of amusement crossed his features. "Maybe."

She grinned. "Maybe?"

"He was standing much too close to you."

"So you were jealous," she purred.

He let out a low growl. "I didn't like it."

Beaming, she replied, "I didn't either. He smelled like cheap cologne."

Sam laughed low in his throat. Then without warning he covered her breast with his palm. "Actually, it's probably more accurate to say I felt strangely possessive, and very worried that I couldn't run down and rescue you because that would mean taking my eyes off of you for several minutes. Minutes where anything could happen."

His thumb brushed her nipple, arousing it to a hardened nub, and heat flooded her again, rushing through her body. She moved her arm and laid her head on the pillow, facing him, aglow with the wonder of knowing he felt that way about her.

"What were you feeling, Livi?" he asked quietly, his gaze taking on a quiet intensity.

She inhaled deeply. "He made me angry, but then I think Edmund enjoys that. He's never really taken me and what I say very seriously. But I think he was also frightened of the fact that I'm here."

"Did he mention your inheritance?"

She brushed loose strands of hair from her cheek. "He says he's in love with Brigitte, which I find appalling."

His brows rose. "You do?"

Her features grew somber as she watched him. "Because I don't think he's capable of love, Sam. He told me he's bedded her, which I find . . . unbelievable."

Smirking, he replied, "Why? Maybe she desires him, loves him enough to give herself to him before marriage."

The mention of such a complication made her uncomfortable because it hit very close to home. "That just isn't something properly bred ladies do, Samson," she remarked, feeling the heat of shame spread across her face.

He unexpectedly lifted her hand and brought it to his mouth, kissing her wrist once, then the back of her fingers. "I think it happens more often than you think," he informed her, his tone low and serious.

She couldn't contemplate that now, what his taking

her virginity might mean for her future, for their future together, if in fact they were to have one.

Deciding it best to return to the more immediate subject, she revealed, "He told me he'd give me back the money he stole from me, all of it, if I don't mention a word of what he did to me, or what I know, to anyone, especially Brigitte."

Sam closed his hand around hers and held it against his chest. "That makes sense, especially if he cares about her, or if he wants to swindle her of her inheritance, too."

She rolled onto her back, staring at the ceiling. "But the thing I don't understand is how he could get her money, regardless of whether the marriage is real. Her *grand-père* is the one who controls the wealth, and he's as strong as an ox." She turned to him sharply. "Unless..."

He firmly shook his head. "I don't think he'd go so far as to kill someone, Livi. And if we are to assume he could never resort to murder, he'd need to marry her legally then wait for the old man's death of natural causes. In the meantime, he'd certainly be living comfortably." He snorted. "That sounds more like Edmund's style."

She ran her fingertips across the coverlet, brows furrowed in thought. "But he knows I can say anything I want, and I'm obviously in Grasse to confront him."

"Not if he pays you off," Sam reminded her. "It seems the money he stole from you is now going to work well with his plans to keep you silent. You need it, and he knows it."

That made her just plain mad. "The snake in smelly

cologne is using my money to blackmail me. I truly cannot *wait* to see his face tonight. I might just kill *him*. Or kick him as hard as I can in the shin."

Abruptly, Sam turned his head to look at her, then grasped her around the waist and easily hoisted her on top of his bare, firm... perfect body.

"What are you doing?" she blurted, attempting to wipe flying hair from her eyes and face.

"I'm feeling you," he replied with a wide, pompous grin.

"Feeling me? Are you insane?"

"Do you know that the most enchanting thing about you, Livi, is your innocence?"

That flustered her and she squirmed, struggling to free herself from the positively enticing feel of his hard, masculine form beneath her, though it proved to be an entirely worthless attempt as he held her securely with strong arms. Eventually she gave up trying.

"I've never considered myself innocent, Sam," she declared sternly. "I take care of myself, I take care of Nivan, I live a respectable life in a modern city—"

He laughed, and she felt it to her toes.

"Let me clarify some things for you, sweet," he said rather mundanely, though clearly still amused. "You married a man you hardly knew, who then easily absconded with your inheritance without your knowledge. You came to me believing I was him without checking your facts. You manage your boutique while someone who works for you tells your aunt your every move—"

She gasped in disbelief, but he ignored that.

"You agreed to travel alone with me, a man, again,

whom you hardly knew, apparently trusting that my intentions were honorable. You're shocked to learn Claudette and Edmund are lovers and likely were lovers the entire time you were together. You lie to me about meeting him alone, then actually do so in a secluded garden where you can't possibly be seen by anyone should a problem arise. And finally, you're the most stubbornly beautiful, *innocent* woman, whose lovemaking ability defies description." He paused, staring into her perfectly stunned eyes. "You didn't even know it was possible to kiss the bottom of your feet. Shall I go on?"

Olivia was speechless, never having considered these simple facts about herself and what she'd done while in his company, and it staggered her a little that he'd been so observant, had thought about her in such a light. But when she finally found her voice, the only thing she could think of to say had everything to do with her vanity.

Coyly, she asked, "You really think I'm beautiful?"

She expected him to laugh again and tease her, but he surprised her by turning remarkably serious, his gaze probing hers.

Finally, huskily, he maintained, "I think you're exquisite—from your body, to your mind, to your little toes, to your laugh, to the perfect way you make love to me. And I will never, ever let you go."

His words and meaning, the intensity in his voice, struck her profoundly. She started trembling faintly, her throat too tight to speak, fearful she might break down into tears in front of him. In an instant she leaned over and kissed him with all the passion inside of her, exposing every deep feeling he evoked in her, loving him with every breath and touch.

It took him only seconds to respond, and when he did, he came alive beneath her, stroking her up and down her spine with his fingertips, returning each kiss with a need unmatched.

She ran her fingers through his silky hair, felt the flexing muscles of his chest beneath her breasts, the growing hardness of his rekindled desire, which she no longer feared but yearned to feel inside of her again.

Finally, he turned her over, very slowly, his lips never leaving hers as she once again lay on her back, the soft pillows cushioning her head. He kissed her until the fire lit anew, until her hunger flamed for him, until her breath quickened and her body ached with urgency. She moved her legs involuntarily up and down the length of his, unable to control the tiny whimpers that escaped her when his hand found her breasts and began teasing her nipples, rolling them between his fingers and thumb. And then he broke away from her mouth to kiss a line of fire down her throat, her chest, and the side of each breast before taking one into his mouth to gently suck and kiss and caress.

Olivia thought she might die of pure pleasure, wanting him more with each gentle touch, each stroke of his hand.

At long last he released her and moved up again so he faced her. "I want to make love to you again, Olivia."

She actually grinned, slowly opening her eyes to the starkness of his gaze. "I give you permission, you silly man," she purred in a breathless whisper. "You don't even have to force me."

He smiled in return as she traced the lines and planes of his handsome face with her fingers, ran the pad of her thumb across his lips until he kissed it lightly.

Gruffly he added, "But you'll be sore from the first time, so we're going to do it another way."

Aching for him madly, her body afire, skin burning from his touch, she couldn't be certain if she heard him correctly. "There's—" She gasped as he placed his hand between her legs. "There's another way?"

He groaned, taking her mouth again, his tongue flicking across her lips before he whispered against them, "My sweet, innocent Olivia..."

Then without warning he released her lips and moved swiftly toward the foot of the bed, quickly placing his head where only a moment ago his hand had been.

Olivia kept her eyes locked with his, then jumped, startled, when he lifted her knees and began to run his tongue up and down the soft, moist folds hidden inside her intimate curls.

Her shock was short-lived, for in seconds he had her reeling from the sumptuous, forbidden touch, stroking her up and down until he found her hidden nub of pleasure. Then he quickened his pace and changed it, concentrating on the center of her desire, rotating his tongue, stroking her back and forth, faster and harder until she relaxed and closed her eyes, giving in to the moment.

She could feel herself nearing her crest almost at once as she began to move her hips up and down to match his steady, focused rhythm. She moaned softly, her hands on his head, fingers in his hair, visualizing his mouth on her, his tongue inside of her, his erection long and hard and ready to claim her.

"Sam..." she breathed, searching for the moment of release, meeting each flick of his tongue with a lift of her lips as the tension within her coiled ever tighter.

"Sam—oh God, Sam..."

He reached up and grasped her hands, interlocking their fingers the moment she reached her peak.

She cried out, squeezing his hands, rocking her hips into him as she gave herself over to the intense pleasure, moaning his name, her eyes tightly shut as wave after wave passed through her.

As soon as he felt her movements start to slow, he quickly raised his body and angled it above her, supporting himself with one hand beside her head, gazing down to her face, into her eyes, as he positioned his erection beneath her moist folds. But he didn't enter her. Instead, he began to rock his own hips, very slightly, allowing just the tip of him to brush against her sensitive nub.

Olivia gasped from the sharpness of the sensation, opening her eyes to look at him, to watch him, to discover the joy in seeing him climax.

He held his body up above hers on one palm, his arm flexed tightly from the weight, his chest and shoulders tense with effort. With the other hand he held the base of his erection to guide him as he stroked her up and down, at first very slowly, then increasing his pace as he neared his release.

Olivia had never imagined anything so erotic in her life. She stared, mesmerized, wishing desperately for him to enter her, filling her within as he had earlier, but finding this ever more intoxicating, stimulating.

He groaned low in his chest, the muscles in his face flexed as he tightened his jaw, his breathing coming in rasps as he closed his eyes to the sensations.

And then, unexpectedly, something wound up inside of her and she felt the sudden building of pleasure once more, quickly this time, taking her to the edge of satisfaction within seconds.

She moaned, and he raised his lids to look at her again, a trace of surprise crossing his features as he watched her.

"Oh God, Livi, come for me again. Come for me, sweetheart."

His voice sounded pained, intense, as he moved himself faster and harder against her.

She reached up and touched his face. And then with a low moan she called out his name in a whisper as he pushed her over the edge for a second time. She whimpered, basking in the delicious brilliance of each pulsing wave of pleasure, made perfect by knowing she was taking him with her.

"Oh God," he breathed. "Oh God. Olivia..."

And then he grunted as his powerful body jerked against her from the sudden rush of intense pleasure, as he rubbed himself against her cleft, his eyes shut, jaw clenched, his head arched back while he moaned and accepted everything she gave.

At last he gradually slowed his movements, then lowered his body beside hers, wrapping his arms around her and holding her close.

Olivia felt her breathing slow as she relaxed, relishing the feel of him beside her, listening to the steady beating of his heart beneath her cheek.

What she'd experienced with him, because of him, this day, would be etched in her memory forever. This marvelous man made the world more colorful, her life worth living for every wonderful reason.

At that moment in time she realized the true nature of love. And she loved him.

Chapter 20

⌒⌒⌒⌒⌒

It would be a night to remember.

Olivia sat across from Sam in what had to be the most expensive and luxurious coach in which she'd ever ridden in her life.

He'd been busy this week, she mused, realizing now where he'd spent his time away from her. He had obviously purchased this beautiful and enormous rig specifically for the ball tonight, and his personal coat of arms had been painted on the black lacquered door in bright gold. The inside was incredibly comfortable, with its plush, ruby red interior, velveteen seating, window curtains, and floor carpeting.

He'd also had spectacular formal wear tailor-made on demand, and he looked positively magnificent tonight, dressed in black Italian silk, a white frilled shirt with silk-trimmed collar and revers, and a black, double-breasted waistcoat.

They'd both ordered baths before they dressed, as the hotel offered a tub and hot water with an hour's notice. Olivia had washed with the vanilla-scented soap she'd purchased at Govance earlier in the week, then splashed a vanilla-based, Asian spice eau de cologne over much of her body as her chosen fragrance for this night.

After brushing her hair dry, she'd plaited it with a gold chain and a string of pearls, twisted together, then coiled the braid loosely atop her head, pulling out a few wispy tendrils around her neck and face to soften the effect.

After donning her undergarments and her tightest corset, which clasped in front and lifted her breasts, she pulled on the golden gown she'd worn the first night she met Sam. It was her best evening dress, with its stunning shimmer, tight waist, and low neckline, which allowed for a tantalizing peek at her cleavage. Sam had helped her by fastening the back buttons without thought. After their early afternoon escapade, she no longer felt even remotely embarrassed by his lingering touch or the kiss he dropped on her neck when he finished.

They left the hotel at exactly half past seven, allowing them ample time for their scheduled arrival at eight o'clock. They'd mutually agreed on the specifics, as they wanted to make their appearance well after many of the guests, giving them an opportunity to blend with the crowd before Sam was noticed. And frankly, Olivia wanted to be late enough to make Edmund stew as he watched for her and her so-called husband.

Sam sat across from her now, looking marvelously sophisticated and more handsome than she'd ever seen him. He'd bathed, shaved, and combed his hair neatly away from his face, and even added a touch of cologne—not because he liked it, she decided, but because it was a unique blend created by her, chosen only for him.

The excitement had begun to build in her the moment she'd seen the coach and he helped her inside. Now, as they were almost upon the estate proper, she could hardly contain herself. They'd spoken little on the ride, Sam lost in his own contemplation of the night ahead, but he seemed amused by her nervousness, commenting once about twisting her ivory fan in her lap.

The coach slowed as they pulled up behind a string of carriages and coaches, both private and hired, the house ahead lit up as it had been last night, only even more spectacularly, if that were possible.

Olivia sat forward with anticipation as she glanced out the window, slipping one gloved hand through the thin rope on her gold-embroidered reticule.

"Are you ready for this?" Sam asked quietly, breaking the silence.

She looked at him and grinned. "I've never been more anxious to attend a ball in my entire life."

He smiled in return, the lights from the house now casting a glow across his face. "You look breathtaking," he murmured.

She practically melted into her seat, staring at him with pure adoration. "As do you, your grace."

His lips twitched up on one side. "And you smell good, too."

"It's a vanilla-based spice, a new purchase from Govance."

"Buying from the competition, eh?" he teased.

In an utterly shocking decision on her part, she lowered her voice to just above a whisper, leaning toward him to ask, "Would you like to know a perfumer's secret of seduction?"

His brows rose with titillation. "Here?"

She shrugged. "Why not?"

Wryly, he repeated, "Why not, indeed?"

Impishly, she said, "Many a seductress through the years has used only one heady, exotic, musky scent to...attract a gentleman when she wants him in her bed."

His mouth dropped open, but he didn't respond verbally, just watched her.

She scooted forward on her seat, perching on the edge. In a husky whisper, grinning broadly, she revealed, "They take their fingers and collect the sexual moisture from between their legs, then place it behind their ears, across their throats, and between their breasts, where, as it happens, gentlemen adore directing their attention." She sat up a little. "The scent of musk has always been a favorite among men. And of course husbands like it because it doesn't cost a penny."

She'd shocked him, and it made her giggle.

He shook his head slowly. "Livi, love, you have absolutely changed my world."

The coach came to a stop at that moment, and just as a footman unlatched the door, she stood and leaned over and kissed him once, quickly, on the mouth.

"For luck, my darling." And then she took the hand

the footman offered her and stepped from their beautiful coach.

Together they traversed the steps to the great front door, behind other guests whose carriages had preceded theirs, her arm through his, clinging to him a bit more firmly than the situation warranted. He seemed calm, but she could read his moods so well now, every different facial expression, every touch, and she knew without question that his anticipation of the events to come had to be eating him inside.

The footmen only briefly noticed them as they entered the foyer among the group of arriving guests, most of whom had yet to meet Brigitte's intended, and so no one paid them any more attention than they might have under normal circumstances, although she and Sam, in their expensive and beautiful attire, made a striking couple.

Instead of taking an immediate left into the drawing room as she did last night, they instead made their way in slow progression down a wide hallway toward the back of the estate.

The Marcotte staff had decorated superbly for tonight's event, lighting candles everywhere and placing freshly cut flowers in colorful, imported vases on every flat surface they passed, the aroma filling the air to mingle with a variety of perfume, sweet cigars, and the smell of delicious food that drifted out of the ballroom just ahead of them.

Sam kept his eyes focused straight ahead, and just as they reached the wide entryway, she gently squeezed his arm.

He glanced down at her and smiled, giving her a

look that sent waves of comfort and serenity coursing through her. She returned it with a smile of her own; not a grin of excitement as she had before, but one of complete understanding and hope that tonight would only be the beginning of marvelous things to come.

Then at last they entered the ballroom, lit brilliantly by a thousand candles, reflecting off long mirrors that adorned the walls and the intricate gilt carvings that covered the high ceiling. Footmen in crimson livery carried golden platters of champagne in flutes and hors d'oeuvres as they worked their way through the crowd. A six-piece orchestra sat in the far northwest corner, now playing a gavotte as a blur of colorful skirts whirled around the dance floor in time to the music.

Olivia adored parties, and beholding the visual beauty in front of her, with the man of her dreams escorting her, made this one simply magical.

Sam began moving to their right, leading her around a group of minglers, laughing and chatting, their voices carrying just above the din.

"Are we going to dance?" she asked, hoping he'd say yes because once the family discovered them, the gaiety of the evening would be over and the drama would begin.

He lowered his head so she could hear him. "Not until they play a waltz. I loathe dancing, and refuse to suffer through any other style."

She tilted her shoulders forward so he couldn't help but look at her. "You loathe dancing?" she asked, surprised.

He gave her a wry grin. "The only thing I despise more is attending the opera."

She laughed. "Then I'll never make you suffer through any of them but *The Magic Flute*. I adore *The Magic Flute*."

He snorted. "I think I could manage to stay awake through one production by Mozart. At least the first act."

"Ahh... what a delight it'll be to make you suffer for my personal enjoyment," she teased, hugging his arm.

"I'd suffer through anything for you, Olivia," he admitted, his watchful gaze directed again toward the crowd.

He'd said that casually, as if it were a passing thought, and yet the meaning behind his words pierced her heart with an incredible, inexplicable happiness. That's when the waltz began, and without comment he led her straight to the dance floor.

Olivia cherished the moment, noting how very much this dance reminded her of their first one, in London, when she'd worn the same gown and gazed into his beautiful eyes, so angry with him because she thought he was Edmund. Now she saw only Sam, as individual as any man, with his own longings and fears and dreams.

She smiled up to his face as he regarded her, twirling her with an expertise that defied his impressive stature or his disclosure that he detested dancing. He was a marvelous dancer.

"I want to tell you something I've never said to you before," she confided, peering intently into his eyes.

His brows furrowed briefly, and then instead of grinning at her, or teasing her, or even looking vaguely curious, his features instead turned solemn, his gaze taking on a depth of intensity she didn't think she'd ever witnessed from him before.

"Tell me," he urged, his voice gravelly, low, and just barely audible above the music.

Her own voice all but trembled with emotion as she revealed, "I've now known you almost as long as I knew Edmund. And with every breath inside me, with every beat of my heart, I want you to know that there is not one thing about him that compares to the wonderful person you are." She inhaled deeply for strength. "If the two of you were standing together, wearing exactly the same clothes, the same hairstyles, the same expression, I would know you with my eyes closed, simply by touching your face."

For a second or two he just stared at her, a cascade of candid feelings spanning his features, his pace slowing as the meaning behind her words took hold and struck him soundly.

And then he swallowed hard, his jaw tightening as he pulled her into him as close as he could, his arm closing around her waist, his chest against her breasts. Then he lowered his forehead to rest it on hers.

"Oh, Olivia..."

His voice, the sound of her name on his lips, enveloped her as a pleading whisper for a lifetime of dreams.

She closed her eyes, their dancing now nothing more than a mere swaying of one heartbeat, one shared soul.

"I love you," she breathed.

His body shook as he replied in a low, harsh murmur of wonder, "I love you, too."

Olivia knew that nothing in her life would ever compare to this moment with him, to the staggering, exquisite joy she felt inside to hear him repeat those words from the depths of his heart, to hear them carried on a whispered wave of tumultuous feelings, always to be cherished as he held her close in a beautiful room full of people, as he swayed with her to the music of a thousand angels that sang in a triumph of everlasting gladness, only for them.

She wanted so badly to kiss him, to run away with him to an exotic land and never return, never look back, to be with him like this forever.

Tears glistened on her lashes when she felt him lift his forehead from hers and kiss her brow, very softly, his lips lingering for a moment or two before he pulled back.

She glanced up, witnessing adoration in his dark eyes, and met his smile, just a faint lifting of the corners of his mouth.

Suddenly his gaze darted over her head and she watched his features change, his smile vanishing as the planes of his face hardened, his eyelids narrowed.

At that moment she realized everything had changed around her. The music still played, but no longer a waltz, and those who'd been dancing near them had all scooted back to form a circle, watching and whispering among them.

Olivia became acutely aware of how they appeared, embracing each other indecently close, like two lost lovers in their own tiny world.

She felt Sam release her, placing his hands on her upper arms, pushing her back a little as her face flushed hot from an instantaneous, acute embarrassment.

And then Sam whispered, "It's time," and that's when she realized they'd all noticed him.

The drama had begun.

Chapter 21

S am felt his blood rushing through his veins, his senses immediately alert, realizing the moment of revelation had arrived.

He gently pushed Olivia to his side, reaching down to squeeze her hand once before letting her go.

He hadn't seen Edmund yet, but he noted how most of the party guests surrounding them were staring, some of them gaping, and he knew with certainty it wasn't because they'd been dancing so closely.

A hush fell upon them, and with it came the greatest villain in the terrible play that had been his life before Olivia, scooting out from among the crowd in a river of pink satin skirts to stand before him. Funny, but he wasn't a bit surprised that she'd come for the festivity of exposing him.

"Samson," Claudette said brightly, smiling, though her eyes betrayed her rage.

After all these years, he had no idea what to say to her, especially here in front of a crowd of the Riviera's elite. Olivia saved him from response, however, as she took a step in front of him, in a manner of protection or possession, he supposed, hands on her hips as she stared at the countess.

"Aunt Claudette, what are you doing here?" she asked in a low, surprised voice.

Before the woman could summon a reply, an aging gentleman Sam didn't know cleared his throat from behind a group of ladies and came forward, his bearing regal, his expression drawn. He tried to smile congenially but his gaze emitted his stone cold anger.

Sam realized at once that this man had to be Brigitte's grandfather and guardian, undoubtedly confused and enraged to see him and not know a thing at all about what might be happening at his granddaughter's betrothal ball.

"Monsieur," he interrupted pleasantly, "would you and Olivia kindly come with me?"

Thankfully, Olivia answered for him. "Of course, Grand-père Marcotte."

The man gave her only the slightest glance before turning his back on them, expecting them to follow without incident.

They met his quick pace through a gathering of people who parted easily for them, and Sam could feel Claudette's sharp scrutiny on his back as she walked closely behind, animosity seeping from her like a river of ice.

The music started playing again and dancers gradually returned to the floor as the four of them neared the ballroom doors. Murmurs and eye-popping still ensued, but grew fainter as guests returned to their conversation and liquor, engaging themselves once again in the party atmosphere.

Silently, they strode down the corridor toward the front of the estate, then took a turn for what Sam assumed to be the drawing room. He heard Edmund's voice from within before they entered.

His moment of truth had arrived, and although his head ached from tension and his mind still reeled from Olivia's confession of love, he felt remarkably calm.

Marcotte entered the drawing room first, followed by Olivia, himself, and lastly Claudette.

"Out," the old man ordered a simple parlor maid, who offered a quick curtsy and left, closing the doors behind her.

Edmund had been in the far corner, standing next to the cold fireplace, speaking to a blond woman who had to be Brigitte, the heiress of Govance his brother had come to court and swindle. But the moment he heard Marcotte's sharp voice, his head popped up and he looked at Sam for the first time in ten long years.

A macabre silence enveloped the room. Nobody spoke for several long, anxious seconds, and then Marcotte moved to a central position, shoved his evening jacket aside and placed his hands on his hips.

"Would someone please tell me what the *hell* is going on?"

His voice shook the beams. Sam reached down and

instinctively grasped Olivia's hand, though he never moved his gaze from his brother.

Edmund had blanched as his mouth opened in shock, his eyes darting to each of them as sweat beaded on his forehead and temples.

Brigitte merely gaped, clearly stunned as she shot a fast glance to her betrothed's face and then back to Sam.

Claudette, naturally, recovered herself first as she lifted her skirts and began a slow saunter toward the center of the room where the old man stood waiting for explanation.

"Monsieur Marcotte," she purred haughtily, "there has obviously been a complete misunderstanding—"

"Misunderstanding?" the old man bellowed.

The harshness in his voice stopped her in mid-stride, her hoops swinging out in front of her and then back again from her sudden halt.

"Who the devil are you?" he directed to Sam.

"Edmund's twin," Claudette said, carrying on as if she were the center of attention, her accounting the only one that mattered.

Marcotte grimaced. "I believe everyone is already aware of that, Madame Comtesse. It appears to be self-evident."

She looked stung, her eyes widening as her cheeks turned even pinker beneath her rouge.

Marcotte exhaled a forced breath, eyeing Sam skeptically. "And so I ask again, monsieur. Who are you?"

Without pause, he replied, "I am Samson Carlisle, Duke of Durham, in France to confront my younger brother, Edmund, whom I haven't seen in a decade."

That should suffice for a moment, he decided.

Silence reigned among them once more as music from the ballroom drifted into the enclosure.

"Grand-père Marcotte," Olivia began seconds later, "I believe there are some things we need to inform you about your granddaughter's betrothed."

Sam noticed that for the first time since he'd made his appearance, Edmund turned his attention away from him as he shifted his gaze to Olivia, his skin tone changing from ghastly white to red in a second's flash.

Marcotte crossed his arms over his chest and replied, "I'm waiting."

Olivia drew in a deep breath for confidence and dropped his hand, taking a step forward, partially blocking his body, arms at her sides. "I met Edmund last summer, in Paris. My aunt Claudette introduced us."

They all glanced to the Countess Renier, whose face had grown as pink as her gown. "I—That's not entirely true—"

"Of course it's true. Stop lying, Aunt Claudette," Olivia ordered, her poise completely returned to her.

Claudette gasped, looking her up and down. "I'm not lying."

Olivia scoffed. "You've lied from the beginning."

Marcotte rubbed a palm harshly down his face as he began to grasp the complexities of the relationships, and certainly dreading the outcome.

Brigitte had started to realize it, too, for she dropped her tight grasp of Edmund's arm and took a step back and away from him.

"Is . . . is *he* your husband?" Brigitte asked Olivia in a

timid, low voice, her eyes widening to round pools of shock.

Claudette flung an arm in dramatic flair, then slammed her hands down on her hips. "Of course he's not. That's a ridiculous notion."

"Actually, I am," Sam replied through a sigh of annoyance, the prevarication coming as easily and naturally to him as breathing.

Nobody did or said anything for a moment or two, then Edmund straightened his shoulders and pulled down on his lapels in an effort to redeem his questionable honor.

"She's *not* married to him, Ives-Francois," he said, at last speaking, directing his attention to Marcotte. "She's lying, he's lying, and knowing my brother, he's come all the way to Grasse to purposely ruin my plans to marry your granddaughter by repeating half-truths and nonsense to confuse everybody." He looked back at Sam, his gaze spilling over with intense hostility he couldn't hide. "It's just part of his nature."

Sam stared at him from across the carpeted floor, his rage increasing with every beat of his pounding heart. "Why don't you explain to your bride-to-be and her grandfather exactly how you came to know my wife, brother," he charged, his voice hard and coarse. "Enlighten them."

"Yes, enlighten them," Olivia repeated, tipping her head to the side and placing her hands on her hips. "I'd adore hearing your telling of the events."

Tension, thick as day-old gravy, surrounded them, igniting the air.

"Edmund?" Marcotte exhorted.

Edmund stared at Sam with narrowed eyes of undisguised fury, his jaw flexing as he warned, "Don't do this, Samson."

It was a defining moment for all of them. Then, in a grating tone of sheer disgust, Sam countered, "The lying stops here, Edmund. Now. All of it."

For a second or two Edmund's face grew so red with frustration and ire, Sam thought he might lunge at him.

"I am marrying Brigitte Marcotte," Edmund asserted in a dark whisper, hands tightly fisted at his sides, nostrils flaring, lips thinned to one long slit. "That is the only truth to say."

Olivia suddenly bristled, and Sam placed his hands on her shoulders for reassurance.

"Grand-père Marcotte," she stressed, her voice surprisingly steady, "your future grandson-in-law lied to me from the moment we met. He said he loved me, he courted me and arranged a fake marriage—"

"Olivia!" Edmund thundered.

"—and then the night of our contrived wedding," she went on, her determination undaunted, "when I was waiting to consummate that marriage, he *left* me. He took a fabricated marriage license, went to my banker, and withdrew the sum of my inheritance as only my *husband* could, then left the city, apparently traveling here to begin the process once again, courting the heiress of the Govance fortune."

Brigitte let out a whimper of shock, looking as though she might actually faint. On unsteady legs she moved farther away from Edmund, then collapsed on a velveteen settee in a heap of purple skirts.

Marcotte simply gaped at Olivia, stunned beyond words; Edmund raged inwardly, knowing the pretense had finally been exposed; Claudette appeared as her imperious self, swishing her fan in front of her face.

Olivia ignored it all, pursuing her revelation without pause.

"Once I realized he'd left me," she continued bitterly, "taking my funds for Nivan to places unknown, I went searching for him, assuming he'd returned to England where he could live a lavish lifestyle spending my fortune. That's when I met his brother Sam, who, unbeknownst to me, was Edmund's twin."

She laughed with a lingering anguish she couldn't hide, then turned her attention to the man who'd scorned her.

"Imagine my surprise, Edmund. Imagine my humiliation when I thought he was you because I had no idea you had a twin." She shuddered, drawing in a sharp breath. "He, however, was a gentleman to me, offering to help me find you and expose you for what you really are."

Directing her diatribe solely to Edmund now, she ignored the others as if they weren't even present in the room.

"You *used* me," she charged through clenched teeth. "You used me, lied to me, and cheated me, and I simply cannot allow you to do that to another naive lady, especially one I personally know and care for." She straightened and glanced to Claudette at last. "The only thing I have yet to learn is whether this despicable scheme was your idea or my aunt's—"

Claudette gasped.

"—a woman I thought loved me as family. A woman who I've since learned has been your lover for years." She paused, then said with solid disgust, "You and she belong together."

For long hours, it seemed, nobody said a word. The anger from everyone present pervaded the room to heights Sam didn't think possible, charging the air to levels of unreality.

"You little bitch!" Claudette spouted, throwing her fan at Olivia, only to hit the hem of her skirt.

Startled by the animosity, Sam pulled her against him, tightening his grip on her shoulders. "Speak to her again like that, madam," Sam warned in a resonant, controlled fury, "and I'll slap that smirk right off your face."

His tone was so cold, his manner so direct and intimidating, Claudette actually staggered back a step, stunned into speechlessness.

Marcotte stared at Edmund, his posture rigid as steel. "Is this true?" he asked tautly.

"Of course it's true," Olivia piped in, exasperated.

The old man cast her a fast glance. "I need to hear it from Edmund, Olivia."

Edmund looked at Sam, his features overflowing with hatred, his lips curled into a sneer so tight his lips had whitened.

"I love Brigitte," he said forcefully through closed teeth.

"I know you're trying to be convincing, but that's not an answer," Sam remarked.

Edmund slowly shook his head. "You've always managed to ruin everything I've ever cherished in my life.

Why do you do that, brother? Because I'm gentle with the ladies? Because they've always taken to me more?"

Sam's eyes narrowed. "Everything that's ever gone wrong in your life, Edmund, has been your doing." He quickly glanced to Claudette. "Yours and hers."

"My doing?" she blurted.

"Yes, yours, too, apparently," Olivia drawled. "Tell me, Aunt Claudette, why are you here? What made you decide to come to Grasse *this* week as opposed to any other?"

Claudette looked confused for a moment, then brushed the questions aside. "I went to visit Nivan, and Normand mentioned where you'd run off to."

"Normand?" Olivia repeated, incredulous.

Claudette shrugged. "He happened to comment on it in passing, that's all."

Sam heard her suck in a breath, and he gently kneaded her shoulders to lend his support, feeling her stiffen beneath his fingers anyway.

"Well, then," she charged, in complete command, "Normand is no longer under my employ. And you, dearest Aunt, are never to step foot in my boutique again."

That enraged Claudette anew, though Sam couldn't be certain whether it stemmed from Olivia's determination and denial of her aunt's right to enter the store her brother had owned or from Olivia's shift in manner, so forthright and swift.

Slowly, Claudette began to walk toward them, her eyes thinned to slits, nostrils flaring, her mouth turned down into an ugly little frown.

"Tell me, darling Sam, have you mentioned the love affair you and I had to Olivia?"

That came out of nowhere, causing gasps around the room. All except for Edmund, who actually chuckled.

"You're a pathetic excuse for a noblewoman, Claudette," he whispered, his tone like ice.

That didn't faze her in the least. "No? Well, I think she deserves to know the truth." She glanced around the room, arms wide. "We are revealing truths, are we not? And you have several dirty little secrets to share."

Oh, God. Sam felt his pulse begin to race.

"Stop this nonsense. Of course he's told me the whole sordid tale," Olivia said in a shaky voice, trying to be blasé about the issue as she lied for him, though Sam felt her start to tremble tenuously beneath his hands.

Be brave, my sweet, beautiful Livi.

Marcotte immediately realized Claudette was pushing beyond the limits of decency. With firm resolve he maintained, "I'd like you to leave, Madame Comtesse. Now."

Claudette fumed, rigidly set, glaring at him. "I'm not going anywhere until my niece hears about the baby."

Brigitte, whom everyone had seemed to forget, suddenly shrieked from her position on the settee.

Marcotte turned pale. "What baby?"

"Leave now, madam," Sam warned, his deep voice reverberating through the walls, "or you will forever regret the day you met me."

"I already regret it," she retorted. "You can't scare me, Samson."

"What baby!" Marcotte bellowed.

"Samson and Claudette's baby," Edmund drawled, a sly expression bathing his face.

Without a word, Olivia tried to pull away from him, but he clenched his hands hard on her shoulders, tightly reining her in.

"You've always been a bastard, Edmund," he said, his voice a deadly whisper.

Claudette clapped her hands together in malicious glee. "Oh goodness, Olivia, dear, I see from your poor pale face that you didn't know Sam and I had a little one together." Her brows rose as she looked at him again. "I wonder why he didn't tell you?"

Sam swallowed his rage. If he weren't so fearful of Olivia running, he'd let her go, take three steps forward, and kill the woman.

"Shut up, Claudette," he warned, clinging to Olivia, who'd started to shake.

Claudette only blinked in feigned shock. "What? And not tell her everything?" She laughed. "It seems you've been keeping some secrets of your own, darling Sam."

Marcotte seemed to quickly gather his thoughts. He straightened, arms at his sides, then walked to within inches of the countess.

"This has nothing to do with my granddaughter. I'm asking you politely, once again, to leave."

Claudette glanced to Edmund. "Darling? I suggest you tell him everything."

Edmund's features relaxed a little, and he gazed at the countess with nothing short of pity in his eyes. "I'm going to marry Brigitte, regardless of what I've done in the past, and regardless of why I came to Grasse to meet her."

Claudette didn't say anything for a moment or two, then murmured, "No, you're not."

"Yes, I am," he countered brusquely.

Claudette looked truly confused, glancing around the room to each of their faces. And then fierce conviction returned; she lifted her chin to bitterly reveal, "Everything Olivia said is true. Edmund and I have been lovers for years, and we planned this ruse to woo the Govance heiress strictly for her inheritance. Edmund is only claiming love to keep his sniveling ass out of prison for fraud."

Brigitte gasped.

"Why?" Sam asked Claudette. It was a simple question, but also the central issue upon which they hadn't yet touched in this horrid yarn. "What is the point of choosing perfume heiresses when you've never wanted for anything in your entire life?"

"Because I want control of the industry, the riches, the supply houses, to control what sells and what does not. I should have been given Nivan at my brother's death. *I* am the rightful heir. Edmund agreed with me, and we... we decided that by having him court and pretend to marry the heiresses of Nivan and Govance, though I may not get complete control, with the Empress Eugenie as *my* patron, I would be the one with status. I would be in charge of what should have been mine."

Marcotte actually chuckled as he pinched the bridge of his nose. "That's the most ludicrous thing I've ever heard."

Claudette turned scarlet again. "And yet it's the truth."

"Madame Comtesse," Marcotte said with ease, looking at her directly, "nothing you could do would give you control of the perfume industry, and certainly not

the kind patronage of the empress. How can anyone
guarantee what her tastes will be next Season? Boutiques and supply houses are bought, sold, or traded
constantly, or they stay in families, as mine has, as Nivan has." He shot Edmund an angry glance. "As for the
part about stealing inheritances, I'd have to say that
dear Olivia, who has obviously been greatly hurt by
the two of you, could and should report you both to the
authorities, though I suppose your titles give you more
respect than you deserve."

Claudette just looked at him; Edmund closed his
eyes and slowly shook his head, clearly feeling the sudden loss of everything he'd tried to gain by cheating.

Brigitte started crying on the settee.

"I am in love with Brigitte!" Edmund fairly shouted.
He looked at Olivia. "Regardless of what I've done."

"You don't deserve her," the old man said in reply.

At that moment Sam actually pitied his brother.

Then standing with rigid bearing once more, Marcotte looked hard at Claudette.

"You have done enough," he said. "You will leave
my estate and never step foot near Govance again, madame. You will leave now or I shall throw you out on
your wicked, deceitful ass."

Claudette took a step away from him, thoroughly
appalled.

He grabbed her arm. "Now!"

And then with incredible strength that defied his
age, Marcotte dragged her, hoops and all, to the door,
opened it, and shoved her out, closing it behind him.

If it were any other circumstance, Sam would have
applauded.

The silence became deafening. Brigitte cried quietly on the settee, Edmund glared at him again, though now looking like a wounded animal. And the greatest love, the greatest woman he had ever known in his life stood in front of him, still trembling, refusing to look at him, emanating raw emotions he thought might actually crush him. But he would not discuss it here, only to embarrass her even more in front of the Govance patriarch, in front of Edmund and Brigitte.

Drawing a deep, full breath, he stood erect and broke the silence.

"Monsieur Marcotte," he said with regal stature, "I offer you my sincerest apologies for the unfortunate events of this night. But the fact remains that I refused to see my brother abuse another lady as he did my wife."

Olivia tried to pull away from him again, but he held her fast.

"Especially one as lovely and innocent as your granddaughter."

Brigitte sniffed, offering him a faint smile.

Marcotte regarded him with narrowed eyes, then nodded once as he simply replied, "Your grace. You are welcome in my house."

Sam hadn't expected that, which made him wonder why the old man hadn't yet thrown Edmund out on his deceitful, wicked ass, either.

"Now," Marcotte expelled through a forced breath, pulling down on his evening jacket, "it seems I have a decision to make."

He strode with purpose to Edmund, who now actually looked sheepish and ridiculous in his expensive black evening suit, probably paid for by Olivia's stolen money.

Without restraint, Marcotte asked, "Have you bedded my granddaughter?"

Olivia sucked in a breath; Brigitte jumped off the settee, her face as white as graveyard lilies. To his credit, Edmund appeared confused and a trifle shaken by the question.

"I beg your pardon?" he blurted.

Although Edmund stood nearly half a foot taller than the Frenchman, he shrank from the man's intensity.

Very slowly Marcotte repeated, "Have you bedded my granddaughter?"

Brigitte came to his rescue, moving to Edmund's side and taking his hand. "Grand-père, your question is *completely* inappropriate."

The old man looked down at her briefly. "Stay out of this, child," he warned in a whisper.

She swallowed, her eyes large as saucers.

He looked back at Edmund. "Answer me!"

"I love her," he replied, his voice dangerously low.

"Does that mean yes?"

Edmund's eyes never wavered. "Yes."

With that, Marcotte pulled his arm back, then shot it forward, ramming his fist into Edmund's jaw.

"Grand-père!" Brigitte screeched, her mouth hanging open as Edmund grunted and fell back, his shoulder slamming into the edge of the mantelpiece before he toppled to the floor.

Sam stared in astonishment. A man nearly eighty years of age had just bested his brother, something he'd wanted to do for years. His admiration for Marcotte grew immensely at that moment.

The old man rubbed his fist, then shook it out, gazing down at the two of them, Brigitte mortified as she bent down and lifted Edmund's shoulders off the floor, Edmund shaking himself, bewildered and in pain.

"Now that we've settled that," Marcotte continued as he straightened his collar, "I will say this. You're a spoiled bastard, Edmund, but I believe you love my granddaughter as she loves you. You *will* marry her, and legally, with me at your side to witness the event, and then you two will make babies and live on my estate until I inform you that you may leave. You will *not* live a life of lazy days; you will work at Govance as I order you to. You will never mention your sordid past to anyone, for if you do, if I learn you've hurt my granddaughter the way you've hurt Olivia, I will have you arrested and will spend every penny of my vast fortune to make certain you die in prison." He huffed, then added, "Or I will kill you myself."

He stepped back and dusted off his coat sleeves, apparently expecting no reply from the man he'd only just floored.

"Now, Brigitte, dear, you will dry your eyes and clean your face this minute," he ordered, pointing his finger at her, his tone growing louder with every word, "and then you and the idiot you're going to marry will walk arm in arm into that ballroom and present yourselves to my guests, who've come to a party that will cost me for the next ten years, as the betrothed couple you are, happy and joyous and in love!"

Sam shook his head in wonder, in keen enjoyment of watching Edmund squirm.

Marcotte turned as Edmund finally stood, trying like hell not to look humiliated or rub his aching jaw, clinging to Brigitte's arm while she coddled him.

Sam remained where he was, Olivia still in front of him. He reached down and lifted her hand, his heart skipping a beat when it felt limp and cold as ice. God, they needed to get out of here, to talk alone. To make love and forgive.

"I'm sure you would have enjoyed that almost as much as I did," Marcotte said lightly, eyes sparkling as he walked toward Sam and Olivia at last.

"You were splendid," Sam remarked with a wry grin. "I enjoyed it just to watch you."

Marcotte nodded, then gazed at Olivia, his smile fading as he clearly witnessed the pain on her face, a pain Sam couldn't yet see because she'd been in front of him the entire time. Suddenly, it scared him.

"My dear Olivia," he said gently, grasping her shoulders and kissing both cheeks. "Thank you."

"Grand-père Marcotte," she whispered, her tone gravelly and choked.

The old man breathed deeply and stood back, clasping his hands together behind him. "You're both more than welcome to stay, but it appears you have much to discuss. Your grace, I love your wife, as I loved her mother, just like my own family. You have chosen well."

He nodded once. "Thank you."

Marcotte bowed, then strode to the door. Placing his hand on the latch, he glanced back at Edmund and

Brigitte. "Out to the party quickly, both of you. And Edmund, if anyone mentions the bruise on your face, tell them your brother hit you. Everyone should believe that."

He opened the door and quit the drawing room, closing it once again behind him.

For a moment nobody did anything, Sam still clinging to Olivia's lifeless hand, desperate now for privacy.

"You...identical," Brigitte murmured as Edmund stood facing Sam, his eyes defiant.

"Enough, Brigitte," Edmund cut in with annoyance.

Sam started walking toward his brother, pulling Olivia along because he was suddenly terrified of letting her go.

"My congratulations to you," he said, his voice once again chilling the air.

Edmund sneered. "Go away, Samson."

"I intend to." He cocked his head to the side. "And I never want to see you in England again unless you come to apologize to my wife."

Edmund snorted, rubbing his jaw, chancing a glance toward Olivia. "You really married her, eh?"

Sam's eyes turned black. "Be careful, Edmund, or I will knock your teeth out. You've done enough damage for one lifetime."

Brigitte grew immediately incensed. "That's enough, both of you."

Sam looked at her and chanced a smile. "Mademoiselle Marcotte, please keep the money Edmund stole from Nivan as my wedding gift to you. I will pay Olivia back for her trouble with my own funds."

Brigitte blinked, then looked at Edmund. "I can't

believe you did something like that, Edmund. It's despicable."

"We'll discuss it later," he groused, never taking his eyes from his brother.

"Until we meet again, Edmund," Sam said lightly, his mind already centered on the lengthy discussion with Olivia to come.

"Until we meet again," Edmund replied sarcastically.

Sam expelled a long breath, then gazed down to Brigitte for a final time. "Mademoiselle, you have my sympathies."

And then clinging to Olivia's hand, he turned and led the two of them out of the drawing room and toward his waiting carriage.

Chapter 22

She still hadn't said a word to him. She'd made almost no sound at all, in fact, since she so gallantly defended him in front of Claudette, lying with such bravery to protect him from ridicule. To protect them.

Now she sat across from him in the darkened coach, moonlight reflecting her flowing, silent tears as she leaned against the cushion, staring out the window.

It absolutely crushed him to see her like this, to know how deeply hurt she was from learning something of his ignoble past from anyone other than him. He just didn't know exactly how to broach the subject now, when she seemed so utterly devastated.

His nerves ate away at his gut. The longer she took to say something—anything—the more concerned he became.

Finally, after the coach had left the Govance estate

and turned onto the main road toward town, Sam decided her silence had lasted long enough.

"Olivia—"

"Don't talk to me," she spat in a forced whisper.

Her quiet rage cut him deeply. "We have to talk," he replied soothingly.

"Not here," she breathed, refusing to look at him.

His confidence started to rapidly diminish by the second. He leaned back against the seat, studying her in her striking gown, seeing the stunning face, remembering each incredible thought, each intense feeling that soared through his body and mind when she had confessed her love for him. He'd never felt anything so extraordinary in his life. And he'd be damned if he was going to lose that now.

Closing his eyes, he leaned his aching head back against the cushion, allowing her the time to contemplate all the remarkable things that had happened to them, and between them, this day. And there were so many. She'd met Edmund alone and had proudly stood her ground; she'd been made love to for the first time; she'd danced, declared her love for him, and then had no choice but to be confronted by Edmund and Claudette and learn that the man she finally knew she loved had a bastard child with a relation she'd never particularly liked and now despised. All that, and then discovering the people she trusted the most had cheated and lied and withheld information with absolutely no consideration for her feelings.

Sam had never hated his brother more.

At last the coach slowed as it pulled up to the Maison de la Fleur. Out of his seat before it stopped, he opened the door himself and reached out a hand for Olivia, but she ignored it, brushing by him and down the steps, proceeding swiftly inside the hotel. He followed with haste, afraid to allow her to leave his view for even a moment, catching up to her as they climbed the stairs to their second-floor suite.

Unlocking the door, she entered first and walked straight to her bedroom in total darkness, slamming the door in his face.

That made him mad, irrationally mad because they had so much to discuss, he had so much to tell her, to explain, and she knew it perfectly well.

Drawing a deep breath for resolve, he opened the door, his eyes quickly drawn to the bed, now bathed only in moonlight, Olivia sitting on the edge of it, ramrod straight, staring at the floor.

"Olivia—"

"Get out."

He set his jaw, hands on his hips. "We're going to talk."

"I never want to talk to you again."

God. Females. He wiped a palm down his face, then in two strides was upon her, grabbing her wrist and yanking her to her feet, fairly dragging her to the center room. He plopped her on the sofa, then turned to the table and lit the oil lamp.

Without looking at him, she tried to stand to head back to her bedroom. He wouldn't allow it, as he grasped her upper arm and shoved her down hard.

"Sit."

"Go away, Samson," she said, her tone coarse and commanding.

She used the same phrase Edmund had, and that stung him.

Pulling out one of the wooden chairs, he sat heavily, his body tense, his thoughts controlled, unbuttoning his shirt at the collar and cuffs. "We are going to talk, Olivia," he murmured, the words coming out harsher than he'd intended. "Or rather, I am going to talk and you are going to listen and respond."

"No," she replied, lifting her head to look directly at his face for the first time since they'd danced together at the ball. "We're finished."

The coldness he witnessed in her defiant eyes at that moment nearly overwhelmed him, and he swallowed hard to keep from choking up in front of her.

"I need to explain some things to you," he said gently, running his hot palms over his thighs to help ease his growing agitation. "And even though they're not going to be easy for you to hear, you're going to hear them anyway."

"I don't want to hear them at all," she replied abruptly, matter-of-factly. "I want to go to bed."

Sam felt his irritation nearing the boiling point. "What you want isn't up for discussion right now. You're going to listen to me if I have to hold you down to do it."

She glared at him, her lips thinned to a straight line of absolute fury. At least that was better than ignoring him altogether, he supposed. Though not much.

After a moment to collect his thoughts, to gather his nerve, Sam began the tale that had so changed his life forever.

"Claudette came to England twelve years ago with her husband, Count Michel Renier," he said, his tone cool, controlled. "I met her at a ball, naturally, as she attended all of them. I won't bother trying to convince you that she seduced me, because she didn't have to. I was quite taken with her and wanted her in my bed."

Olivia started crying again, silently, and it startled him because he hadn't even gotten to the difficult part. He carried on anyway, knowing she needed to hear the truth from him and to hear it all at once.

Leaning forward in the chair, he placed his elbows on his knees, interlocking his fingers in front of him.

"We had a love affair for several months, and I truly believed we loved each other. Yes, she was married, but at the time I didn't concern myself with that. I was young and arrogant, and she was beautiful and French and...exotic to me, different from the young English girls who played coy with me, if they talked to me at all. Claudette seemed to want me desperately, and I was willing to step in and be her lover."

Olivia cupped her mouth with her palm, squeezing her eyes shut as she shook her head in denial, tears streaming down her cheeks now, ripping him apart inside.

In a suddenly shaky voice, he maintained, "I was naive, Olivia. Naive and stupid and blinded by a beautiful woman who actually pretended I was the only man in the world she'd ever loved."

"Where is the child?"

He'd barely heard the words as she spoke them into her hand, but her disgust filled the room like a tangible thing.

"There is no child," he whispered in return, his panic continuing to mount.

She dropped her hand to her lap with a thud and

stared at him, her features hard and cold as marble in winter. "Now, which liar am I supposed to believe?" she purred sarcastically.

Her animosity took him aback. She'd jumped ahead of him, but he should have realized she'd be most upset about him fathering a bastard and would want those answers first. Trying to remain calm, he stared at the floor, squeezing his hands together because they'd started shaking.

"There is no child," he repeated gravely. "Claudette and I were lovers for about a year. I knew she couldn't marry me, and frankly, I never really thought about it. I was just...obsessed with her, I suppose, and didn't want it to end."

He drew in a sharp inhale and closed his eyes to the memory.

"Claudette became pregnant and came to me with the news. I was...stunned, I suppose, but then I rationalized that many an aristocrat had bastard children, and I would simply accept it because I loved her, or thought I did. At the time, I considered the baby to be nothing more than a nuisance for which I intended to always remain financially responsible."

"That's disgusting," she interjected.

His head shot up. "Yes, it is," he agreed irritably, "but then I was young and pompous and had my whole life ahead of me, Olivia. I also knew without question that because of duty I would have to marry one day to produce legitimate heirs. I could not be bothered with a bastard child. I was privileged, and privileged people often do disgusting things they're later not proud of. I'm one of them."

She had nothing to say to that as she turned her head away from him, resting her elbow on the arm of the sofa, her fist on her mouth as she closed her eyes.

Sam rubbed the back of his neck, feeling the tension, his head pounding with every fast beat of his heart. Deciding he could no longer sit, he shot to his feet and began to pace the floor.

"When her husband learned she carried a child that wasn't his—and he knew it wasn't because he hadn't bedded her in months—he appeared on my doorstep. I took his arrival in stride, of course. Men and women have extramarital affairs all the time, especially in the aristocracy, and I just assumed he'd tell me he expected me to reward him financially for raising the child, which I was prepared to do." He laughed bitterly. "That's not what occurred. He instead informed me that he was leaving her, that he'd had enough of her antics, that he would return to France posthaste and live as a bachelor. To say I was appalled is an understatement."

"No more appalling than your escapades, apparently," she quipped.

Sam shot a quick glance in her direction, noting how she hadn't moved a muscle, refused to look at him. And the most difficult part for him was knowing he couldn't go to her and offer comfort, to murmur his love and the tumult of emotions he felt right now, because she'd surely reject him. And rejection was the one thing he could never take from her. It would utterly shatter him.

With resolve, he stopped pacing in the middle of the room, deciding he'd simply tell her everything before he made any attempt to win her trust anew. His hands shook badly now, so he shoved them into his coat pockets.

"That was the day my innocence died, Olivia," he revealed, his voice barely above a whisper as he stared at the carpeting. "Claudette's husband told me—and with great pride and delight, mind you—that she had been my brother's lover for almost as long as she had been mine. That she had been using us both and loved nobody but herself. Being the fool I was, I didn't believe him and more or less tossed him out of my house. Then I went to see Claudette."

Sam inhaled deeply, trying to remain composed as all the anger and humiliation of that time long ago came flooding back to him as if it had taken place yesterday.

"Claudette had a town house in London then, and I marched up the steps in the middle of the afternoon, as I hadn't ever done before because we'd been so discreet, and walked into her home."

"You found her in bed with Edmund," Olivia said for him, wiping a palm across her cheek.

Sam's heart ached for her, for the sweet innocence he so cherished in her that he was about to destroy of necessity, just so she could understand him better. No lady of her beauty and upbringing should be so exposed to the degradation of human nature, but he could think of no other way to explain his actions without revealing the blacker side of life.

He walked to the chair again, quickly turning it around to sit on it backward so he could face her and be able to place his arms somewhere. He stretched his legs out a little and rested his forearms on the hard wood running lengthwise at his chest, studying her carefully.

"I did find her in bed with Edmund, but they weren't alone. Two other women were with them, and all four were engaged in the sex act while two other men, half dressed, watched them from the corner. I—I was shocked, and appalled. But more than anything I felt suddenly lost and alone and ashamed because the woman I thought I loved had not only lied to me, she had laughed at me as she did it. Not only was she Edmund's lover, she was everybody's lover, apparently."

Slowly, as he'd confessed his disturbing revelation, she'd opened her eyes to look at him, her face now deathly pale, her brow furrowed in an odd stupefaction. He waited for his words to sink in, for her to come to an understanding of what he must have felt at that moment.

"I don't believe you," she charged quietly, her tone spilling over with revulsion.

He looked directly, intently, into her eyes. "It happened, Olivia. It happens all the time, in every country and in every walk of life. There are people in the world who can be very base with their desires, very loose with their morals, and very indifferent toward the true nature of lovemaking. And again, those of the privileged classes often have the time and money to appease their sexual fantasies. Some of them will do just about anything with anyone." He sighed, and added in a soft murmur of regret, "One of the great dangers to the love between a man and a woman, especially in marriage, is uncontrolled lust and the desire for self-gratification at any cost. I learned this by having it slapped in my face."

She shuddered, shaking her head. "This sickens me," she whispered.

Rubbing his tired eyes with his fingers, he returned, "It should."

"And you were ... bedding her the entire time."

She said that so flatly, with so little emotion, he wasn't sure how to react. Instead of meaningless words that would do nothing to appease her, he simply nodded.

A long silent moment passed between them. Then she pulled her legs up and onto the sofa, tucking them under her gown, hugging her knees into her chest.

"Have you ever done that?" she asked, her gaze locked on the carpet at her feet.

He should have expected the question. "No, I never have, and never want to."

"But you've bedded other women," she stated rather than asked.

He wasn't about to lie to her now. She wouldn't believe him anyway. But he could give her the details gently. "Olivia, it's complicated—"

"Answer me!" she shouted in anguish, her eyes tearing up again as her gaze pierced his.

He pulled back in shock, swallowing his fear, afraid suddenly that he might break down in front of her. "Yes," he replied quietly.

She just looked at him, then moments later asked caustically, "How many bastard children do you have, your grace?"

He clenched his teeth. "None."

She scoffed. "You don't know that."

"Yes, I do. That's one thing I know with absolute certainty."

She hesitated, wondering if he spoke the truth, looking him up and down as she wiped a rolling tear off her cheek. "What about Claudette's baby, the one you and she had together. Or are you now going to tell me she never carried?"

"Claudette was indeed pregnant," he said, trying not to lash out at her in anger. "She began showing very shortly after the day I walked out on her and her group of lovers. She actually laughed at me when I did that, Olivia. She thought it was funny that I'd found her like that, and with my brother who looks exactly like me." He lowered his tone, his throat now dry and cracking as he spoke. "From that moment on I refused to acknowledge the baby. Perhaps that was wrong, but I had been so sickened by what I'd seen, so heartbroken to be betrayed like that, I just did not care."

She looked away from him again, closing her eyes.

"Edmund and I have never lived peacefully together; we're just too different. But what made me despise him was his indifference toward my feelings for Claudette, and his hiding the fact that the two of them had become lovers directly under my nose. When I learned the truth, when I discovered that he'd been with her all the time I had, it occurred to me that even if the child looked exactly like me, he would also look exactly like Edmund. I would never know if it were truly mine, and so I refused to accept it."

He stood again and walked to the other side of the room, near the window, where he could view the moonlit garden alcove by moonlight, where he'd seen his hateful brother with the woman of his dreams, arousing every memory of him and Claudette together, every pain because his fear of losing Olivia would have been the greatest tragedy of his life.

"Claudette became furious with me when I stopped communicating with her, when I refused to acknowledge the child she carried." He hesitated, then at last said aloud, for the first time in years, what started the scandal that would follow him always.

"Just a few days after rejecting her for a final time, she was discovered accidentally in one of her sexual parties by several upstanding members of the elite, and Edmund was with her. When the rumors started to spread..." He fisted his hands tightly at his sides, gritted his teeth. "When the rumors started to spread, not only did she claim the child was mine and I refused to compensate her as a good nobleman should, she also insisted it was I who had been with her the day she'd been discovered with three other people in her bed. She claimed *I* was the deviant, not Edmund, and because he was my brother, I felt honor-bound to keep my mouth shut. I never denied it. Who would believe me anyway? We look *exactly* alike. From that day on I was the social fool, the man mothers kept their daughters from, the man who other gentlemen joked about at cards. Stories were created about my escapades, made worse because they were exaggerated." He laughed, tasting the bitterness of irony to this day. "I have always been accepted socially, Olivia, because of my title. But I will never, as long as I live, be accepted as a person one wants as a friend, or a love."

He stared out the window, gazing at the darkness of the garden, seeing nothing.

"Claudette gave birth to a boy she named Samuel,"

he proceeded, his tone thick and hushed, "but it had been a very difficult delivery and the child had shown his feet first. He only lived for two days. I don't think Claudette really wanted him anyway. She was never very moved by his death. She left for the Continent with Edmund shortly after that, and I never saw her again until that night with you on the balcony in Paris."

A heavy, enveloping silence grew around them. Olivia sniffed and he glanced back at her. She just shook her head slowly, her eyes closed, her palm covering her mouth again.

Sam moved away from the window and walked toward her a little, closing his own eyes and tipping his head back.

"Olivia, you have to understand—"

"Understand?"

He jerked his head up, numbed by her outburst.

In one fluid movement she abruptly stood, facing him with her hand on her hips, glowering at him with scorn. "*Understand*? What is there for me to understand? I could accept a bastard child. I could raise him if I had to because he'd be yours. But what happened to me tonight went far beyond anything Edmund ever did to me." She choked back a sob.

"I don't even really care that you've...indulged yourself with other women. My heart *aches* for you, for the pain you've felt all these years, for having to live with horrible people who spread rumors and destroy lives." She braced herself, lowering her voice. "But I *loathe* knowing that the things you did to me this afternoon, all those marvelous, wonderful, beautiful things, you...you also did with my aunt," she said in absolute anguish, her face flushing, her hands cupping her cheeks. "You made love with my *aunt*. And the worst part is, she and Edmund knew it all along. Tonight, during this...this...huge confrontation that I'd been dreaming of for months, she and Edmund were *laughing* at me."

"No!" He reached for her, grabbing her by the shoulders and shaking her once. "It wasn't like that at all."

Using all the force within her, she shoved his hands aside. "It *was* like that," she asserted through a husky growl. "You're such an idiot if you think I didn't look like the fool tonight, Sam. The innocent little virginal Olivia who had no idea that the man she thought she loved with everything inside of her had bedded her aunt, had a child with her—"

"Goddammit, Olivia, that isn't the point," he cut in, grabbing her shoulders again.

"It is the point!" Her tears flowed freely now, her body shaking with uncontrolled fury. "Do you have any idea how *humiliated* I was tonight? For nearly a year now I've been lied to and humiliated by people I truly believed loved me, and tonight I learn that you've done exactly the same thing. Humiliated me, lied to me—"

"I never lied to you," he whispered thickly, his throat tight with a new flood of emotions. "I admit to withholding facts, but that's not the same thing."

She scoffed with disgust and turned away from him.

He yanked her against him, holding her so close she couldn't help but look into his eyes.

"I love you, Olivia," he said huskily. He shook his head minutely. "What I felt for Claudette doesn't begin to compare to what I feel for you."

She closed her eyes and he hugged her, holding her tightly, his face in her hair. "Please don't do this. Please try to understand that I was a different person then, that the wrong things mattered to me."

She shook her head vehemently, pushing with all her strength against his chest. "All this time you were with me, after you met my aunt again on the balcony, you should have told me."

"How? How exactly was I supposed to tell you, Olivia?"

She wiggled against him, and he finally let her go. She took a step away and then turned her back on him.

Sam had had enough. Placing his hands on his hips, he lowered his voice to a husky whisper, revealing everything inside him.

"I want you to know, Olivia, that one thing Edmund said tonight was true."

He waited, and after a moment or two she peeked at him over her shoulder.

"I've forever been jealous of the easy way he's able to talk to the gentle sex, to attract the ladies, to flirt and woo them and get them into his bed." He drew a shaky breath. "But never had I been more envious of him than I was the first night I met you, Olivia. To think, to learn, that he'd married so well, to someone so goddamned beautiful, someone so smart and engaging and witty, made me jealous of him like I'd never felt before." He paused to control his raging thoughts, then whispered, "Do you know why I made love to you today?"

She said nothing, and so he reached out and clasped her arm, yanking her around, forcing her to face him. "Do you?"

She gazed up to his face, her eyes glassy pools of confusion and anger she couldn't yet reconcile. "Because you thought he'd bedded me and you wanted what he'd had?" she returned sarcastically.

That made him furious. "I knew you'd never been with Edmund."

"How?" she asked through batted lashes.

He tried very hard to ignore her sarcasm. "Because Claudette told me when we danced together at the Brillon ball in Paris. Thinking I was Edmund, she warned me not to bed you so I wouldn't run the risk of ruining their plan."

That shook her a little. Her brows furrowed and she tipped her head negligibly. He took that as a sign that she was beginning to understand.

"I made love to you, Olivia, because I was so terribly afraid Edmund would earn your trust again. I saw you together in the garden and it scared me. I didn't want to run the risk of losing you."

She backed up a step, lowering her lashes, trying, at least, to absorb his disclosure.

Standing tall, he boldly whispered, "In all the years since my affair with Claudette ended, I have been with many women, Olivia."

"I don't want to hear this!"

He lunged for her, pulling her against him again, forcing her to know.

"I have been with many women, but until today, until *you,* I haven't been *inside* a single one of them. Not in ten long years. Not one. I will not have another bastard child, to run risks of more rumors. Since I became the scandalous nobleman whose unusual sex acts are legendary fodder for horrible jokes, lovemaking ceased for me. I occasionally took a woman to bed for her pleasure, for the touch, for the superficial sexual release. But I didn't know what *love* was until I needed to be inside of you, Olivia. Until that desire became so strong I *needed* to become one with you and gave you everything I am."

He took hold of her face, feeling the wetness on her skin.

"I've never known another woman like you, and I wanted to share myself, to leave my seed in you, to make you mine. Being with you was the most wonderful thing I've ever experienced in my life, and I refuse—*refuse*— to lose you now."

She didn't say anything, but she trembled, nearly sobbing now, shaking her head, her eyes squeezed shut.

And then she jerked away from him and swiftly walked to her bedroom, shutting the door to the torment inside of him, the anguish that he'd hoped, with her love, she'd want to soothe away.

Sam closed his eyes, overwhelmed by her pain, uncertain if he should go to her, but deciding after a moment's thought that she needed the time alone.

She loved him. He knew that beyond any doubt. She would accept his past and share his life with him. He trusted her that much—and he refused to think otherwise. Not after all they'd been through.

His chest tightening, hands shaking, he walked to

the table and extinguished the lamp. Too wound up to sleep, he sauntered to the sofa and sat heavily, staring at the darkened floor for a long time, hoping she'd come to him, wrap her arms around him and hold him close in silence.

Finally exhaustion overcame him and he curled up on the cushion, still wearing his entire evening suit, closing his eyes for only a brief moment. When he opened them again, daylight streamed in through the window.

Sam shot to his feet, looking toward her room, noting the wide-open door, the neatly made bed. And it was then that he realized she'd left him.

Chapter 23

Their dinner was to be a quiet affair, just the four of them, as Sam had been invited to Colin's town house along with his only other close friend, Will Raleigh, who, along with his wife, Vivian, had come to London for the Season.

They'd met in the foyer at seven, but had since moved to the study for casual discussion and whiskey, Will's wife sipping only a taste of champagne.

Colin, of course, had been carrying on about his latest venture for the government, the talk between them regarding his trip to France all but over weeks ago at his return.

Although he'd given them details of the events, especially as they pertained to Edmund, Sam hadn't disclosed much of his personal thoughts, and none of his feelings regarding Olivia Shea, and his friends had been wise enough not to probe for answers. Still, his memory of the weeks he'd spent with her surfaced constantly to bring back all of the guilt, frustration, and anger, but mostly the love they'd shared as it grew between them during the course of their adventure. At least he would always have that.

Sam didn't think he'd ever felt such fear as on the morning he awakened in the hotel to find her gone. He'd immediately returned to the Govance estate, only to be told they hadn't seen her. They'd supplied him with names of two of her late stepfather's relatives who lived in Grasse, and he checked with them, learning more of the same—she'd visited no one. He then returned to Paris and stayed for three weeks, but she never came back to Nivan. She'd simply vanished, and after spending as much time as he had, Sam eventually gave up the pursuit and returned to England alone.

His heart ached constantly. Never in his life had he considered that he'd one day fall in love as deeply as he had, and then lose it, and no pain, he decided, could compare to such a devastating blow.

Every day he experienced a twinge of anger at her stubbornness that kept them apart, that she made him worry about her constantly. He'd been carrying the hope that she might simply walk back into his life, but as the weeks passed with no sign of her, no word or correspondence, that hope was beginning to fade.

Now as he sat with his friends in Colin's study, sipping whiskey and listening to the three of them chatter on about something completely mundane, he couldn't help but think what a joy it would be to have Olivia by his side, as his wife, blabbering on about sachets and perfume bottles, the scent of the season and the fragrance she used to keep her stockings smelling like flowers.

"What are you smiling about?"

Sam blinked and looked up from where he sat behind the desk, first glancing to Will and then to Colin, who'd asked the question.

"Smiling about?" he repeated.

Colin smirked and then took a sip of his whiskey. "We're discussing the civil unrest in France and you obviously think it's amusing." His brows furrowed, and then he added, "I guess the French are always funny, however. Carry on."

Vivian laughed softly from the wing chair in which she sat beside the cold fireplace, her husband behind her, leaning on the chair's back with his arms crossed.

"He's probably smiling because it hardly matters what *we* think about France," Vivian mused with a crooked grin.

Sam snorted and in one long gulp finished off his whiskey. "Actually, I was thinking about spice."

"Spice?" Will drawled.

He shrugged, setting his empty glass on the desktop. "I'm starved."

"Me, too," Vivian said through a sigh.

Will leaned over and kissed the top of her head. "You're always hungry."

"One must feed the baby," Colin offered nonchalantly. "How marvelous to have an acceptable excuse to eat all the time."

Vivian scoffed. "That's the only acceptable thing about carrying."

"You seem to be handling it with ease," Colin replied.

"With *ease*?" Vivian repeated, wide-eyed.

"Well, it looks easy enough," he bantered back.

"Good God," Will muttered, "I can't wait for the day when you take a wife and you have to suffer—"

"It'll never happen," Colin argued as he took a long sip of his drink. "I don't have time for a wife and all her little..." He waved a hand toward Vivian. "...things."

A slight rap at the door interrupted them.

Sam smiled. "Thank God for dinner. I'm suffering just listening to the three of you."

Colin said, "Come."

The door opened softly to admit the butler, a new one, Sam thought. Always new servants for Colin. He would never understand that.

"Your grace, you have a visitor," the man said, his expression staid.

Before Colin could offer a reply, the butler moved to his side a little and in walked Olivia Shea, formerly of Elmsboro.

Colin reacted first. "Good God, it's the vision in gold."

Sam just stared at her, suddenly mesmerized. And then he felt the blood drain from his face as his hands began to shake.

"Olivia?" he murmured, attempting to stand, supporting himself with his palms on the desk in case his legs gave way beneath him.

She looked radiant, dressed entirely in sky blue, from her day gown to her shoes to the ribbons tying her shiny black hair in twisted plaits atop her head. And the moment she offered him a hesitant smile, his heart filled with tenderness and his mouth went dry as his throat tightened from a swell of suppressed emotion.

She'd come to him because she loved him.

She had never been more frightened in her life. Frightened—and excited. How she ever managed to stay on her feet the moment she set eyes on Sam again, she'd never know.

He looked marvelous, dressed casually for dinner in navy trousers and an ecru shirt with the neck unbuttoned. His hair seemed slightly longer than when she'd last seen him, though he'd brushed it back from his face the way she liked it. His eyes, so dark and aloof, gazed into hers intently, and it made her knees go weak. She had to swallow with difficulty to fight back tears of exhilaration and happiness, only hoping to the depths of her heart that he would forgive her for being so callous as to walk out on him, a truly wonderful man.

She couldn't take her eyes off him as she took a step into the room.

"Set another place for dinner, Harold," someone said.

"Right away, your grace," the butler behind her replied before closing the door and leaving her alone with him.

Only they weren't alone, she realized as if living in a dream, moving her gaze at last to note the man she remembered as Sam's friend Colin, who'd just spoken to the butler, standing near the fireplace, and two others she didn't know near the window on her right.

"I—I'm sorry if I'm intruding," she managed to say.

"Not at all," Colin returned with a wry smile. "We adore surprises. Don't we, Sam?"

She shifted her gaze back to the man of her desire, lingering on his handsome features, remembering the way he teased her, the way he laughed with her. The night he told her he loved her.

"Are you going to introduce us, or shall I?" the woman in the chair said rather sharply, her brows lifted in question.

Sam seemed to suddenly collect himself, the shock of seeing her standing before him vanishing as an aloof formality quickly returned. He stood upright, arms to his side, then gestured with a lift of his hand.

"Lady Olivia Shea, formerly of Elmsboro," he said in a cool, deep voice, "I'd like to introduce you to William Raleigh, Duke of Trent, and his wife Vivian."

Olivia curtsied. "Your grace. Ma'am."

The corner of Sam's mouth twitched up. "And of course you've met Colin Ramsey, Duke of Newark."

"Your grace," she replied with another curtsy. The three of them remained silent for a few seconds after that, and so she smiled broadly and added, "My goodness, so many high-ranking noblemen in one room. And all so handsome, too, which I find quite unusual—"

"Why are you here, Olivia?" Sam cut in, his tone thick and low as he eyed her intently.

She inhaled deeply for strength. He was obviously going to make this difficult for her.

"Perhaps we should leave the two of you alone," Vivian interjected, looking at Sam.

"No, please—" She twisted her fan in front of her.

"I'll just be a moment. I—I wanted to tell Sam that the...um...political climate has changed in France."

"Actually, we were just having an in-depth discussion about it," Sam maintained, finally moving as he walked out from behind the desk.

Olivia noticed at once that everyone was staring at him with furrowed brows.

Sam cleared his throat and leaned his hip on the dark wooden edge, crossing his arms over his chest, waiting for her to say something more, she supposed.

"I see," she remarked as casually as she could. "Well, then, you must be aware that the Empress Eugenie has been banished from the country and the British government has been kind enough to allow her to take up residence here."

"Yes, we'd heard," Sam said coolly, his expression guarded.

"Oh, the antics of the French," Colin declared as he took a sip of the drink in his hand. "Always giving the English something to discuss at parties."

Olivia decided at that moment that she really, really liked Colin.

"Where have you been?" Sam asked quietly, his gaze never straying from hers.

The question gave her pause, and she shifted from one foot to the other. "Did you look for me?" she asked in return, her voice sounding timid to her ears.

He didn't respond for a moment, then whispered, "Yes."

She grinned broadly. She couldn't help herself. "I've been staying with Lady Abethnot for the last three days, but before that I was in Cornwall."

"Cornwall?" the three of them repeated in unison.

Her eyes widened and she took a step back. "Yes, well, I have family there, cousins on my father's side, and since Eugenie won't be a patron in Paris any longer, I came here to...consider my options."

"Consider your options," Sam repeated.

She sighed. "I suppose the boutique in France will carry on without me, but I thought I'd consider opening a new Nivan branch here." She shrugged. "For the Empress Eugenie, of course."

"Of course," Sam agreed, his expression lighting a little with a shade of amusement.

That gave her confidence. "Naturally, I don't want to lose her patronage. She simply adores what I create for her and I've just recently blended a new eau de cologne for her, in spice, actually."

Olivia noticed how, aside from Sam, the others in the room looked confused.

"I'm sorry, Nivan? Spice?" Vivian asked from her chair.

Olivia looked at her closely for the first time. A beautiful woman, older than she, with dark hair and striking eyes. And quite obviously pregnant.

She offered her a smile. "Nivan is a house of perfume that I manage—or did manage—in Paris. And spice is the scent of the Season. It's my favorite as well."

Vivian's husband actually chuckled as the other two looked at Sam. He, in turn, seemed to flush, flooding her with the memory of how he looked when he made love to her—flushed and vibrant and intense in his pursuit to satisfy her. The thought made her suddenly hot all over and she squirmed in her shoes.

"Would you like to sit, Lady Olivia?" the Duke of Trent asked her kindly.

She shook her head. "Thank you, no. I'm not here to—"

"Why are you here?" Sam asked, his cool demeanor returning.

He still hadn't moved away from the side of the desk, leaning against it with his arms over his chest. He was making her nervous, and a little annoyed that he kept asking as if he wanted her to confess everything before he even said he'd missed her.

She straightened and opened her fan, swishing it slowly in front of her. "I see you're expecting?" she said brightly to Vivian.

The woman grinned beautifully. "In four months."

Olivia gaped at her. "Four months?" she repeated.

Vivian placed a palm on her overlarge belly. "I'm huge, I know."

Olivia frowned and began to walk toward her. "Are you experiencing any swelling? I know that can be a problem when it's so hot as it's been lately—"

"Olivia, stop rambling," Sam ordered, stopping her in her tracks.

She fairly glared at him.

At that moment the butler rapped on the door again, then opened it. "Your grace, dinner is served."

"In a minute, Harold," Colin acknowledged as he looked at her. "This is fascinating."

"As you wish, sir," the man behind her said before taking his leave once more.

"Are you going to get to the point?" Sam asked her, his voice cool again.

She pushed her shoulders back and cocked her head to the side. "Why do you think I'm here, Sam?"

He shrugged negligibly. "I've no idea."

Her eyes narrowed as she crossed her arms over her breasts. "You can be such a cad."

"Him?" Colin said, placing his glass on the mantel-piece. "My lady, do you have any idea how long it takes this man to find the nerve to just talk to a—"

"Enough, Colin," Will admonished him.

Olivia glanced back to Sam, who now peered into her eyes intently, watching her for reaction, waiting.

Swallowing her pride, she closed her fan again and said, "Then I can assume you've not been courting someone else in my absence."

Sam's forehead creased as he looked her up and down. "In eight *weeks*?"

"Ah, l'amour," Colin said lightly, running his fingers through his hair.

She blushed. "Are you married, sir?"

He gave her a sly smile. "No, but I'd suddenly like to be. Are you looking for a husband?"

She stared at Sam. "Yes, I am."

Sam only raised his brows, and it infuriated her al-most as much as it begged her to rush to his arms and kiss his face.

Curtly, she said, "Actually, I had one once, but he turned out to be a scheming liar." Nobody said any-thing, so she added, "And then I learned I wasn't actu-ally married to him at all."

Her voice had grown serious as the mood in the room changed.

She inhaled deeply, lifting her chin a little, the

emotion of the moment instantly striking her full force. "Then I chanced upon another man, a better man, so completely different from the first." Her voice shook a little as she continued. "He was wonderful to me, so smart and handsome. He cared about my feelings, my work, my life."

Sam's features had softened considerably as he watched her, his gaze melting hers, and she swallowed hard to hold back tears.

Slowly she began to walk toward him. "He changed my world," she said in a husky whisper. "He actually loved me, needed me, but I—I said some horrible things to him that I'd give my life to take back."

Deadly silence pervaded the room as she now stood only a foot away from him, gazing into his eyes with all the love and longing she felt inside, hoping with every breath that he'd witness it for himself.

"I want to marry him so much," she breathed, the intensity she felt overflowing from her words, her body trembling, her eyes filling with tears of their own accord.

She fisted her hands at her sides, gritting her teeth. "I love him so much. I love him so much more than I could ever say to him because I left him. I want him back, loving me like he said he did, forgiving me for being so naive and stupid." She sniffed, then whispered, "I love him with everything inside of me, but I'm so scared he doesn't feel the same way about me anymore."

Olivia could actually see the pain and rush of feeling that rippled through him from her disclosure. His jaw tightened as he inhaled a shaky breath, squeezing his arms with his hands to keep from reaching out to her until she'd finished.

That's when she knew, with a profound relief, a profound joy, that she had never lost him.

A slow smile of a radiance she couldn't possibly conceal spread across her face. And then she took a step away from him and looked at Colin, who remained standing by the fireplace, amused.

"But if he doesn't want me, sir," she admitted lightly, "I suppose you'll do."

Sam was on her in a second, grabbing her by the shoulders and yanking her against him so hard it fairly knocked the breath from her.

Gazing at her, a crooked grin upon his mouth, he whispered huskily, "He doesn't care for ladies with blue eyes."

She heard the faintest laughter around her, and then he kissed her deeply, drowning out all sound, returning every feeling she had for him, saying everything he wanted to say in that one gesture of stark meaning, of love. She dropped her fan to the floor and wrapped her arms around his neck, holding him tightly, afraid to let him go.

When at last he pulled away, he cupped her cheeks and kissed her forehead, her lashes and chin, the tip of her nose.

"You scared the hell out of me, Livi," he whispered forcefully, his lips to her skin. "Don't ever leave me again..."

She shook her head, tears stinging her eyes as he looked down at her, his eyes glazed with love and desire. With relief.

"I missed you so much," she breathed.

He swallowed. "God in heaven, Olivia—" His voice cracked with emotion, and with that he pulled her head into his chest, cradling her with his palm to her cheek.

She closed her eyes briefly, relishing in the solid sound of his heartbeat, in the feel of his tall, strong body holding her close.

"Everybody's gone," she murmured softly.

He chuckled. "They're smart people, and right now they're in the dining room eating all the food."

She giggled against him. "I'm only hungry for you anyway."

He drew in a long, slow breath, then tipped her face up to meet his, his expression turned grave.

"Are you carrying my child?"

She felt like crying all over again. "No," she whispered.

He grinned. "Good. Then we can have a proper wedding."

She beamed, leaning back a little. "A real, *legal* wedding."

"A real, legal, lavish wedding that will cost me a fortune in ball gowns."

She laughed again. "And perfume."

He smirked. "Naturally."

After gazing into her eyes for a moment or two, he dropped his forehead to hers just as he had the night so long ago when they'd danced as if there were no one else on earth.

"I love you," she whispered.

"Livi…" he breathed. "I love you, too."